Winter Solstice

Dan Wright

My Fat Fox
MMXIV

My Fat Fox Ltd
86 Gladys Dimson House
London E7 9DF
United Kingdom

www.myfatfox.co.uk

Winter Solstice © 2014 Dan Wright

The rights of Dan Wright to be identified as the author of this work have been asserted by him in accordance with the Copyright, Designs and Patents Act, 1988

Cover design © 2014 Paul Holloway

ISBN 978-1-905747-35-1

Also by Dan Wright

The Marian Visits

Five Themes in the Alien Abduction Transcription Project

THIS PAGE INTENTIONALLY LEFT BLANK

CONTENTS

Foreword

Growing up Catholic in the Midwest during the Cold War, a few intrinsic matters beyond the Church's immediate realm were in one's consciousness: Russia was godless and America's profound enemy. China, and Asia generally, were ridiculously overpopulated and the epitome of "foreign." Africa existed in Tarzan movies and the collections of change by nuns at school for the Church's missions to save "pagan babies." The Middle East consisted of dunes and windblown tents, plus swirling-robed riders on camels and horses, brandishing scimitars.

All Muslims believe the Koran (Qur'an in Arabic) consists of Allah's revelations conveyed through the angel Gabriel – yes, *that* Archangel Gabriel in Christian thought – to the prophet Muhammad. The education of this Arabian merchant in the 7th Century AD consisted initially, he later told his followers, of an intensive two-week instruction by Gabriel. That was followed by the angel's intermittent visits and conveyances over a period of twenty-three years.

Muhammad segued from commercial trader to evangelist and warrior following that original fortnight of seminars. Since he could neither read nor write, he recited the revelations to scribes – but much later. Over fourteen centuries since, Muhammad's latent recorded words have been the final authority in all matters Islamic.

Therein lies an argument by nonbelievers. The Qur'an – as with the Bible – is riddled with lengthy direct quotes attributed to Allah/Jehovah/God. That gives rise to legitimate skepticism about retaining such a prodigious amount of material verbatim in one's long-term memories. If not retained, as it were, "photographically," where did later paraphrasing leave off and substituting his own ideas begin?

Muhammad did not claim to be God. Whether Jesus did is debatable, but as with the words attributed to the one known as the Christ, six centuries later Muhammad outlined a path for living appropriately.

They both set in motion, in modern-day parlance, "policies" and "best-case practices," some of which had unintended consequences:

- Institutionalized sects replete with wildly differing dogmas

- Scandals within

- Unswerving devotion made sacrosanct

- Suspicion of those who followed other faiths or none at all

- The hope of bliss yet the fear of misery after this life

The 21st century is destined to further expand and shift several technologies and quite likely scientific paradigms as well – at risk of further dehumanizing societies. On the sidewalk or in a restaurant, heads bow to a small hand-held screen, essentially oblivious to immediate surroundings, driven evermore inward.

Across the industrialized world, a primary challenge is to fuse what is left of our spirituality with new i-pod apps. In the Middle East, North Africa, South Asia and the Pacific Rim, Islamic men and women in the street confront the reverse, attempting to meld all these new technical and scientific realities with a rigid and austere 7th Century belief system. Our psyches, Judeo-Christian and Islamic, respectively, continue to forge opposite paths.

In America, the United Kingdom and Western Europe, Protestants live next door to Catholics, Jews, agnostics and atheists. Despite our continued stark differences spiritually, we cheer as one at youth ball games, laugh together at the school musical and share parental commencement tears. We agree to disagree on religious concerns. It wasn't always this way, but we've adapted — to the betterment of our cultures.

In contrast, Sunni and Shi'a Islam remain at loggerheads, stuck in an internecine dispute after nearly fourteen centuries and billions of lives. This can be easily scorned from afar as silly and pointless. But it's not at all silly or pointless to them.

Fair or otherwise in the post-9/11 world, Middle Eastern Islam in particular is viewed suspiciously by westerners through a prism revealing senseless bombings, sobbing mothers and vengeance — always the revenge motive, provided conveniently by Muhammad's own words all those centuries ago.

To be sure, Muhammad spent only a tiny fraction of his teachings on that subject, the remainder championing ethics, charity and love. Yet extremist groups around the world with axes to grind have latched onto those few vengeance-sanctioning phrases: Smite thine enemies in the name of Allah.

What an altogether different world we might live in if retribution were beyond reason in the collective human spirit.

Statements, actions and perspectives portrayed here are not intended to characterize any particular individuals and, where apparent, are coincidental.

About the Author

Dan Wright is a retired civil servant for the State of Michigan where he served as a senior analyst and policy writer in the Department of Human Services.

For 25 years beginning in 1978, he was a member of the Mutual UFO Network, Inc., an international not-for-profit organization dedicated to resolving the enigma known as unidentified flying objects through direct investigations and research. For seven years he served as MUFON's deputy director, overseeing all North American investigations. In that capacity he provided oversight on hundreds of locally conducted investigations. He authored two chapters in the MUFON Field Investigator's Manual and was instrumental in designing the organization's computerized database of completed and approved investigative case reports.

From 1992 through 1997, Wright conducted a seminal MUFON effort to organize and examine over 900 recorded sessions of hypnotic regression across the US and Canada regarding suspected alien abduction of human subjects.

Wright is the author of "Five Themes," his final report on the MUFON abduction transcript study; and "The Marian Visits," analyzing historical accounts in Roman Catholic history of claimed miraculous appearances by the Virgin Mary. He was a guest speaker at the 1995, 1997 and 2003 MUFON international symposia.

He resides in Athens, Georgia.

Acknowledgments

Astronomer and geologist Sandra Miles offered hardheaded input on the scientifically possible.

Two preliminary readers contributed highly valuable insights and support to the final product: mysteries author Jennifer Patrick and Dr. Paul Gurian, associate professor of political science at the University of Georgia.

The National Oceanic and Atmospheric Administration (NOAA) and U.S. Air Force websites contributed a wealth of important material.

Historical information and fact checking were assigned primarily to an Internet treasure trove: Wikipedia, the encyclopedia of everything. To the extent that any information derived is incorrect, such is not likely wrong by much.

Two civilian investigations and research organizations afforded a myriad of opportunities to learn: the Mutual UFO Network, Inc. (MUFON) and the J. Allen Hynek Center for UFO Studies (CUFOS). Their unsung but essential ongoing roles in our society are hopefully represented faithfully in these pages.

THIS PAGE INTENTIONALLY LEFT BLANK

Chapter One

Rayan Traboulsi awaited word, patiently checking pent-up anticipation. He was not a courageous man. He knew why he'd been chosen: Most importantly, he was no longer youthful; a young driver would draw immediate suspicion on the road. Also, he had a passable knowledge of Yiddish, had learned how to manage a two-ton truck from working Lebanese fruit and vegetable fields, and over these many years had shown unshakable loyalty to the organization and its credo.

Following the day's final call to prayer and a strategy session, Rayan accepted heartfelt congratulations before heading to his tent for some solitude. After tidying his bed roll, he knelt once more, this time on the small prayer rug he'd held onto since childhood.

Allah, I am your servant always. Prophet, I beseech you to guide my path. He proceeded into a ritual mantra to free his mind.

The right side of Rayan's face bore the scars of youthful dissent. In November 1982, months into the Israeli occupation, the then 12-year-old fell victim to an Israeli soldier's anger for straying a bit too far from home after dark then trying to run when caught. The blow sent him head first onto the cobblestones and curb. For want of basic medical care, his broken jaw wasn't properly set, resulting in a misaligned bite and a myriad of dental problems ever since. His torn ear had been stitched roughly. Deep facial abrasions left a discoloration that would always attract a stranger's first notice.

Upon recovering from his injuries, a still seething adolescent

Rayan joined *Hizb' Allah* (in the West, Hezbollah), the Army of God as a message runner. He received a continuing small stipend for his efforts. In the years to follow, fashioned after the Iranian Shi'a revolutionary movement, *Hizb'allah* gained strength and sway over the impoverished south Lebanon.

Rayan's Shi'ite parents had lived and toiled in the port city of Sur. Known as Tyre at its founding around 2750 BC, the city boasted two expansive archaeological sites, both Romano-Byzantine. Once part of Phoenicia, the city and surrounding region had endured successive and lengthy occupations by the Romans, Persians, Ottoman Turks and, more recently, Syrians and Israelis.

At the conclusion of a civil war in 1990, Hizb'allah's military wing, Islamic Resistance, escaped the Lebanese government's call to disband all militias. It claimed not to have taken part in the internal Muslim-Christian conflict, that its sole purpose was ongoing resistance to foreign occupation, namely Israel's.

Thus did Rayan proceed into his twenties and beyond as a part-time soldier for Allah – support roles mostly. In June 1996, four years before Israel would ultimately relent and withdraw to its border, Hizb'allah scored one of its greatest successes, an ambush that killed or wounded all thirteen members of an Israeli patrol. As in numerous operations leading up to that triumphal incident, Rayan drove a getaway vehicle.

While he was not a man of natural courage, over three decades he had repeatedly demonstrated calm under stress. Now with Allah's blessing and Muhammad's guidance he would once again find the inner peace to perform his role and help smite the Zionist entity.

Practical inventions make their way to commoners eventually. That truism manifested itself in the darkest manner on Wednesday, December 6, 2023, a day before the onset of Hanukkah, in the form of synchronized bombings in Tel Aviv and Jerusalem. The twin attacks essentially removed Israel from the Middle East political equation for the foreseeable future.

Identical, they consisted of 35 kilograms (77 pounds) of 20-percent processed, i.e., still industrial-grade, plutonium oxide (PuO2) – well short of the 95-percent pure plutonium for undisturbed fission to occur but powerful enough to level several city blocks. Each device was the ultimate "dirty bomb."

The PuO2 crystals had been pulverized at the Natanz underground enrichment facility in the Iranian desert and encased in tubular molds of pewter from a Tehran foundry. Sealed only with welds, the instruments leaked radiation detrimental to the long-term survival of all those who would handle them.

Delivery was arranged by a Syrian arms dealer. In the continued chaos of an interminable civil war there, the merchant was free to ply his trade in the lawless Golan Heights. The cargo arrived in early November at an airstrip in Lebanon's Bekaa valley, near a Hizb'allah compound. With social programs in place, that organization was by now the longstanding de facto and popular authority in southern Lebanon.

Technicians at the encampment blanketed each metal tube with 80 kilos of high-energy plastic explosives and a dozen, evenly spaced simul-flash detonators to form the trigger. They buried their wrath in a pit and waited for the go instruction.

Their efforts, apart from the predictable and devastating, would coincidentally settle an academic argument among nuclear physicists across the globe: In terms of low-volume destructive potential, any distinction between reactor-grade (five-to twenty-percent pure) and ultimate weapons-grade plutonium was largely rhetorical. These were crude constructions, to be sure, yet capable of immense havoc. Israelis, Americans, and Western Europeans had long obsessed about megaton-bearing nuclear missiles erected by Tehran, all the while ignoring the potential of such a backyard design.

An ever-growing addiction to sugar by the Israeli populace, combined with an infestation of the country's sugar beet crop that year, quickly drove up prices on all naturally sweetened products. Sugar beet processors soon prevailed on the agriculture ministry to relax its rules on imports from the bumper crops in Lebanon and Jordan. A new directive to crossing stations allowing beet trucks to enter relatively unfettered took effect December 1. It was the break Hizb'alla's secretary-general, Jawad Rahal, had prayed for. "Allahu Akbar!" (God is great), he cried.

When word came to proceed in the early hours of the 6th (the voice on the phone saying only, "three, two, one"), the men at the compound dug up and loaded their vengeance onto a pair of two-ton trucks, which were then filled to overflowing with sugar beets from nearby Lebanese fields. Sporting the logo of a prominent Bekaa Valley farm on their doors, Rayan Traboulsi and a second driver set out for the Israeli border and their separate destinations beyond.

Using standard telescoping mirrors, the Israeli border crossing guards panned the trucks' undercarriages, which were clean, and spoke briefly to Rayan.

Calling on an inner peace, the middle-aged man cast a wide smile at the guards and, in broken Yiddish, explained that these deliveries and more to follow would keep the farm in business for another year. Rayan's practiced delivery was flawless and disarming. The manifests appeared to be in order as well.

In that fateful moment, with a long line of Lebanese day workers still to cross over, the guards might have conducted a full inspection, a process tying up two men for an hour. The officer in charge knew he would ultimately field more angry complaints from Israeli employers about needless delays and inefficiencies at the crossings. Aware of the new directive regarding sugar beets in particular, he instead waved the vehicles through.

Using a cell phone, at 1:35 PM local time on the eve of the Jews' hallowed period, Rayan set off his weapon while driving past the Tel Aviv stock exchange. In a final cogent thought, he wished for one of the blasts to somehow find its way to that soldier from the cobblestone streets of Sur. He recognized that, on the far side, he would greet seventy-two virgins – though what he would do with such a contingent now seemed problematic. He had never really been that sexually oriented.

Two minutes hence, the second truck erupted along the thoroughfare separating the Israeli Knesset and U.S. Consulate General – barely far enough removed from Jerusalem's Old City to spare the Dome of the Rock and Al Aksa mosque from outright destruction.

Small even by Hiroshima standards, both low-grade nuclear devices produced an effective yield of nearly 200 metric tons of TNT – approximately forty times larger than any terrorist bombing anywhere in the world to that point. The Jerusalem and Tel Aviv downtowns were leveled in horrifically magnificent fashion.

Shi'ites everywhere would rejoice, Rahal was certain, having crippled their ancient Zionist enemy and likewise put all Sunnis on notice. Let the path to the 12th Imam's appearance go forward.

WINTER SOLSTICE

Israel's Knesset had near full attendance at that hour, wrapping up business before the Hanukkah break. The initial concussion, a second later followed by a monstrous wind, searing fire and countless tons of debris, tore into the building and its ranks. The Prime Minister and her top six ministers in succession were later found incinerated in the remains of a conference room. All but the few MPs not there that day were lost, as was the American consulate and its entire staff.

In the tumult, Israel's ministries of defense and foreign affairs likewise essentially ceased to exist. Most other central government offices as well as the home office of the Bank of Israel were also victims of the massacre.

Israel's powerful military suddenly found itself without clear direction, its nuclear deterrence stranded in scattered silos. Whom to punish for these foul acts? Hamas? Hizb'allah? Egypt's Muslim Brotherhood? Some nondescript al-Quaeda cell? And where had the fuel source originated? Iran? Pakistan? North Korea? The Jewish homeland had its share of enemies. Anything approaching firm answers could not be known in those critical first hours and days when the world might have excused a limited nuclear retaliation.

Inescapably, Israel's highly trusted intelligence service, Mossad, had failed its primary mission, and the nation paid a dear price. Now, for want of a verified villain to attack, its vengeful sword remained sheathed.

Media coverage of the debacle in Israel's principal cities was understandably limited to satellite images initially as many governments and television networks shared resources to survey and broadcast the conflagration.

An estimated thirty to forty thousand residents of the two metropolises were dead or would die soon, according to optimistic assessments in the first hours. (A far more comprehensive analysis two years later would tally a quarter-million victims in outright deaths and shortened lives, plus twenty thousand more in Jordan and Saudi Arabia.) Radiation-related cancers accounted for most of the walking dead. Disfigurements among newborns would tax hospitals and social agencies for years to follow.

Across Israel's remaining cities in those first hours, workers from factories, shops and offices – anyone with a means of travel – scrambled away into the desert, panicked by rumors that the evil doers would continue to prey on population centers. Of the country's 6.6 million surviving citizens, over a third embarked on a run to nowhere. Local aid stations and camps sprang up haphazardly as the world's established relief agencies diverted desperately needed supplies bound for African and Asian venues.

An openly nuclear-tipped, Shi'a-dominated Iran had used a hidden-ball trick to fundamentally change the region's dynamics, political commentators suggested ad infinitum. But the proof of it would be elusive as the Iranian president, Nazila Fadavi, and heads of other governments hostile to Israel denied any knowledge or involvement.

Up close, the consequences were beyond polite description. Torn-away arms, legs and entrails mingled with fallen streetlights, cash register receipts, handbags and television sets.

Chapter Two

"Good morning, this is NPR." The Reverend Estefan Bernardo Tolavares awoke as usual to the news reader's first words. He'd never been a very heavy sleeper.

The radio voice's normally flat affect was tinged that morning with concern which perked the priest's immediate attention. The host proceeded to describe the attacks on central Tel Aviv and Jerusalem.

Oh, Jesus, this isn't good, Estefan quickly concluded. *Teacher, please watch over those who are fleeing.* His eyes suddenly glistened as he stared at the crucifix in his room. His body felt the weight of compassion – for the dead and the maimed, for all the families dispossessed or soon to be, for the hate-filled minds of those responsible.

As did everyone else in the West in those first hours following the dual bombings, Estefan fretted that a counterattack – by an apparently intact Israeli military – could launch a wider conflict. Still, Armageddon scenarios had never begun in this fashion, he reasoned. With his enhanced awareness of Muslim cultures, over a first cup of coffee he considered the Sunni-Shi'a tension underlying the region's affairs.

He gazed out a window at the New Mexican desertscape and sighed heavily before turning his thoughts to necessary parish routine.

Estefan was foremost a Midwesterner. The first born to an immigrant couple from Puerto Rico, he had called a brown brick walk-up on Chicago's south side his home. Serious-minded even as a little boy, he had quietly excelled in parochial schools while serving within the Tolavares home as "assistant mommy" to four younger siblings. Both parents worked six nights a week in nearby restaurant kitchens, serving up Cuban sandwiches and Italian pasta, respectively.

Estefan attended Chicago's Jesuit Academy beginning in 2004. A favorite teacher there, Reverend John McDowell, recognized this young voracious reader for the seeker that he was and took the adolescent under his wing. Father Jack's seminal advice to him one day would play over and over in Estefan's mind in the years to follow:

"You'll come across many credible writings, across a spectrum of subjects, arguing both for and against the legitimacy of Christian faith. In the end, what stands out, I believe, is what Jesus really said. You have four accounts to choose from. The insights you're seeking are there in His actual words."

Of average height and build but quick on his feet, Estefan might well have excelled on Jesuit's strong soccer team, but he ran cross country instead, discovering a bit of courage while in hopeless pursuit, finding solace in a personal best. He'd always loved baseball as his spring sport but found curveballs mystifying. Nonetheless he practiced his way onto the academy's varsity as a good-glove-no-hit reserve infielder.

Thanks to Father Jack and some other fine teachers, over four years Estefan's eyes opened to the enormity of the universe. It was to them, and to him, the vast expression of God's will.

The Big Bang, now argued by many in Catholic thought as the creation, occurred 13.567 billion years before. Yet scientifically, the stuff that fused into an unimaginable eruption necessarily had to come from somewhere, the young scholar reasoned. So there must have been a prior period. Maybe the Big Bang was mischaracterized as a singular event, when in actuality it was the eightieth or the 80,000th repetition. An eternity past was impossible to really grasp, he knew, yet perhaps it could be no other way.

He wondered, too, whether our three-dimensional universe is all that exists or is just one of many in a "multi-verse," as some theoreticians suggested. Cyclotrons had proved the existence of several additional dimensions of space-time, after all, but only at the subatomic level of quarks and gluons and such. Were those extremely temporary deviations from an otherwise singular universe within our familiar three dimensions? Or was God holding out on us, showing us only the spectrum our telescopes could detect?

The magnificence of it all was a rush to him.

In his junior year of high school, Estefan was selected to the National Honor Society largely on the basis of a submitted paper critiquing scientific and religious doctrines. After scoring a 33 (out of 35) on the ACT, he quite suddenly began receiving promotional literature from dozens, then hundreds of colleges and universities across America, including a Who's Who of strong engineering and physical sciences programs. His father brought home an empty lettuce-shipping box from the farmer's market to store all the promotional materials – then another.

To his parents' dismay, Estefan didn't respond to any of the offerings by Christmas. He remained vague about his procrastination while continuing to ponder privately a central question.

On a starry night in January, following hours of caffeine-induced freewheeling discussion at the Tolavares dining table,

Father Sancho "Sammy" Morales halted at the bottom of the stoop outside the Tolavares home before ducking into his car, a streetlight faintly illuminating his brown bomber jacket. He looked up the snow-swept steps toward Estefan and, with a sweep of his hand skyward, broke into a smile.

"Young man, you're asking about the true nature of God when we only know a tiny fraction so far of what He set in motion. I hear you! The Church and its belief system are constantly evolving. We're not your grandfather's Oldsmobile." Leaning forward in a final gesture, Father Sammy concluded, "Join us and you just might find some answers."

Estefan was convinced this was where he needed to be. He would become a Jesuit.

Along the way he had learned that the Society of Jesus was founded outside Paris in the early 16th Century by Iñigo López de Loyola (now Saint Ignatius) and six other Roman Catholic priests as a reform movement within the Church in response to the Protestant Reformation. With a 500-year heritage of good works since then and over 14,000 practicing clerics, it was the largest priestly fraternity. In the past half-century in particular, though, its progressive commentary and practices had sometimes called into question the order's devotion to the Church's chain of command. Estefan was impressed with that facet as well.

Following his high school graduation party at a White Sox home game, Estefan was off to The Jesuit School of Theology in Berkeley, California – all expenses waived, given his academic accomplishments and his family's size and finances.

There he continued to excel, turning his primary attention gradually from the physical sciences to world affairs. But the young scholar was principally a pupil of the Teacher, Jesus, and His words. That foundation, with encouragement along the way, allowed him to feel comfortable in exploring the borders of his beliefs.

Early in his stay, Estefan was taken aback by the mention in a lecture one day that Islam's Qur'an actually contained more words about Mary, the mother of Jesus, than the New Testament did. The Shi'a sect in particular held Mary in considerable esteem, he learned – though she was not, of course, listed among its saints.

The very fact that there *were* saints in Shi'a belief fascinated this student. Some of their biographies, he soon discovered, read very much like those his mother had brought home to him from the parish rectory: innocents put to the test. But more were enshrined for their gallantry with a sword, martyrs for the Islamic cause.

Shi'ites, he learned, were far more demonstrative to this day than Catholics in their continuing adoration of various saints, regularly celebrating feast days *en masse* at elaborate shrines not unlike Lourdes, carried over to dozens of venues.

The young student likewise found remarkable similarities among the core principles espoused by Muhammad and Jesus, beginning with the axiom of a single, all-knowing, omnipresent god force. "There is no god but God," proffered Muhammad. The Muslim concept of heaven – a oneness or unity with the Creator – was obviously in line with Christian belief. That Islam rejected the notion of an eternal hell was actually not so far from progressive Christian thinking. More than one Jesuit over the years argued that hell lay perhaps more in superstition than objective reality.

Another Islamic principle – the perpetual remembrance of

Allah in everything the believer does, thinks, and says – might well have been taken from an age-old Catholic primer, the Baltimore Catechism. In daily practice, Estefan recognized, the Muslim man in the street was far more pious than nearly all Christians.

He found ample evidence that Muslims regard Jesus as an important early prophet, a status never returned in kind by Christians to Muhammad.

A central difference dividing the faiths, Estefan affirmed, rested in the mindsets of the two founders. Jesus was a gentle man who preached nonviolence regardless of the circumstance. In contrast, at his core Muhammad himself was a warrior, and he spent brief yet stark remarks on the concept of justifiable revenge. That Muslim tenet, to modern-day jihadists, excused all manner of mayhem rained down on others.

As to an eternal resting place for the billions of non-Christians who had occupied Earth these many centuries, published Christian thought was all over the board. But Estefan was certainly mindful of the Vatican's official, still unbending message: Everlasting life for souls not baptized into one or another Christian faith was impossible; they were beyond the reach of heaven.

Muhammad had expressed that all religions discovered fundamental truths. Concurrently, though, and with evangelistic (military) fervor, he and his followers had warred against atheists, pagans and Christians alike. The Rome-inspired crusades centuries later, Estefan discovered, were not exactly an original idea.

His studies inevitably brought him to the great Islamic divide: Sunnis, far outnumbering Shi'ites worldwide, plainly regarded the latter as heretics – and vice versa. It was an argument dating back to Muhammad's demise and the choice of his rightful successor.

In remarks to followers before his death in 632, Muhammad seemingly chose his father-in-law, Abdullah ibn Abi Quhafa, nicknamed Abu Bakr, as caliph, the leader of all Muslims. Successors as caliph would be selected through a Sunni process called *shura* – consultations among community religious leaders.

To every Sunni, the Shi'a claim that Muhammad's son-in-law, Ali ibn Abi Talib, had been the rightful heir as caliph (Muhammad had sired only a daughter) was nonsense, at once ignorant and malicious. The Prophet had never spoken of Ali in those terms. Shi'ite shrines, furthermore, were simply idolatrous. Muhammad had strictly forbidden any attempt to cast his own image in any medium. By extension that principle applied to any of his followers – "saints" or otherwise.

Sunni faith had remained remarkably decentralized over fourteen centuries whereas Shi'a followed the Roman Catholic model of hierarchical authority.

By the onset of the third millennium Islam claimed upwards of 800 million adherents worldwide. But the Shi'a-Sunni schism over ascribing Muhammad's original authority had never healed. That age-old drama of rightful succession, along with disparate Islamic practices, continued to play out in a sickening ongoing scene which no amount of prayer seemed to alter.

On one level, the seminarian reasoned, the only change in 21st century Islam was a preference for exploding vests, cars and trucks over the traditional sword. The principle of honorable aggression framed in Islamic teaching – in contrast to unadulterated Christian compassion or, say, Buddhist acceptance – allowed each Islamic sect to continually wave a litany of grievances at the other. Rigid discrimination in housing, employment and access to daily resources was historically cast in Sunni or Shi'a molds wherever they shared a city. And the prospect of retribution forever awaited just a spark to ignite.

At a level Estefan and all Westerners could relate to only in terms of "the troubles" in Northern Ireland, Sunnis and Shi'ites viewed one another as infidels, incapable of discerning the true Islamic path. With that assurance, individual lives were justifiably expendable. The essential concept of compromise for the sake of peace had never taken durable hold among the faithful of either side.

Sadly grasping the Sunni-Shi'a gulf, as a seminarian Estefan looked with fresh eyes upon the differences among Christians and their beliefs. As with Muslims, their clashes over the centuries had been less a matter of interpreting the Bible's words, more about the legitimacy of their respective leaders. Likened to the several sects now comprising their Sunni counterparts, Protestants had fractured into numerous denominations.

During his long stay at the seminary, Estefan devoted a series of research papers to parallels in Catholic and Shi'a history and tenets, including their claims of miraculous happenings. At the suggestion of Father Jack, who continued to fill a mentoring role from afar, the seminarian also enrolled online for UC-Berkeley classes in comparative religions, emphasizing Islam. For his sparse free time, the young scholar ordered a set of language disks, "Arabic for Dimbulbs."

Had he been born in Saudi Arabia, Egypt or Jordan, Estefan knew, he almost certainly would be Sunni today. In Iran, Iraq or Azerbaijan, he would more likely be a Shi'ite. Accident of birth, perhaps, he reasoned. Or not.

In his personal and final analysis, the student left open

whether Muhammad had genuinely received a series of visions and instructions from the Angel Gabriel on behalf of the God Estefan knew. After all, self-proclaimed prophets and mystics abounded for several centuries following Jesus' death. Some of their works were even legitimized eventually in the Apocrypha: eleven books only recently accepted in the Church's canon as addenda to the New Testament.

The student, however, could not get past Muhammad's claimed instruction from Allah to spread the Islamic faith by force where necessary. It was just too remindful of the Old Testament's wrathful Yahweh – and contradictory to the essence of Jesus' words. As Father Jack had expressed one day at the Academy, "In my heart of hearts, I can't square some of what is ascribed to Yahweh with anything the Teacher said. Violence is still violence, no matter how you couch it." Thus did Estefan view Muhammad and Islam with the same respectful yet jaundiced eye.

After several years at the seminary, two months apart, Estefan Tolavares was ordained into the Society of Jesus and awarded a Master of Arts degree in international relations from UC-Berkeley. The topic of his master's thesis: "Roman Catholic-Shi'a Muslim Discord and Arabic Relations with the West."

Leading up to his ordination, he had applied for and was hopeful of snagging one of the favored entry-level posts at the North American Jesuit headquarters in Washington D.C. to continue his research. He frankly envisioned a series of published papers, employing the Jesuits' immense storehouse of historical documents there, and to perhaps further the background dialog among clerics in the United States and Iran.

Instead, without explanation he was assigned by his order to a different front line of sorts: Saint Javier Missionary Catholic Church in Columbus, New Mexico, attached to St. Gregory Parish in Deming, both mere miles from the Mexican border. Not only did it bear no relation to his interest in the Middle East, these were not even his native people. He was of Puerto Rican heritage, with a different Spanish dialect and a fundamentally separate culture and history.

Following a day or two dealing with a bit of anger and self-pity, Estefan regrouped. The Mexican border it would be. And there he remained, too busy from the outset to think about what might have been.

Logic and contemplation had driven Estefan's decisions since his arrival, stemming from before the completion of the electronic fence and the onset of Predator drone aerial patrols along the border. His priorities were to organize and maintain a food pantry, a used clothing exchange, a child care co-op and literacy classes for those already on the U.S. side. While immersed in his work, he managed to gain a working knowledge of three Mexican dialects, plus a bit of the Guatemalan and Honduran tongues.

Most evenings he was free to enjoy a glass of cheap red wine or two as he contemplated this world's dire circumstances and his tiny role within them.

Now, over a decade having elapsed since his appointment here, prayer was reserved for thanks, mostly, just to carry on for another day. But his heart struggled to believe that the prayers of these immigrants were being answered. There were simply not enough jobs back home to go around. In the states they would have at least the hope of opportunity – those that made it through.

They weren't *illegals* to Estefan. They were young men whose rigid jaws masked fear and suspicion, pregnant teens and sad-eyed mothers, three-year-olds already staring vacantly in the absence of enough toys. Here and there were the grizzled veterans of the fence war – fonts of practical wisdom on where to proceed, which employers to solicit.

The U.S. Border Patrol, he understood, was only carrying out policy in its regular sweeps for the residual numbers of undocumented immigrants still coming this way. The men in uniform did so with respect and minimum force. Estefan in turn had long since posted bilingual signs warning of necessary credentials. The officers, to their credit, recognized that he didn't check IDs before scooping a plate of beans and rice or handing out a 12-pack of recycled baby socks.

The local self-styled vigilantes, rifles with infra-red scopes at the ready to gun down a Honduran kid looking for a job, were another matter entirely. In his gut, Estefan loathed their hyper-patriotic attitude. But finally, the ACLU had challenged their tactics in the New Mexican state and federal courts.

He rinsed out his coffee cup on this morning, shaking his head slowly at the carnage in Tel Aviv and Jerusalem. In light of that chaos where Jesus had once walked, he would struggle to find the right words to celebrate the official birth of the Savior two weeks hence.

Chapter Three

President Adrian Vander Kamp was familiar with The Book: short- and long-range intelligence estimates on the military capacities and political instabilities of every country and territory in the world. These roll-ups, a composite from hundreds of sources, were, in effect, betting odds on our nation or any other going to war over a given set of issues.

On hearing the particulars of the twin attacks and consulting The Book's new entries, Vander Kamp deduced that the bombings were unsophisticated, the likely products of a radical insurgency of some sort, quite possibly al-Qaeda, not the direct work of a nation-state.

In a best-case scenario, an American spy satellite overhead might have captured the dual scenes of destruction. But none was within close enough range at that hour to resolve the particular type of vehicle responsible and perhaps its origin. Ubiquitous cameras stationed on the immediate downtown streets of both cities, of course, were obliterated.

American intelligence soon located the seventh in line of succession in the Israeli cabinet, Education Minister Asher Goldfarb, who was about to lecture at a conference on autism in Bruges, Belgium. Via Skype link the shaken Goldfarb cried out, "They're trying to kill us all!" Van der Kamp offered a cryptic response, in effect a directive: "Do nothing for now."

Within 36 hours, USAF ballistic missile techs, Defense Intelligence Agency operatives, State Department veterans and the first of several battalions of combat-ready U.S. Army soldiers were camped well upwind of Tel Aviv and Jerusalem, respectively. In a scenario never revealed to the Israeli cabinet, Operation Failed State would swallow Israel whole and regurgitate it several years later. Martial law was the order of the day.

Remaining Israeli air force and army generals were furious but offered no armed resistance. To be hamstrung following the most wanton and egregious intrusions in the country's 75-year history was unacceptable. But they were good soldiers; they would not launch a retaliatory strike without firm evidence and administrative plans, and those were not soon forthcoming. They instead complied with the sudden American dominance of their command and control structure.

Israel had long been an icon of liberty and democracy in the face of tyranny. But that was not a factor in the real world of commerce. While massive, if haphazard, charitable outpouring took shape, world markets would turn a predictably businesslike cold shoulder to Jewish officials' appeals for unabated trade. Israeli container ships would be turned away, contracts for its important exports — especially electronics and assembled toys — canceled, penalties be damned, in an unfounded but generalized fear among the world populations of radioactive contamination. The Israeli tourism industry, meanwhile, came to a standstill. Beyond the immediate humanitarian crisis, the nation's competitive edge was destined to be crippled for years to come.

In the short run, Israel's fate domestically rested with Education Minister Goldfarb. Some deft diplomacy by American and British diplomats and that clamp on his military response potential convinced the interim PM not to retaliate against someone — *anyone* — for the moment.

Jordan's Crown Prince Odeh, meanwhile, had been sharing afternoon tea with his wife and twin daughters at their palace in Amman when royal guards burst into the room. A waiting elevator swept them all to the roof where other family members were gathered and a helicopter strained to warm up. Ten minutes later they were rumbling down the Amman International runway reserved for the royal family – headed to their Swiss retreat.

From a cell phone en route, the prince railed at his ambassador from America (himself in flight) that this had to be "the work of those Persian bastards, I am certain of it. It is no accident that countless among my people are suffering and will suffer more in the days to follow. The ayatollahs were not satisfied to extend a Shi'ite crescent from Iran to Lebanon to Syria. Now they would try to push their will down the throat of every righteous Sunni."

The US ambassador tried to cool the ardor of his Jordanian colleague but to little avail. Ancient grievances and hatreds were running roughshod over reason and notions of diplomacy.

Odeh went on, "Iran has called us 'Jew lovers' for building the Aqaba-Eilat Airport with Israel. Once again we see where moderation toward the Jewish state has left us. Tell the president I am calling an emergency meeting of the Arab League. We will deal with the Shi'ite infidels in our own style, the Arab way. *Allahu Akbar.*"

On the morning of Thursday, December 7, snow squalls continued across the Midwest and Northeast, the nation's weather otherwise passive. But vacations in the winter wonderlands and on Caribbean beaches alike had been cut short. Only one senator – caught in an Austrian blizzard – was not on hand for this extraordinary session.

"For what purpose does the gentleman rise?"

"To address the chair."

"The senior senator from Connecticut is recognized."

President Pro Tempore Arthur Rosenbaum had first run for a vacated Senate seat during the crescendo of the Vietnam antiwar movement. Now, half a century later, halting in his gait, his voice half an octave higher with age, he had relinquished the chairmanship demands of the foreign relations committee. This would be his final term in office, he'd already announced.

Per protocol dating back two centuries, Senator Rosenbaum addressed the nation's vice president individually as the chair, officially the chamber's president and chief officer.

"Mr. President, my friends on both sides of the aisle, I have been here a long time, longer frankly than any of you, which grants me the privilege of speaking first. 'Just wait your turn', my father would say." He pushed a few strands of white hair from his brow. Behind sagging eyelids, dark brown eyes still flashed.

"I first ran for this seat as a reasonably young man intending to be a voice for sanity in our foreign policy. According to those campaign placards and pamphlets back then, I was the 'Peace Now' candidate.

"Well, over the course of these many years, I have endorsed war-making – on this floor or in some budget mark-up, directly deploying U.S. troops or supporting one ad hoc ally or another – more often than I care to recite. … And what has it all accomplished?"

Uh-oh, a few insiders contemplated on hearing those introductory words, was a death bed confession of sorts to follow? Journalists' pens were at the ready.

"Parenthetically, I would note for the record that it was 82 years ago today when the United States was suddenly and wantonly attacked at our naval base in Hawaii.

"The people of my ancestry have forever been at odds with surrounding societies. Isaac and Ishmael and their separate roads, a continuous clash of cultures and religions over *four millennia*. I happen to be from Isaac's lineage, but what does that really matter if we are searching for the truth?

"How does one go about calculating and rendering overall justice to cover such a history of unbridled hatred? Spitting at one another, refusing to hire or rent to a person of that other faith and culture. How does one factor in all the lives needlessly lost or stunted, Jewish and Palestinian properties alike seized over the centuries, the indignities sprayed as if from a water cannon?

"In short, there is no formula. No claim of righteous retribution, no peace treaty, no amount of reparations can heal the hearts of the wives and mothers, the sons and the daughters over such a span of time.

"Awash in the afterglow of our victory in World War II, the United States was the driving force to establish a new world governing body, the United Nations. The UN has shown itself to be an imperfect body, surely. Clashes of ideologies and ill-conceived alliances were inevitable, and reasoning sometimes gave way to power broking.

"Then and now, however, the UN as an institution has offered the only framework we have as a planet for settling international disputes. It has especially proved its worth over the years in assisting some of the world's downtrodden. It was and is the antidote to total chaos on Earth.

"Very early in its life, on November 29, 1947, in the midst of Israel's War of Independence from surrounding Arab peoples, the UN proclaimed the establishment of a Jewish state. President Truman and the Congress wholeheartedly endorsed a legal homeland, finally, for my ancestral people.

"In its acceptance and reply, the provisional Israeli

government declared then," as Rosenbaum reached for a notecard in a breast pocket, "that it 'will ensure complete equality of social and political rights to all its inhabitants irrespective of religion, race or sex; it will guarantee freedom of religion, conscience, language, education and culture.'

"That declaration, Mr. President, went on to offer assurance 'to the Arab inhabitants of the State of Israel to preserve peace and participate in the upbuilding of the State on the basis of full and equal citizenship and due representation in all its provisional and permanent institutions.'"

"Yup, he's going for it," whispered one journalist to a colleague in the gallery. "This'll be above the fold tomorrow."

The aging politician took a moment to reposition his legs and regain physical strength. "At the conclusion of the War of Independence in 1949," he continued, "the Arab countries who had invaded two years before signed cease-fire agreements specifying interim borders, as decided by the outcome of the battles. The previous borders with Lebanon and Syria were restored. Egypt retreated to its earlier border but retained control of Gaza. Jordan held the West Bank, the hill country traditionally known as Judea and Samaria, and Jerusalem's Old City. That 1949 'Armistice Line' later became known as the 'Green Line.'

"Vengeance, however, seethed in the hearts of the vanquished, and minor clashes continued on and off until 1967 when Israel showed itself as the *baddest* dude on the block, as it were.

"The Six-Day War, a maxim of superior Israeli strategy and American weaponry, adjusted those 1949 borders for practical purposes. Gaza, the West Bank, the Golan Heights and the Sinai Peninsula became occupied territories under Israel's administrative control – buffers of desert, as it were, against threatening nations, the Senate heard then. And the members of this great deliberative body said that was only reasonable."

The entire chamber had grown exceptionally quiet, conversations concluded, notes set aside. Rosenbaum appeared to be taking Israel to task, if latently. This was certainly a first. The cagey old dog had to be up to something.

"America and Israel by 1967 were joined at the hip," the Pro Tem continued, "bulwarks of democracy in a largely undemocratic world.

"And so it was that this body looked the other way in the decades to follow when our close democratic ally went beyond mere military control of those occupied territories. First a few simple Jewish communes sprang up. Later came major housing developments, temples, shopping centers, policing and all the accouterments of modern Jewish living. Desert land was transformed and made fertile – and thereby precious aquifers under the desert floor were strained."

Rosenbaum's spindly legs were more than a little shaky from a few minutes on his feet. He grasped the side of his desk, resolute to finish the task at hand. The chamber was in a state of pin-drop silence.

"The upheavals in my ancestral homeland came at the cost of displacing another people, Arab Muslims all. Some were driven out of East Jerusalem in 1947 and '48, others fled in '67. They and theirs were never compensated for their property losses.

"Refugee camps sprang up, of course. Children there would eventually foster their own refugee children and then grandchildren. Those who managed to remain in the City of David did so in the certain knowledge of continued poverty.

Over the years, they shared in few of the benefits bestowed by municipal and Israeli federal governments."

His sad stare intersected that of one startled colleague and the next. "By means of housing ordinances, banking restrictions and a general absence of educational and employment opportunities, the continued underclass status of Arab Israelis in East Jerusalem and elsewhere in Palestine was ensured.

"As we should have expected, reprisals followed and have continued, essentially unabated, over three generations – the intifadas.

"Mr. President, I was a young child when I first heard the word *lebensraum* – living space – as Hitler's justification for land grabs in the late 1930s. Unfortunately, 'Zionism,' by dictionary definition the justifiable support of an Israeli homeland, has like *lebensraum* instead become synonymous with expansionism.

"Two years ago I co-sponsored Senate Resolution 141, which called on the Israeli parliament to accept a UN-brokered arrangement to formalize 'home rule' for the Arab-dominated section of East Jerusalem in return for the West Bank lands comprising Jewish settlements. This was a deal applauded by Egypt, Jordan, Saudi Arabia and moderate Arabs everywhere.

"But the prevailing Israeli leadership, true to its myopic party vision of an expanded Jewish homeland in Old Testament terms, turned away that offer as it had previous attempts to find a two-state solution. In so doing, Israel forfeited its final chance to render a permanent peace between the cultures.

"I have loved and still love the nation of Israel. I have visited there, including the villages of my post-World War II forebears, some three dozen times.

"This week, distant cousins of mine were among those who perished in Tel Aviv and Jerusalem, in office buildings and neighborhoods that will remain radioactively off limits for years to come. There is no easy solace for the way in which they died, for the insanity of it."

Slump-shouldered now but still with a fire smoldering, Senator Rosenbaum lifted his shaggy unkempt eyebrows and declared, "My heart ached for revenge! ... Then I checked myself and considered the consequences – all those premature deaths, Muslim and Jew, that have resulted from *four thousand years* of revenge!

"Last evening, in a moment removed from the news and politics of the day, oddly I recalled part of a line from a Celtic ballad: '... another eye and another eye 'til everyone is blind.' I was reminded then that a simple longing for peace cannot forestall unbridled hatred.

"Mr. President, for decades I have been wrong – across a series of public pronouncements and budget deals that excused *lebensraum* in the name of Zionism as originally constructed. For that I am deeply humbled and greatly apologetic."

"He's going 'bad neighbor' says ten bucks," the AP reporter hushed in a challenge to his Reuters seatmate.

"You're on, he won't go that far."

"My friends on both sides of the aisle, the book we must all live by as disparate societies is not the Torah or the New Testament or the Qur'an, for they all give us parochial yet contradictory rules. Instead, we must adhere to the book of *common sense* and the record of laws in *our own* time. That must prevail.

"Hence, it is with a very heavy heart that I make clear now: My religious homeland, Israel, despite all its grievances born in millennia past, was a bad neighbor in the latter half of the twentieth century and beyond."

"Oh, yes! Give me some greenbacks!" The AP reporter whispered with glee, barely containing his excitement at having nailed the exact phrase "bad neighbor" in the senator's remarks. "Do I know the mind of a speech writer or what?"

"Senators sitting here, including myself, have been tepid in our response or altogether silent. And so we have continued a course that was on the wrong side of history and wrong-headed. Why? Because of a 'towel head' mentality, a fundamental sense of superiority held by the Judeo-Christian community over Muslims.

"Well, the Muslims matter now.

"I say this to those who conceived the dastardly attacks this week in response to what they perceive as a pattern of Israeli injustice: Incinerating many thousands of lives in Jerusalem and Tel Aviv, disabling an entire nation's economy, reduces you to a status below your sworn enemies. You are now accountable to God – Allah."

The chamber was still rapt. The old man had a way with audiences.

"Mr. President, colleagues, I ask this of the survivors in Israel and Muslims across the Middle East: Even by the most perverse standard, is this not enough bloodshed? Must we continue to extract an eye for an eye until everyone is blind?"

With halting fingers, the aging senator removed the microphone from his lapel and fell back into his desk chair. His eyes were cast downward, his frail body spent.

This recognized foreign affairs guru and ever-strong Democrat had cut the knees out from under every other member of his party to follow on mic or otherwise on record. The venerable Jewish-American senator had called out his ancestral homeland, critiqued it as a bad neighbor.

Bloggers and conspiracy theorists would rail in the aftermath that the Connecticut senator had struck a deal to help the administration stifle enthusiasm for an Israeli counter-attack against an as-yet unknown enemy and perpetrator.

The cable commentariat suggested four militias and five countries as potential culprits of the attacks on Tel Aviv and Jerusalem. Fox News but virtually no other major outlet directly challenged Rosenbaum's reasoning on Israel's substantial culpability.

Looping footage of the erudite Pro Tem's astonishing remarks on the Senate floor had an immediate and significant effect on the nation's populace. Overnight polls showed a precipitous drop in support for a potential American military action on Israel's behalf.

On December 27, three weeks after the twin blasts, the Arab League fought for its life. Twenty-two representatives sat solemnly around a massive conference table in the administration building of Riyadh's King Sa'ud University. The walls were lined with banded cables leading to Al Jazeera and Al Arabia cameras.

Less than two hundred kilometers north, Saudi joint military evacuations were wrapping up in the cities of Tabuk, Ha'il and the Persian Gulf port at Ra's al Khafji. All three and the desert between lay directly under the light but broadening path of radioactive fallout. In pressing his will on the League to host this emergency meeting, Crown Prince Irfan bin Khazandar might well have chosen Mecca, well to the southwest. Instead, he felt it important to bring the delegates to the precipice, subject to Arabia's shifting winds.

Amman, of course, was completely out of the question as the meeting site. Its hospitals and those across Jordan were overflowing with the stricken, an awful consequence of bordering Israel downwind. With the world's focus necessarily on the disasters in Jerusalem and Tel Aviv, Jordanians had been uprooted in comparative obscurity.

The Iranian ambassador to Saudi Arabia, Hassan Dabir, had accepted Crown Prince Khazandar's forceful invitation to appear before this emergency assembly. Addressing his Persian guest indirectly, the prince was unusually candid in his introductory remarks:

"*Salaam aleikum* (Peace be upon you)," he began. "The Khazandar family and our nation have justly earned a reputation for moderate policies toward our neighbors near and far. Together over the past century we have fought the infidels with the scimitar when necessary but with patience, guile and the weapon below our feet as well. My family and your families are first and always Arabs. For two hundred generations our bond has been strong.

"Hear me now. Three decades ago, immoderate thought sprang from the Lebanese sand in the form of Hizb'alla, bearing the watermark of the Iranian Shi'ite ayatollahs. You know of what I speak. Their relationship dates to Beirut and the 1983 bombing that drove the Americans out of Lebanon.

"It is clear for all to see that Hizb'alla is a wholly owned subsidiary of Iran – the western flank, some say. These malcontents have spread their message of hate onto my family's peninsula. I speak of the Hijaz cells -- which as of this morning are no more."

A stirring among the attendees and reporters grasped the importance of his words. Overnight five dozen key, Shi'a-loyalist

Hijaz combatants, the key players from a tiny but rowdy minority in Saudi Arabia, had been rounded up and held as part of coordinated police raids. They would undoubtedly be put to death in due course.

The Saudi crown prince continued. "It requires no satellite imagery to track those attacks on Jerusalem and Tel Aviv back to the Lebanese border." Eyes narrowed around the silenced room at this apparent confirmation of Hizb'allah involvement.

"My family weeps for the many lives lost among ordinary Israeli citizens. But few of us here truly grieve over the destruction of the Zionist government. One can fairly say they have now reaped their bitter harvest. However, that is not why we sit at this table. The poisonous radiation unleashed has sickened our Muslim brothers and sisters in Jordan and scattered my own people from the northern reaches of our peninsula. Too many to contemplate across our two nations are already suffering and will experience tortured desperate futures."

Many gazes in the room shifted first toward the Iranian Dabir then to the Lebanese delegation. Lebanon's NATO-propped government continued to control Beirut and little else, long since having consented to a de facto power sharing arrangement with the grassroots Hizb'allah movement over much of the southern land bordering Israel.

"We have a choice," Prince Khazandar continued. "We may continue to cooperate with the West, to receive just compensation for our resource and forge bright beginnings for our children, a future filled with technical expertise, robust commerce and fulfilled lives. Or we may turn away from Allah's blessings to lash out at one another with weapons our ancestors never knew, weapons which – if I may speculate – the Prophet himself would have condemned.

"With that, my family and the Arab League offer welcome to the ambassador from Iran. We await his answers to our questions."

Dabir, a slight man even among his Iranian compatriots, stepped lightly across the room to the rostrum. His full, prematurely graying beard belied his age of 32. Standing below one of the hall's magnificent crystal chandeliers, he pulled sheets of prepared remarks from a breast pocket.

"Distinguished delegates, I bring you greetings from Grand Ayatollah Alireza Vahid Shirazi, the Council of Guardians of Islam, President Nazila Fadavi, and the Iranian people.

"My country is shocked and saddened by the recent events that have befallen our region. I wish to assure you that the Revolutionary Guard Corps commander, General Emad Kadivar, has undertaken a thorough investigation in response to the unfortunate rumors that Iran had anything at all to do with this despicable act of savagery against the nation of Israel and the great difficulties it has caused to Saudi and Jordanian citizens.

"In the long and exalted histories of our peoples, the nation-state of Iran has sought mutually beneficial accords wherever possible. We respect every—"

Jordan's foreign minister, Adnan As-Sahm was on his feet. "'Respect'? 'Shocked and saddened'? You mock the words!" the distant cousin of Saudi Arabia's Prince Alsahm screamed.

Collective breaths and rustling sounds overtook the room momentarily. Arab League gatherings were renowned, if not for productive international accords, at least for their civility and decorum in difficult times.

Taken aback by the outburst, a flustered Dabir returned his attention to his text, but before he could find his place again the rotund As-Sahm stepped away from his seat as if to physically challenge his younger rival.

"Persians know *nothing* of respect, only conquest and blood spilled across the sands and the seas for thousands of years! You have created 'saints' from hooligans! Now your theocracy has falsely read the Qur'an once again."

Dabir stepped away from the rostrum, flustered, arms flapping, his eye sockets wide, looking from left to right for assistance in quelling this outburst.

"For too long," As-Sahm continued, "you failed to develop facilities to extract and process your oil and thus robbed the proud citizens of Iran of the better life Muhammad promised. Instead you export mayhem!

"Your infidel ayatollahs were not satisfied with Shi'a influence across Iraq, Lebanon and Syria. Now they would war on the original and true Islam. One can reach no other conclusion but that they seek ultimate regional domination, not by peacefully spreading the righteous words of Allah expressed by Muhammad but through terror. I condemn you! My government and all Sunnis condemn your false beliefs and your illegitimate rulers!"

With that, As-Sahm removed his Italian loafers and hurled them, one after the other, at Dabir. By mere chance, the leather heel of one clipped the Iranian ambassador on the left ear, drawing a trickle of blood. This extreme insult was unmistakable. An Arab throwing a shoe was tantamount to the denunciation, "You are lower and dirtier than the soles of my feet, you dog!"

Dabir pointedly spat in the general direction of As-Sahm as he made his exit.

In an anticlimactic gesture of unity, the representatives from Oman and Bahrain, both Shi'a-majority countries, arose and followed Ambassador Dabir through the exit.

WINTER SOLSTICE

For all the bravado, however, nothing of substance would be decided this day or in Arab League gatherings to follow. For all Arabs, including Saudis, Egyptians and Jordanians, quietly exulted in the 'downsizing' of Jewish hegemony in the region.

Chapter Four

The pre-dawn darkness of March 9, 1916 had concealed hundreds of Mexican revolutionaries under the command of General Francisco "Pancho" Villa. At that hour they attacked the New Mexican border town of Columbus and its longtime protector, Camp Furlong, a leftover U.S. cavalry outpost. It was the first armed invasion of the continental United States since the War of 1812. The village and Army post were left in smoking ruins; dozens lay dead.

Within hours word of Villa's attack flashed by telegraph across the nation, displacing the next day's routine newspaper headlines. In short order, President Woodrow Wilson and the U.S. Army organized a punitive force of 10,000 to track down Villa. The troops ventured into Mexico under the command of General John "Black Jack" Pershing, who a year and change later would command the successful American Expeditionary Force in World War I.

Pershing eventually rose to the highest Army rank ever held, General of the Armies, equivalent only to the posthumous rank accorded George Washington. But in this Mexican "tune-up," he and his men came away with no medals. After tromping for eleven months across the sand, tumbleweeds, cactus and hills of northern Mexico, rousting dozens of settlements to no avail, they came to the bitter conclusion that Villa had vanished.

Addressing *realpolitik* in 1959, as a potential tourist attraction the New Mexico state legislature approved the creation and funding of Pancho Villa State Park on the grounds of the old Camp Furlong just outside Columbus. Eventually a 7,000-square-foot exhibit hall was erected, and in 1999 expedition-era vehicles and other military artifacts from Pershing's march were added.

Each winter brought a trickle of motor home traffic to that desert terrain and the 62 spartan campsites there, adjoining the one-stoplight village. Hampered by an average January high under 60 degrees Fahrenheit – with summer highs often over 100 – the Pancho Villa theme never really caught on. Short of such a tourist boost, Columbus remained a hardscrabble footnote in the American Southwest, another way station for Mexicans moving north for work.

Never having prospered generally from its part of the bargain in the North American Free Trade Agreement, the skewed Mexican economy left ever growing millions of its citizens uneducated and without enough solid entry-level employment. Inevitably came a renewed surge across the largely unprotected borders of New Mexico as well as Texas, Arizona and California.

Columbus and the U.S. Border Patrol station located just south of town became embroiled in NAFTA's failure as young men and whole families by the hundreds and then thousands, on word of mouth, found their way every month to the shower and toilet facilities at Pancho Villa State Park.

Eventually – several years after the federal crackdown was ordered – a long-delayed electronic fence, aerial drone sweeps and regular ground patrols essentially put an end to the crossing practice. But not before a widely aired shooting of four unarmed individuals in the park's restroom by a pair of self-styled militia men – Anglos with a hateful purpose. The shooters later claimed they had broken up a drug transaction. In an electric courtroom six months later, they were exonerated by an all-Anglo jury. Pershing, effectively, had the last word.

A century after Villa's attack and now well removed from the recent nuclear madness in the Middle East, southwestern New Mexico this July morning was tranquil, warm and dry. Having reached a low of 73, the thermometer would climb to 101 by mid-afternoon. With humidity just under 20 percent, men working outside wouldn't appear sweaty; the droplets of perspiration instead crystallized into a light salty grit just below hairlines and across cheekbones. But no one in the village of Columbus talked much about summer weather. These were age-old conditions, expected and tolerated; this was the desert.

Attesting to the adaptation of human spirit, the long months of heat here had little effect on children's play. Bicycling and running in some form remained favorite pastimes all summer. With median household incomes at just over $27,000 per year and homes valued at $85,000 on average, most of the seven hundred youngsters in Columbus had no laptop to occupy their time, no portable games to engage in thumb combat, no mall to loiter in. Instead, joyful moments were found on the cheap, with a rubber soccer ball, a bat and worn-out gloves, or lines of chalk on a vacant driveway for a variation on hopscotch.

Eighty-three percent of the 2,000-plus Columbus residents had listed Hispanic origins to 2020 census takers. The proportion of Anglos was considerably higher back in the '70s and '80s. But with the migrant influx prior to the *valla que rodea el perimetro* (perimeter fence), the village's population grew 165 percent from 1990-2000 alone, all Latino. Still, the great majority who now experienced Columbus soon moved on to hoped-for prosperity – north to Albuquerque and Denver or east into Texas.

Only 35 percent of Columbus' adult residents had a high school diploma. Nearly half were without work, and most of the rest were underemployed. A debit card swiped at the local market was less likely to draw on a checking account than on the individual's monthly allotment from the USDA's venerable Food and Nutrition Service – electronic food stamps.

The village tavern, Cisco's Hideout, was one of the struggling Columbus enterprises. The décor was set to the simplistic fifties TV western, "The Cisco Kid." Large black-and-white posters across two walls featured action shots taken on the Arizona sets where Cisco and his sidekick Pancho – that *other* Pancho – dispensed justice every week. Draft beer and tequila shots remained at happy-hour prices sixteen hours a day. The Hideout's clientele, a sadly happy regular gathering of settled-out Chicanos, spent much of their time on the premises one-upping each other in Spanish with tales of what might have been. A jukebox in a back corner played salsa continuously, at no charge.

Before sunrise every morning, a score of old pickups, each with six to eight brown-skinned men in the cargo box, headed north on Highway 11 toward Deming, the county seat 35 miles away. A community of 16,000, Deming itself was two-thirds Hispanic and not prosperous by any stretch. Less desperately poor might have better depicted its stature. Some of the day laborers from Columbus would find work there. The rest hoped to catch another ride fifty miles east to Las Cruces to look for construction sites more promising.

<hr />

Fourteen-year-old Miguel Flores slapped his alarm silent at 5:30 AM, the 21st of July, and immediately slipped into faded lycra shorts and well-worn Nikes. Following leg and torso stretches, by 5:45 he was out the kitchen door of his family's small ranch home on the outer reaches of Columbus.

From Windsock Avenue he reached State Hwy 9, heading west out of town. It was his weekly long run, a 10-miler that took him first to County Road (CR) 6, a craggy two-track suitable for foot traffic, the sturdiest off-road vehicles and little else. Miguel picked his way north along the rutty, hard-packed sandy path, heading northwest toward the South Sister.

This route was ideal for gaining leg strength: It climbed from less than 4,100 feet at his home to over 4,700 at the mountain's base. The South Sister rose another 1,500 feet — a little shorter than the Middle and North Sisters beyond and out of sight.

Finally reaching its base where the path angled right, his challenge became mostly one of balance as the rough trail, no longer suitable to any vehicular traffic, gradually descended to the desert floor. Featuring ubiquitous stones and larger rocks, ruts and washouts, conquering CR-6 would put him in good stead for any autumn cross-country route.

The youth continued his balanced left-right dance, tapping his way gradually downward around all the irregularities in this undulating yet doable path. At the end of the long promenade, the two-track would change, in official number only, to CR-9, leading him east to Columbus Road, the southward highway home.

Miguel was feeling strong and exhilarated as he carefully loped along, picking his way around more ruts and rocks, the hardest part behind him. Maybe next time he'd try this course in reverse, starting northward from Columbus, he thought. His breaths were measured, his quads and ankles firm and responsive as he leaned back slightly on the descent.

He thought again about six weeks from now when he'd be enrolled at Deming High as a freshman and starting the cross-country season. Some of his adult neighbors already referred to him good naturedly as a single-minded youth on a mission to impress the coach. He didn't mind the banter; running made him feel good about himself.

With an age-group win – 16 and under – in the Deming Days 5K, his first road race last April, Miguel realized he had better-than-ordinary stamina. What that might ultimately mean (possibly a scholarship to some college far away?) was vaguely in his consciousness at this juncture. Quietly confident, he just knew he loved to run and didn't easily tire. From a school library book on distance running and fitness he followed, Miguel's training pace was down to 7:10 per mile for his routine 4- and 6-milers on flat-and-fast weekday routes. But today he had intentionally cut back to 8:30 miles for this longer, rougher trek.

The U.S. Space Surveillance Network was sophisticated radar with optical sensors to detect, identify and track some 10,000 man-made objects in space – mostly the sixty years' worth of debris from space launches that remained in orbit. Pieces as small as a basketball, 20,000 miles up, were detectable.

The network predicted the paths of this myriad of objects from orbit to orbit, warning other agencies of an impending collision when occasionally necessary. More than an afterthought, this agency was likewise responsible for the early warning of any potential foreign attack using space.

Because it could not realistically track every piece of space trash circling Earth, the system's operations core, the Space Surveillance Center inside Cheyenne Mountain, Colorado Springs, routinely updated a prioritized list of selected objects to observe. As a rule of thumb, those were mostly in the latter stages of decaying orbits or with "high-value" purposes. That data was forwarded among other places to stations located near Socorro, New Mexico; Maui, Hawaii; and Diego Garcia in the Indian Ocean.

Those three facilities constituted the mid-range arm of America's Ground-based Electro-Optical Deep Space Surveillance System (GEODSS). Their telescopic TV cameras each scanned two degrees of the sky overhead on a given night, watching for fly-bys of the known objects chosen for that hour. Gigabytes from their rapid-fire cameras were sent instantly to Cheyenne Mountain to electronically wash of all visible stars, leaving only artificial objects. The precise position, speed and declination of each targeted object were then calculated relative to its previous orbits. A computer program predicted the next orbital coordinates, and the new set was passed back to the three stations for the next pass.

Separately, the Navistar Global Positioning System was the world's map, a moving yet static "constellation" of 36 satellites (including four used as back-ups) circling the globe in so-called medium earth orbit, forming a spherical net of eight overlapping rings in space, 12,550 miles above the Earth. In unison, all continuously circumnavigated the globe every twelve hours.

With their rubidium-cesium atomic clocks, they provided continuous worldwide triangulation – GPS – for use by ships, planes, hikers, drivers and telecommunications everywhere. A Navistar satellite was the size of a large van and weighed nearly a ton. Its smallish solar panels spread over seven square meters.

On this early morning, 21 July, a duty officer deep within Cheyenne Mountain, Lt. Bradley Williams, was collecting readouts, among them the latest on a Navistar machine. It had already served four months beyond its 7.5-year predicted life but was still performing flawlessly. In perhaps another year its orbit would begin to decay inexorably until the machine finally fell out of orbit. For now, it was about to cross over the Socorro facility, which awaited an update on its path.

Lieutenant Williams had graduated a year before from the Air Force Academy, just across town, with a degree in avionics and astronautics. He aspired to attend astronaut school one day.

It was now 6:27 AM Mountain Daylight Time.

The Navistar was just into its pass over southwestern New Mexico when a monitor attended by one of Williams' airmen began flashing an alert; he was picking up something unexpected. Readouts quickly showed an unidentified under the 22,000-mile GEODSS ceiling and on a steep descent. By rough initial calculations it was arcing generally on a path toward the Navistar satellite.

With four rapid mouse clicks Williams brought up the "General Wash" program, manually removing any planet, all the stars and all the known debris from his screen, leaving only the Navistar, the unexpected interloper and bordering graphics. He used successive screen overlays to speed through and catch up on the photographic sequence – split-second images since the bogey was first detected half a minute before. Whatever it was, this was *not* on his priority list.

The lieutenant's software quickly calculated the intruder's velocity as just over 190,000 mph – way, *way* beyond the potential of a ballistic missile, even beyond the potential of any known NEAR (near-earth asteroid) pulled in by Earth's gravity. An incoming comet from the far reaches of the solar system would've been detected long before now.

Images from Socorro's telescopic camera continued to relay onto Williams' monitor, one overlying the next, showing an ever more sharply downward trajectory. Earth's gravity shouldn't be pulling a static object this hard, he knew.

Bradley strapped on his earpiece and tapped out a five-digit number on his i-pod. "Stacey, this is me. I know this isn't protocol, but if you ever did care for me, please put the colonel on *right* now. It's that important." She read the tension in his voice and quickly complied.

Waiting, he wondered hard how costly it might be – doing the right thing if not expedient – at this moment in his young career. The Air Force didn't take kindly to ignoring the chain of command. But there was simply no time to find the captain or major. They weren't in sight and could be in an extended men's room session reading the sports section or outside the building having a smoke. *There wasn't supposed to be anything unusual!*

Finally he heard a not unexpectedly grumpy voice. "This is Colonel Lemke, what's the problem, Lieutenant."

"Sir, I realize I've skipped a rung or two and I apologize, but there's something here you need to be aware of. It just came down over Socorro in camera range. We were routinely tracking a Navistar when this – whatever it is – came into view suddenly on a steep decline, an improbable one. Its speed is, uh, well, so far beyond an ICBM and well past any asteroid we know of. It's something very peculiar, sir. The readouts plot it at close to 200K, sir. We have no clue what it might be, but it seems to be angling toward a possible intercept with the Navistar we were tracking."

"You said 200K, Lieutenant?"

"Yes, sir."

"Not 20,000 miles per hour. Two *hundred* thousand miles per hour?"

Williams hit the refresh button on his keyboard and quickly

reassured himself as to the absurd velocity and trajectory numbers appearing along the bottom of his relay screen. His linked airman across the room looked at him and offered an exaggerated shrug of his shoulders. Williams repeated, "Ah, around 191,700, sir. That's what we have – and descending at now over an 87-degree trajectory."

"Lieutenant, this is explainable – first of all because it's ludicrous!" Colonel Lemke tried to reassure the young officer in typically hard-nosed fashion. "Could be a computer snafu, y'know. If it is, we'll get it straightened out. What's the status right now?"

"One moment, sir." Williams glanced at his monitor, spoke briefly with his airman then responded. "It looks to be still above the satellite on a nearly vertical angle of descent. Less than thirty seconds to potential intercept. It looks like ... sorry, Colonel, the overlays of the new screens are delayed a couple seconds behind real time."

"That's all right, Lieutenant, just keep your focus and figure this out." Lemke pondered for a moment. Nothing Chinese or Russian was possible; the Pentagon would have been onto such an advancement before now. Whatever its origin, destroying an American GPS satellite would be a grave provocation. He spoke again. "Lieutenant, are you suggesting I contact Be-Mews?"

The Ballistic Missile Early Warning System, age-old radar, really, had been part of NORAD in the years before 1982 when the Space Command was formed to combine U.S. missile defense efforts with space operations.

"We've heard nothing from them," Lemke continued, "at least to my knowledge, but it would be worth ..."

The colonel's words trailed away when he heard a commotion of voices. Several seconds hence the lieutenant spoke again. "Sir, I believe the intercept threat is over."

"How's that?"

"Well, the screen overlays are showing the bogey. ... Ah, it looks like the bogey veered around the satellite and continued toward our floor, almost straight down. And it ... it just vanished all of a sudden at about 4,500 miles. Sir, Socorro can't see below 3,000 miles, as you know. But the target was gone well before that.

"There's nothing left on their screen. Socorro no longer has a target – except for the satellite. ... And that's progressing in its normal orbit. ... It seems to be unaffected."

Lemke displayed a growing irritation. "Well, did the bogey just burn up or what?" He waited for a response.

Williams demurred. "I just can't say for certain, sir." Reciting now, "The Leonids shower in November produces the fastest meteors in the solar system, sir, about 160K. No rock from the asteroid belt or comet from way farther out in the solar system should get enough whip from a planet, even Jupiter, to reach close to 200K.

"Sir, the Air Force taught me that nothing in our solar system moves that fast – and the progression of slope was just way too steep to be from Earth's gravitational pull alone," this junior officer skilled in mathematics rapidly added.

"Sir, its movement as it grew closer to the Navistar reminded me of how a nasty slider drops across home plate, if you know baseball. Just a sharp movement. Something responding to natural forces like our gravity really wouldn't do that, not at that speed. Plus we should've seen it breaking up at that velocity, but whatever its surface shape, it was maintaining its integrity throughout. And then, Colonel, after it veered past the satellite, at 4,500 it just winked off the screen."

An uncomfortable silence ensued. "That's the way I viewed it, sir," Williams finally said.

"It veered, you say. It was angling directly toward our Navistar and then it veered. Like a slider."

"Yes, sir."

"Purposefully?"

"I can't say that, sir. I'd need some real metal on my shoulders to make that call."

The colonel pressed his point. "What was Socorro looking at, Lieutenant?"

Williams cleared his throat. "We just don't know, sir. We haven't experienced anything quite like it in my fourteen months here."

"Fourteen months," Lemke sighed. "Okay, well, if we don't get word of a mighty blast in the next few seconds," the colonel reasoned, "I believe your *superior* should call in your IT unit to do a thorough diagnosis of hardware and software and coordinate with Socorro as they do the same. Maybe some hacker finally broke in and ran a game on us. If that's the case, we'll all have a laugh over a beer this evening, right, Lieutenant?"

"Uh, yes, I guess, so, sir."

Lemke flipped his phone off and sat down firmly in his desk chair as long-ago memories rushed back. *Christ, it's not starting again, is it?* He was no stranger to unidentified objects reported in the sky. Over his 37 years in the Air Force, the last 24 with Space Command, he'd seen lots of computer screens and statistical readouts indicating lots of unexplained blips and streaks. On occasion it was more than that. Like now.

UFOs were the worst-kept secret in Space Command. Every year a hundred or so enlisted men and women separated from the Air Force, and this surveillance effort, after a stern warning never to reveal what they had seen or heard of a sensitive nature – on penalty of certain court-martial and imprisonment.

In moments the colonel was on the line with "Be-Mews," which had no activity whatsoever to suggest a ballistic missile had been launched toward the United States. More checks by his staff assured Lemke that no explosion of any sort was being reported in any Southwest state or Mexico's bordering state of Chihuahua.

The Maui Optical Tracking Facility, the Passive Space Surveillance System, and various phased-array and mechanical radars in the western states were accessed in the hope that some documented triangulation would be forthcoming. There would not be.

Lemke's final call was to General Washburn at the Space Command Directorate. It was now 6:34 AM Mountain time.

Miguel's lithe but solid 130-pound frame danced and weaved, his steps issuing a light percussion against the sand and rocks, breaths still measured. Focused on foot placement he loped along, constantly adjusting to maintain efficient form.

Snake hole, a glance ahead alerted. He'd seen a diamondback in this section just a few weeks ago. He gave it wide berth.

As on many past occasions, Miguel was drawn to the utter silence here. Boulders as big as houses had, countless eons ago, crashed down these slopes to their current resting spots. Mr. Vasquez, his eighth-grade science teacher, had explained all about mountain building and deterioration last year, using the Sisters as an example. Miguel once more imagined for a second the enormous force necessary to catapult them upward. But now it was so quiet; footfalls and steady breaths were all he heard. He couldn't wait for the cross-country racing season at Deming High.

He pulled his ballcap lower to block the morning sun ahead. His breathing was a little elevated, he took note, but easing on the descent, not a concern at this point. He checked his watch: 6:38. He was confident of holding his pace the rest of the way. Endorphins were in his bloodstream; he was feeling the subtle "runner's high," a general sense of well-being with every stride.

Just then, something (a reflection?) caught his eye and jarred him to keen awareness. In front of him to the southeast, not far removed from the eastern sun's glare, a brilliant light was coming his way. He held his pace, sharing glances between his upcoming footfalls and this new detail. Airplane headlights? he wondered. *Awfully low.* This curiosity seemed to move past Columbus Road and continue over the desert terrain in his direction.

Gradually Miguel's glances defined an outline. It was a ball, a glowing amber ball! Six feet in diameter, more or less, he reasoned. It slashed from his right to left across the flat expanse then upwards. In a second or less it was lost from sight behind the South Sister's long eastern ridge on the boy's left.

Miguel stopped abruptly and stared up the slope. Meteor? He considered. No, it couldn't be, no explosion. Besides, this was a perfect sphere! And meteors were fantastically fast, Mr. Vasquez had told the class. Faster than a speeding bullet, he liked to say, many thousands of miles an hour. Whatever he had just seen – for what, ten seconds? – was fast but not *that* fast.

He thought again about the absence of an explosion. On impact, a meteor that big would've blown him off his feet or worse, even from the other side of the ridge. Plus it looked almost, well, graceful, he considered.

His heart raced as he stood there, trying to account for what he had just seen. It was something he couldn't begin to explain, and he figured Mr. Vasquez probably couldn't, either.

In that moment, undecided whether to be frightened or brave, he heard his name called: "Miguel." Where had *that* come from? It was a young female voice – as if right next to him. *Or was it in my head?*

Again the voice intoned, "Miguel, do not be afraid. You will not be harmed." The globe of intensely glowing yellow-orange light rose up without a sound over the cascade of boulders that formed the eastern ridge. The sphere settled into a rocky niche within a jumble well above where he stood, less than a hundred meters angularly upward.

To his further amazement, momentarily the upright figure of a woman somehow emerged from the light and proceeded to float slowly through the air, angling lower toward him, moving neither her arms nor legs. As she approached, he could see that she was barefoot, that her hands were folded at her waist. She was no older than late teenage – and certainly looked real enough. Yet someplace in his consciousness he remained skeptical. *She's not translucent or anything*, he reasoned, conjuring up the specter of a ghost. But quickly he shouted back at himself, *People don't float!*

The youth cried out softly under his breath and subconsciously stepped sideways, stumbled into a rut and nearly lost his balance. He was overcome with a witch's brew of emotions: stark fear mixed with intrigue and something approaching elation.

As the young female figure approached, Miguel detected a subtle but unmistakable aura of yellowish-white light completely surrounding her, extending out several inches from her torso. Her eyes were now fixated on his. He seemed unable, or unwilling, to break their mutual gaze, which deepened the closer she came. His thoughts were slowing; he was captivated in the truest sense.

The diva's feet were skimming a few feet over the spiny, ground-hugging cactus plants.

She was not unattractive in a girl-next-door sort of way, with light olive skin, dark eyes and eyebrows and thick dark hair falling in waves beyond her shoulders. But it was her manner of dress that struck the boy as she neared. An ankle-length, formless yet elegant white gown reminded him of his mother's winter nightgowns except for its silky, flowing look. Pulled over most of her hair and dress and extending toward her bare feet was a sky blue veil, likewise silky-looking.

Santa Maria! He caught himself. *Santa Maria?* the youth pondered.

The figure halted in mid-air, just over a cactus plant twenty feet away. For a timeless moment she continued to stare at him, her face pleasant but unsmiling. Miguel struggled to form a thought, to make sense of the moment. She seemed real – here and now – and yet somehow couldn't be, his mind was slowly processing.

The teen spread her arms outward, hands open to the sky. Still gazing at the boy, she began to speak: "Miguel, you must help. Tell your priest that I have returned. Bring him here."

Miguel's mind absorbed the words, but the core of his being remained awestruck. Finally summoning the will to utter a phrase he asked, "Are you … her?"

"I am the one known as Miriam."

Huh? Transfixed, his mind was sluggish. *Miriam?* He could no longer formulate a cohesive thought and so simply listened.

"Your world is greatly troubled. The final battle has begun. There can be no winner. Bring your priest here tomorrow at this hour," she said emphatically.

With that, the figure clasped her hands again, then she retreated angularly and swiftly upward toward the ball of light, vanishing within its glow. The sphere then raced vertically into the clear morning sky and out of sight in less than a second.

Gathering himself, Miguel fled down the path for home, checking the time once more as he set out: 6:40.

Chapter Five

Kenna Nowitzky rocked pensively in her cordovan leather chair and, as was a regular part of her routine, prioritized the world's events and situations in her mind. Rust-tinted highlights in her short-cropped dark brown hair glinted in the morning sun through her window. The effect rendered her almost pretty.

Kenna had one of the six prestigious corner offices on the fourth floor of the Pentagon – a recognition of influence over authority. She held the formal title of Special Assistant to Thomas Hagelthorne, Secretary of the Department of Homeland Security. For security reasons Hagelthorne's suite was located in the building's interior.

In daily (and evening) practice, Kenna was the filter and funnel – and a first among equals in a building stacked with specialists. She possessed a phenomenal memory, exceptional multi-tasking skills, and a cool if too often sarcastic demeanor.

By Hagelthorne's directive the previous year, Kenna was to be copied on all internal emails, FAXs and reports "concerning events or developing situations potentially or substantially threatening to United States interests in the short term – whether of a commercial, political or military nature." Thus her essential role: triage.

Hagelthorne trusted Kenna to cull the most pressing new information from the world's hot spots and produce, on 24-hour cycles, a descending list of priorities. These he would massage into his portion of the President's daily security briefing. If sufficiently critical, Kenna could even interrupt departmental schedules.

She had reached this post by making a name for herself outside government. Following post-doctoral work in political science and international relations at Indiana University, she taught undergraduates and then grad students over fifteen years at the University of Illinois in Champaign-Urbana. Along the way, she gained a reputation among political insiders for her no-nonsense, pragmatic, insightful critiques of U.S. foreign relations. She became a popular guest on AM radio talk shows emanating from Chicago and St. Louis, simulcast on the Web.

Kenna took a leave of absence from the U of I to serve as foreign policy advisor for the reelection bid of Wayne Johnston (R-Illinois), a member of the Senate Foreign Relations Committee. Following the senator's November victory, she took the plunge from academia to hands-on administration with this high appointment, at Johnston's behest, in Homeland Security.

She found the transition from a college town to D.C. living manageable, the faster pace at her office exhilarating. A year and a half later, the swirl of issues emanating from far-flung places held her interest through seven-day, 70-hour weeks. This was her pinnacle and dream job.

The Middle East, forever and always, it seemed, still predominated – though more recently the crumbling of Ukraine and the South American puzzle were stealing real attention.

Already a grizzled veteran of internal HSA policy disputes, she evaluated the events of every day in terms of overlapping chess boards.

The "temporary dissolution" of Israel, as agency parlance now portrayed it after all the hands were wrung, posed a new set of geopolitical circumstances, no simpler but different. This was not merely a matter of one less participant in a regional restructuring underway. Israel's effective demise had created a sudden and enormous power vacuum.

America was still sorting through the diplomacy of it all. Life, and politics, went on.

Back from a first meeting this morning, Kenna poured another cup of joe. A forwarded message on her secure screen had originated from Space Command, bumped over by the Air Force liaison office. The yellow flashing light bar suggested priority attention.

She scanned the text of the memo, sent forty minutes before from a Colonel Lemke at NORAD to the Space Command director, Lieutenant General Raymond Washburn. Then she flipped to the attached log entry. Lemke had ordered a thorough debugging, which would take hours. Rationally it was a false reading. She consigned the communication to her low-priority e-folder. It was likely another factually challenged suggestion squeezed into the cracks of real crises ongoing or imminent.

Kenna turned her attention back to the latest details from overnights on the pirating of a European luxury liner off the coast of St. Thomas, now in its second day. Had the guerillas in charge seen the manifest, they might well have recognized one of its passengers, the second-born son of Karl Gustaf, King of Sweden. A quietly introduced news blackout there had kept his identity from reaching the greater Euro and American press.

She processed the piracy factoids: good blackmail potential but implications for U.S. policy were negligible; no direct threat to any American interest for now; no reason for concerted involvement. She sent this one to her late-afternoon follow-up folder, leaned back in her chair and arranged all the morning's news again in her mind.

Miguel burst through the kitchen door and skidded to a stop before his mother, who was in the midst of rolling tortillas for breakfast. It was 7:12 AM. "Mami! I ... it ..." Suddenly he had no words for what had happened.

Rosalinda Flores realized only that something was terribly wrong. She hastily rinsed her hands under the sink then reached to hug her oldest child, knowing that whatever it was, he needed to collect himself first. "Was it a snake?" she finally whispered. She felt him shake his head no. This was very unlike him.

After more seconds, their embrace having calmed his nerves somewhat, Miguel broke away and looked at her intently. Heaving a sigh, he began in rapid fire:

"I was on my run, and just after I turned back east and was passing by the front of the South Sister, I saw this ... this ... I don't know *what* it was! It was a ball – I mean a glowing light. It was both! It was glowing really, really bright and it was a perfect sphere!" His words tumbled out ever faster.

"First it came down toward the Sister and ducked behind the ridge. Then it came back up over the ridge and went into a notch there, and right in there somewhere I heard my name called. 'Miguel,' like that, 'don't be afraid.' But it was crazy! I heard this voice like it was right next to me, Mami. No, even closer; it was like wearing earphones for the hearing test at school, where the tones are right there in your brain. But there was no one there! Just this ball of light up the slope.

"And then I thought maybe I dreamed it up or something, the voice. But it happened again, 'Miguel,' like that," imitating a soft female tone. "And then this older girl came out of the ball and just floated down to me! But she wasn't dressed like us. She was dressed like really olden times. And—"

"All right, my son," Rosalinda interrupted. She placed her hands firmly on his upper arms. She saw the anxiousness in his eyes; there was more to tell, she knew, but he needed to slow down. Miguel didn't frighten easily, this she'd always known about him. Whatever had happened out there, she was convinced that, with a few moments to reflect, he would find the truth of it himself.

"I love you and respect you," she said reassuringly, "and I want to hear the whole story. Now, settle down and start at the beginning."

Miguel poured out every detail he could recall, including the diva's exact words. When he had finished, Rosalinda let out a heavy sigh before responding. "How tired were you when you saw this ... girl? Did you get enough sleep last night? You push yourself with this running."

"Not tired at all, no!" Miguel blurted. "This was *not* my imagination," he said emphatically, his eyes widening.

"All right," she soothed, "we will go see Father Estefan."

"When?" the boy's voice filled with exasperation.

"After you have something to eat," she replied soberly, "and take a shower!"

"Padre Estefan, thank you for seeing us this morning," Rosalinda Flores began. "I do not know what you can do, maybe nothing. But my son feels he needs to speak with you."

"Do you prefer that we converse in Spanish," the priest opened as always.

"No, we use English in this Anglo country. That is fair to

everyone."

"Miguel, sure, hello," the cleric said to the young runner. He reached across his worn wooden desk centered in the home's small living room that served as the parish office and grabbed the boy's smaller hand. Adolescents, regardless of ethnic background, had never been famous for their firm handshakes. "I hear you might be the next Alberto Salazar."

The Cuban-born American Salazar had won three consecutive New York City marathons in the 1980s and set American records in the 5,000- and 10,000-meter runs. The youth flushed and smiled at the absurd comparison with America's greatest distance runner. "I do okay, I guess, Father," he replied with a shy grin.

The priest looked firmly at his young visitor. "You don't come to Mass much, Miguel. Why not?"

"I don't know, Father," the boy mumbled, taken a little aback. Then, summoning a bit of nerve for a second, "Um, maybe I don't get much out of it, I guess," his words trailing away with his gaze.

"Fair enough," Estefan smiled. "I'll try to work on that." Turning back to Senora Flores, "And how is Renaldo? Is he finding enough work?"

"Oh, yes, sixty hours a week and more," she responded. "But that is not ... Miguel, tell Father Estefan what happened."

After a brief moment to collect his thoughts, the young runner spoke continuously for five minutes, offering all the factual details he could recall of the incident. He moved nervously in his seat, feeling that what he was saying didn't make enough sense.

When he had finished, the priest looked hard at him for a

moment then rose and strode easily to a north-facing window, his footfalls creaking on the old wooden floor. He raised the blinds and looked out toward the Three Sisters on the distant horizon.

"How you doing in school, Miguel?" he asked without looking back.

"I had four A's and two B-pluses for spring semester, Father."

Estefan continued. "Good, good. You like VH1?"

"We don't get cable, Father," Miguel said with the knowledge of a youth who had seen the venerable music channel on rare occasion in a larger town.

"You tell friends hi on Twitter?"

Miguel didn't look down. He wouldn't see his lack of Web-calling devices as a point of shame. "We don't have Internet at our house."

For half a minute the only sounds were those of Estefan's fingers drumming on the window frame. Plan B. He spoke again while continuing to stare out at the mountains four miles away. Hopefully, he thought, the youth was open to a little coaching.

"You're throwing your right foot out on your kickoff. As your mileage increases, that could lead to shin splints or stress on your knees, if not problems with your hip joints. You're also throwing your right arm out a little more than your left; that's why your right foot is flying out. I think if you concentrate on your arm carriage you'll be okay."

Miguel's jaw fell agape a bit. *How could he know that?*

"But that was a nice win in the 16-and-under at Deming. Congratulations."

"You were there?" the boy asked.

"Mm-hmm." Estefan turned to face him and offered an explanation: "Diocesan meetings that weekend." Then, "I ran cross-country at the seminary, Miguel. But tell me, how did you feel out there?"

"You mean—?"

"When the presence was there," Estefan added, choosing his words judiciously.

Miguel hesitated, thinking back again to the encounter. "Um, it's hard to say, Father. Maybe a little weird. Like, I wasn't real tired or anything; I still had a lot in the tank, y'know? But nothing like that ever happened to me before, so I don't know how I was supposed to feel."

"How many senses do we have?"

"Physical senses? Uh, sight, hearing, smell, taste, touch. Yeah, five, why?"

"Isn't there a sixth? Just knowing?"

"Well, hmmm, I don't know. Maybe," Miguel pondered. *Where is this going?*

Estefan moved back across the room and sat on the front of his desk, directly before Miguel. "Senora Flores, would you mind waiting outside for a few minutes?" his eyes fixed on his main guest.

When Rosalinda and the girls had exited, "So, who was she, Miguel?"

"The girl? I don't know. Like I said, she called herself Miriam. I don't know about any Miriam." He paused, renewing the picture in his mind. "Maybe it was a ghost, I don't know. I mean, she was floating, y'know? But she looked real and everything, like you could touch her, I think. Except I couldn't on account of something that was like invisible that was pressing on me when she was close to me there."

"Uh-huh, hmmm."

"Um, she didn't look Latino, really, y'know, like Indian in her blood, but she had some, like, complexion." He thought some more. "But there was something strange about her. Like she was really there, y'know, but like at the same time there was something that made me think maybe ... I don't know, like she wasn't real or something. Does that make sense, Father?"

"Just knowing," Estefan countered. "Did her dress surprise you?"

"Well, yeah, sure. At first it reminded me of the robe Mami wears for bed in the winter when it's cold out, y'know, all the way to the floor. But it was like olden times, like you see on a statue or like that. We've got a picture in our house of Our Lady of Guadalupe. It was kinda like that, y'know, a robe almost – and real nice, like silk or something. And the long blue veil and everything."

"How familiar are you with the history of Guadalupe?" Estefan threw into the exchange.

"Um, Mexico City. There's a big cathedral, and there's always been a big parade every year, I think."

"Yes, there's a feast day parade and festival. But what do you know about how that all came to be?" he pressed.

"Hmmm, you mean about the Virgin Mary? Um, well, ... I think a peasant man, he saw her and she made like a print of herself on his shirt, and so they built a chapel there and later on the cathedral – at that place where they first met."

"It was his poncho, Miguel – actually a 'tilma,' they called it back then – cactus fiber," the priest corrected.

"Well, the picture in my parents' bedroom doesn't look quite like that. It's like all cleaned up, maybe, y'know?"

The priest held the adolescent's gaze. "It was faked."

"I know, that's what I'm saying. The picture in their bedroom, it's like a copy or something."

"No, the impression on the original tilma was a fake, Miguel. The image of Our Lady of Guadalupe on that poncho was painted by a Catholic convert, a Tarascan Indian named Marcos Cipac. He was a skilled local painter but he didn't have nice canvasses to work with, so he painted the image of Mary, based on what some priest from Spain told him, onto his poncho. That poncho ended up in the bishop's possession and much to-do has been made of it ever since.

"It would be wonderful, Miguel, if that were a real image of the real Virgin Mary, like a laser imprint or something similar, but unfortunately it was just paint and it's been crumbling over these past five hundred years – and now looks like it, all cracked." He paused, seeking a response to his near-heretical statement. "What do you think about what I've just said?"

"I don't know, Father. If it's a fake, it's a fake, I guess."

Estefan grinned and clapped Miguel's shoulder. "You're right. How about Lourdes, does that name mean anything to you?"

"Um, that's over in Europe someplace, I think. You want to know what I know about that, too?"

"Please, if you would."

"Well, uh, there was this girl – Bernadette, I think, yeah, that's her name. And she saw the Virgin Mary, too. And there was a stream or something there, and people take baths in it and stuff, and they say it gets rid of a lot of their arthritis and being paralyzed and like that. I think that's all I can remember, Father."

"Where did you learn this?"

"In fifth and sixth grade when I used to go to Wednesday night devotion classes with Sister Conchita from Saint Gregory's." Realizing the import of what he had just said – that he hadn't attended catechism classes in two years – pushed Miguel's eyes toward the floor.

"How about Fatima?"

"Who's Fatima?" the youth looked up. "I know a kid at school who has a sister named Fatima, but she's still a little girl."

"Medjugorje?"

"What's that?"

"Okay, enough with the names." Estefan rose and began pacing softly around the room before speaking again. "Tell me more about Miriam."

"What else do you want to know?"

"Well, for instance, how tall was she?"

"Mmmm, not very tall, maybe five-foot-two or -three. A little shorter than me."

"Was she pretty?"

Miguel reddened a little before replying. "I guess, a little. Not really. I mean, she was kinda pretty with the robe and the veil and everything but, y'know, just sort of like average, I would say."

"Hmmm, discriminating taste." He smiled at Miguel. "Not the kind of girl you might fantasize about, then?"

"Father, no! It wasn't like that. I mean, she's maybe a few

years older than me, but no way!" Still a touch indignantly, "I wasn't thinking that way. Is that what you think this is about?"

"No, Miguel, I don't. I just needed to ask so that all the possible bases are covered, all right? Let me be more specific. Ah, did she move her mouth when she spoke to you?"

"Of course."

"But you said there was something unusual about her voice."

"Yeah, well, it's like I couldn't tell whether her voice was a voice or not, y'know? Like, she first called out my name before I even saw the ball of light come back over the rocks. And yet it sounded like it was right inside my head maybe. But that was impossible because she was still on the other side of that slope there. Inside that light, I guess. That didn't make any sense to me. And after it was over, after she went back inside the light and it left, I started thinking about that again, y'know? That part of it just wasn't normal, I think."

"I see. Were you frightened when she came closer?"

The boy looked up at his priest. "Well, that's the thing, Father. Okay, I admit I was a little bit scared at first, like when that light was flying around and getting closer to me on my running path out there and then dropping below the ridge. But then when she called my name, I don't know, it was like I got more relaxed or something and started feeling really good."

"You weren't thinking about running away at that point?"

"Huh-uh, no, Father."

"So, when the girl came out of the ball of light and drew closer to you, what were you thinking about then?"

"Uh, hmmm... nothing in particular, I guess, Father." He

pondered for a moment. "It was more like a feeling. There was this sort of pressure pushing on me. But it was sorta like a runner's high, y'know, where you just feel really good in the middle of your run – before you start getting tired."

"That's from endorphins: natural drugs your body releases into your bloodstream to protect you from fatigue and injury," the priest offered.

"I know."

"You do?"

"They get *Runner's World* magazine at the school library. I always read it over lunch hour. ... But there was something else, too. It was more like my whole focus was on just her, y'know? In fact, it was hard to think at all. And she was real serious when she was talking, so I just listened real close to that. And, um, so I wasn't like thinking about much of anything else."

"Good description, thank you." Estefan smiled. "So, was it more like being stoned?" he countered.

The youth jerked visibly and locked eyes with his pastor. "I haven't ever smoked that, Father. Not even tobacco. Me and my friends are clean."

"Good for you," the priest responded warmly, his smile broadening. *This really is a good kid.* "You said there was a bit of light around her. Tell me more about that."

The boy relaxed again and stared vacantly for several seconds at a drab wall beyond Estefan's desk as he focused the scene in his mind. "It wasn't bright at all, not like she had strings of Navidad lights around her or anything like that. It was, um, faint, I think." Miguel thought for another second. "Y'know how, when you have a night light in the little kids' bedroom and it just has a little bit of glowing around it? It was like that, y'know? Like that dim glow in the air, only it was all the way around her. And it was sort of yellow, like yellow and white."

"Okay. So the colors you saw …"

"The big ball of light was like amber. It was like that kind of yellow-orange – more yellow – like at the traffic light in town, yeah. And then the light around the girl was more like a light yellowish white maybe. Only not bright, it was dim. Maybe six or eight inches out from her dress and her head and everything. Mmmm, I'm not sure, maybe more like five inches; and after that it kinda faded away, y'know?"

Estefan recognized the boy's striving for exactitude. "You enjoy focusing on details, don't you, Miguel?"

"I guess so, Father." The youth was finding himself a little more at ease in the priest's presence. Lots of teens around Columbus didn't attend Mass; it wasn't a priority and Mami didn't lecture him about it. Still he had found no strength in those numbers this morning. A bit of guilt still tugged at his conscience, advanced by the respect he was gaining for his pastor.

Estefan broke their brief silence. "If you could have any kind of career, what would you be?"

"A scientist," Miguel replied without hesitation, "but I'm not sure what kind yet."

"Well, you have awhile to decide. And with your eye for detail, you'll have your choice of science careers to pursue, I'm sure. So, when did you first notice this dim glow, this aura around her?"

"Hmmm, it was already there when she was partway down the slope, I'm pretty sure," the youth replied matter-of-factly. "She was standing up the whole way, y'know? That was the weirdest thing. She didn't, like, walk or anything. Except her whole, uh, figure kept coming closer toward me ... just floating," he ended a little bashfully. "But I don't know if that glow, the, uh, aura around her, was there when she first came out of the ball of light or not," he added. "It was pretty bright – the sphere, y'know."

"That's fine. She said, 'tell your priest that I have returned.' ... I'm not expecting anybody, Miguel."

"I don't know, that's what she said," the boy responded a little defensively again. "I don't know any other priests. I figured it must be you."

"Returned from where?"

"Wherever that ball of light comes from, I guess. Like, I didn't really think about that, Father."

"Okay." Estefan began to pace slowly back and forth again, his footfalls lightly creaking. "Now, you said this Miriam spoke about some 'battle' and that," looking down at his notes on a small pad, "'no one can win.' What do you think she meant by that?"

"I have no idea, Father," Miguel replied soberly. He leaned forward in his chair again, elbows on knees, looked over and locked eyes. "Father, I'm not lying. It's too crazy to expect anyone to believe this, I know. It would be crazy to me if Carlos or Ivan told me this stuff. Those are my best friends," he clarified. "I mean, like, this just doesn't happen! ... But I'm not making it up," he added with his most serious look.

Estefan noticed dimples appearing in the adolescent's chin, the auto-response of a sensitive boy who only wanted to be believed. The priest looked warmly back at his young visitor. "Who said anything about lying? I believe you, Miguel. Now tell me more about how you felt physically during your conversation out there."

The student relaxed again and sat back in his chair. "Well, it wasn't much of a conversation, Father. Like I said, she talked and I listened. But physically? You mean how my body felt?" The priest nodded. "Uh, like maybe kinda slow, um, like sluggish – uncoordinated maybe. Yeah, definitely uncoordinated – my legs and everything. But not tired. And mentally, it was like, maybe, um, hard to make a thought of my own, y'know?"

"So, this sluggishness in your body and your mind, when did you first notice all that?"

"Hmmm." A long pause as Miguel adopted a second thousand-yard stare at the wall. Then, "As I'm thinking about it now, I think it got stronger the closer she came to me. Yeah, that's right, it was the strongest when she was real close. Huh, I didn't think about that until just now."

"All right. By the way, you described her hands as being folded. Was she holding anything?"

"No, Father," the boy said assuredly.

"… Mm-hmm, okay. And how about her feet? Did you notice them?"

"Yeah, they were sticking out of her robe sort of. She was barefoot."

"Nothing else there at her feet that you noticed in particular?"

"Hmm-mm, no, Father."

Estefan proceeded to the door and opened it, smiling at Rosalinda, realizing he had a phone call to make. Looking back, "Do you plan to go out there tomorrow morning?"

"I think so, yes, Father. … I mean, if you do."

"Wouldn't miss it for the world. By the way," he added with a wink, "should I be afraid?"

The adolescent shuffled his feet and paused for a second. "Like, maybe a little, I really don't know. Father, can I ask you something?"

Estefan nodded at Rosalinda standing on the porch, pushed the door closed and turned. "It's okay to be apprehensive, Miguel."

"I know. No, it's not that. See, the thing about Guadalupe and Lourdes and like that, well, Carlos and Ivan and the guys I hang out with, we never pay much attention to that stuff, y'know? That's like the spooky side of the Catholic Church, just like Jason and the Argonauts and mythology and Atlantis and stuff like that. To us it's just stories." The boy looked down at his feet again before lifting his gaze. "So, was that, like, the Virgin Mary, Father? Or was she like some kind of ghost or something?"

Estefan extended his hand to the teen. "Couldn't tell ya'. We'll be fine, my friend. All right, I'll pick you up at, say, 5:30 just to be safe. But not to go running," he chuckled. "I have a Wrangler."

"I know, Father. Me and my friends all say it's sweet."

Chapter Six

Iraq desperately needed a patriot in the wake of Saddam's fall, during the long American occupation. But none stepped forward with the stature and vision to displace tribal and sectarian loyalties with a genuine sense of Iraqi nationhood, to substitute ethical practices for corruption, reason for vengeance.

Three disparate cultures occupying the landscape – Sunni, Shi'a and Kurd – had never been a good fit. And the prolonged occupation only complicated matters.

Within a few years of the 2011 American withdrawal, this post-WW1 political creation devolved into three informal cantons – Sunni, Shi'a and Kurd. Cultural-sectarian aggressions across soft borders continued unabated. With the radical Sunni's ISIS finally defeated, in 2022 came a UN-sanctioned division creating separate nation-states. As an incentive to their achieving a peaceful future, oil revenues in Shi'ite and Kurd lands would be proportionally distributed over 50 years.

Shi'ites had long been concentrated in a handful of countries. Fully half (over 60 million) resided in Iran, the ancient Persia, comprising 93 percent of the population there.

Shi'a faith focused on a strict hierarchy. The Guardian Council of ayatollahs served as jurists in all matters of a legal or moral nature. Its grand ayatollah wielded enormous influence.

Majority Sunni populations in over a dozen Middle East countries remained restive toward their misguided Shi'ite brethren and their strictures of religious authority. The average Sunni man regarded Shi'a saints and shrines as nothing better than silly, their passion plays in the streets as abominations. In the hardened Sunni view, there was only one name to follow, to pray to, sacrifice and offer penance to, and orient one's mind to, and that was Allah. Believing in intermediaries like so-called saints to petition one's prayers was false and dangerous. Idol worshipers all – infidels – from the Sunni perspective.

Whereas Iraq's Hussein had been a minority Sunni dominating the nation's Shi'ites for a generation, the reverse situation continued unabated in Syria. Al Assad, from the minority Alawite sect (a mystical offshoot of Shi'a), was willing to murder hundreds of thousands of his country's Sunnis to remain in power.

The latest renewal of the interminable, now regional Sunni-Shi'a feud could be traced to a single ill-timed quip at an annual all-Arab conference.

The 22-nation Arab League Council had gathered that year in Medina, Saudi Arabia, recognized by all Muslims as the "city of the Prophet," Muhammad. Originally a double-walled fortress 110 miles inland from the Red Sea, Medina had been Muhammad's home base after the merchant-turned-warrior fled Mecca in 622 AD. Nearly fourteen hundred years later, this lovely city was still an enormous engineering marvel, an artificial oasis whose vast reaches of bountiful fruit trees, vegetables and herbs belied the harsh reality of Arabian desert beyond.

The League's heads of state and selected ministers once again had slogged through a week of discussions on a host of political and cultural matters. Numerous among them were progressive measures either tabled for further study or politely voted down with oratorical ruffles and flourishes. The most strident of those was a "Pan Arab" revenue sharing proposal for oil profits from the wealthier to more impoverished states. Intended to emulate the agreement struck in the partitioned Iraq, it was nonetheless turned away by the OPEC-member nations with an ambiguous promise of alternative aid.

Afterward a few among the attendees from the have-not countries grumbled privately that the League hadn't done anything decisive since 1996 when it called on Turkey to share the Tigris and Euphrates waters equitably with Iraq and Syria. Dissatisfaction, even occasional outbursts aside, the League's yearly sessions had seldom been a font of momentous policymaking.

Al Jazeera television network went live at 8 PM, awaiting the after-dinner testimonials on this, the final evening. Sipping exquisite (nonalcoholic) fruity drinks, the various leaders and their lieutenants fawned for the three cameras in the room as the dishes were cleared.

Near the end of the front table, a busboy misjudged the off-centered weight posed by his tub full of dishes. He fought to regain a balance but too late; a corner of the vessel clattered hard against the edge of the table, spilling a few dirty plates and knocking over a microphone in front of the Saudi Oil Minister, Abu Bakr Pachachi. The minister smiled gratuitously at the embarrassed young man and turned again to the Egyptian on his right.

The kitchen staffer flushed and quickly set the tub on the floor. Head bowed, he apologized softly, gathered Pachachi's dishes and those that spilled, then righted the microphone. In so doing he inadvertently depressed its power button.

Ammon Farouq Shehab, Egypt's Foreign Minister, ignored the upset as well and continued their banter before the now hot mic. "Tomorrow comes the celebration of Shirazi's birth," referring to Iran's controversial imam and Shi'ite firebrand, Alireza Vahid Shirazi, who had risen to grand ayatollah five years earlier. "Did you send him a gift?"

"Yes, of course," Pachachi answered with a wry grin, "a box of patchoulis to burn at the shrine of his patron saint, Benito Mussolini."

The two Sunni men, regional heavyweights, laughed with contrived gusto as a conference host hurried over to turn off the mic. But an Al Jazeera camera was trained on their section of the table at that moment and the signal was beamed to the network's Cairo headquarters. Technicians there, not grasping the potential political ramifications, relayed the exchange without deletion to affiliates League wide. Over ten million viewers overheard the exchange.

The flippant comments by Pachachi and Shehab were the story of the week in an otherwise drab conference within a year of relative quiet. Tape of the provocative faux pas was shown repeatedly throughout the evening and into the night. Impassioned commentary from both Shi'a and Sunni spokesmen and political apparatchiks increasingly cited old wounds and slights. Al Jazeera's competitor, Al Arabia, cobbled the footage onto its broadcast in a game of ratings one-upmanship.

By mid-morning outside the Egyptian and Saudi embassies in Tehran, Shi'ite protesters numbering many thousands chanted slogans and shook fists in unison. Hand-painted placards called for dismissing both men from their respective governments.

Concurrently, bullhorned voices raked the air in central Cairo at the University of Al-Azhar, an educational centerpiece of Sunni Islam. Its grand mosque, featuring an onion-shaped dome and splendid spires remindful of European Renaissance cathedrals, was a majestic focal point of the campus and surrounding cityscape. On this day, however, minority Shi'ites – unemployed street people mostly – had amassed outside to vent their scorn.

The protesters demanded an apology from Safiyah Abu Muttalib, the highly revered Sunni cleric and leader of the Supreme Council of Al-Azhar. For the better part of the day, Shi'ite rabble-rousers milled about the mosque and surrounding campus property. As the chanting of one insulting slogan faded, another rose somewhere else in the gathering.

Shortly after noon Cairo's mayor consulted with police administrators to divert personnel and resources to the mosque as a precaution. Meanwhile, over the course of several hours, Muttalib himself, likely acting on the advice of lesser clerics, failed to appear outside as a gesture to quell the huge throng.

By 4 PM, a few thousand Al-Azhar students had gravitated to the scene after their final classes of the day. Soon brickbat insults were flying between the uniformly Sunni students and Shi'ite demonstrators. Predictably their accusations called up the original question of Muhammad's successor: "Go home, infidels!" came a chant among the students, followed quickly by a Shi'a rejoinder, "Your faith is false, Allah does not hear you!"

Words in this environment were indeed equivalent to sticks and stones. Denying the validity of Shi'a or Sunni faith – mockery attached to condemnation – quickly dehumanized the situation. The underclass status of Shi'ites in a Sunni-dominated city fueled eternal resentments.

In short order fistfights broke out on the grounds between Sunni students, largely from wealthy families, and Shi'ites of a lesser stripe. Privileged against underprivileged. Carefully tended flower gardens were quickly trampled underfoot, severely scarred as the two sides grappled, tearing at each other's faces and garments.

The assembled city police needed no further prompt. Tear gas was lobbed from the perimeter, and the Force moved in systematically. Three hundred strong, they sported helmets with attached gas masks, flak jackets, shields, night sticks and holstered Helwan pistols. Soon they made their way to the worst of the fighting, supporting the students, beating back the Shi'ite swarm in spots and holding their ground elsewhere as the courtyards and grassy sections quickly filled with bodies overwhelmed from telling blows or the disabling gas. Some of the less hard-bitten on both sides were beginning to stagger away.

Then, above the tumult, three ear-numbing explosions in rapid succession toppled spires of the mosque. One collapsed harmlessly onto a walkway adjoining an administrative building away from the scene. The other two spilled out into the multitude. Their huge blocks bounded, trampled and crushed indiscriminately. The students, having protectively surrounded the mosque, were more immediately in harm's way, but many a Shi'ite combatant was struck down as well by the cascading, splintering limestone.

Two blocks away, three cell phones were tossed out a side window; the car moved slowly into the street. A fourth device sent a text message to a number manned by an aide to the *nom de guerre* Ali Abdi, the secretive Iranian warrior and head of the Revolutionary Guard's elite Quds Force. The message: "It rains in Cairo."

Gunfire now rang out on the campus – sporadically at first but in seconds with more crackling consistency. Whether Shi'ites in the protesting crowd or Sunni police first pulled their guns would be debated later by an Arab League special commission. For now, men both young and middle-aged were falling at point-blank range or as stray bullets found hapless marks.

Most of the remaining upright students, their rage replaced by panic, ran toward the safer havens of campus residence buildings. But the retreating wave was slowed by its sheer numbers, many limping or carrying their fallen brethren – easy targets for the Shi'ite intruders.

The staccato sound of pistol shots raged for ten minutes. Police laid down intensive volleys at the street crowd, while those Shi'ites who were armed, when not firing at students, aimed at the officers' vulnerable legs, toppling many.

Shortly before 5 PM it was over, in part owing to ammunition finally running short but also a growing realization on all sides. Hatred had turned to nausea as most who could still do so took in the carnage around them. The air grew quiet except for moans and cries for help.

The slaughter was sickening. Over two hundred Al-Azhar students lay beneath tumbled blocks or from gunshot wounds. Muttalib's own grandson was among the dead. A greater number was seriously injured, many in fetal position, unable to evacuate; seventy of those would later die of their wounds. Forty policemen were dead or wounded. Well over a hundred Shi'ites were expired. The courtyards and sidewalks of this cherished Sunni mosque were awash with intersecting pools of blood.

Finally the Shi'ite mob dispersed, carrying their own as they could, a retreat striking most among them as a disgusting but preferable course at this juncture. As ambulance sirens wailed, police captains at the scene, to avoid an eruption anew, chose not to arrest those with weapons who fell back.

Al Jazeera and Al Arabia TV crews with telephoto lenses had shared the roof of a nearby office building. With live feeds and a clear view to one of the areas of greatest violence on the campus, they captured the unbridled hatred of two sects that prayed to the same God. For good measure, tag teams of studio

WINTER SOLSTICE

guests, Sunni and Shi'ite in turn, offered unceasing rants, no
quarter offered, no notion of compromise extended.

Chapter Seven

Jerome Terrell "J.T." Seymour, second-term Missouri governor, was at first a curiosity in the 2024 Democratic presidential primary cycle.

Raised amid 200 acres of corn and soybeans outside Jefferson City, as a young man he'd witnessed the Great Flood of '93 when the levees holding back the Missouri River collapsed and a year's income drowned. J.T. and his kin had known hard work and hard times.

On the campaign trail he cut out a separate niche, championing primarily two green commercial causes. He drew ever larger audiences as he went.

Recent upgrades to the vanadium flow battery, when wedded to industrial windmills, would resolve the longstanding challenge of generating power after the winds die down. Storing enormous wattages for release as needed, vanadium batteries could prompt forests of those giant blades on remote tracts owned by the Bureau of Land Management in the windy Great Plains and Rocky Mountain states. Those would all feed into a new electrical grid with buried trunk lines on more federal land – the medians and banks of the nation's interstate highways. Thus, he proclaimed, could a gale in Colorado or Nebraska reach Chicago, Boston, Miami, Houston or L.A.

In his quest to transform America's energy consumption, Seymour's second strategy stared down foreign oil producers and domestic refiners thereof. He would offer matching federal grants, production tax credits and excise tax relief to introduce fleets of American cars and trucks burning methane: ultra-compressed natural gas.

CNG technology was not new but had languished in the years encompassing oil-promoting administrations and the concurrent rush to an elusive all-electric, high-mileage vehicle. Seymour's stump speech, keying on a third way, trumpeted America's own natural resource as a near-term alternative.

"My fellow patriots, a century ago we were driving Model-Ts. Let's all give a nod to what American ingenuity has accomplished since then. Yet – hold on – what's that? We're still burning the same sulfur-rich fuel? That's insane!

"America has *a hundred years* of confirmed natural gas reserves to supply both our home and transportation needs. Now that we've resolved the shale fracking problems, we're the world's foremost leader in natural gas production. We don't have to be *slaves* to Arab and South American oil! Good gosh, just how long have we been talking about this? Well, I'm here to tell ya', there's a better way.

"Natural gas is much cleaner for our environment. And it's odorless; think about *that* for our inner cities. Further, it won't ignite in an untimely highway crash.

"CNG can now take you just as far on a tank full – still *way* farther than on a battery alone. And it's *quiet*: A diesel-burning 18-wheeler is over 80-percent louder than on natural gas. Lots of folks who live along our nation's highways will appreciate that.

"All this aside, friends, at long last we Americans can achieve real energy independence with just two changes. And you'll have your choice.

"First, for everyone with natural gas supplied to their home, a machine the size of a dehumidifier can appear in your garage, free of charge after a tax rebate, to refuel your own car or truck from your own gas line. Second, within a year after I become president, CNG pumps will appear at a fuel station in your neighborhood. We once made the conversion painlessly to unleaded gas; we'll do the same with methane.

"Fellow patriots, with all its other practical advantages, natural gas is *cheap* – on average about half what we've been paying for Arab and South American oil! And as if it needed another selling point, engines burning methane last at least *twice* as long as gasoline engines. What's not to like?

"Now, our acquaintances, bless their hearts, on the extreme end of the environmental movement, they're already saying CNG emissions still contribute particulates to the ozone layer. And they do – not nearly as much as gasoline, but they do. Friends, CNG isn't a permanent or perfect solution. But until that elusive hydrogen fuel cell – the one that's reliable, *crash-resistant* and affordable – magically appears on the scene in our lifetimes, this is the road we should travel.

"By the way, did you know there are now over ten million CNG vehicles worldwide? That's a fact, neighbors, and the folks in just one western country, Brazil, will sure tell ya'; they've switched over entirely, from farm machinery to sports cars. In the U.S. we do have well over 100,000 CNG cars and trucks on the road – mostly busses and trash haulers – but that's just the beginning. I see more than just fleets of city government vehicles burning CNG. I envision America's next-generation family sedans and SUVs, with a long buffer until we need to find something better.

"By comparison, electric cars pose a *real* national security risk. Those lithium-ion batteries will put us on a collision course with a certain Bolivian socialist – a patron of that old scoundrel Che Guevara, no less, and a *fine* example of international civility," he added sarcastically. "From the dumb luck of having an inland sea eons ago, more than half of the world's remaining lithium rests in Bolivia. Now, as America's need for lithium goes from tiny batteries for i-pods to *big* batteries for electric cars, whattya think the odds are that he's gonna trade fairly with us?

"We have enough lithium here in the U.S. to run our electronic gadgets, but an enormous influx of electric cars would soon take us on a fool's errand. We'd find ourselves hostages once again, just as we've been captive to OPEC for generations.

"Plus, big rigs aren't even *suitable* to those puny electric motors. They'd still need that smelly, noisy diesel engine."

Dismissed as a fanciful gimmick initially by other candidates, Seymour's plan did envision ten million new jobs divided among the auto industry, construction trades and a new civil engineering corps – jobs at a living wage, not the pittance of service industry employment. Seymour's plan would arguably slash the unemployment rate.

"Neighbors, we've put up with a federal government all these years because it can move the country forward in difficult times. This is about us!" To raised fists protruding from flannel shirts and overalls, Seymour reached the crescendo of his stump speech.

"I need to tell you, as governor I've had one overriding rule. I just won't sit through a four-hour meeting that could and should be wrapped up in thirty minutes! We're going to get all this done – the windmills, the electrical super-grid, Detroit's switch to natural gas – in four years' time. This is *America*, after all. We *know* what we're capable of. Now let's get to work!"

Thunderous applause tinged with anger, defiance and xenophobia would sweep Seymour to his next stop on the trail.

In April he donned bib overalls and climbed aboard a well-used John Deere field tractor in central Oklahoma to decry the influx of Asian farm vehicles, and loyalists knew he was no stranger to the controls. He disked a long row for good measure. J.T. was salt of the earth, plain spoken, brusque and direct – equal parts Teddy Roosevelt, Harry Truman, George Wallace and the Udall environmentalists.

Seymour's fairly brilliant strategy beckoned the nation's utilities, construction and auto trades, anti-nuke activists and ecological centrists. Streams of contributions from each source formed a strong river. In a contested convention, he won the Democratic Party's nomination on the second ballot.

As the November election's "open season" kicked off with patriotic speeches on the Fourth of July weekend, a campaign of pranks and hijinks by Democratic party guerilla Dick Compton went into high gear. The target: Senator Patrick Dunnaway, the presumptive Republican nominee for president.

In the weeks to follow, Dunnaway's microphone or amplifiers repeatedly malfunctioned. His rally goers were diverted by road signs to the wrong site. Misprinted placards distributed to his crowds proclaimed "Dunnawho?" "Dunnawhy?" and "Dunnahuh?" to assembled cameras. At one site before an all-white crowd, a very pregnant African-American woman wandered around wearing a t-shirt sporting the campaign slogan "Dunnaway's the One!"

On a runway in Dayton, Dunnaway was answering a local TV reporter's question on government waste and mismanagement when his chartered jet sped past him and climbed into the sky.

Then came August 25, the night of Dunnaway's acceptance speech at the Republican national convention. Just past 10 PM, he uttered his climactic line and the assembled throng burst into cheer.

From a signal offstage, 36,000 balloons in overhead nets

rained down onto the floor of the Omaha arena. A dozen among them – late additions by someone seen in the rafters in a stage crew uniform – were exceptionally delicate and destined to burst at the slightest jostle. Those were inflated with sulfur dioxide.

The 22,000-seat arena was cleared in just over 20 minutes and in fairly good order. Most delegates recognized the age-old trick by its rotten-egg signature and so remained calm. But here and there panicky cries of "terrorist!" rose above the general din. The nominee himself knew the real culprit. "Compton!" he was heard to shout in the tumult.

Television commentators and newspaper editors uniformly condemned the spectacular stunt, of course, but the damage was done in the minds of convention viewers everywhere. Though entirely outside a prospective president's ability to control, scenes of chaos were not at all persuasive politically. He was destined not to recover.

That act would be forever hailed in Democratic political circles as the "Omaha Overture," the utter disruption in the public's mind of the 2024 Republican convention.

Seymour's sparse but shrill foreign policy statements along the way echoed those of a country disgusted by intermittent yet interminable Third World strife. During the most-watched early October debate, Seymour stirred long-simmering passions and fears in response to the moderator's pointed question about his perceived intolerance of non-Christian cultures.

"Sir, I'm a Christian, all right?" Seymour began, glaring at the questioner. "Now, I don't mind that the majority of the world goes by other religions. A firm spiritual conviction in any legitimate form is good, I think. Keeps us out of trouble, y'know – at least most of the time," inserting a grin.

"So, do understand, I'm not talking here about the good people of the Muslim faith or any other who have settled in these United States, found work, bought a house, put down some roots. Law-abiding citizens, most of them are, and dang patriotic. Their Koran talks about love and charity, and these people practice it every day – more fervently than loads of Christians, I might add.

"That aside, the Middle East today is still rife with Muslim radicals who've been at each other's throats and ours for too long, plain and simple. Some cultures over there exist simply to hate, and that's a fact. Religious intolerance – Shi'a, Sunni, doesn't matter. All they know is revenge and the gun. Or the cowardly bomb.

"We're not going over there looking for any more fights, that's for dang sure. But I revere that *other* motto from the early days of our country: 'Don't tread on me.'

"Now, as for Iran in particular, with their ayatollahs as judges of everything and absurd laws that keep their own people down, especially their women, and with that stand-in president they have, I'll deliver this message right after January 20: 'Hey, all you mullahs, we can squash you like a bug. This is America! Get it? Got it? Good!'

"As to Russia and their guy Trukhin, oh, right, he's a badass. He got bent out of shape a decade ago when some former Soviet republics turned to the West. So he made noise, rattled some sabers trying to recapture lost ground. Yeah, he wanted peace, all right – a piece of Ukraine, a piece of Belarus, a piece of Latvia and Estonia.

"Hey, welcome to the new order, Mr. Trukhin. You lost, we won, okay? We're a superpower, you're not."

Seymour wouldn't be accused of isolationist tendencies in

the campaign's final weeks. Words such as "jingoist" peppered the cultured media, but to no avail; they loved him on talk radio and on factory floors.

Seymour's side strategy of organized harassment to shut down the GOP message worked exceptionally well. None of the angry lawsuits arising from campaign hoopla were heard prior to the general election – which Seymour won handily with 54 percent of the vote.

In February 2025 the Democratic Party provocateur Dick Compton pled guilty in an Omaha municipal court to a misdemeanor charge of reckless endangerment. He paid a $5,000 fine plus court costs.

Chapter Eight

Kenna's i-pod chimed. The screen ID revealed it to be the private line of General Raymond Washburn. She glanced down and read the face of her chronograph: Fri, 7-20 7:15 PM EDT. *Damn, missed another gym appointment.* She busied herself, prioritizing the disks in her satchel for tonight's home reading as she took the call.

"Kenna, hello. Keeping busy?"

"And then some, General. I got your note and read the Cheyenne log. I found the duty officer's remarks and the film unconvincing," she led off matter-of-factly.

"Well," Washburn's voice softened, "you haven't had a month of training on reading telescopic footage. I suspected you wouldn't appreciate what you were looking at." The general paused then added, "Ordinarily material such as this would remain in Space Command. This one's different, Kenna. Thought you might find it useful."

"Okay, sure, I'm intrigued," she replied flatly with a touch of sarcasm. "So, convince me in one minute. I have a date with my garden tub and laptop." *Damn it, don't give him any visuals. Maybe he'll ignore it.*

"Okay. First, this wasn't a meteor; it never disintegrated in the slightest and approached too fast not to. It wasn't ballistic; we have no recorded path in low space from any known strategic source prior to entry, and nothing exploded. We've reviewed every frame for a thousand miles above and below our GPS satellite. There's definitely a wrinkle in the bogey's path: When it was within just miles of our machine out there, it veered over eight degrees from its arc. I see that as an avoidance maneuver.

"The new heading took it into southwest Texas. From there, following a blank period, airborne infrared radar found it again at an obscure trio of mountains in extreme southwest New Mexico, where it settled for a few minutes. Then it shot straight up at great speed – off the scale, Kenna. Socorro managed to catch it for just seven seconds before it rose above their 22,000-mile ceiling; you do the math on velocity. It was just a smear on the camera footage, then gone. We have nothing from any longer-range camera at that point."

"No sonic boom reported? Don't you get a sonic boom when you go much past something like 700 miles an hour?"

"Yes, you do – normally – and no, we don't have a reported sonic boom."

"So, is there a point to all this, General? At least beyond serving as grist for whatever the Air Force calls its 'X Files' unit these days. Should I be putting a 'UFOs Are Real' bumper sticker on my car?

"Besides, I read that those air base intrusions you once brought up were nothing more than special ops testing perimeter security. Now, if you'll excuse me, I have a half-dozen actual hot spots to catch up on this evening."

"Special ops was the cover story internally back in '75, Kenna. Couldn't have all our base commanders jumpy. We had to keep all those stories local.

"But I'll be succinct here," Washburn continued, feeling both admonished and offended by the brusqueness of a political appointee he had once befriended. "The thing this morning, whatever it was, demonstrated velocity and sudden maneuvers beyond any prototype, ours or anyone's; those are documented facts.

"Just as important, it moved from visible light into infra-red, according to a weather satellite, when it first approached the Texas surface. Which is to say it became invisible to the human eye. We're still at a rudimentary stage of engineering that kind of stuff. Then it was back in the visible spectrum as it shot up from New Mexico past our satellite camera."

Still unimpressed, Nowitzky countered, "Klingon cloaking device, General? Or more like an electronic glitch in some of our machinery, just maybe, hmmmm? You did say 'succinct.' I'm shutting off my computer as we speak."

"We did a full IT diagnostic. I have the results right here — came in an hour ago. There's nothing wrong with any hardware or software at any facility, ground-based or in the sky. Kenna, I get nervous when something shows a clear intent around our equipment in space. Besides," he now mellowed, "I thought you and I had an understanding."

Of course he wouldn't let it pass. Damn it! she chided herself. "One weekend at Vail three years ago doesn't constitute an understanding, Ray."

Washburn's sense of duty tried another appeal. "Back in 1967, March 5, NORAD tracked an uncorrelated target descending over a Minuteman site at Minot. That's in North Dakota."

"Thanks for the geography lesson," she replied harshly.

Undeterred, Washburn continued. "Two strike teams witnessed it. They agreed it was a metallic disc with flashing lights that circled 500 feet over the launch control building. It moved away laterally and they gave chase in the only things they had handy, a few big trucks. It stopped and hovered, then, before our scrambled F-106s were in the air, it climbed vertically out of sight.

"This was two years before the sham Project Blue Book was mercifully disbanded. Blue Book never got the report on Minot, by the way. Security-related incidents were handled elsewhere.

"Then, yes, in '75, which you may know *part* of, I'm here to tell you all hell broke loose across our northern-tier bases over a few months' time. Bogeys intruded a missile site in Maine, hovered over nukes stored underground in Michigan, and intruded a Canadian air base in Ontario. After another incident at a Montana missile site, the final strike was a nuclear silo in New Mexico. A disc hovered over that one and corrupted the warhead's targeting mechanism. A security guard there took in that episode at very close range."

"Ooh, corrupted the targeting mechanism, I like that," Kenna's words played to the melodrama.

"I'm just giving you the facts. We were at elevated security more often than not for quite some time there. But after reports were written and sent up the line, like Minot they just faded away. No request for follow-up, no reply at all from above, really. It officially became a non-issue.

"It was one thing to tell the public we quit investigating UFOs because there weren't any, but when the airbase and missile site intrusions just dropped into a black hole within the Force, well, that bothered the hell outta me.

"Okay, that was all back then," the general went on, "but what I'm trying to impress upon you now is this: Whatever we picked up this morning, it may have more tunes to play – maybe several events in short order."

"And so you've shown your hole card, Ray: 'UFO.' It's still a spook story. May I leave now?"

"You don't believe a quantum advance in technology, threatening a U.S. satellite and intruding our airspace, is worth paying attention to?"

"Not if it means taking our eye off the bouncing ball in Persia and thereabouts, Ray. That's called regional sectarian war, and we're right at the edge and we hope it stays just that, a potential regional war. With Russia and China itching to find any edge, I devote myself to the here and now, thanks."

"Oh, this is here and now, I assure you, Kenna. I intend to push this up to the Air Force Secretary tomorrow, to the joint chiefs next week. Alerting you was a personal courtesy."

"Do *not* do that, Ray, are we clear?" she spat out in her firmest tone. Her worst nightmare would be a new Homeland Security responsibility to guard against space alien attack. That would be disastrous – the giggle factor and all that, both for the Department and for her personally.

Following a silence, she added only a bit more softly, "That's loose cannon stuff, friend. You really don't want to go there – unless you'd prefer to be known as General Ufonut. Need I recite your own creed? The Air Force doesn't investigate UFOs anymore because there is no national security threat and because there isn't – and never was – any firm evidence of a technology beyond our own. We're officially alone in the universe, don't you *get* it?"

Long seconds passed. Kenna consciously lowered her tone. "Look, Ray, that's the party line in both the Democratic and Republican camps: UFOs don't exist. Need I say more?" She heard only the sound of breathing in return.

"Ray, you're a nice man and a patriot, and it's certainly your call whether you take this up the line. If you have no discretion by your own code of honor or whatever, then go for it, I guess.

But think about what you have: a few fleeting frames, long-range shots of what could be anything, a reflection off the lens, whatever.

"And since you brought up old UFO scare stories, remember 1980 over in England – at our Bentwaters base? The supposed glowing pyramid in the woods, the radiation readings, the depressions in the ground and all that? Whatever happened to that brave Air Force colonel, the deputy base commander, who insisted it had to be extraterrestrial, Ray?" knowing full well that Washburn was familiar with the incident. "He was laughed into retirement, wasn't he? Left to make his case on those so-called UFO documentaries on cable TV." Kenna paused again, this time for effect. "Isn't that where you're going with this, friend? You've had a fine career. You'd be throwing it all away."

One more pregnant pause preceded the general's two-word reply, "We're clear."

Chapter Nine

Friday night, shortly after 10 PM Johnson Selby threw his freestanding, camo backpacking tent into the short bed of his Land Rover Hybrid then secured his photography gear inside.

Digitals had made significant strides, but he still preferred his single-lens-reflex camera, a Canon XL-Y, for long-distance shots. Onto a rear bucket seat he belted the complementary "Big Guy" telephoto lens, secure in its own custom velvet-lined case. Only a few dozen Big Guys were scattered across the globe; Johnson felt fortunate to have acquired one for $80,000. With the XL3 EOS adapter in place – extending the reach of the formidable 5-inch lens by a magnitude factor of 24 – this setup was as much telescope as camera. Including a heavy-duty titanium tripod, it all weighed in at about 30 pounds.

Attributes of the equipment aside, for peak efficiency (reading an eye chart from a mile away) it needed low humidity and plentiful sunshine at Johnson's back, which the morning to come would fortunately provide.

He was also stowing a Canon HV-90 ultra-high-def digital camcorder and its tripod. He would set it to the maximum 320-power zoom to afford a continuous look at the general site in question, regardless of what he picked up closer with the XL-Y.

On his vehicle's dash were two screens: a GPS road map to direct him southward from his estate outside Albuquerque, plus Google Earth satellite images of the Three Sisters and surroundings. The overall area was mostly flat terrain broken by a haphazard chain of minor mountains. He had chosen to situate himself on an unnamed rise two and a half miles east of

Columbus Road, in line with the South Sister five miles away.

Johnson's destination was officially part of the Sierra del Potrillo Mountains, a landscape used in the forties movie classic, "Treasure of the Sierra Madre." From the easily reached summit he had in mind, he'd have an unobstructed view of the Sister.

He dropped eight 36-frame rolls and two 90-minute disks into the console of his vehicle, shifted into Drive and pressed the remote to open the wrought-iron gate at the end of his driveway.

This bachelor and adventure freak lived what he readily described as a "comfortable life." His tastes were simple, he was fond of saying: "I do like the best." Sole heir to the Selby Mattress fortune, the toned and blondish attractive 30-something had long since put some of his many millions to the best use he could think of: having fun.

Since he could remember, Johnson had always realized his great good fortune financially. Both a cook and separate housekeeper weren't commonplace in American society. Yet he had no "poor little rich boy" complex. In fact, he recognized early, both of his parents took time to dote on him, individually offering a block of time every day of his life to be himself in their company. Moreover, they introduced him to just about the best of everything: a Montessori school, lessons in piano and horn, junior league soccer and Junior Achievement commerce among them.

But none of it took, not really. Johnson grew up bored.

He recognized by middle school why certain girls who should have been out of his league instead cast him a "come hither" look. It was his dad's and granddad's money. But in adolescence, he also found, wealth acquired in the wrong business could, like an ethnic surname, still be mocked. Decades of 20-second TV and radio commercials for Selby "Golden Goddess" mattresses had taken their toll. At his exclusive prep school, he was transformed in short order and hallway whispers into a mocked "Golden God." Some of the well-to-do cute girls turned away in cliquish fashion even as those of lesser status fluttered in with sympathy and claws.

The hodgepodge of favored circumstance, recognition of both the positives and negatives his wealth attracted, absence of any athletic skills and uncomfortable fit socially led Johnson to try the Jesuit seminary in Berkeley after an undistinguished four years of prep school.

There he was roomed with Estefan Tolavares, a third-year seminarian. The Puerto-Rican-American Estefan's example, rather than having an intended settling effect, soon led Johnson to grasp that he'd likely always be too self-centered to lead a genuinely spiritual life. Then there was that rule about priestly abstinence; a year away from the scent and feel of a girl was long enough.

The year in Estefan's company taught Johnson a valuable life lesson about genuine respect for another. He developed the utmost admiration for his roommate's brilliance, quiet confidence and compassion. Estefan, to Johnson, was the whole package.

The two met up again by chance a year later at Berkeley where Johnson was dabbling in photography classes. Over coffee in the student commons he explained how he'd come to love the outdoors – removed as it was from people and their invariably false assertions – fawning, critical or otherwise. Animals in the wild, by contrast, reacted to their basic needs. Nothing was false in nature.

Johnson and Estefan had maintained fairly steady contact

ever since.

Without a formal photo-journalism degree but a keen eye with cameras and plenty of family contacts, Johnson had managed to publish a number of spreads in modestly popular travel magazines, depicting his treks to various wilderness locales. He was especially proud of a feature article in National Geographic on summer's beauty in the Chilean Andes.

Johnson enjoyed and appreciated life to the fullest he could find. Along the way he'd managed to avoid impregnating anyone and remained ever mindful – selfishly, he recognized – that the "right girl" would ultimately steal his time if not his money.

An hour before this departure, he had picked up the phone while devouring a mid-evening bowl of homemade chili and a second Dos Equis in his home theater. As his attention shifted across four big screens – from tape-delays of a soccer match in Madrid, cricket in Cape Town and jai alai in Havana to the sixth inning live of a Diamondbacks home game in Phoenix – he smiled on recognizing the caller ID.

"Estefan, my main hombre!" he fairly bellowed. "What's up?"

"Hello, Johnson," the priest opened seriously. "Say, listen, I don't want to bother you and if this will be inconvenient, just say so, I understand. But I have sort of a situation here and could use your help. I hope I'm not calling too late."

"No big deal, my friend. Situation, huh?" the affable acquaintance beamed. "Well, I don't think you're gay, Estefan. At least you never came onto me in our bathroom." He laughed at his own quip. "So, did some young lady finally turn your head? My friend, remember, as a good Catholic boy, if she's with child you have to marry the girl. They let you do that now, I hear," referring to a recent Vatican edict.

The cleric always appreciated his friend's outrageous informality, dispensing with any pretense over his own role as "Father Estefan".

"I do love your humor, Johnson. No, nothing like that." He proceeded to relate the substance of Miguel's account.

The wealthy rascal's demeanor had settled into somber as he said, "So, I gather you believe the boy."

"I accept that he truly believes he witnessed something extraordinary and that I'm supposed to go back out there with him. I did consider the practical joke possibility, you know, an adolescent in a way-station village. He's a good-hearted kid, Johnson, a fine student and exceptional runner. He has some things going for him, so I really doubt he'd pull a stunt."

Estefan changed the focus. "Miguel is basically familiar with the Guadalupe myth and the Lourdes healings. He hasn't heard of Fatima or Medjugorje. But I think it's important that he didn't leap to that kind of conclusion. No doubt the name Miriam confused him; he even asked whether it could be a poltergeist."

"Yeah, Miriam, ghosts. Okay, if he truly doesn't make that connection, it could be a calling card right there, fella. You're sure he doesn't get it?"

"I don't think so. I believe him at face value."

"Okay. Well, wow. This is all just still sinking in. So, ah, in short, why you?"

"Well, I've been asking myself that. ... Johnson, one part of Miguel's description about the image bothered me."

"What's that?"

"She wasn't holding anything."

"No rosary?"

"Nada. And no roses at her feet."

"Oooh, yeah, those are flags, all right. So, maybe Bernadette made up that part, Padre. She was a strange one, that girl, a loner. Today she'd be staying after school for counseling."

"But not Lucia and Francisco. Fatima was genuine."

"Agreed," the adventurer replied, "genuine in some fashion, anyway," as he recalled the event on October 13, 1917, outside a remote village in Portugal, the last of several monthly incidents in what was hailed ever since by the Church as the 20th century's most spectacular, miraculous Marian appearance. In those claimed visions by three young shepherds, the older two being nine- and ten-year-old cousins, the Virgin was said to be holding a rosary, with roses adorning her bare feet.

"There was something genuinely anomalous going on that fifty thousand people witnessed on that final occasion," Estefan reasoned. "Those primitive photos did show an eclipse, and the reported temperature drop there would seem to confirm it."

"Except that every European observatory at the time and NASA since then said it never happened," Johnson retorted, reminding the priest of what he already knew. "It wasn't the moon blocking the sun, guy. The moon eclipsed in 1912 and again in 1919 – nothing in between. All that aside, how may I be of assistance to my favorite priest?"

Stemming from their one year together at The Jesuit School of Theology, sharing a small dorm room, late-night popcorn and emerging philosophies, Estefan and Johnson would forever have a mutual trust and understanding. It mattered not a whit that one was poor, the other privileged. They had something indefinable, a connection centered in frank, sincere honesty. They'd never needed frequent conversations since then to maintain such a bond.

Johnson remained in awe of his brilliant friend who had accepted a godforsaken assignment along the Mexican border without any outward protest. It was just like Estefan to think lemonade. The wealthy shutterbug would do most anything for his Jesuit friend. But this was not simply a favor. It was likewise a potential opportunity, even if a long shot, to capture something genuinely anomalous on film or disk. A jaguar in the wild and travel magazine spread were one thing, a hallowed personage quite another.

The call concluded, Johnson had climbed back onto the massage table before heading out. His deceptively powerful masseuse reentered the room. She pressed her left elbow into a muscle along his right shoulder blade. He groaned and winced as thoughts turned back to a decision several years before.

Scouring a bookstore one evening in search of a Christmas gift for Estefan, he'd found something unusual, a two-volume set of New Testament gospels with dispassionate, detailed commentary throughout. In their subtitles the books asked respectively what Jesus actually said and did. Which of the stories and declarations could be set apart from those of much older cultures, their truisms and legends? Over a chocolate mint latte in the bookstore's lounge, Johnson marveled at the roster of contributors – nearly a hundred veteran Bible scholars from prestigious universities, theological schools and think tanks.

The assemblage endorsed a timeline of 35-80 years after the crucifixion as the period of gospel writing. Only Paul's letters had come earlier, and even those were not contemporaneous with the life of the main character, Jesus. The New Testament was simply devoid of firsthand testimony.

In a six-year effort to assess every chapter and verse, taking into account influences from Greek and Roman mythology as well as factual contradictions, the scholars had reached a consensus that less than twenty percent of the New Testament was objectively true – and none of the claimed miracles.

These modern critiques were tantamount to heresy in either mainstream Catholic or Protestant thought. Would Estefan be offended? Shocked? Both? Johnson hesitated before sliding his debit card but ultimately took a chance.

In a holiday period phone call from his Albuquerque compound, Johnson tentatively broached the subject: "So, did I manage to rankle you with the books?"

"Not at all, my thoughtful agnostic friend," the cleric soothed. "These are wonderful texts. I'm very appreciative and happy to have my own copies."

"You mean you've ..."

"Read them already, yes, back at the seminary, actually. You didn't stick around long enough for the good stuff, Johnson. But if you're looking for an emotional response, I would ask this:

"So what if He didn't really turn water into wine at a wedding or raise Lazarus from the dead or calm a storm on the Sea of Galilee? So what if His own family doubted His abilities or His heritage?

"That wasn't the point, dear friend. It's about what every Christian agrees on. He gave us a way to conduct our lives. All the rest – the debates about what He didn't say or didn't do – that doesn't matter as much to me."

Tari, a forty-something skilled technician, had done lots of repair work on Johnson's generally sturdy physique over several years. "Now if you'll turn over, mister mountain climber, before you leave for your next trip I'll work on that knot in your left quad again. And if I may add, a timeout from scaling and repelling would do your structure a world of good," she said for at least the twentieth time.

Recognizing the contradiction in terms, Johnson was indeed an avowed agnostic. He had long since found himself unable to square the writings about Jesus, by Muhammad or from any other sage in history with the deteriorating circumstances of his 21st century world. And he doubted that any all-revealing certainty would ever present itself in his mind or heart. In the face of scientific advancements and insights, religions and religious dogma from millennia past seemed evermore primitive, properly consigned to the "Magic and Superstitions" rack in the bookstore.

For Johnson, absolute proof of the supposed savior's true nature wasn't really necessary; a preponderance of factual evidence would do. In its absence, he would continue to suspect that the New Testament's authors were more storytellers than scribes.

While Johnson had long ago punted on all matters spiritual, he couldn't quite quell the seeker inside. Whatever it was in the New Mexico desert, he would try to record this new actor on stage using the best available equipment. It was indeed as much for himself as for Estefan.

On this short notice, he'd drive through the night, which he was more than glad to do. But, for lack of both enough time and familiarity with the terrain, setting up a proper triangulation was out of the question. This would be seat-of-the-pants photojournalism, and there was a great chance nothing would come of it. Estefan's endorsement aside, they were, after all, asked to take the word of a 14-year-old Latino boy.

At 5:30 AM the young priest pulled into the driveway of

Miguel's home, a smallish drab four-bedroom ranch on the outskirts of Columbus. A big mixed-breed dog bounded over to the gait of a chain-link fence that enclosed the back yard, parched and trampled. The dog woofed twice, then padded out of sight.

Miguel flew out the front door and into the Jeep. "Hi, Father." He looked around at the simple dashboard and interior. "Sweet," he repeated from the day before. This early morning excursion, he knew, was altogether set apart from any experience he'd ever had with Carlos and Ivan or the rest of his village friends or with any relative he'd ever known. He felt weird in a way because of that. But he knew what he'd seen and heard. He just had to follow through, regardless of any consequences.

The two moved through the neighborhood and west on State Hwy 9, headed for CR-6. "This must be messing up your running schedule," the priest led off.

"That's okay, Father. I'll do my run later."

Now on the two-track, Estefan began negotiating the constant and severe ruts produced by flash floods over many years. He was grateful to have this high-axle vehicle for the purpose. Nonetheless, it would be twenty minutes or more to the mountain.

He looked over at Miguel and grinned. "You didn't tell me about the washouts," as he eased the Wrangler over an especially tough one. "I hope we're not late."

"She didn't say a particular time, Father, just 'this hour,'" the boy answered a little distantly. He was staring at the south peak in a new light.

"Anything else you thought of since yesterday?"

"Um, yes." Miguel turned his head the cleric's way. "I mean, like, nothing more that she said or anything. But … I think this is all about you, Father, not me. She said 'bring your priest here', so I was thinking—"

"That you're off the hook?" Estefan injected with a wink. "But that could mean any priest. I happened to be here."

"I don't think so, Father. It was more the way she said it, or – I don't know. But it was like she meant *you*, Father Estefan, y'know, especially." Their eyes fastened for half a second, followed by a long silence amid the racket of the Wrangler's engine and tires.

Finally, at Miguel's instruction, they pulled to a halt along a bend in the trail near the foot of the South Sister where CR-6 moved eastward. Immediately north was a 10-degree waning eastern slope of tangled granite boulders and shards. Estefan had retained enough knowledge from a long-ago geology class to comprehend that these rises in the landscape were molded from multiple geophysical upheavals perhaps millions of years before.

Farther north rested the Middle Sister a quarter-mile away. The valley between was no doubt likewise rock strewn. That peak and the North Sister's beyond were not especially attractive.

Estefan exited the Jeep and walked a short distance to an area of scattered stones and larger rocks on flat ground. Sizing up one, then another, he was finally satisfied and picked up one that was palm-sized, fairly spherical and weathered, slipping it into the right rear pocket of his jeans. Diamondback rattlers called these mountains home, and a sudden confrontation with a coiled serpent was not the time to be searching for a suitable weapon.

The cleric rejoined his young companion to absorb the broad silent scene before them. The South Sister was not majestic by any stretch of the meaning. It would be climbable most of the way with patience but no special equipment. Nonetheless, it was impressive in its own way. The ubiquitous rocks – giant boulders, minuscule stones and all sizes between – along this eastern slope rendered it dangerous to novices.

After standing around awhile then sitting, their vigil extended to over half an hour. The youth began pacing, looking over at his pastor less and less. This was when Miriam had appeared before him. If nothing happened pretty soon, he would have to be a liar in his pastor's opinion, he was sure. Father was a good guy, but this Miriam craziness was too much to ask anybody to be cool with. If their roles were reversed, he wouldn't believe it, either, and he'd be mad at being hauled out here early in the morning by some kid and made the fool. *Teenagers and their bad jokes, that's what he'll think for sure*, Miguel concluded.

Estefan now came to notice a subtle change of some sort, using his self-described sixth sense of just knowing. It was not obvious yet it was palpable. Something was about to happen. He looked over at his young companion, receiving no indication in turn that the boy sensed it, too.

Then quite suddenly it appeared. The priest and boy were continuing to look northward when the amber light simply winked on above this same ridge as the day before. The witnesses stiffened with expectation as it angled slowly in their direction. Gracefully arcing downward, the light settled into the same niche as then, a little down the slope and two hundred feet away.

Estefan noticed immediately that, while the six-foot sphere itself was nearly as brilliant as a welding torch, it was curiously not hard to look at. Its glow stretched less than a foot, and none of the surrounding grayish boulders reflected any of its light.

In seconds a separate image moved out of the radiance and skimmed over the rocks, headed their way. It was a female figure, upright in stature, her legs not moving, yet she glided as if silently propelled, keeping a steady pace. Cognizant of what the youth had said about eroding awareness, the priest tried to cement in his mind all the physical details he could before the visitor was upon them.

She was indeed of an olive complexion, he considered. Her thick, black wavy hair, prominent eyebrows and nose were also consistent with Middle Eastern descent. Her flowing gown of white and an overlying sky blue mantle were simple yet elegant in a seemingly fine fabric.

The air now felt lightly supercharged with something like static electricity, but the witnesses' hair wasn't standing on end. Estefan felt a pressing force of some kind, as if he were standing on some alien planet with multiples of Earth's gravity.

As the figure drew still closer, staring directly at the priest, he strained to remain upright and sensed a slowing of his thought patterns. With the uncomfortable realization of mind control he fought to break his gaze and looked toward the ground. *I believe in God, the father almighty, Creator of heaven and earth …*

The young female figure halted twenty feet away, levitating over a spindly cactus protruding from the jumble of rocks. Estefan's evermore sluggish mind recorded that he felt no heat from her yellowish aura.

"You would stone me, priest?" came her first words, soft but accusingly – directly into his thoughts rather than vocally, he managed to ascertain. He clutched at the implication in her remark, struggling to form a thought. *She saw me ... pick it up,* he reasoned in his mind.

"True," the figure posed, "perhaps that is how I know. Your blood pressure at this moment is 152 over 106, your pulse is 98 beats per minute. On most mornings you consume a bowl of oats with cow's milk and burned wheat with mashed oiled nuts.

"At 31 years you lied to a law enforcer about five people hiding in your home. At 25 years you considered leaving the priesthood when you received an unfavorable assignment to this place. At 17 years you spurned the sexual advances of a human female. At 16 years you recorded an intelligence quotient of 144 and placed last in a foot race when your right lower leg muscles tightened. At 13 years your left ankle was damaged when you fell off your porch. At nine years you killed a rodent in your home then felt remorse. At six years you were frightened by gunshots outside and urinated in your garment. At four years you were punished for using a form of glue inappropriately."

Estefan heaved a resigning sigh at the telepathic interception of his thoughts plus the extraction of long-term, mostly long-forgotten memories. More than a little befuddled from the surrounding force on him, his innermost core of awareness dictated that he stagger backward across the two-track and well beyond. The figure remained in place. As twenty feet became a hundred, the priest felt the electromagnetic effect diminish.

Now, feeling the stone in his pocket, on impulse he plucked it out and, with a whipping side-arm motion, let it fly. The pebble tumbled on a line and passed directly through the figure's midsection. It clattered off a boulder beyond her before coming to rest. He turned toward the ball of light, still tucked into the higher niche, and shouted defiantly, "This is a projection, a holograph! Speak to me openly, no control!"

secondarily recognizing that he probably didn't need to shout at all.

The image of the young woman before them abruptly vanished. Simultaneously the powerful energy field ceased its hold on the cleric and the teen.

For his part, Miguel remained slack-jawed, hands on knees and speechless. He was clear-headed still as to what had just happened; his mind had recorded the extraordinary exchange.

Estefan continued to monitor the glowing sphere above them and to their left where it rested in the rocky niche. He wondered whether he had just accomplished something or instead reserved himself a place deep in Dante's inferno. He moved unsteadily forward, shaking off some muscle tension, and clapped the young runner on the shoulder.

"You okay?"

"Yeah, Father, uh," clearing his throat, "fine, y'know, I'm good," the boy now straightened. "Father, when you threw that rock, it went straight *through* her, I swear! I was standing right here looking at her and it went through her belly! What's going on?"

"A test, I think," the priest answered quietly, with more assurance than he really felt.

The adolescent looked warily at the amber ball still resting above, then at his pastor with growing admiration. "You really fired it, Father! Wow, you've got an arm!"

"I played the infield at seminary," Estefan offered, collecting himself and breaking into a brief smile. "No big deal, I couldn't hit a curveball. And I'll be feeling that throw tomorrow – didn't warm up." They both chuckled nervously.

Another moment passed as the man and boy continued to

look on. "It can read our minds," the priest posited to his young companion.

"Who's 'it'?" came the youth's reply.

"I don't know yet, son."

Miguel unconsciously balled his hands into fists. Paraphrasing the priest's words from the day before, "Father, are we supposed to be scared now?" The boy realized that, whatever might be going on, they were probably powerless to stop it. Even knowing that, he wouldn't have traded this moment for a World Series ticket to see the Diamondbacks.

With a deep breath to quell his own anxiety, Estefan paused before answering. "I don't know that, either. Just concentrate and focus. Don't let your mind drift. Remember everything. Just focus."

A voice telepathically intoned, "You have courage, priest. You are unsure what to believe. You have pondered questions from your sciences and the words of your Old Ones." Neither male nor female in its timbre, the voice in their heads offered only minor inflections and modulation.

"I know the God I pray to doesn't have anyone behind the curtain, pulling levers," Estefan shouted, testing with an analogy while insisting on a vocal exchange, at least on his part.

"You know nothing of the greater awareness," came the telepathic rejoinder. "Your brain is not sufficiently evolved to comprehend. You seek confirmation: The Wizard of Oz wore a black tuxedo."

This did confirm that it was reading his mind. In formulating the Oz reference, he had for an instant envisioned that grainy scene with the professor dressed in a black cutaway tux, pulling levers. There was no defense in the human arsenal against such a power.

The cleric pressed on regardless. "Why did you pretend to be Miriam?"

"Manifestations are made suitable to the culture and individual. Miriam is a comfortable image for you."

The priest stared hard at the luminescent ball, a bit more at ease if only because he was still upright and lucid. Reverting to his Jesuit seminary background, he verbally threw two more high hard ones: "Do you represent the one known as Yahweh? And how is Yahweh connected to Jesus?"

"That is your quest. Know this."

Immediately a dreadful, ghastly scene filled the cleric's mind: wasteland, smoking ruins stretching to the horizon, charred bodies everywhere, burning rubble near and far. Astonishingly, he smelled the overpowering, putrid stench of it all and involuntarily retched. Then, as instantly as it had appeared in his mind, the horrible scene and smells were gone.

Estefan was shaken, no longer resolute.

"No one can win. Your species would repeat this until it is no more," the voice intoned. "If you fail to act as your winter solstice approaches, soon after your world will have no Christians, no Muslims, no Jews, no Hindus, no Buddhists, no Taoists, no agnostics, no atheists. Most will starve or die slowly, painfully. This need not result. It is your choice."

The Jesuit's mind thrashed about for rationale. *Fail to act? How? Jesus, what does this mean?* "Why me?" he rasped, still sorting what he had just experienced.

"This will be your time," came the firm yet ambiguous reply.

"My time? I don't understand, please explain," Estefan

managed, his voice lowering.

"You agreed to this."

Seconds became a moment while the priest processed the apparent allusion to the metaphysical. *Agreed? ... As in before this life? Teacher, you really didn't bring up past lives!* Then in quick succession: *Could be playing on my faith. Why do I feel so distrusting? It knows these thoughts as I think them.*

Politely now but still boldly he insisted, "Who was Jesus?"

"A messenger," came the response without hesitation.

Estefan considered the answer ... and the source. "There were others?"

"You suspected this."

Another fastball as the cleric regained some confidence: "Have you manipulated our species and, if so, how?"

"You are a protectorate," was the initially imprecise response. "Interventions have been necessary. Human development is erratic."

Yeah, tell me about it. Then, on behalf of Johnson and agnostics everywhere, "Tell me of God."

"You cannot perceive the greater awareness."

"Yes, you said something like that before; a thousand pardons but that's not an answer," Estefan pressed. He looked left and right across the bland eastern slope of the South Sister and shifted his feet, assuring himself that he still had all his faculties.

"At 28 years you attempted to describe the sky to a blind child who came to your village," the voice intoned. "You were unable to convey color."

Estefan now recalled the moment, a frustrating one.

"It cannot be conveyed, that which cannot be conceived."

Estefan tried a more concrete approach. "There are other worlds like this one?"

"More than your highest number.

"You will become aware of a message to deliver. ... When you remember, it will be your time; then you must act."

The cleric was momentarily lost between thoughts. Vague neural signals from his left foot, cockeyed against a stone, returned him to the here and now. *Huh.* He shifted the foot to flat ground and looked over at Miguel, who was staring back, perplexed.

The globe of light began to rise slowly from its rocky niche.

"Wait!" The priest groped for something else reasonably intelligent to query. Failing that, he proffered another challenge: "Yahweh was cruel and evil!" he bellowed. "Yahweh ordered death and destruction. The Israelites were sent on a crusade to decimate Arab cities, to kill old men and women and children, the dogs, the sheep, to leave nothing alive in their path – all because Yahweh assigned Palestine to the Hebrews. That is not the way of the Teacher! Again, are you from Yahweh?"

Estefan was warming to a prosecutor's role as the light continued its casual ascent. "You have used trickery here but you forgot the beads! In the visions, Mary always holds a rosary!" aware that he might yet be struck dead in his tracks for this insolence. "And there are roses at her feet!"

The glowing ball paused a few hundred feet nearly overhead. Estefan looked over at the boy, who was still amazed at his priest's audacity and at the sum of what had just transpired. Miguel flashed the hint of a trembling smile.

Summoning one more bit of gall, Estefan looked skyward and hailed, "Tell me now what it is you seek! Who are the parties that cannot win?"

"You will know when it is your time." With that, the sphere shot silently straight up and out of sight, faster than their eyes could follow. The priest and teen looked at each other, neither knowing quite what to say, struck by what had just transpired.

They turned to head back to the Wrangler, picking their way across the mountain's rock-strewn apron when, faintly at first, they became increasingly aware of a low rumbling noise from the east. Then it erupted into a thunderous roar. Two F-22 Raptors in tandem flashed over the South Sister, barely clearing the peak. A sonic boom followed.

They reached the Jeep and were pulling away when that pair of jet fighters blasted across the sky again, retracing their path, another booming clap of thunder closely behind. In seconds the planes were out of sight.

As he had monitored so often on his runs, Miguel looked at his watch face: It was 6:45. *She came back at the same time after all.*

For several minutes the priest and boy drove in silence eastward across the equally rough two-track of CR-9 toward Hwy 11, aka Columbus Road, that would take them south to the town. Finally Miguel spoke, referencing the telepathic communications they had both heard.

"Father, that voice, um, the ball of light, it seemed a lot more powerful than us. But it was like you didn't trust it very much."

Lost in thought to that point, nervously holding the steering wheel in a death grip, Estefan shook himself to full awareness and the boy's observation. "Well, ah, yes, that's fair to say." They drove through another big rut. "I guess we shouldn't believe everything we see in the movies, eh?" he inserted lamely with a weak smile.

The young runner understood. "But you were talking about 'Yahweh.' Is that somebody from the Bible?"

"Yes. Yahweh was also called Jehovah, God the Father – or so the Old Testament would have us believe."

"But you were kinda saying Yahweh was bad, like evil."

The priest searched for an appropriate response. "Evil may be too strong a word. Let's just say some things attributed to Yahweh don't square well with what we're told Jesus said and did."

"So do you think the light was maybe sent by Yahweh?"

"I'm not sure."

"Because it wouldn't answer you?"

"You've got that right. You'll probably find as you grow older that it's hard to trust someone who won't give you a straight answer."

"Gotcha. ... So who's Miriam?"

"Well, in Hebrew, the language of the Jews, Miriam was Mary, the mother of Jesus. But Jesus and the people of Galilee spoke a somewhat different language called Aramaic. And in that tongue his mother was known as Mariam, not Miriam. I would've told you sooner, but I thought it better not to influence you by the connection."

"So why did that voice say Miriam instead of Mariam? Wouldn't it use the language Jesus really spoke?"

The cleric looked over and winked. "Have I mentioned that

you're a pretty bright kid?" The absence of a rosary and roses, the mispronunciation of Mary's original name: Whatever the source of this presence, it appeared capable of mistakes. *Or were those more tests?* he wondered.

They pressed hard against their harnesses several more times on the still rugged path back to the paved road before the youngster spoke again.

"That voice, the one from the light, it talked about the winter solstice. That's December 21st, I know, the shortest day of the year. So, can I say something else, Father?"

"Of course, Miguel, every thought has value. Go ahead." Estefan eased over an especially rough washout.

"Um, well, I was thinking the voice was, y'know, a little mean, too." He looked away, out over the desert expanse. "Well, maybe not mean so much, but maybe just, um, like stern and all business. I don't know 'cause I'm still a kid, y'know, but that's not like how I was taught about the Virgin Mary and Jesus and stuff. They're supposed to be all nice and everything, but that voice didn't give you much respect, Father."

"You noticed," Estefan replied wryly, unsmiling at first before brightening. "Do you think my Levi's were too baggy or something?"

They shared the laugh and the teen was buoyant again. "Father, I think you proved it wasn't, like, God and that Miriam was just a holograph or something. How could you have known?"

The cleric fell serious again. "I didn't; it was a calculated risk. And besides, throwing that stone didn't prove much."

"Why not?"

"It answered nothing about the source, the light – what it is or what it represents." *Teacher, I could use some guidance here.* "Miguel, did you see something in your mind back there, a disturbing scene?"

"No, huh-uh. I heard the voice say 'Know this,' and then 'This does not need to happen,' or something like that, but I didn't know what that meant. Besides, I was kinda out of it, y'know?"

Estefan breathed a sigh. *Thank God for that, at least.*

Miguel went silent and was still contemplating as the Wrangler finally reached Columbus Road for the balance of their journey home. With the warm morning breeze blowing his hair through the open window, the youth finally spoke again.

"So, if Yahweh wasn't God, then who was he?"

"Hmmmm." Estefan slowed the Wrangler and brought it to a gradual halt along the shoulder. He looked over at his passenger and replied, "Sometimes a ruthless warrior, if we're to believe the accounts in the Old Testament. But keep in mind, those stories are from three and four thousand years ago. Still, Yahweh did set down some basic rules that we all try to keep today: the Ten Commandments."

"But why would Yahweh choose Palestine to give to the Jewish people?" the boy insisted. "Isn't it just all desert and everything, like here?"

"Yes, mostly. Not exactly the Garden of Eden, eh? I've wondered that myself."

Miguel gazed away again in a tangle of thoughts. He looked down at the floorboard momentarily, then, "That wasn't fair — about killing everything and everybody just because they were in the way. So why is that stuff even in the Bible? I'm a little lost." The youth thought fleetingly of his own family and the discriminatory practices accorded to his grandparents and those before them. Injustice seemed to have no bounds.

"It doesn't mesh well with what Jesus told us in the New Testament, you're right." The priest retrieved the rosary from his left front jeans pocket and clasped the simple pewter crucifix between thumb and forefinger. "I just know I feel at home with this guy."

"Yeah, me, too," the boy replied seriously. "So, what happens next?"

"We need to speak with your mother."

Five minutes later Estefan followed Miguel through a door into the Flores kitchen.

"Father, hello, sit down, tell me what happened," Rosalinda rattled off. "I heard two explosions from that direction and I was worried."

Estefan offered an abbreviated account, explaining the sonic booms, shortening the desert discourse, trying not to be alarming, remaining factual – and omitting the scenes of destruction shown in his mind.

He concluded, "Senora Flores, understandably you're concerned for Miguel's safety. And nothing that happened today suggested that he needs to be involved further."

Miguel traded glances with his priest. He folded his arms disapprovingly and turned his head away. He realized it was his pastor who was at the center of the experience, but he wanted to help in any way he could.

"I wish Renaldo were here," Rosalinda sighed.

"Where is he now?"

"In Michigan; they are finishing the strawberries. He was

farther north until this month, for the cherries. Soon they will move to the vineyards over by the big lake."

Estefan reached for her hand as she went on. "He calls at night from his cellphone – the cheapest plan he could find. He saves every dollar." Tears welled at the pride she held for her spouse. "He is stubborn, Father. He says we must stay here, that our children must know the same home and the same schools."

She paused then added softly, "He should be home in late October, after the pumpkins." She dabbed a sleeve of her blouse to her eyes. "Renaldo is a proud man, Father. He wants to be the last migrant worker in our family."

Rosalinda looked lovingly at her oldest child and spread a strong right arm across his shoulders. She kissed his temple then turned to the priest again.

"If you are finished with my son in all of this, it is a mother's relief. But if this is God's work, and if you need Miguel's help, I will not be the one to stand in the way. I know you would do your best to take care of him."

"Thank you for that, it's very gracious of you. But I doubt that will be necessary."

Estefan drove away from the Flores property toward the rectory, not at all sure himself what the coming months would offer.

Johnson was waiting in Estefan's driveway when he arrived home. "My main man!" They hugged hard. "Did you know you're developing a bald spot on the crown of your head? Perfect. My guy, the Chicago monk!" he bellowed. "Now you just need the brown cassock and knotted belt."

The priest smiled and nodded but remained reflective. "You're saying you had an unobstructed view?"

"Damn straight! Like standing just beyond you and to your right, friend. Intense, man, like a mini-sun, yet curiously it wasn't hard to look at through my lenses. I noticed you didn't shield your eyes, neither of you. So, it wasn't searing your eyeballs either, I take it."

"I've been giving some thought to that, Johnson." Estefan leaned against a fender. "You're right, it wasn't hard to look at, not at all. The brilliance had a different quality somehow – nothing I learned in physics class."

"Strange. Hey, at one point early on, you backed up a ways then threw a stone at a pile of rocks. A minute later you walked back toward the kid. What was that all about?"

"I was reacting to the figure, obviously."

"What figure? You're talking about the ball of light up high, right?"

"No, I mean the young woman – close to us."

"Fella, I don't know what you're talking about. ... Yes, I do. Of course. A certain teen in a flowing dress, white perhaps, with a blue veil?"

Estefan nodded.

"I see! Hmmm. Holy cow. ... Wait, I wasn't referencing anything religious by the cow." The old seminarians shared the chuckle, recalling Ancient Religions 101. "Anyway, you musta missed 'cause I saw the stone clatter off the rocks."

"Actually my aim was good and the stone went through its midsection. It looked opaque and tangible, but it had to be a projection. And it didn't react at all."

"Well, excuse this Fatima bystander, bud. Damn, that took some *cajones*. So, I'm picking up that you had concluded by then that it wasn't really her. You did say 'projection' and not 'vision.'"

Estefan pressed his point. "You *didn't* see her – it – hovering near us, just over a cactus?"

"No, I didn't, friend." Johnson's humor was gone now. "There was just the ball of light up higher. Look, in retrospect I wish I'd thought to pack an infra-red unit – my bad. Even in daylight it might've detected something. Regular cameras pick up only visible light, so I'm not shocked that I didn't get anything. But my own eyes didn't see it through the lenses. Both you and Miguel did?"

"That's right. But the crowds at Fatima didn't see Mary, either."

"Yeah, true. Hey, I could tell you were shouting up at the ball of light a few times. What was up with that?"

"I wanted to know who sent it, frankly, whether it represented quote-unquote God in terms of the wrathful Yahweh. But it wouldn't give me a straight answer. It kept telling me humans aren't capable of understanding God."

"Ouch, that wasn't a polite thing to say to a priest."

"Tell me about it."

"Then, near the end it rose to maybe 500 feet and paused for a moment. Then it boogied straight up – or I think it did, anyway. It went up so fast, I don't know if my cameras caught part of that or not. It was literally wink-of-an-eye stuff. We'll see when I get back to my photo lab.

"So, guy, what were you looking at? And talking to?"

Estefan considered the scene in his mind again for a long moment. "I didn't ... I don't know quite what it was, I guess. I need to pray on that.

"By the way, the light could read my thoughts. It responded to some of my particular misgivings though I didn't speak the words."

"Okay. Huh. I don't know what to say, fella, that's a pretty powerful thing to have in your bag of tricks."

Estefan looked hard at Johnson, his darkish features tightening. "My friend, this was not a positive presence. I know you remember all those volumes of Marian literature. She expresses concern for our world and its future, and that was sort of shown here. But from what we have to go on, there was always a profound compassion conveyed by Mary and a corresponding reverence toward her. I felt only sternness, no warmth at all. As Miguel said afterward, it wasn't quite mean but all business."

"So he witnessed the whole exchange as well?"

"Not quite. I saw some awful images in my mind that he didn't experience. I'm grateful for that. It was an end-of-the-earth scene. I saw and smelled utter destruction; it was beyond horrible and it was as if I was right there. Everything and everyone incinerated. The voice implied it wouldn't happen in a single event but apparently in spreading wars that eventually annihilate the entire planet.

"There's one other thing, friend, it was a moment ... I don't know quite how to describe it. I felt a stone under my left foot, uncomfortable. I didn't recall stepping on it. I got confused there for ... I don't know, maybe a few seconds. Then I'm hearing this internal voice saying when it's my time I will act. And I don't know what that means."

"Bro, we'll figure it out, eh?" Johnson reverted to his enthusiastic self. "Hey, I was flyin' through those rolls of film, man, I'll tell ya'. Toward the end I had the Canon on auto-repeat, a frame per second. I was at about thirty frames on the seventh roll, figuring to save the last roll for something climactic to happen, when the light boogeyed straight up and that was that.

"I was just about to crawl out of my camo tent there when this godawful roar came from behind. So I settled back and caught the jets with those final frames. Got 'em on the return flight with the last roll. Ya' think they had something to do with this? 'Cause that's damn coincidental."

Thoughts were swimming in Estefan's mind. He and Miguel had clearly seen what his wealthy acquaintance with expensive cameras apparently had not. Just like Fatima, it was a projection. A vision? Just as Lucia and Francisco had claimed to interact with a tangible presence of the Virgin that no one else could see, Estefan's sentinel had had no clue the diva was there.

A "familiar form," the voice had offered. Was his suspicion correct, that this was really a copycat event, borrowing Marian lore but overlooking the rosary and roses at her feet? A superior but not supreme intelligence? Or had he fundamentally misread the situation, castigated a divine presence? No, he couldn't have; there was no love shown, he reasoned.

"Yoo-hoo, Estefan, front and center, please. The planes. You think the jets were reacting to this thing?"

The priest agreed. "Ah, I guess it'd be pretty odd otherwise to see those fly overhead just then," he offered vaguely. Beneath the particulars, he was buried in the metaphysical.

He, but not the boy, had been shown an end-of-days scene, a vivid mind picture. Was that another tactic, fake like the figure, or a real event to come? Could this still somehow have been an envoy from God? If not, was it good or evil? There were too many unknowns, there was too little to surmise, to trust.

The bachelor photographer said, "I'm gonna head home. I'll

start running the stuff through my processor asap." After another short silence, "The rolls of film, Estefan, and the videodisk. I presume you want me to develop them."

"Uh, sure – sorry. Yes, if you would take them to an Insty-Pix, I'll pay you back."

"Your money's no good, friend. Plus I have better processing equipment back at the house. I'll just go ahead and—"

"Thanks, but if it isn't too much trouble, I'd appreciate it if you'd have them processed commercially. The date stamp might be important, I don't know. Just thinking out loud here."

"You got it, guy, but I'll use the best place in Albuquerque, a professional film and disk processor I know.

"Hey, guy, I'm leaning toward the UFO theory myself. It was certainly flying in the beginning and at the end, and we sure haven't identified it. I happen to also know somebody who's into all that. He's with a credible civilian group, the Mutual UFO Network. They have lots of professionals involved who do this on the side. I went to a weekend symposium there a couple years ago and made some acquaintances, this one guy especially. But, y'know, if it's something else, like, oh, I don't know, the *Virgin Mary*, man, that's ... You're a good guy, Estefan. I'm at your service, okay? Anything you need, I mean it."

Chapter Ten

Ray Washburn placed the handset back following his video conference call, a departmental budget meeting. He had figuratively sat along the wall for two hours, his hands clasped, one of a dozen seen-but-seldom-heard functionaries, feigning interest in the proceedings as General Townsend held court.

The Air Force Secretary certainly enjoyed center stage with the best of them, Washburn knew. The Force was in serious need of upgrades in its fighting apparatus, Townsend had conveyed, but that was an uphill battle for now against a public gone completely sour on foreign adventures and military matters generally.

He set aside the charts, slid back in his chair with a fresh thermal pitcher of decaf, two large onion bagels and cream cheese – brunch. After briefly massaging away the meeting's posturing from his neck, he opened his email directory. One titled "Incident Report" was flashing.

Colonel Luther Ferguson, base commander at Holloman, west of Alamogordo, had forwarded a message which read starkly, "Pursuant to your personal-review directive, attached is a report of an incident involving Holloman AFB active-duty officers this morning." The attachment read:

```
To:     Lt. Col. Hugh Stone, Commander
        49th Operations Group

From:   Major Sylvester Millen
        8th Fighter Squadron

Re:     Unknown Light
```

21 July 0622 MDT squadron office received an
alert: At 0621 base radar painted an
infrared target of suspicious origin, range
~ 150 miles SW of Holloman near the Mexico
border. Capt. Rhodes and this pilot
scrambled F-22 aircraft; wheels up at 0627
with low-altitude-flight and sonic-resonance
clearances; target coordinates 31.90 N,
107.66 W. Activated GPS receivers and laser
gyroscopes.

0637 aircrafts' over-horizon infra-red
radars locked onto a stationary target at
ground level, range ~ 60 miles; permission
to arm weapons. Target not yet visually
identified.

0640 both pilots observed a stationary
yellow-orange light 7 miles distant, 300'
aloft and phosphorescent in appearance.
Light immediately rose at great speed and
out of sight in less than one second.
Neither aircraft's height-finder radar was
able to track the object.

0641 pilots passed the coordinates, a
grouping of three minor mountains. Nothing
visually threatening at the location;
nothing further on radars; one ground
vehicle and two pedestrians observed.

0645 on return pass ground vehicle observed
leaving the area; nothing else visual or on
radar.

0648 pilots received permission to
deactivate weapons and continue to base.

Washburn stood up and let out a long slow breath. *It's beginning again*, he thought. *Cat and mouse, '67 or '75 reprised.* But for now there was no point in taking this back to Nowitzky; she'd just ridicule the radars or drop a "General Saucer" line again. He'd wait for an opportunity to buttonhole Townsend, especially if this crap in the skies continued.

Damn this stranglehold on the military by the White House, Washburn chafed. With everything that was security related now filtered through Hagelthorne's office – or, rather, Nowitzky's – the armed forces command structure was stifled. Joint chiefs meetings were narrowly structured as never before, their agendas always cast in concrete, with short shrift given to new business.

How could he have reached the pinnacle of his career yet allowed himself to be dressed down by that woman? *A damn political operative! They're even worse than the politicians themselves!* He sighed again. *And she wasn't even very inspiring in the sack.*

Washburn printed the attachment and set it aside.

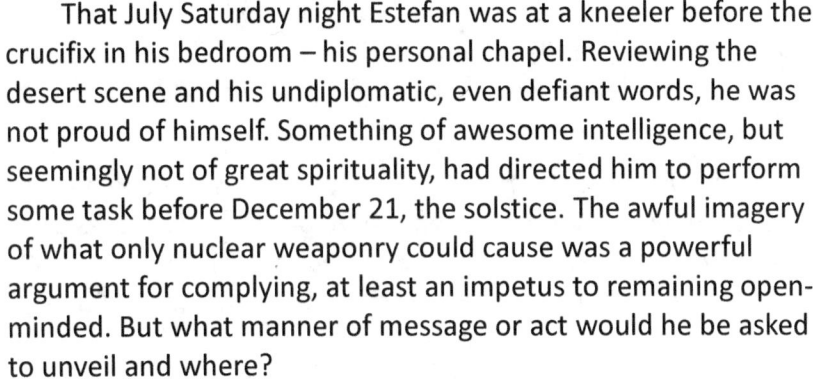

That July Saturday night Estefan was at a kneeler before the crucifix in his bedroom – his personal chapel. Reviewing the desert scene and his undiplomatic, even defiant words, he was not proud of himself. Something of awesome intelligence, but seemingly not of great spirituality, had directed him to perform some task before December 21, the solstice. The awful imagery of what only nuclear weaponry could cause was a powerful argument for complying, at least an impetus to remaining open-minded. But what manner of message or act would he be asked to unveil and where?

Teacher, I don't know what to do. ... I never had a vision before; I don't know what one is supposed to be like. Was it even a vision from You at all? Is it "aliens," as Johnson implies?

If this was our Blessed Mother, I behaved very badly; my penance may never be complete. But something was terribly wrong, sweet friend. Like the boy Miguel said, there was a bit of meanness – and mind control instead of compassion. Rightly or wrongly, I decided it couldn't be Mary, that it was a ruse.

If instead this was an angelic presence, bad demeanor or not, why would You call on me? My station here is nothing. Refried beans and secondhand clothing, those are my life here. Plus the Border Patrol. At least their manners are a great improvement on the Romans'. But, what purpose could I possibly serve?

I just don't know what to believe, and I'm a little scared that I'll do or say the wrong thing. Maybe I already did some of that. It's all very confusing right now.

He pulled the beads from his jeans pocket, kissed the small crucifix and made the sign of the cross. "In the name of the Father and of the Son ..." When he had completed the rosary, thoughts flooded his mind again.

Teacher, I'm at a loss, humbled before You. This ... yes, of course, it was an intelligence; it had to be an intelligence. Maybe even beyond my imagination of what that means. But our Father created all things; wasn't this of Him?

Yet my heavens, Mary is Our Lady of the Rosary! Could that have somehow been an oversight? And there were no roses at her feet. Accessories "they" forgot to add to the projection? ... Or was this a test, leaving out details to convey a message? But if so, what? Jesus, what did it mean?

A fractured scene intruded his mind for a second: looking

down to see his foot cockeyed on a rock.

Teacher, You said we are all God's children. Everything emanates from the Father. By the providence You afforded, I know I've been in fortunate places in my life, with a wealth of resources to draw upon along the way. For these blessings I thank You again.

But who is it that called on me today, sweet friend? Is it evil? Like Miguel suggested, it was authoritative, and it disrupted my thinking. As I depict You in my mind, I'm having a difficult time accepting that anyone You send would act quite like that. Something just wasn't right; there was no compassion. Is that what humanity could devolve into eventually, a species devoid of emotions?

The priest's thoughts suddenly turned once more to those revolting images of nuclear cataclysm.

Teacher, the scenes in my head were horrifying. And the smell. I don't believe I could conjure up all that on my own. Whatever the nature of this power, it must've put them in my mind. It implied this will be the end of humanity. Was that truly a prophecy? … Or merely a trick?

Remaining on the kneeler, Estefan slumped back onto his heels, his face contorted at the enormity of his worry.

There was something else, my dear friend, and I'm struggling to define it. … Just before the light shot into the air, I think maybe something happened – or should have happened, I'm not sure. There was a shift in my gaze; I was looking up at the ball of light and then – instantly? – I was looking down. And my foot was off-balance on a stone. And then the light receded. That's gnawing at me, like I missed something momentarily. If You find it appropriate to afford me some insight on that, I'd be most grateful.

Master, I haven't contacted my bishop yet. Surely I have to. Why am I delaying? Why do I feel uncomfortable telling anyone else about this?

Then he thought of Johnson Selby and the acquaintance he had spoken of. Estefan needed information.

I am Your student always. Whatever You wish of me, I gladly accept. If this was but a once-in-a-lifetime "UFO" experience, I'm grateful for having participated; it was fascinating. If something more is expected of me, I seek Your guidance. Amen.

———

"Okay, Estefan, your camera and mic are operating fine. And hey, man, thanks for letting me drag you into the 21st century."

"I'm most grateful for the laptop, Johnson." The priest sat back in his bedroom easy chair and looked at his friend.

"My pleasure. And it's okay that your eyes are cast down at your screen right now. It's natural to look there, but the camera's the little dot at the top." He pointed an index finger upward and chuckled good naturedly, "Rookie. Now, through the marvels of Skype, we'll go to split screen. Estefan, this is Dr. Paul Palmatier. He's chairman emeritus of the sociology department at Boston U."

"Glad to meet you, Father Tolavares. 'Emeritus,' yes, I love that word, generally reserved for old coots well past their prime. Oh, how we do love titles – a worldwide phenomenon, indeed." The professor laughed at his self-effacing lines.

"The honor is mine, and thank you for agreeing to speak with me, Professor." Estefan felt a charming quality about the older man.

Johnson interjected, "Estefan, I took the liberty of filling in

Paul about your encounter. Thought it would save time."

"Yes, then," the seventy-something former department chair vocally gaveled them to order. Thick salt-and-pepper eyebrows thrust upward in sync with his loose jowls and ever-moving facial muscles. Broad white sideburns crept onto his ears; white locks cascaded over a navy turtleneck and lapped at the collar of his brown tweed blazer.

"I suppose I ought to begin, Father, by saying tonight I represent two organizations: the Mutual UFO Network and the Center for UFO Studies. Boston University is in no way involved. In fact, harkening back to those sixties TV spy programs, they would no doubt disavow any knowledge of my actions pursuant to these matters." He laughed heartily again then cleared his gravely throat. "Colleges have been a hard sell, yes.

"These civilian organizations do some fine work on very limited means. Some of the best scientific minds – physicists, engineers, psychologists – have been involved. Cutting-edge stuff. Highly qualified people bringing solid evidence and analysis to bear. It's been my privilege to do some research for them, to speak at their conferences from time to time. Wonderful gatherings, yes, absolutely stimulating conversations!

"But to the point, Father," the old professor rose in his chair, again clearing his throat, "I need to ask whether you'd be willing to complete a few sighting forms and have your experience entered in a computer system."

"Ah, I hope you understand that, ah, no, that might not be a good idea."

"That's all right, I kind of expected that. So, we're off the record.

"Now, by way of explanation, in UFO research circles a close encounter is something anomalous that occurs within roughly

500 feet or so of the witness, a length at which lots of ordinary things at a much greater distance – aircraft, meteors, all that – can be ruled out as an explanation.

"Five categories of close encounters are generally accepted in the field, from a simple momentary appearance of an unconventional craft in the air nearby – a close encounter of the first kind – to quite intrusive behaviors.

"Johnson spoke of a ball of light, several feet in diameter and orange to red in coloration, is that correct?"

"No, well, yes, the size is about right; I would say maybe six feet. But the color was actually closer to yellow – amber."

"Thank you. Yes, then I shall dispense with further illusory queries, if that's all right. 'Illusory query,' yes, that's academia-speak for a trick question," the professor chuckled. "And how far away from you was it at its nearest point?"

"About 200 feet, on higher ground."

"Now, please characterize the physical nature of the light source and the 'glow' that Johnson mentioned was emanating from it, if you would."

"Well, it was intensely bright yet not hard to look at – if that makes any sense."

Dr. Palmatier grunted a noncommittal response but with a perceptible facial intimation.

Estefan continued. "The luminescence, I would say, extended less than a foot from the outline of its shell, which was a perfect sphere. It appeared to be tangible, but beyond that, I wouldn't speculate on the makeup. No markings that I could see through the brilliance. It was producing a lot of volts, as we understand the concept, so I wondered why it wasn't illuminating the rocks around it."

"Uh-*huh*." The prof's brow pinched a bit more. He was very familiar with the factor in UFO archives of a brilliant yet non-disbursed light source. Many witnesses to roadside encounters over the years had remarked that nearby trees or fields were inexplicably beyond the glare's reach.

To eliminate an age-old trait attributed to spherical sources in particular, Palmatier asked, "Excusing another leading question, Father, what about an undulating effect, like burning coals?"

"No, it was just a constant glow, no pulsating, no undulating. It was more like the glow around an incandescent coil – just a lot more intense."

"Hmmm. That narrows the parameters a bit, yes." The academic stroked his white evening stubble. This was remindful of 1967 in particular. He thought of amber lights and structured unconventional crafts cavorting all over the country. From time to time they had even bumped Vietnam as the lead story on the evening news. He recalled the CBS anchor, Walter Cronkite, getting all puffed up one evening about UFOs and the government's failure to come clean about what it knew.

Palmatier smiled and lifted a glass of pinot noir at his side, twirled the dark red contents and sipped lightly.

"I backed into the field, myself, to be sure – as most of us did. Wrote my dissertation on crowd behavior in the early seventies and continued to dabble in it. Fascinating stuff, how individuals subjugate their will to the mob, engage in behaviors they would never do on their own. Many lessons to be learned, yes."

The professor paused for several seconds, scenes from long ago filling his mind.

"A close encounter of the *fifth* kind, Father, involves

communication with a nonhuman entity. Johnson says you were greeted personally out there, and from what he expressed, one might say there was some mild hostility. You threw a rock at the being before you. Am I correct in assuming you doubted this was a religious experience?"

"I ... Yes, it's fair to say I had doubts. And do. I guess I'm not sure what to believe at this point. But I wouldn't say the stone I threw was a hostile act. I took a calculated risk to confirm a suspicion. The figure didn't react when the stone passed through it, as if it wasn't programmed for the unexpected. That led me to conclude it was probably just a projection, not a vision as I understand the term."

"All right, but let's stay with the figure for a moment. How would you describe her relative to, oh, a normal person standing next to you? What struck you as being exactly the same or somehow different than that?" The prof's brow knitted again at the prospects.

"Ah, well, for all intents and purposes, sir, it looked like a real woman – actually a teenager, maybe seventeen or so. Long dark wavy hair, olive skin, dark eyes, quite short. A pale yellow-white aura extended a few inches all around. Her robe and veil ... Dr. Palmatier, they were precisely as Lucia dos Santos described. Are you familiar with the events in 1917 at Fatima, Portugal?"

"Father, you jest! It's one of the most *staggering* accounts of crowd behavior in modern history! Besides, I live in Boston – home to a million Catholics. Oh, yes, psychological, even apparent physical effects were laid on that throng at Fatima – fifty thousand strong, they say, on that final day, October 13, 1917.

"But, Father, did you ever come across the Lisbon newspaper accounts? Two reporters were there from those two competing dailies, yes. They were standing off to the side, somewhat removed from the crowd."

"No, I guess ..."

"Permit me a second to recall the passage from the next day's O Seculo edition." Palmatier leaned back in his chair, looked up at his ceiling. ... "'The immense multitude turned toward the sun, which appeared free from clouds and in its zenith. It looked like a plaque of dull silver and it was possible to look at it without the least discomfort.'"

Looking back at his camera, the retiree continued. "That reporter speculated in his article that a solar eclipse might have taken place. Except, of course, there was no recorded eclipse that day or on any day or month near it. Astronomers and observatories around Europe were pretty good about those things by then. And, of course, now we have marvelous software to plot the sun and moon positions back as far in history as you'd care to go. No, this was not an eclipse – at least not of the variety we're all familiar with."

Estefan considered the phrasing "a plaque of dull silver" in the professor's reciting of the newspaper account.

Dr. Palmatier had the priest's full attention. "O Seculo's reporter went on with phrases familiar to you, I'm sure: '... the sun trembled, made sudden incredible movements outside any cosmic laws – the sun danced according to the typical expression of the people.'"

The aging educator was in mid-semester form now, retrieving long-stored data. "Then there was the second account printed the next day in O Dia, the other Lisbon paper. That reporter on the scene, a distance away from the first, also described the sun." Palmatier closed his eyes, finding the passage. "'The grayish tint of mother of pearl began changing as if into a shining silver disc that was growing slowly until it broke through the clouds.'"

The prof hesitated, opened his eyes and stared at his camera lens, recalling the final line. "'And the silvery sun, still shrouded in the same grayish lightness of gauze, was seen to rotate and wander within the circle of receded clouds!'"

The priest sat fairly enraptured. Some of this was new information.

"Now, we have essentially two possibilities, yes, relative to the, shall we say, tantalizing object in the sky that midday. The ordinary sun is one. Something blocking the sun is another.

"The reporters from O Seculo and O Dia might themselves have been fooled along with the rest and caught up in the excitement, yes, though their words belie that notion. Perhaps it was some wispy layer of remaining cloud cover at work, nothing more. We've all witnessed as much from time to time – looked directly at the sun through a thin cloud layer, seen its face diminish in radiance, even darken a bit, perhaps, yes. But fifty thousand people at once fooled and sent into a frenzy by a wispy cloud layer, with no other stimulus?

"The crowd reaction, of course, is what drew my interest initially. Some were obviously terrified, wondering at that moment whether their world was coming to an end. Panic! Screaming and carrying on, oh, indeed."

Estefan was highly impressed. The professor had obviously not been reading from any script or even prepared notes; he was simply bringing back verbatim quotes and obscure facts about the incident. What a mind he still has, the cleric marveled.

"Finally," the aging sociologist said, still not finished, "I would add the thoughts of a college student who was present that day, a young man who went on to become a science professor at a university there in Portugal, yes."

Palmatier looked up, dead-on at the camera lens. "He wrote, 'Its appearance was of a sharp and changing clarity, like the orient of a pearl. It did not resemble in any way the moon on a fine night. It had neither its color nor its shadows. You might compare it rather to a polished wheel cut in the silvery valves of a shell. This is not poetry, I saw it thus with my own eyes.'"

Estefan was a bit overwhelmed, not only by the professor's phenomenal retrieval of direct quotes but also the implications.

Palmatier went on, paraphrasing now. "Then came the shafts of light sent all around, illuminating the landscape far and wide in every direction and in all the primary and secondary colors. Why, students at a school a *dozen miles* away witnessed the display.

"This polished wheel in the sky then appeared to plummet toward the ground three times, that is, growing in *apparent* size. Hold a quarter at arm's length then move it closer to your eyes; it seems to grow larger.

"Importantly, as it came closer many in the crowd afterward reported sensing a downward pressure. But no lasting effects, no radiation burns or the like. Most curious, wouldn't you say?"

"Yes, fascinating," Estefan reacted without elaborating. Downward pressure, like he'd felt at the South Sister. He'd heard some of these phrasings at the Jesuit seminary but didn't realize they originated in the Lisbon press. Was it the professor's emphasis on the physical particulars that now gave him pause?

Palmatier wasn't finished. "I once had the privilege of viewing first copies of several photographs taken by a few who were present that day. Fascinating, yes. The originals, of course, are locked away in the Vatican. Most of those images were of the assembly itself. Many of them were looking up and pointing at angles roughly approximating the sun's position at that hour. One frame aimed at the sky included a darkened circular feature suggestive of an eclipse. Cameras and film were in their infancy then, to be sure."

Palmatier now emphasized, "Crowd behavior can be very misleading, yes. Monkey see, monkey do, to coin an old truism. Misjudgment of an actual circumstance by a few is picked up by more, then still more, reinforcing one another's delusion as valid observations. The chain is set in motion, beginning with emotional discomfort over the unfamiliar sensory input and finally proceeding to widespread panic. We do fear the unknown, yes.

"Skeptics have claimed that what we think of as Fatima was nothing more than a sundog — a reflection of the sun elsewhere in the sky under the right atmospheric conditions. But all things considered, given a sundog's fleeting and hazy nature; that seems far too simple an explanation."

Palmatier lifted his eyebrows again and stared into his camera lens. "This, of course, wasn't the first visual display at Fatima, as you know, Father. A smaller but substantial number in attendance witnessed a similarly colorful light display across the same field two months earlier on August 13. Then on the 13th of September, 25,000 there saw a globe of light move across the terrain, followed by a freak atmospheric event — a sleet storm under a sunny sky in late summer. Coincidence?"

A globe of light, Estefan considered. He decided to just listen further.

"So, whatever happened in the initial months of claimed visits to the children alone, we do have substantial documentation for an extraordinary experience on the 13th of August and September and certainly the 13th of October.

Multiple sensory phenomena, witnessed by many thousands.

"I apologize, Father, for having dominated the conversation. May I answer any questions you might have?"

Estefan's line of inquiry went to Dr. Palmatier's sources. "Not many years before Fatima, the Portuguese overthrew a Christian monarchy, as I recall," he began.

"Correct, in the 1910 revolution. King Miguel the second was allowed to remain on as a titular figure for another decade."

"Wouldn't it be fair to characterize the Portuguese press in 1917, then, as reflecting the more secular government that had taken control – actually quite virulently anti-Vatican?"

"To be sure, Father, there was no love lost, as I understand it. I love a good round of deductive reasoning; please proceed, yes."

"So, following this 'coincidence' of unusual happenings witnessed by thousands on the same day of the month as the two previous months, the O Seculo and O Dia reporters appeared on October 13. Is it fair to suggest they might have had a jaundiced eye, a view that precluded the possibility of the miraculous?"

Dr. Palmatier smiled into his lens. "Said another way, Father, perhaps those three educated men – from separate locations, mind you – were attempting to describe an aerial phenomenon in physical terms, scientific principles of the time at work, if you will."

Estefan caved and smiled. "What do you think really happened in that meadow, Doctor?"

"Ah, my youthful seeker, I'm neither a physical scientist nor a member of the cloth. I've studied crowds alone. Assuredly, something extraordinary intrigued and then horrified the throng at Fatima that day in October 1917. Physical effects reported were not lasting, therefore science is left without a final answer to offer. Perhaps, then, the source and implications are better left to your profession."

Chapter Eleven

"Enter in peace," boomed the baritone voice as the bishop's secretary opened the heavy mahogany door with its intricately carved Spanish flair.

Estefan stepped into a well-appointed office in a semi-high-rise in downtown Las Cruces, around the corner from Immaculate Heart of Mary Cathedral. "Thank you for seeing me on short notice, Excellency."

"The pleasure is mine, Father Tolavares, you've come a long way. Now, if this concerns those surplus work gloves you asked about last month, I did make an inquiry to the New Mexico National Guard, and they've taken it under advisement. I read the same newswire as you – the order for 3,000 pairs and 30,000 delivered. I agree that shipping 27,000 excess pairs back east, then storing and reissuing them, would probably be as expensive as simply giving them away here. But dear Lord, it does raise a substantial question, you'd concede, about federal assistance to a parochial entity. Not to mention they'd have the Baptists and Methodists breathing down their neck. So, as I gather, the whole matter has been kicked up the line of their command structure. I haven't heard anything back, sorry. You knew it was a long-odds request, certainly."

"No, Excellency, this isn't about that," Estefan finally found a pause to interject.

"Oh?" as the portly bishop finally reached across his ornate desk and shook the pastor's hand. "Is this about the Border Patrol, then? Has there been further trouble?"

"Again, no, Excellency," Estefan replied. "Something's

happened that I need to inform you about."

"Oh, there I go again, jumping to conclusions. I'll simply shut up now and allow you to explain. And please, enough of the 'excellency' bullroar. We're not in a diocesan meeting now. Please call me PeeWee; that was my nickname back in high school in Pittsburgh. I was a 5'6" point guard. I kind of got attached to it, the name PeeWee. You're tall for a Chicano, Estefan. What, about six-one?"

"Ah, well, yes, thereabouts. Actually, I'm Puerto Rican by birth."

"That's right, that's right, I remember now."

Bishop Stevens had always been a jovial man, considering the strains incumbent on any bishop's weekly schedule, the quarterly objectives and the still-creaking wheels of Catholic hierarchy. He had been a young Episcopal priest who, in the wake of Bobby Kennedy's death, converted to Catholicism. Never regretful of his decision, Stevens had long since accepted bureaucracy on either side of the Catholic-Protestant divide.

In Estefan's opinion as a backbencher, his bishop's administration had been good for southern New Mexico in the so-called "post-immigration" years. Stevens had acquired his share and a bit more in funds from the American Catholic Conference. Though not well acquainted, Estefan had developed a certain fondness for the now 81-year-old. He was not a great man, but he was a good man.

"Excellency, I can't call you PeeWee, I'm sorry."

"That's all right. I've had very few takers on that. How 'bout Phil? That's my given name, Phillip. Anyway, what's on your mind, Estefan? Please, have a seat. I am going to go silent now."

"Excellency – Phil – something happened last week,

something that … This has nothing to do with any day-to-day administration of anything. … There's this boy in Columbus, Miguel Flores. He's a little shy, a nice young man of 14, a runner. In fact, he demonstrates a real capacity for running. Unquestionably, colleges will be recruiting him soon enough.

"Miguel is Catholic and has fine parents, though his father is a migrant laborer and gone more than half of the year. Like any boy his age, he doesn't take the Church seriously."

"Yes, of course. We haven't had a good rock group on our side in all these years to help us out. And 'Christian' talk radio and their evangelistic bullroar is light years ahead of us."

"Yes, well, ah, anyway, the boy was on a routine weekend training run, which took him along the edge of a minor cluster of mountains outside Columbus, the Tres Hermanes or Three Sisters. When he returned, Miguel came to my rectory with his mother and said he had seen an amber light out there and heard a female voice calling him telepathically, as if the voice were in his mind. He then witnessed the image – a vision, seemingly – of what we know as the Virgin Mary."

Estefan paused a moment to allow his words to be absorbed. "The lady before him called herself Miriam. She told Miguel to fetch his priest and return the following day."

Bishop Stevens was focused now on the village priest's account. "Uh-huh. Miriam. I haven't heard that name in a while. Go on."

"The next morning at the same hour, he and I drove out to the location, a few miles from the nearest highway. And together we had," he sighed, "an encounter … with a globe of amber light that projected a figure, again what we've all been taught is Mary. Blue veil over white. She came out of the ball of light, floated over some rocks and came to rest over a small cactus. The exchange lasted a few minutes."

Stevens rose from his chair, unable to sit any longer. He looked hard at Estefan, absent-mindedly fingering the edge of a hardback resting on a bookshelf. "Miriam. *Mary*. You saw Mary?"

"Yes ... well, I don't think so. That's how the figure was presented." He waited for a further reaction but, receiving none, continued. "She told me a dark hour is upon us, that I must help."

"Huh," the bishop responded with now downcast eyes. "I really thought we had a few more decades, at least. But that nicety aside, do continue."

"The image referred to December 21, the winter solstice, as an endpoint. All hell will break loose, as it were, unless something prevents it by that date."

The bishop had a thought. "That's the Mayan calendar date, right? But a number of years too late."

Several years himself removed from the comfortable surroundings of the Portland, Oregon, diocese, Stevens had learned scattered details about Latin American history, including the Mayan Long Count calendar said to end on that day in 2012.

"So, have you contemplated on this imagery, this 'figure' as you say – Miriam?"

"I've thought of little else."

Stevens stood next to the desk. "Hmmh. ... Was she pretty?" he asked whimsically.

"More handsome than pretty," the parish priest offered honestly. "She had long wavy hair, Mediterranean complexion, thick dark eyebrows, a prominent nose."

"Yes, well, we always figured the statues and paintings were a little *Euro*-centric," the bishop chuckled. But am I picking up some hesitation? Estefan, was she the real article or not?" In Church parlance and in accordance with Church doctrine, Stevens was asking whether this was a claimed miraculous appearance by the Virgin Mary or something else entirely.

Estefan clasped his hands tightly as he again felt his sidearm motion, saw the stone leaving his hand and passing through the figure, noted the absence of any reaction.

"I really couldn't tell; I'm sorry to confuse you. See, I threw a rock at the figure and it went right through and it didn't react. The image looked tangible, like a young woman, but it was really a sophisticated projection from the sphere of amber light, which had remained high in the rocks."

"Say again?" The bishop leaned a hand onto the corner of his desk, his legs weakened by Estefan's words. "You threw a *rock* at the Virgin Mary?"

"When the figure first drew close, I felt something like static electricity, then a pressure, an unseen force pressing down on us and slowing my thoughts. The boy had spoken of a mild euphoria the day before in its presence. But for me this wasn't at all a joyous or wondrous feeling. Frankly, it wasn't what I'd expect from the Teacher's mother – no love, no compassion, no emotion whatsoever. Plus the figure held no rosary, nor were there roses at her feet. So, yes, I was suspicious."

Stevens moved over and leaned his ample butt against his book shelves. This was quickly developing into the crisis of his administration.

The parish priest continued. "The light source behind the figure could read my mind and tap my long-term memories. It revealed moments I'd long since forgotten. But my essential feeling was one of distrust.

"Bishop, the force was oppressive. While I could still think, I backed up to a place where the pressure diminished somewhat. I grabbed a stone from my pocket without thinking about it and threw it at the figure. It went straight through the midsection and clattered on the rocks behind. The figure didn't react in any way, as if it were oblivious to what I had done."

"And you happened to have this stone in your pocket ..."

"For rattlers. But the ball of light knew I had it. The first words I heard were, "You would stone me, priest?""

"I see. But you winged it at this 'figure' anyway." Stevens sat back down and leaned forward, fingering the desktop lightly. "So, are you here for a reconciliation, perhaps, Estefan?"

"Thank you, Bishop, but no, I don't think I sinned. I just needed to know if the figure was genuinely Mary. When it didn't react I concluded it was a programmed projection, not a sentient being."

"You're not going to call me Phil, either, are you?"

"No, sorry."

"That's all right. So, is that important, then, whether 'Miriam' or 'Mary' held to the age-old pattern of *exuding love*? Whether she brought a rosary this time? Whether someone placed flowers at her feet? Whether your stone struck something solid, caused a painful reaction?"

"Uh, hmmmm... I'm not sure. Until this moment I was inclined to think of it as a holographic image or the like, projected by the amber globe – with a programming glitch. Besides, the light said, 'Manifestations are made suitable to the culture and individual. Miriam is a comfortable image for you.'"

Bishop Stevens looked seriously at his visitor. "And so she should be a comfortable image to you. God acts in mysterious ways, or so I've been told."

Estefan reconsidered now whether his expectations for an intellectual discourse with his bishop were reasonable.

"Bishop, I thank you for that counsel. I should have mentioned that a friend of mine photographed and videotaped the scene from a distance. He and his equipment picked up the sphere of light but not the figure. That at least would be consistent with a holograph."

"Wouldn't it also be consistent with the accounts of a certain French girl and three young Portuguese shepherds? The crowds around them didn't see our Blessed Mother, either," frowning, "though no one *threw a rock*, to my knowledge."

Stevens leaned back in his swivel rocker. "You distrusted this image; that's the central point, isn't it?

"Now, God knows an official investigation of a potentially miraculous appearance would be a pain in the butt for both of us. And we wouldn't hear the Church's conclusion until I'm long gone and you're middle-aged. So, I'm sure not pushing you in that direction, believe me. But, Estefan, so far you haven't convinced me one way or the other whether you and the boy experienced something truly metaphysical or – what? – extraterrestrial, I guess."

The boisterous elder adopted a lighter tone. "It's okay for Catholics to believe in ETs now, Estefan – the 'Greater Glory of God' doctrine, as it's been called. I'm sure you're familiar."

"Yes, of course. I ... I don't really know what to think. ... I need more information. Bishop, I recognize that I was suspicious when Miguel first told me of his encounter. And, yes, the absence of a rosary and roses were markers in my mind.

"Um, to finish the account, after I threw the stone, the figure vanished and then I argued with the voice coming from the ball of light up in the rocks."

"You ... *argued*." Stevens' face shook with the word. He looked hard at the parish priest now. "And what if anything did you learn from it?" He clasped his hands on his lap, a this-better-be-good gesture.

"Well, first the light said humans will annihilate themselves, and images appeared in my mind of what would surely be civilization's end, like the aftermath of an all-out nuclear exchange. It was horrible. Then the light said that Earth is a protectorate – of what, it didn't explain – and that 'interventions' in human development have occurred before. It said we humans don't have the mental capacity to understand what the all-encompassing god force is."

"Oh, just that much!" Stevens laughed. "All right, that's fine. We're Jesuits, after all. We explore the unknown, right? Our forebears discovered new galaxies at a time when that wasn't very popular. We pushed the envelope in the wider priesthood about other dimensions of space and time.

"Estefan, things happen beyond our ken. Oregon won the FBS title game. And the stock market may finally recover next spring to the point that I can retire comfortably. Wondrous things do happen."

"It wasn't like that." Estefan was a bit irritated by his Bishop's flippant remarks.

"No, Estefan, it wasn't like that," Stevens agreed. "So, again, where have your prayers led you as to the nature of this visitor?"

"To your office." The parish pastor leaned in. "But there was another factor I need to mention. After our, uh, verbal exchange, the globe of light rose into the sky. Then, while Miguel and I were walking back to my Jeep, two jet fighters raced by, very low. And a few minutes later they came back in the opposite direction. I believe they must have been alerted somehow."

"Physical or metaphysical in origin, then, a fine quandary," the bishop deduced, casting a warm smile.

"Father Estefan, I'm sure you realize we don't need any more Guadalupes. Even the Mexican faithful are finally taking that old painting to task, as you're no doubt aware."

"Yes."

"And meanwhile we're hanging by a thread in this area of the world." Stevens' levity was gone now. "The Protestant evangelists have been eating us for lunch. Our most recent surveys show we're still sliding with the under-30s and even worse with the middle-aged crowd. We're losing, Estefan. They're not buying what we're selling anymore."

"Recognized," the border priest agreed simply.

"But you're here telling me we have another Fatima – or an ET – on our hands."

"I only know what happened to the boy and to me. I know we both felt that something … wasn't right. When we were both in the presence of the figure … Let me put it this way. I had always assumed that Mary's presence would bring gladness, sheer joy, however serious the message. Instead this was more like, ah, tension. That's the best way I can describe it."

"An absence of spirituality, then?" the bishop probed.

"Exactly, thank you," Estefan said, "no spirituality. There was an urgency expressed, certainly, but I distrusted the motive behind the message."

The young priest now rose from his chair and slowly paced

the room, gesturing. "I can feel the tension between a husband and wife that aren't doing well in their marriage, between a mother and teenage daughter at odds. But this was far more visceral." With an exhale, he stared out a window at the abbreviated Las Cruces cityscape.

"Estefan, well before our time, priests survived the Reformation. My generation survived the shake-up of Vatican II. We've rolled with the punches of the Rolling Stones and Pink Floyd and the grunge bands – God bless them all for their clarity.

"We Jesuits represent something that's better than most of us ever achieve. But we keep trying to make sense of it all, to incorporate new experiences and views and react appropriately.

"Whatever the true nature of this, God willing, you'll find it."

"Bishop, thank you so much for your insights." Estefan realized no further guidance would be found here. He left Stevens' quarters, glad that he had done the expected by informing his superior. But now he was probably further from a firm conviction on the nature of the light and how to proceed.

Following a long drive back to Columbus, Estefan opened an email from Johnson Selby concerning the late astronomer J. Allen Hynek. Long since deceased, Dr. Hynek had served as astronomy department chairman at Northwestern University.

From his early brilliant days at Ohio State University in the fifties, and for two decades to follow, Hynek had also volunteered his time as the scientific consultant to the Air Force's Project Blue Book – the government's semi-public and wholly contentious inquiry into the UFO subject.

To the military's dismay, Hynek's thinking on the subject evolved over the years, from initially and routinely debunking all UFO reports sent his way to eventually founding the Center for

UFO Studies after he left the Air Force's employ. A flood of cogent close-encounter reports – by police, pilots and other observers deemed credible in any other circumstance – influenced his thinking along the way.

The text of Johnson's message was a few quotes taken from interviews with Dr. Hynek in 1976 and '77, respectively:

"The conclusion I've come to after all these years is that, first of all, the [UFO] subject is more complex than any of us imagined. It has paranormal aspects but certainly it has very real physical aspects, too."

"[The extraterrestrial] theory runs up against a very big difficulty, namely, that we are seeing too many UFOs. The Earth is only a spot of dust in the universe. Why should it be honored with so many visits?"

"I am more inclined to think in terms of something metaterrestrial, a sort of parallel reality. ... I have the impression that the UFOs are announcing a change that is coming soon in our scientific paradigms."

Attempting again to present Estefan with views contrasting traditional Church doctrine, a month later Johnson arranged a Skype conference call to someone he knew across the Atlantic.

Johnson began the call at 1:45 PM Mountain. "Estefan, may I introduce Dr. Andrew MacKinnon, a folklorist and full professor of history at the University of Edinburgh. I first came across Andrew in a downtown Edinburgh pub several years ago when I was doing a spread on a chain of lochs. He took notice of the photos on my table, set his pint down and filled me in on some of the local lore. He's a learned man, Estefan."

"Ye're much too kind, my adventuring friend. Hello, Father Estefan, 'tis good to make ye'r acquaintance," Dr. McKinnon began in a high-pitched, scratchy brogue.

The prof was rocking lightly in a century-old rocker built of Scottish ash. In his left hand glowed a sea captain's bent-stem meerschaum. A pair of antique floor lamps softly illuminated a floor-to-ceiling wall of books behind him. Labels along the edges of the sycamore shelving revealed its organization: Legends, Myths and Superstitions; Faery Tales and Ballads; Ancient Art and Dance. An adjoining wall supported the cultural histories of Great Britain and the European continent in the Dark and Middle Ages.

Wisps of gray had invaded McKinnon's thick auburn hair, cut short to counter its natural wave. He stroked a full speckled beard. "I understand ye've had an experience ye might wish to talk about. Johnson forwarded a few of his photos and informed me a bit about the circumstance. Quite interesting.

"Normally I would proceed through an interview with a series of open-ended questions. In this instance, may I dispense with that and presume that Johnson has accurately portrayed the basics of ye'r account?"

"No doubt he has," Estefan replied. "I'm grateful for your insights, Dr. MacKinnon."

"And they're free!" he laughed. "Johnson thought it might be useful to relate a bit of historical perspective and perhaps a few trends in human-nonhuman encounters I'm familiar with across the ages."

The folklorist bore in. "The sameness in themes is rather numbing, I've found. The subject, if that's the appropriate usage, is temporarily rendered physically helpless or mentally slow or both. This has been something of a constant. The distance necessary for the effect to take hold may vary, from several meters to a hundred or more, but the effects are similar. In modern accounts, friends or family may ask afterward why they didn't, say, pick up a camera lying nearby, even pull a cell phone from their belt. Hah! Most of the time, lad, they couldn't tell ye the *day of the week*."

Andrew stared at the sober-faced cleric in his monitor. "Father, ye don't claim to have been taken anywhere but instead simply to have had an extremely proximate encounter with a nonhuman being. It's remindful, if ye'll excuse the hackneyed expression, of older tales involving so-called faeries and the like."

Estefan replied, "Really? How's that? I'm genuinely interested."

"Father, a brilliant French mathematician, the late Jacques Vallée, compiled a tome of such legends the world over, several centuries' worth. He demonstrated commonalities in those stories which, despite the obvious retellings, remain intriguing. For example, a small humanlike yet oddly attired person emerges from a ball of light – the leprechaun of legends, as it were – to speak briefly with his human subject."

MacKinnon had truly piqued Estefan's attention. He'd never made such a connection.

The prof continued. "Several factors – the ball of light, whatever its energy source, the emergence of animate beings or inanimate objects, the light or projections or both vanishing into thin air – they're part and parcel of folk tales stretching back thousands of years across every continent but Antarctica, right up to the present day.

"Much of what Celtic history, in particular, tells us, lad, comes from the *Book of Invasions*. That was a 12th century epic based on 8th and 9th century documents that were in turn transcribed from the earlier works of the bards. Those were said to be based on still older legends.

"They tell of faerie folk who first arrived in Ireland, descending from the sky in flying ships. They brought a darkness over the sun which remained for three days."

This new parallel to the final appearance at Fatima in October 1917, the shrouding of the sun that day, intrigued Estefan and Johnson.

"The visitors were known as the Tuatha de Danann – people of the goddess Danu. They were said to be tall, graceful and elfin, greatly intelligent, musically gifted, possessing secrets of magic. They were treated as gods by the human populace. Following a lengthy period interacting in the Celtic lands, the Tuatha retreated to their parallel dimension of reality.

"Lad, whatever truth lies in Scottish, Welsh and Irish legends, I've managed to locate impressive and similar oral histories in China and from the Australian aboriginals, among other places.

"To me, the most striking feature of all these tales across the centuries is that the subjects themselves recognize afterward the absurdity of their stories. The ball of light doesn't behave according to known scientific principles or common sense: It levitates without a sound or any visible means, it traverses the sky at great speeds, and so on.

"The beings themselves – whether ye'r talking about 5th century faeries or the ubiquitous 'greys' of modern lore – appear or disappear instantaneously; they converse telepathically; they tap into the subject's memories. I expect some of this rings the proverbial bell for ye."

"Yes, I ... I hadn't realized the parallels. Please go on."

"Well, I have to say, from what Johnson told me, stowing that stone beforehand, then throwing it on impulse without first forming a thought in ye'r mind, was brilliant. Had ye contemplated for even one second, ye might not have been able to retrieve it from ye'r pocket."

Estefan's thoughts flashed back to the first encounter by Bernadette Soubirous with the Virgin Mary at Lourdes. Upon recognizing the figure before her as the mother of Jesus, the young girl had made a conscious decision to pull a rosary from her pocket, but her arm was effectively paralyzed momentarily while the diva made the sign of the cross with her own beads.

"The lesson, it would seem," MacKinnon continued, "is that the intelligence, or intelligences, behind all these encounters have always had difficulty countering human spontaneity – or irrationality as the case may be."

Johnson spoke. "Andrew, explain more about the continuity through all this. I mean, were people reporting saucers and cigar-shaped crafts and glowing spheres back in the dark and middle ages?"

"Oh, indeed, yes. Not at all with the frequency of 20th century accounts, mind ye, but yes. Their reporting media, though, were limited to hand-scribed accounts and the occasional painting. Few of either have survived firsthand.

"Some colleagues and I have long since concluded that intelligent visitors present only that which can be grasped by the human imagination. With the exception of a few brilliant men and women along the way, Earth's inhabitants, after all, have only recently reached any sophistication in what we can imagine.

"As to aerial vehicles, before the twentieth century the world's populace had only balloons as a frame of reference. By the 1940s, rockets, though initially for war purposes, inspired thoughts of space travel. The A- and H-bombs, the first Univac computers and so on announced that our basic sciences and technologies were making strides. We as a general population came to grasp that reaching for the stars was no longer fanciful; it could actually happen one day. Which is to say all of that seeped into the collective imagination.

"Accordingly, our visitors seemed to adjust their presentation as well: Unconventional vehicles maneuvering marvelously in the sky became far more commonplace. Sprites and leprechauns from the days of yore morphed into the large-headed jumpsuited alien. They looked futuristic, to be sure, yet they were upright and bipedal, with arms and hands and a head at the top with facial features. Their appearance was still within modern imagination."

Estefan depicted such a "grey" in his mind. Instead of focusing on the differences relative to humans, MacKinnon's thesis looked for similarities.

"They show us only what's next, it would appear, not what our descendants ten thousand or a hundred thousand years from now might fathom as possible. The visitors appear to limit their message to what we can intellectually conjure."

Estefan found himself enthralled by another of Johnson's acquaintances.

"The, ah, figure in my experience mentioned something like that, sir."

"Oh, I'm not a sir, Father, no pretense to royalty here. Simply Andrew will be fine. But tell me her precise words, if ye recall."

"Ah, well, I believe she said, 'Manifestations are made suitable to the culture and individual.'"

"That would indeed be consistent," MacKinnon nodded, "thank ye for sharing."

Estefan leaned forward. "Andrew, if I may ask, then, how would you characterize my experience from what you know of others through history?"

"That would depend on what all was spoken to ye. Do ye recall everything?"

"I ... I guess so, yes." Estefan's mind curiously returned to the moment at the South Sister when his foot had moved inexplicably from solid ground onto a loose rock. He was probably making too much of such a detail. "She talked about a confrontation that no one can win, whatever that means. This was just after the scene came into my mind of total destruction. That's about the most important thing that was said."

"And ye have no idea why this happened to ye?" the Scot pursued.

"No, none. I'm a simple priest in a small missionary parish. I say Mass, counsel families, hear their reconciliations – confessions, they were once called – coordinate a day care, run a clothing exchange and a food pantry. Normal duties of a priest. I'm nobody special."

Johnson spoke up, addressing MacKinnon. "Well, he does have at least two additional attributes. Estefan is an expert in Shi'a Muslim history and culture, and he's fluent in Arabic."

"Languages come easily for me. But that was a long time ago," Estefan quickly inserted. "There was one additional remark I should bring up. The voice implied that I had agreed to do whatever this entails, ah, before this lifetime. But that's impossible for me to accept as a Christian."

"Yes, religious tenets do get in the way when a reality buster comes along, Father," MacKinnon intoned, his accent gradually having grown more familiar to Estefan. "Like most Scots I was raised Presbyterian. We have no history of Marian visits and attendant miracles. Does it not strike ye as odd that only Roman Catholics have these miraculous happenings? Never any Protestants?"

"Well, that may depend on whether you accept Catholicism as the one true faith."

"Hah, good, a fair statement!" Andrew replied jovially, stroking his beard again. "But wouldn't that have been a reasonable way for God, from ye'r perspective, to pick off some Protestant converts along the way?"

"Point well taken," the priest replied.

"It's been a pleasure speaking with ye', lad. I do hope I've been of some use, and good fortune to ye, Father."

Estefan proceeded to bed that night still pondering a central tenet of the Scot's remarks. That the intruders in Celtic lore emerged from balls of light was at once disturbing and fascinating.

Chapter Twelve

"General Washburn, this is General Jeffrey Gash. I head up the Research and Development Board for the Joint Chiefs of Staff. Shorthand, I have one more star on my shoulder than you do."

"Yes, sir. How may I help you?"

"Are you aware of what the R & D board engages in?"

"That would be related to high-performance vehicles, General."

"*Extremely* high performance – off the scale, as it were.

"I'm given to understand that you intend to make some noise about a bogey that intersected our airspace over Texas and New Mexico awhile back."

"Well, I wouldn't characterize it as noise, General, I'd just appreciate the opportunity to—"

"You intended to move it up the line, and so you have. Let me be eminently clear: It stops here, with this conversation."

Washburn understood their respective roles and authority, but he was not going to be intimidated by the moment. "Sir, may I remind you that this was and is a legitimate matter of national security. Multiple radars recorded the same wrinkle in its downward trajectory. This was not an explainable event, by any means."

"Apparently you understand our black projects over here better than I do. Fine. So, what if you're right and this wasn't one of our prototypes? What would we do with that information? How about if President Seymour reserves an hour of prime time TV to lay it all out for the nation, would that satisfy you? Should he announce that those Phoenix lights in '97, for instance, were actually alien – a triangular vehicle three city blocks to a side?"

"Yes," Washburn responded coolly. "The truth is always acceptable and accepted in the end. I remind you of the Military Code of Conduct, sir."

"Well, which turnip truck did *you* fall off? All right, let's go further back, then. How about 1967? You weren't even yet a radar jockey at NORAD, but I expect you know what came up on those screens. Should we flank the President with some of those aging state troopers and deputy sheriffs to tell their stories of objects setting down silently in farm fields – when the best we had still used jet engines and runways?

"And what about 1952? Does the President tell America how our very Capital was under siege for two nights?"

"That's an overstatement, sir."

"Like *hell* it is. As the saying goes, you don't know the half of it. But, okay, let's have him reveal the big enchilada, Roswell. How's that sound?"

"We're already on record that Roswell was an errant Project Mogul balloon."

"Yes, and before that we called it a weather balloon. But you want the *whole* story out: the dual crash sites, the dead beings, the one we captured but couldn't keep alive. You've assumed a balloon was the cover – not a very convincing one. So be it.

"Now we're back to World War II. Does Seymour talk about 'foo fighters,' those glowing balls harassing both Allied and Axis fighter pilots? Does he reach still further back to throw in the mystery airships of the 1890s? How far back does he go, General? Because it is indeed a long and slippery slope once you take that first step."

"Well, depending on how you structure it, there's certainly a way to tell the story without—"

"Without *what*? Without revealing what our black projects do and don't consist of? Much to the benefit of the Russians and Chinese, it goes without mentioning. Without the Dow Jones losing half its value in a week? Who will invest long term, General? Who will take out a damn life insurance policy, for chrissakes!

"Beyond all that, think of congressional hearings from here to eternity. They'd haul out doddering old men to tell what they knew, specifically who gave the orders to classify the subject. How many good men do you care to implicate, General?

"Still more central to the point, what does Seymour follow up with after explaining that Earth is monitored by vastly superior technologies and vastly more intelligent beings? 'Go about your business'? The whole idea is political suicide, which every president since Roosevelt has recognized. And that's why it will never be acknowledged – not by Seymour, not by me, and *not* by you!"

A pause ensued as the two bureaucratic warriors ruminated.

"General Gash, I believe something is afoot right now. If the American public isn't told, the shock and the rumblings from that shock will only be worse in short order."

Gash breathed heavily into his mouthpiece. "I understand your concern, General, I really do. It's duly noted. Now I'm telling you to be a soldier and put a sock in it."

"Begging your pardon, General, but I'm not in your chain of command."

"Oh, if you want a direct order, I can arrange it within the hour. But that would come with a note of threatened reprimand for your file and all the rest. So, are you onboard?"

"... For the moment," Washburn hushed.

"The moment, indeed," Gash finished. "Think real hard before you let that moment expire."

Kenna Nowitzky is behind this, Washburn seethed as he switched off his handset.

For nearly half a century radical Islam, Sunni and Shi'a, had threatened the brittle structure of nation-states throughout the Middle East, North Africa, South Asia and the Pacific Rim. Their separate interpretations of the Qur'an each envisioned a universal theo-political organization. Democratic republics had no adequate response for such revolutionary movements – at least not one true to civilized principles.

Jihadist Islam rejected the national sovereignty of all secular state models, extending its reach and allegiance wherever populations professed the Muslim faith. Since neither an international body such as the United Nations nor the internal structure of individual governments had legitimacy in that unrestrained view, its ideology rejected all Western notions of negotiated compromise. Diplomacy was not in its lexicon.

In the long view, both Sunni and Shi'ite leaders foresaw an entire world fashioned in their own righteous, austere molds. In the short term, each was an infidel's sham faith to the other.

On October 31, 2025, as moms across America sent children

off to school with costumes and treats, a trick devised an ocean away drew no notice.

In a beautifully appointed conference room at the rear of the Grand Mosque of Tehran, a collection of ayatollahs and military commanders from four nations rose from their chairs in unison. Handshakes and enthusiastic kudos carried over to an anteroom and finger foods. The long-anticipated Shi'a Accord was finalized.

Party to the secret talks were the leaders of two longstanding, sometimes warring factions from central and southern Iraq; Hizb'alla's secretary-general Jawad Rahal from southern Lebanon; Syria's famed Subcommander Mounir Tariq Haziz, an Alawite-Shi'ite; and representing the Quds Force of the Iranian Revolutionary Guard, its rarely seen guerilla warrior known only by the *nom de guerre* Ali Abdi. Grand Ayatollah Alireza Vahid Shirazi had overseen the negotiations.

Each of the participants promised an elite contingent of two hundred to carry out separate and simultaneous strikes in a Night of Fire. Using purloined maps detailing weakly guarded points along Saudi pipeline routes, the plan called for the Iraqi militias and the Syrian contingent to spread across the landscape, placing numerous incendiaries to cripple oil production for months. Meanwhile, one Quds contingent would set ablaze supertankers in the Persian Gulf.

While those courageous forces severed limbs, Quds assassins would arrive concurrently at palaces across the Arabian Plain, overwhelm the light security forces stationed there, and decapitate the Sa'ud royalty, Sunni lapdog to the U.S.

To adapt a naval phrase from the Great Satan, this would serve as a shot across America's bow. *Allahu Akbar!*

Egypt, Jordan, and the puny sheikdoms in Kuwait, Bahrain

and the Emirates would quickly and wisely assess their tenuous positions on or near Iran's borders, their prospects of being overrun, the reach of Iran's nuclear missiles.

Shi'a's homeland of Iran would be restored, righteously, as the dominant force in the region, to dispense its own generous reserves of oil at unseemly prices as the West scrambled to form new treaties.

Beyond savage power politics, these coordinated, decisive actions were designed to advance the conditions preparatory to the return of the Twelfth Imam – successor to the Prophet Muhammad – who died in 785 AD.

In a view not shared by Sunnis, Shi'ites interpreted the Qur'an and related prophetic words as promising a messiah for humankind, al-Mahdi, the "Rightly-guided" or "Redeemer." He would be the last in the line of caliphs to guide believers following his return from centuries-long occultation.

In the final days before al-Mahdi appears, all the world's political ideologies will have failed, leaders and governments neglecting their people. It will be clear to all that no one is able to establish justice.

During those "last times," according to the belief, unprecedented calamities and misfortunes will occur. Injustices, persecution and distress will engulf the planet. Civil wars of every cause and stripe will be waged. Many Shi'a true believers will be in shackles, tortured.

Following his long occultation, Muhammad Abul Qasim – al-Mahdi – will appear in Mecca, wielding Allah's double-edged sword, Zulfiqar, the Blade of Evil's Bane. He will protect all right-thinking Muslims from further harm and convince the remainder of the world that Islam in its Shi'a form is the one true path.

Decapitating the Saudi whore and further weakening the

Great Satan were necessary to set the stage for al-Mahdi's emergence. *Allahu Akbar!*

⌢⌢⌢

Estefan came to full awareness, sitting up in bed, his pajama top damp with sweat. He glanced at the clock on his nightstand: 4:18A Dec 8. Predawn light was still far away.

He began organizing the day's tasks in his mind. This was the Feast of the Immaculate Conception, of course, a holy day on the Church calendar; he'd be celebrating Mass at 9 AM and again at 6 PM. In between, parishioners' reconciliations were scheduled for noon. His Sunday sermon was only begun, and he hadn't finished the parish food pantry's weekly inventory. Plus the rectory's set of screens were overdue for removal and winter storage; maybe he could call on a volunteer for that.

But there was something else, something vaguely not right. The word "signs" kept intruding his thoughts.

He padded into the kitchen and started a pot of half-caff then pulled a box of cereal from a cupboard. When he opened the refrigerator door, his jaw fell slack. Not a trace of milk was left in what had been an unopened gallon jug. The plastic container was instead stuffed with several large apples. *How in the… ?* He pulled it out for closer inspection, finding the cap's ring seal intact at the neck. Flipping it over, he expected to find a slit or hole in the bottom as telltale evidence of someone's practical joke – not that anyone came to mind as a perpetrator. But there was no evidence of tampering; the jug was undisturbed from bottom to spout.

He'd seen one or two ship-in-a-bottle demonstrations on TV, of course, employing a string to collapse then re-hoist the sails inside. But these appeared to be real fruit – plump and untouched – inside the flagon. He wasn't much of a fan of apples, really, and rarely purchased them.

"Johnson, I'm sorry for waking you so early but you asked me to call right away if I experienced anything out of the ordinary. Well, a strange thing happened here overnight. I'm holding an unopened milk jug that's filled with apples, and I can't for the life of me figure out—"

Selby's guffaw on the other end of the line cut him short. "Oh, my word! Golden delicious, right?"

"Yes, but how would you know that?"

"I got up in the night to take a leak and then decided to snack on an apple; I had just brought a bag of golden delicious home. The produce bag was half empty, left out on the counter. I figured maybe my overnight housekeeper pilfered them. Friend, this sounds like a marker," his tone suddenly somber.

"What do you mean?"

"Have you discovered anything else out of place?"

"Not ... not really. I mean, there may be something I can't put my finger on, I'm not sure. I did wake up in a sweat. Actually, I wasn't lying down at that point, I was sitting up, still under the covers."

"Any sand on your sheets, down by your feet?"

"Hang on, I'll check." After a moment's pause, "No, they're clean."

"Good, you probably didn't go anywhere, at least. But it sounds like maybe this was a home call. We're within two weeks of the solstice, y'know, so ..."

"My work right now is more geared to Christmas, but yes, friend, the date has crossed my mind."

"If you're up for finding out the whole deal, I have an acquaintance that might be able to help. Ever been hypnotized?"

By mid-morning Estefan was busily inventorying foodstuffs, wondering still about the word "signs," when an image flashed into his mind: slender hands holding a rosary, the decades of pearly white beads separated by delicate gold chain links. He immediately thought of St. Francis Cathedral in Santa Fe. A life-size porcelain statue of the Virgin there displayed just such a rosary, a replica of the one Mary held at Lourdes and Fatima. For whatever reason, this time the imagery wasn't comforting.

The cleric returned to his ledger. He was recording the sixteen institutional-sized cans of diced tomatoes on a shelf when his pen paused on the page. *These hands moved.* The mental picture seemed like more than just a forgotten memory from the cathedral. There was a change in arm carriage in his mental picture; the white rosary moved fluidly from waist to breast, pressing a fold into the cloth – a silky white dress. The visual snippet seemed all too real. *Oh, sweet Jesus, what is going on?*

Now Miriam's full countenance blazed from the recesses of his brain: the same facial contours, same dark wavy hair, the concerned look, the surrounding aura, all just like the figure at the South Sister – the projection, as it were. The backdrop this time, however, was not a mountain but the simple furnishings of his bedroom. "Miriam" had been at the foot of his bed.

Estefan's pen clattered to the floor as he pondered the brief scene in his mind. It felt neither like a dream nor a recollection of that July morning at the South Sister. But the same tension in the air had been present last night.

Signs. Did that mean the encapsulated apples? Even so, that would be only one. He was certain he'd heard the word in plural form.

The cleric strained to remember more. Her lips moved, yes, her lips did move. But what were the words? "Signs," that's all he could come up with. No message at all, not a single phrase.

He momentarily tried mentally piecing together a sequence, more than merely a rosary being lifted, but none came forth. The lightly irradiated figure was out of context. Now he recalled being a little antsy prior to retiring, expectant, but with nothing obviously troublesome he had dismissed the feeling. Was that tied in somehow?

He returned to the rosary. The figure by the South Sister had held nothing. That's what prompted him to risk throwing the stone at it. Yet last night's visitor, if he wasn't simply imagining all this, definitely held a beautiful white rosary. She even raised it up ... to show him? Was that it? Was this then the desert projection again – whatever its source – having added a missing detail, making sure he noticed?

Or have I actually – for some reason – been blessed by your presence, my Lady? Bishop Stevens' cautions about how the Virgin might vary her presentation came flooding back. In his heart Estefan still wanted to be utterly wrong in his suspicions. He wanted it to be Mary. *Was the rosary a sign that this was truly Thee, yet I deny it with all this cynicism? What kind of faith is that for a priest? Sweet Mother of Jesus, I'm confused!*

Estefan slumped to his knees and pulled his plain black rosary from a jeans pocket. Grasping the small pewter crucifix with trembling fingers, he made the sign of the cross. "Our Father who art in heaven, hallowed be Thy name ..."

Chapter Thirteen

Luis Hurtado was at it again. In a bid to secure sufficient tonnage of bauxite for his struggling aluminum industry, the Venezuelan strongman had first cajoled officials in neighboring Guyana, a leading bauxite exporter. Failing to reach agreement on a suitable price, Hurtado amassed troops along the border and threatened to blow up several of the mines. No doubt his men would take hostages as well, including some Alcoa representatives on site, to underscore his resolve.

Guyana was appealing the matter to the UN. Knowing that a full airing there could take weeks, its Secretary General, Ricardo Graveande, contacted the U.S. State Department, whose liaison to Homeland Security cc'd Kenna Nowitzky.

Direct threat to American interests? Yes, certainly, Alcoa's CEO must be having a hissy fit. Diplomatic instability potential? Oh, yeah. Hurtado's the biggest jerk in the western hemisphere. She was still waiting for him to call back all his major league ballplayers. *That would cause one helluva diplomatic uproar. Border threat potential? None.* Nothing else on her triage form applied. She filed it as a Priority 2 in her 24-hour alert cycle.

Just then her i-pod chimed; it was Tom Hagelthorne.

"Kenna, glad I could catch you here so early on a Saturday. Be sure to take a comp day down the road when things are slack. Would you join me, please?"

Comp day, she laughed silently. She hadn't taken a day off in well over a year, let alone a compensation day for extra time put in. She probably had three months of comp built up, but who was counting? She really did feel privileged to be here, to be a voice in shaping policies on far flung matters every day. She had no life beyond these walls, nor was she seeking one.

She pulled on her suit jacket, fluffed the satin scarf cloaking creases in her neck, and strode swiftly down the hallway to the director's office. She brushed past his secretary's vacant desk and opened the ornate mahogany door.

"Hi, Tom, what can I do for you?"

Hagelthorne combed his fingers through thinning silvery hair, a nervous habit left over from a time when he displayed a much thicker mane.

"I just took a call from Senator Sybrandt. He chairs the subcommittee—"

"On Space, Aeronautics and Related Sciences, yes, I know."

"He dropped your name, Kenna."

"Well, gosh, I guess I should be flattered."

"Don't be. He was royally pissed off. His top aide spoke with someone from NOAA's Space Surveillance Center this morning. It seems one of our satellites fell out of orbit overnight. Dropped like a rock – unnaturally so, he said. Landed in the New Mexico desert."

"Huh. That's odd, I guess. But what does it have to do—"

"With you? Maybe nothing. Maybe everything. Their contact at NORAD, a Colonel Lemke, apparently referred to an event last July. He told his boss, General Washburn at the Space Command Directorate, that something – who knows what? – had buzzed that same satellite from above, from deeper in space, months ago. You ever hear anything about that."

"No, I don't believe so," she lied.

"Well, that's understandable. I didn't ask you to keep track of all our hardware up there. But Sybrandt seems to think you knew about it. I don't recall seeing anything like that in your dailies, but frankly I don't usually get beyond your Priority 2s. Tamika logs the rest.

"Anyway, if this is the Chinese or somebody else having some fun with us, I need to know, so I'm afraid I have to add this to your duties. Those machines are expensive, y'know. I realize you've been pretty busy, but I want you to contact Washburn and find out the Directorate's latest thinking on this. And stay on it, wherever it leads, okay?"

"Yes, of course." *Your secretary logs the rest?* Now she had to call Ray Washburn. "Christ," she muttered as she walked back down the hall.

Miguel took a few extra minutes this December Saturday morning for leg and torso stretches preparatory to a long easy run. His mother had insisted he sleep in; now the sun was midway up his window frame.

He had finished sixth the day before in the state cross-country meet — well behind a pair of seniors headed on scholarship to Texas A&M and Arkansas, respectively, as well as a district rival, a junior from Santa Teresa.

A few coaches from other schools had approached him afterward to offer assurance of his potential. One even mentioned that the recruiter for a PAC-10 school was overheard asking about him. As a freshman, he was too young to be contacted; NCAA rules forbade it.

He'd managed to maintain running poise and monitor his

oxygen debt amid the exhilaration of competing with the best. And it was fun; he'd had a blast. Still, sixth wasn't first, and only the top three medaled. On the long uphill fairway to the finish line, his legs hadn't responded when he needed faster turnover.

Now he would set his sights on the track season and the two-mile. He wanted sprinting speed – a kick. More 200-meter intervals were in his future, he knew.

The mid-December air was crisp but the sun's rays warm as he stepped off the state highway and onto the dirt two-track of CR-6. He was replaying yesterday's race in his mind, the rolling fairways of that suburban Albuquerque golf course, the parents and girlfriends cheering those around him, his disappointment in not closing on the frontrunners.

Lost in thought, his gaze lowered in deference to the constant ruts and rocks, he failed to immediately notice the scene ahead. Suddenly a dark blue sedan pulled across the path from behind an oversized bushy cactus. A white-lettered decal on the door read United States Air Force. The driver, a stocky forty-something MP, stepped out and held up his left hand in a gesture to stop. His other hand was snapping open the cover of a holstered revolver.

"Whattya doin' here?" he barked as the boy came to a halt.

"Uh, running, sir."

"Who you runnin' from?" the man drawled, peering suspiciously southward down the path.

"Nobody, um, just running. I'm on the cross-country team at Deming High.

The MP's voice softened a degree. "What's your name, son?

"Miguel. Uh, Miguel Flores."

"You got some ID?"

Dressed in only nylon shorts and cotton turtleneck, the youth thought the answer should be obvious. Slapping his arms to his sides, he replied nervously, "No, I, I don't carry a wallet out here."

He looked past the car. In the distance, just this side of the South Sister he noticed a depression in the ground, like a crater, and several more vehicles around the edge of it. Something bulky was on a flatbed truck under a tarpaulin. A number of men in fatigues were meandering about, sweeping their arms back and forth with what, from this distance, appeared to maybe be metal detectors.

"What's going on?" the high schooler asked.

"You'll read about it in the paper – if you can read," the man added condescendingly.

"I can read." The young runner cared neither for the tone nor the implicit ignorance in this redneck's remark. It was his friend Carlos who had introduced him to the epithet "Gringo." This guy fit the description.

"Fine, now git," the MP barked again with a dismissive wave. At least his right hand no longer toyed with the butt of his pistol. "And if any friends of yours have ideas of coming out here, tell 'em they'll find nothing but trouble."

"Got it," the young runner scowled as he turned to make his way back toward the highway. Agitated but holding his emotions in check, Miguel ran past his Columbus home and headed straight for the church.

"Miguel, hi, what brings you here?"

With one deep intake of air to quell some heavy breathing, "Father, something happened out there." The teen panted some more. He had sprinted the final blocks.

Estefan sensed his young parishioner's visit wasn't related to the state meet. The boy, he knew by now, wasn't one to gloat or seek attention. Besides, his demeanor was visibly serious.

"Sit down, please, take a load off. By 'out there,' do you mean the Sisters?" The priest leaned back against the front of his desk as Miguel nodded.

"I was doing my run this morning, y'know, when this Air Force guy stopped me. He was li—. He was sort of a cop, and he pulled out from the tall scrub there. Got out of his car and I thought maybe he was gonna shoot at first. He was a mean hombre."

Miguel proceeded to relate the entire account: his confrontation, the truck and its tarped load, the men in khakis with what looked like metal detectors.

Signs burrowed back into Estefan's thoughts. He had awakened abruptly in the night. Was it from a distant explosion? He wasn't sure.

The boy stood and walked over to the window facing the Three Sisters. He leaned against the adjoining wall with both hands and moved his right foot back, beginning his leg stretches. He knew it looked odd, but his calves were tightening. Post-run stretching was even more important than pre-run. Besides, he figured, Father would get it.

The priest had to smile, harking back to that morning five months ago when he himself approached the same window of his office, stared at that same minor mountain chain, and proceeded to ask Miguel some tough questions about his first experience there.

Something had apparently come to abrupt rest in that

desolate place which the military was hellbent on retrieving. *Signs.*

Momentarily, Miguel came back to the old desk, started to raise one leg then stood up straight again. "Is this okay, Father?"

"Sure, I had it pre-scuffed; ya' like the effect?" Estefan laughed, looking down at the worn surface. "Gotta keep those hams loose."

The boy raised his right heel onto the corner and bent forward at the waist. "Father, this is all weird to me, I don't understand."

"Tell me about it," the remark going over the adolescent's head.

"Well, there was that morning when I saw the ball of light come down outta the sky and the lady out there and everything. And then the next day when we both saw them. And now this. I mean, I don't know what went on before I got there this morning, but something metal must've blasted that hole, 'cause they had what I think was maybe metal detectors out there. There must've been something they wanted to collect every bit of. But the light, y'know, back in July sure didn't look metallic to me, so this had to be different. Anyway, that's three times out there."

Estefan nodded.

Miguel continued. "What I want to say is, I mean, we're kinda out here in Nowhereville, y'know? Nothing ever happens here. So, I don't know. But I said back then, I think this is about you, Father. I mean, otherwise that's a pretty extreme coincidence, y'know? Whatever it is the Air Force was looking for, they already had something on that truck."

Ignoring Miguel's supposition for the moment, Estefan

switched the subject. "I hear you, yeah, I do. Hey, the Deming paper this morning had a little write-up on the meet yesterday. Congratulations, young man! I'm proud of you. And your arm carriage has improved; I see you on the streets now and then."

"Thanks," he blushed. "But I need a kick in the late stages when I'm tired. I just couldn't catch those guys out front."

"You'll get stronger, and you're not done growing yet."

"I don't know about that, Father. Nobody in my family is very tall." Assuming they were finished, the runner headed for the door.

"Before you leave, ah, that was some disrespect you encountered from the MP, Miguel. It won't be the last time, I'm afraid. Be proud of your heritage, okay? The Mexican people are proud and rightly so; that's the first thing. But understand as well, lots of young people tend to confuse respect from others with self-respect. 'He disrespected me, so I had to punch him out.' Those who truly respect themselves don't need to go there. I hope you always remain a gentle soul."

"Got it," Miguel repeated from half an hour before, this time with a faint smile.

The teen was opening the door when the priest called after him again. "By the way, I noticed you didn't say 'like' when you were describing what happened. 'This is, like, what I saw.' What's up with that?"

Miguel turned around and flushed. "My English teacher, Mrs. Frazier, says using 'like' shows immaturity."

"Well, good for her. And good for you. Now, remember, you're into the off-season. Time for lots of slow easy runs and some off days, too. Let your legs recoup for a couple months. Then you can resume a hard-day, easy-day schedule. It doesn't do any good trying to run a personal best between seasons. Save it for when it'll count in the spring.

"And thanks for the information. I really am grateful."

"You're welcome, Father. I'm grateful, too, y'know, that you're here. Take good care of yourself, okay?"

"Got it," Estefan replied, grinning.

Miguel stood in the door jamb for several seconds, looking around, then stepped back inside. "Father, can I ask you a question? Maybe it's come up before."

"Fire away."

"Um, okay, if we just had the day of Mary's conception, December 8, y'know, when the angel told her she was pregnant with Jesus and everything, then how come Christmas is just seventeen days after that? I mean, that's not much time. Shouldn't she have known she was pregnant by then?"

"Yes, it's come up once or twice," Estefan winked. "That's a misconception, so to speak. See, the Immaculate Conception doesn't really refer to her carrying Jesus in her womb. What it means is that Mary herself was born immaculately – without what the Church calls original sin. Does that make sense?"

"Uh, sort of. So, then, she really got pregnant in maybe late March, nine months before December 25th?"

"Actually, quite a few scholars now believe He was born in springtime, around 6 BC. They're just dates on the calendar, Miguel; that part doesn't really matter. It's about what we feel in our hearts on a day like Christmas, feelings we know we should try to keep year round."

"Thanks for the explanation, Father," Miguel smiled. Father Estefan was a good guy. Carlos and Ivan thought so, too.

"Well, well, Kenna," replied the general to her tepid greeting. "I'm a little surprised you'd call me directly. I thought your playbook was limited to end runs to the joint chiefs," he said acidly. "So, does this reference a certain satellite falling to earth last night? We've had a cleanup crew out there all day. Should be wrapping up by nightfall."

"Tom Hagelthorne directed me to phone, Ray. I need your assessment of how it happened. Did the power supply fail?"

"Not a chance. I needn't remind you this was the same one that was buzzed last summer. But a power outage will likely be our storyline. I don't make those decisions. What does Hagelthorne think of that little coincidence?

"He wasn't aware of the earlier incident until yesterday."

"You didn't *tell* him? Anyway, that begs the point. Does he get the connection now, at least?

"Yes, he does. Your Colonel Lemke saw to that. What's the scene in New Mexico now?"

"We had to chase a couple film crews outta there just after our men arrived. A satellite the size of a minivan makes one helluva fireball through the atmosphere. They spotted the crater by air; not much we can do about that."

"So, what did happen?"

"I don't have anything definitive yet, but that GPS machine was performing flawlessly, I'm told. It covered LA, Vegas, Phoenix, San Antonio and everything between. All of a sudden it dropped out like it was shot from a cannon. But that's not all. The angle of descent was all wrong. Gravity should've taken it over south-central Arizona, but this thing angled on a beeline for southwest New Mexico. Came down precisely where that bogey ended up last July, the one our F-22 pilots confirmed. Sure as hell looked like it was guided there, don't ask me how.

"GE and NASA had to scramble to position a backup. Handhelds were down for well over an hour for lots of folks on the ground. Don't you catch the news?"

"As little as possible. I get enough here."

"Anyway, funny you should call just now. We've been getting radar returns on unknowns for most of a week, entering airspace all over the Southwest. Newspapers and local TV are picking up on sightings by the public, including some low-altitude stuff and cell-cam footage. Still think I'm full of crap, Kenna?"

Nowitzky's breathy sigh was evident over the secure phone line to Boulder. "Tom asked me to coordinate with you on any further satellite complications and anything like it for a while, maybe months, I'm not sure. Please keep me informed, if that's a convenient arrangement."

"Anything for madam," Washburn fairly cackled. He pulled the figurative sock from his mouth and tossed it aside.

Chapter Fourteen

"Come in, come in," the cleric called out as he rose from behind his desk. Johnson Selby and a very tall companion stepped into the rectory's living room and office.

"Estefan, I'd like to introduce Ricki Atwood. Ericka, really. Ricki is a state-licensed hypnotherapist and family psychologist. Plus, she's an author twice over on the particular subject of false memories – hope that's not intimidating," he chortled.

Dr. Atwood nodded at Johnson with confident appreciation, her carriage erect on a svelte 6'5" frame. She extended a long well-muscled arm Estefan's way. "Pleased to make your acquaintance, Father."

Johnson added wryly, "Oh, and Ricki was a spiker on the Cal State Fullerton volleyball team, in case you wondered."

The priest motioned his guests to the old couch along a wall. "Thank you for coming all this way, Dr. Atwood, especially on short notice."

"Please, just Ricki. We're still a week and a half away, but Merry Christmas, Father. I do have a full schedule of clients tomorrow, so I'll be flying back to San Diego tonight. I'd truly love to learn all about your life here, but that may have to wait until another time."

The counselor pulled a notepad and pen from a large leather handbag and crossed her willowy legs. Brown-black hair with the first streaks of gray curved around high cheekbones, cascading past her shoulders and well down her back.

"Johnson summarized your experience last week, as you

related it. But first of all, are you amenable to a hypnosis session this evening? We shouldn't presume you have nothing else to attend to or that you haven't changed your mind."

"No, no. Yes – I mean, I guess … I haven't done anything like this before," he said sheepishly.

"She's not going to make you cluck like a chicken or anything, my friend."

"That's right," Ricki followed. "I should explain, there's a fundamental difference between 'stage' and regressive hypnosis. See, in your forebrain, in the medial temporal lobe, is a region called the hippocampus. That's where long-term memories are stored – subconsciously so that they don't interfere constantly with your daily activities. In practical terms, anything you ever paid attention to, longer ago than, say, yesterday, is a long-term memory. The hippocampus is basically like a steel trap; nothing escapes. All it requires is a deeply relaxed state and concentration to emerge back into conscious awareness.

"However, false images and distortions can spill out as well. Let's say, years ago your favorite football team lost the big game when a normally sure-handed receiver barely bobbled the climactic pass in the end zone." She smiled at Johnson and his ever-present televised sports from around the planet. "And, for the sake of argument, we'll ignore the advent of instant replay.

"As a big fan, you might have replayed that if-only moment over and over in your mind. Eventually you convinced yourself that your guy probably caught it cleanly, that the ref must've been wrong and his bad call cost your team.

"In that circumstance, under hypnosis your notion of a clean catch might well substitute itself for the actual bobble that was originally on your mental movie screen.

"I mention that because, Father, you're in the priesthood, after all, which the last I knew came with a full set of doctrines – preconceptions, undeniable conclusions from your perspective. So we need to guard against letting those interfere."

"Yes, of course."

"Tonight you'll be returning to review a scene that was a first-run feature just nights ago. Hopefully that intricate grid of synapses in your brain has retained those particulars fresh and clear. There certainly hasn't been a lot of time for contamination to enter, though that's still possible. I just want you to understand that regressive hypnosis isn't foolproof; it's not like pulling a clip out of a YouTube folder."

"Sure."

"Lest we get ahead of ourselves, though, how familiar are you with hypnotic procedures?"

"Not much, I guess."

"Well, in shorthand it's all about relaxing your mind – nothing paranormal or mystical. I can assist you with that. We'll begin with a routine to relax the rest of your body. I'll ask you to focus on your feet, your lower legs then your knees and so on up your torso until you're a fairly limp dishrag, so to speak. Then we'll go from there with suggestions I offer.

"Father, I'm not Catholic, but I'm fairly well aware of its traditions with regard to the mother of Jesus. For both our sakes and to the extent you can, I can't overemphasize that you should leave your belief system and presumptions at the door and just describe what you experienced, okay?"

"That's reasonable, sure."

"Since we do have the actual setting available – your bedroom – it may be advantageous for you to stretch out on your bed for the session. Are you okay with trying that?"

"There might be a pair of dirty socks on the floor."

In due course the handsome Latino priest lay calmly on top of his comforter, shoes off, belt loosened, eyes closed, well-relaxed. Ricki's hypnotic induction was nearly complete.

"As I count from three to one, you will be ever more at ease, free from cares. Three, perfectly at peace, not a care in the world. Two, wonderfully relaxed. And one.

"Drifting back now to that night and the moment you became aware of something. Please speak in the present tense and begin whenever you're ready."

Over a minute elapsed before Estefan's lips first trembled. Then in hushed voice, "I'm waking up. Opening my eyes. … Something nearby. … A feeling, like a weight pressing on me. … I felt this before."

"Felt this somewhere before, all right, go on."

" … Coming through the wall, something coming right through the wall into my room."

Estefan abruptly sat upright on the bed, his mouth parted, a thousand-yard stare canvassing his expression. Seated on a straight-back chair beside him, Ricki started to extend an arm in front of his chest to ease his torso flat again. But Johnson, knowing this was part of the original sequence, shook his head; he wound circles in the air with an index finger to let the scene play out unimpeded. She trusted his judgment and nodded. The priest's eyes remained open throughout their silent exchange but took no notice.

"All very clear, Estefan," Ricki reassured. "Continue to observe the scene, relaxed and focused."

"... White dress, long sky-blue veil. Yellowish light around her. ... Can't see her feet. She's at the foot of my bed. ... Must be floating above the floor – too tall otherwise."

"This isn't the time to analyze," Ricki cautioned. "At the foot of your bed, wearing a white dress and blue veil. Describe her further."

"... Dark hair, long, ... wavy, parted in the middle. ... Olive complexion. ... Young, still a teen. ... Serious face. ..." He lowered his head slightly. "Something moved. ... She's showing me her rosary, ... white, like perfectly formed pearls, gold chain and crucifix. ..."

"Here and now. No cares, you're perfectly relaxed. The woman is in your room, just past your bed, showing you her rosary. What happens next? Whenever you wish to continue."

"... She's looking right at me. She calls my name, 'Estefan.' ... I want to – part of me wants guidance from the Teacher." His head turned for half a second toward the crucifix in beautifully carved teak affixed to the wall, a gift from his parents at ordination. "My thoughts, they're ... slow. Can't think ... how to react. ... Must listen."

"Mm-hmm, go on to what you notice next."

"She wants me to pay attention. 'This is important.' ... Hard to concentrate – the force on me; she's so close."

"Estefan, use the remote we talked about, the one you're holding in your right hand. Now push the button." The priest's index finger pressed into the comforter. "The pressure on you is starting to subside. Less and less now, nearly gone."

"... Better."

"Good. Your focus is much clearer now. Perfectly relaxed. Does she speak to you further?"

"... She says, 'The great battle Bernadette was warned of is upon us. Signs will confirm your resolve and guide your path.'"

"Mm-hmm, signs, all right." Ricki looked across the bed at Johnson, who nodded a confirmation and brought a hand to his mouth, taking a bite from an imaginary apple.

"... I must take the boy. He will clear a final hurdle. ... We must go to Smyrna ... soon before the solstice. ... I will know whom to speak to there.

"... 'You have lost your way.' I must say that. 'Your hateful paths lead to Allah's wrath upon all Muslims. Allah controls the sun, all the stars and all life. Look to the northern sky in the mid of solstice night for proof that His wrath is near. Find peace and justice now or perish.'

"... She's backing away now."

"Do you see the wall of your room through her?"

"No. She's real – opaque, real in every way. ... She's just backing through the wall now. Gone. ... I look at my clock; it's 4:18."

Ricki sensed this was the moment to intervene. "Well done, Estefan. Left your room, everything back to normal. Feeling contented." She was about to suggest that he lie flat again in order to bring him back out of the hypnotic stupor when his eyes grew wide once more. She leaned back and waited.

Estefan's movie screen was now filled with the eastern slope of the South Sister back in July. "She's floating out of that amber ball. It's a sphere of light, but there's a shell inside the glow. ... The radiance is really intense, like a welder's torch. ... But I can look right at it – not stinging my eyes. ... Not even shining on the rocks.

"... She's gliding down over the boulders ... just standing

upright and floating toward me. ... The light stays up there under the outcrop. ... What about the roses? At Lourdes and Fatima there were roses at her feet."

"No analyzing now, just describe what you see."

"... Same pressure, an energy. ... I feel ... dull, slow witted. Mesmerized. ... 'You would stone me?' ... Knows I have that rock in my pocket. ... Maybe saw me pick it up before. It was just a precaution – rattlers. Jesus, protect me. ... She's really close now, standing over a shrubby cactus. Serious. Concerned look.

"'Miriam,' she calls herself. I'm impressed by the Hebrew name. ... She knows all about me, little things I did ... when I was much younger. How can she know all that?"

"Analysis is for later." Ricki studied Estefan's features. "Go on."

"... I must help."

Now Estefan drew a sharp breath.

"Perfectly comfortable, able to describe what you're experiencing. What's happening, Estefan?"

"It's horrible. Everything – buildings just leveled, like a tornado but it's not. People in the street, sprawled and dead, horribly burned. Cars smashed and turned over.... Oh, sweet Jesus, this is *my* street! I recognize those porch steps. This is my neighborhood on the south side.... It goes on as far as I can see. ... And the smell, a putrid stench.... More scenes coming into my mind, other places, everything ruined, people in agony, ... so much sorrow. Awful scenes, flashing one after another.... A partial dome – must be a nuclear power plant – what's left of it, smoke billowing out.... Oh!"

"What's happening, Estefan? Relaxed and focused."

"I see it all from way above now, like I'm in orbit somehow.... Huge areas on fire across our whole country, across Europe.... Dark clouds starting to cover the planet. Must be nuclear winter coming."

"No analyzing. Go on."

"... She recites the world's religions. Everyone will perish. ... It doesn't have to happen this way. She says 'no one can win.' She's asking – more directing me to help." He squirmed slightly on the bed. "... But somehow I don't trust. I'm without faith."

"Does she say that to you?"

"No, that's what I feel, sort of. ... Hard to process. ... Force is still pressing on me – too close, she's too close."

"All right, you're standing near Miriam. Use your remote. Press the button and the force on you will slowly fade away."

Estefan pressed a finger into the comforter again.

"... This isn't good. ... No compassion, no loving energy, just tension. ... And no rosary! No roses at her feet. ... Gotta move away. ... Backing away, past the two-track. ... Better. I can think again."

"Clear headed now, all right. What happens next?"

"I get an impulse and just react. 'Oh, Jesus, let me be right about this!' I pull the stone out of my pocket and throw it. Goes right through her midsection, tumbles across some rocks beyond. She doesn't move. ... It must be a trick, a projection somehow. She didn't react. ... Maybe I'm being tested, not sure. Something's not right. ... She looks so real, just what I expect Mary to look like. ... But she can't be the Virgin."

A tear dropped from one eyelid and crept down to the corner of his mouth. "'Teacher, what is going on? You are love and this image is not.'

"... I look over at Miguel in front of me. He's got his hands on his knees, looking up, staring."

Ricki sat in amazement herself as she softly uttered, "Hands on his knees, all right."

"... The figure disappears. Didn't move, just vanished before us.... Now I'm yelling at the light up there at the outcrop. I challenge it. I demand more.... I take a step forward and my foot lands awkwardly on a stone there.

"The voice from the light tells me Miriam will come again before the solstice. She will tell me that my time has arrived, that I will travel to a meeting.... I must deliver a message, an ultimatum.

"The voice says, 'A tall woman will assist you to remember what I've told you to say. Now you must forget. When you remember, it will be your time; then you will act.'"

"I look down. My foot is cockeyed on a stone, uncomfortable. When did I step on that? I move my foot...."

Ricki looked at Johnson in disbelief. A tall woman? Was this priest confusing the here and now with then?

"The ball of light, it's moving up and out into the open.... I ask if it comes from Yahweh, but it doesn't answer.... It moves slowly straight up then stops overhead. I challenge it again, shouting, but it doesn't reply.... Now it streaks upward, faster than I can follow.... No love, no compassion....

"Miguel and I are walking back to the jeep now. ... We hear a sound, a roar. Two jets go nearly straight over us and head west." A very long pause ensued. "Now they're coming back. They race to the east. They're gone."

It was time. Ricki gradually brought Estefan back to alert consciousness, and the three returned to the front room.

"I always like to begin the debriefing this way: Without looking at your watch, Father, how long do you think you spent in there on your bed?"

"Mmmm, after you performed the relaxation exercise with me, maybe ten minutes."

"It was over an hour, man," Johnson laughed. Those pauses were pretty lengthy sometimes."

"And that's fine," the psychologist added. "That shortfall of time is a good indicator that you achieved a pretty deep hypnotic state.

"Now, you threw me a bit of a curve midway through the session, but I shouldn't have been all that surprised." She looked over at Johnson. "Thanks for the cue. Clients often venture spontaneously to another place or time in addition to the one they set sail for. Father, you returned to your first encounter with this young woman – or image – at the mountain."

Estefan was only partly listening. He was still considering that stone underfoot. It had been only a moment he'd lost out there, but one of seemingly great consequence. In those blank seconds, he'd been told of a second visit to come, near the winter solstice, for further instruction, and that a tall woman would help him recall it – as in tonight. But he had to forget that part for the time being, the light had said.

"It knows our future," the cleric finally offered.

Grasping the inference, Ricki replied, "Well, I seem to be the only tall woman in the room. You're suggesting that, back in July, you learned of tonight's session, right?"

"It would seem so, yes." The priest shook his head slightly.

"Until now I only knew that my left foot came to be lopsided toward the end, and I didn't know how."

"Hmmmm," the therapist responded, unconvinced. "That's kind of turning this process inside out. Again, I'd caution you that a preconceived notion can cause a false recollection, a story woven out of whole cloth. You had two similar encounters with the same figure, this Miriam, one in the desert and one here. It's understandable that you might take the factor of my presence tonight and add it to your first exchange in order to account for the misplacement of your foot."

"I understand, yes, but I don't perceive it that way," Estefan replied.

Johnson chimed in. "Well, one thing's for sure, if you hadn't phoned me about waking up in a sweat, or if Ricki couldn't make it over here tonight, you'd still be waiting on particulars.

"Now, as to just who or what this Miriam and the light represent, first of all, guy, I know *you* know that in the days surrounding her initial encounters, Bernadette referred to the presence before her as '*aquero*,' not Mary or Miriam."

Looking over at Ricki, Johnson continued. "In the colloquial French of that region, *aquero* meant literally 'that one,' a bland nondescript usage. Curious word choice, I think, from a girl who completed a rosary every day, including those *fifty* Hail Marys. Later, when she moved to the convent and wrote it all down, of course, she said it was the mother of Jesus all along."

Switching gears, Johnson continued. "Hey, I happen to know that Smyrna means Izmir, a Turkish port city – the 'Pearl of the Aegean,' they call it. Thought about doing a shoot there once. Anyway, Smyrna was its name dating back to Old Testament times – the Hittites in those days of yore." Glancing over at the priest, "Whattya think is up with that?"

"No idea," Estefan replied simply, then, "Pearl of the Aegean, huh?" He saw the rosary of pearl beads again in his mind. *Sign?*

"Yeah, but I mean, that's pretty far removed from Bernadette's letter." Johnson turned back to Ricki. "In 1879, shortly before she died – essentially from asthma, by the way – Bernadette Soubirous, by then Sister Maria Bernarda, wrote a letter to the pope. Or so it's claimed. Bernadette is the girl at the center of the Lourdes story."

"I see." Ricki busily scribbled notes.

Estefan picked it up from there. "In 1858 at Massabielle Rock – a stone outcrop, or grotto, along a stream outside Lourdes, France, where Bernadette lived – the Virgin came to her several times. One of two cathedrals there today rests on top of that grotto. In her memoirs she spoke of secrets given to her.

"The letter Johnson mentioned was allegedly written to Pope Leo XIII. It is said she predicted wide uses of electrical energy, also the rise of Hitler and the Second World War, plus a moon landing she said would happen around 1970."

"1969, yes," Ricki responded, looking up from her writing. "Hmmm, you said 'allegedly' about her writing the letter. Should I be impressed or not?" She turned back to her pad to add more notes.

Johnson stood and began to pace. "Well, there's a catch or two. You see, the actual letter she supposedly wrote has never been shown to the public. The text was finally publicized, first in a newsletter for German clergy, but not until 1998. A French priest named Antoine LaGrande, the story goes, discovered it tucked away in the Vatican Library." He looked at Ricki's pinched eyebrows. "Yeah, we know. But if there *is* such a letter, that'd be really impressive, for sure. Otherwise, well, predictions are a whole lot easier to make after the fact, I've always said.

"Meanwhile, Father LaGrande either went underground or never was; he hasn't stepped forward to this day. More recently came word that no Father Antoine LaGrande used a Vatican Library card for that time period in '98."

"So, it's a hoax," Ricki supposed.

"Probably. Anyway," Johnson continued for Ricki's benefit, "Lourdes has long been the most visited Catholic shrine in the world, a few million a year. There are over four hundred hotels in and around the town. Plus a host of websites offer replica artifacts, y'know, a twig from a bush *like* the one Mary stood over at the grotto. You can even buy the water online – well, not really the water from that little spring, but genuine Lourdes *city* water just the same," he said with a smirk. "This was a cottage industry until the middle of the 20th century when it swelled into a major enterprise. There's big money at stake in keeping the story alive."

He stopped pacing and smiled at Estefan. "Sorry, bud, I don't believe it went down quite the way the Church has portrayed it all these years." The priest nodded in return.

Johnson went on. "More to the point here tonight – which is to disregard questions of the letter's and Father LaGrande's existence. In the letter Bernadette supposedly said that on the eve of the year 2000, a 'final clash' would occur between Muslims and Christians. She even specified the number to die, something like five million."

"Five million, six hundred fifty thousand, four hundred fifty one," Estefan clarified.

Johnson added, "The big number is due to a 'bomb with great impact' dropped on Persia – meaning Iran. And I'd have to agree, the way things are proceeding over there, something like that wouldn't surprise me, I guess, not with this yahoo president."

Ricki spoke up. "Pardon me, Father, not to throw cold water on what this Bernadette may or may not have said or written a century and a half ago, but the eve of 2000 is long past, and I sure don't recall any climactic religious battle just then. I'm pretty certain I'd have remembered if a nuclear device or something like it fell on Iran. Instead, it was no doubt Iran behind the near demise of Israel awhile back."

"Your point is certainly well taken," Estefan replied quietly. "It doesn't make enough sense to me, either."

"And again, friend," Johnson offered, "that Bernadette was an odd child – few friends, always making up bible stories. Pleasant enough, by all accounts, but sickly most of her short life, not to mention cloistered in a convent the last fifteen years. Who knows what all influenced her? Plus, those 'miraculous' curing waters never helped her a lick. She drank from the spring, washed in it repeatedly, yet her asthma continued and finally caught up with her before she was even middle-aged."

For Ricki's benefit again, Johnson said, "Still, folks have come to Lourdes from everywhere to drink and bathe in the water. The cathedrals there have walls filled with crutches and braces and whatnot that people left behind. Miracles? The power of positive thinking? Who could know?

"The Church eventually set up a commission, then another, to separate the wheat from the chaff, so to speak. Lots of what had been written up at first as miraculous healings turned out to be psychosomatic illnesses or temporary remissions from cancer, those sorts of things. In the end the second commission certified several hundred cases as unexplained cures."

Estefan offered his perspective. "You can measure Lourdes by the high proportion of claims that were later rendered false or by the raw number that do appear to be miraculous."

"That's a good way to put it," Johnson conceded, "a lot like UFO reports by the hundreds of thousands over the years: ninety percent mistakes, ten percent that, well, make you shake your head."

Ricki leaned forward on the old sofa, setting her notepad aside. "So, we have a dubious claim to a 19th century letter, somehow overlooked for 140 years, predicting a planetary crisis and allegedly authored by a young, seriously ill nun shortly before her death – a prediction whose time frame passed without incident. Does that fairly capture all of it?"

Johnson laughed heartily. "Yup! Other than that it's airtight!"

Ricki pinched her brow again. "And now, here, we have a seeming repetition of that general storyline by a Mary-like figure which you, Father, suspect is a trick, if I listened correctly tonight – a projection from God knows where."

Estefan bit on his upper lip. "In the reported Marian appearances over the centuries – and I believe some are genuine – the figure has always been said to exude love and compassion in addition to distress over the fate of humankind. What I've experienced doesn't generate that. The energy it gives off is powerful but without a trace of warmth. That's why I've been distrustful. I don't know how else to explain it."

Ricki queried further. "If you accept what came forth this evening as accurate, yet it wasn't an appearance of the Virgin Mary, then what do you believe it was?"

"I can only say that the figure Miguel and I saw and heard – and felt – seemed all too real but wasn't."

"Whoa, friend," Johnson jumped in, "my reputation as an agnostic precedes me, but just because you blew her off, so to speak, that doesn't necessarily go to the question of reality, does it? I mean, Bernadette and the kids at Fatima didn't wing a rock at her to test whether she'd react, y'know? Plus at both places they described a ball of light as her mode of transport."

"Really?" Ricki asked, lifting an eye at the parallel.

Johnson nodded, "Oh, yeah."

Estefan looked at each of his guests. "Part of me, the side that distrusts this figure and the light and the underlying intelligence, considers what was shown and told to me as a high-jacking of Church history. I keep coming back to the figure's flat affect – the absence of love and compassion. Then there's the part of the account that's not even close to Church tradition. The voice said I chose this, implying some time before this life."

"And the other part of you?" Ricki inquired.

Johnson spoke for his friend. "The other part, Estefan's heart and not his head, wants her to be the real deal, Mother Mary – in business mode, as it were. The ball of light had to be the actual intelligence, or something stemming from it, and told him that 'Miriam' was the vehicle because it's a familiar form to him. The headliner, as it were. Right, compadre?"

Estefan nodded. "I'm just a priest out here in the desert. As Miguel said the other day, this is nowhere. And certainly, I'm nobody special." He shook his head slowly and looked down.

Johnson broke a brief silence. "Hey, bud, beyond the 'Why me?' Turkey strikes me as, well, sort of a turkey, y'know? That's a Sunni-dominated country with a small Christian minority that doesn't have a major beef. Turkey's even in the European Union now. Last I paid attention, the BBC gave an all's-well after Istanbul finally allowed the region in the south to secede and join with their Kurdish tribesmen from northern Iraq. Anyway, to me the notion of your going to a resort city like Izmir doesn't make a whole lot of sense. Are you sure you heard the name Smyrna right?"

"As sure as I can be," Estefan responded. "That's what it sounded like in my mind. But like you, I'm at a loss as to why Miguel and I would have reason to go there."

The cleric pondered his old roommate's critique moments before of the events at Lourdes. On that final morning years ago, when Johnson was packing his bags to leave the seminary, he offered the excuse of being just too hedonistic for a life as a priest. But it was more than that.

The Jesuits always presented the whole nine yards, nothing unturned in Church lore. They wanted only those of unshakable faith to remain. Johnson's faith had wavered; it was better for him, and for the order, that he leave the seminary.

Now Estefan was experiencing doubts of his own about the real nature of Marian visits over the centuries. Dr. Palmatier's earlier seeming certainty that Fatima was a contrivance further tested his mettle as a Jesuit. Were the Marian visits spanning centuries somehow a mix-and-match of the Blessed Virgin and some other intelligence at work?

Ricki Atwood was belting herself into the rider seat of Johnson's sleek BMW roadster while he stood in the driveway and bear hugged his friend.

"Sure hope I didn't come off as too cynical in there," the adventurer apologized.

"Not to worry, all insights are useful and welcome, my friend. I don't have any final answers about this, either."

"That's what makes for a great mystery, eh?" Johnson

clapped Estefan's shoulders then slid behind the wheel.

"Say, ah," Estefan hesitated, "Johnson, I might need to ask you for a loan. I don't know what the airfare for two would be to Turkey, but—"

"You're so funny! I'll say this once more, okay? Your money's no good here. I have a jet and 'time-share' pilots who really haven't been earning their keep lately. I can get the landing clearances on short notice. Just give the word."

Chapter Fifteen

Primetime network programming across America was dominated by the now-annual retrospective on the so-termed "Second Holocaust," the Hanukkah-Eve leveling of the Tel Aviv and Jerusalem central districts.

Early into the evening's retrospectives, electronic banners began streaming across the viewers' screens. Soon aerial views showed distant roiling clouds and monstrous flames rising from desert locales as well as from ships in the Persian Gulf. Separately, reporters stood in the darkness on sprawling lawns – Sa'ud royal palaces their backdrop. The attacks on Arabian soil and shipping appeared to be the work of Shi'ite extremists, agreed the quickly assembled studio commentators.

For over 250 years since Abdul Aziz (referred to as Ibn Sa'ud) founded that desert kingdom and consolidated power over Arabian tribes, the Sa'ud family had dominated the peninsula. Eventually the monarchy became that rare country to attach its surname to a nation's identity. Now it was no more.

Two attackers killed outside one of the family compounds, reporters soon learned, were clothed in the long shirt-robe and burnoose-type headwrap of the Al Murrah, a centuries-old tribe of camel-herding nomads who roamed the Arabian east and south. Surviving palace guards and oil company employees far afield described their invaders as uniformly dressed in the same Bedouin garb. But weapons found next to the few fallen attackers – CQ assault rifles of Chinese manufacture – belied any involvement by that peaceful tribe, instead throwing suspicion where it belonged.

The various strikes had been carried out almost flawlessly. Only four Hizb'alla militiamen and six Quds Force personnel were killed across all venues. Four more had put pistols to their temples upon imminent capture. None of the dead, of course, carried any identification. The remainder had slipped back into the desert night, fleeing in Chinese-built armored vehicles, another clue to implicate the Iranians as architects of these latest assaults.

Quds attackers had found and slain seven families of the Sa'ud clan vacationing in foreign lands: Swiss chalets and London high-rises, a New Zealand seaside retreat and a villa outside Sao Paulo, Brazil.

American forensics specialists raced to catch up to the evidence: primarily shell casings and slugs from victims to weigh and tire tracks to be cement casted — uniformly Dunlop, an international tire brand, as it turned out. Photographs of the dead attackers would be FAXed to the State Department and Interpol for potential computer match.

The ploy set out in the Shi'a Accord, to spread confusion in the initial hours as to the assault teams' origins, was limited. Tehran and the grand ayatollah gambled that the incremental passage of days would be enough, that American and European public sentiment would soon and predictably cool. They would shrink once more from the wretched affairs of the Middle East, grudgingly accept the new reality and turn on their leaders over continued oil dependency.

As was their habit, American TV network commentators offered thumbnail sketches of Saudi royal history and the victims throughout the following day, set to somber music and splendid coffins on screen. Since September 1932 when the Aziz clan officially renamed its land the Kingdom of Saudi Arabia, these princes of oil had weathered World War II, the failed 1967 Six-

Day war with Israel, an OPEC boycott, and tenuous alliances with the West.

Before bands of marauders shattered its pipeline system in the early morning darkness of December, the kingdom was producing seventeen percent of America's crude oil imports, about 1.5 million barrels per day. With an additional ten million barrels a day of oil and petrochemicals sent to Europe, Asia and elsewhere, the black gold had constituted nearly eighty percent of Saudi revenues.

Dating back to the original rule of Ibn Sa'ud, the nation had always adhered to the Wahhabi doctrine, a structure of Sunni teachings formulated by Muhammad Ibn Abdul Wahhab. That austere code of personal behavior and societal institutions was utilized by successive monarchs within the clan to legitimize itself and crush reform movements aimed at such notions as fair trials and a free press. Summary executions and amputations awaited dissenters.

In this century, lower-level Saudi officials had frequently been criticized in the news. But never the royals. Now they were all gone, over four hundred in all, slaughtered to the last cousin.

***

3:04 PM EST, December 17, 2025, two years and 11 days since the demolition of Israel's two major cities and less than 24 hours since the latest upheaval, 42-year-old Vice President Justin Turnbull gaveled a special Senate session to order. Across the way and under a separate parliamentary procedure, the House was assembling as a Committee of the Whole. Despite the challenges of flight connections through tough winter conditions across the Plains and Northeast and from far flung vacation sites, all but four sitting members of Congress had managed to return from holiday recess.

Turnbull, the handsome political moderate from Oregon, he of the smooth-jazz delivery, had appealingly offset the gruff, temperamental J.T. Seymour during the campaign. In his first session as titular President of the Senate, he had performed only perfunctory duties and cast one tie-breaking vote, per instruction from the West Wing, on a banking bill. Now, officially at least, he presided over a watershed moment in the nation's history.

In the first hours of the crisis, it was Turnbull who had suggested these extraordinary sessions to Seymour. Leaders of both houses were already expressing outrage wherever a camera could be found. With prospective outcomes not seriously in doubt, the dialogues would be viewed as a gracious gesture on the administration's part, allowing the entire legislative branch into the executive province of emergency decision-making.

Meanwhile, some political posturing before the networks would buy a little time, providing the president a day or two of cover to allow everything to sort out. There were military logistics to consider, after all, while counter-intelligence operatives needed time to make contacts and piece information together.

"This evening," the VP began in his pleasantly serious tenor, "we meet to discuss the events of the past day in our world. President Seymour, by written transmittal, is supportive of our gathering and seeks the guidance of this chamber and that of the House of Representatives in these perilous times. May God watch over our deliberations.

"For what purpose does the gentleman rise?"

With shaking hand the elder statesman clicked on his lapel

mic. "To address the chair," came his thin reply.

"The senior senator from Connecticut is recognized."

The President Pro Tem, Arthur Rosenbaum, now 90, rose slowly. These final years of his eight-term tenure as United States Senator had not been kind to him physically. He realized also that his short-term memory, though not his wit, was fading. In halting high-pitched voice he began with a few pages of notes scribbled on the afternoon train.

"Mr. President, I am retiring from this body. And I must say it is a trifle awkward to be back here now after the wonderful retirement parties and the marvelous hyperbole your aides wrote into your congratulatory remarks only weeks ago."

From his center-front desk, with a sweep of his head the old man winked and nodded at his colleagues. "I assure you these are definitely my final comments for public consumption."

His seminal speech on the Senate floor in the previous biennium – broadly characterized as condemning Israel for being a "bad neighbor" inviting attacks – had left him open to criticism as senile, a traitor or both. He aimed to set the record straight.

"In 1979 radical Shi'ite students rampaged through our embassy in Tehran. Two decades later, in the first years of this century we removed a dictator next door in Iraq – a minority Sunni – ignoring the few voices here in this chamber who realized that would probably do Iran a great favor.

"It has been some years since we – sort of – vanquished the Taliban, that other lingering Sunni thorn in Tehran's side. And we finally found and killed the tallest man in Afghanistan, that poster boy and benefactor of al Qaeda insurgencies – also a Sunni. One might have expected a congratulatory note from Iran's ayatollahs, but no.

"More recently, Lebanon's Hizb'allah, a protégé of the Iran regime, rearranged the regional political landscape, destroying Israel's cabinet, its entire Knesset, its national bank and finance industry as well as decision-makers in its military.

"I was here two nights later, the first to speak as now, with all the networks looking on – as now. It was I who called for an international tribunal of disinterested parties to determine who was responsible for those cowardly acts. I felt the sidelong glances and heard the whispers. Was I betraying ethnicity? Why hadn't I rallied us all to the fight?

"I did not call for knee-jerk vengeance then. As we were all witness to, some wild suppositions expressed here and in the media were subsequently proven wrong. Hamas had nothing to do with those bombings. Egypt's Muslim Brotherhood, we would learn, had no involvement, nor did South Africa as a weapons supplier.

"Hizb'alla, however, did have everything to do with it. That criminal gang all but left an invitation to chase it down. But I knew that, for different reasons, America and Israel were not up to another protracted fight over there – and all of you did, too."

A stool was brought for Rosenbaum to rest on as he continued.

"The failure of Lebanon's elected government to quell that renegade sect remains a major concern to the interests of the United States.

"The roads that might have led to Tehran for the attacks on Tel Aviv and Jerusalem reached evidential dead ends. There was no direct link to a supposed mastermind of the attacks, no incriminating phone call, text message or email, no confirmed movement of components across borders, no confession offered by any person in U.S. or Israeli custody – despite, I suspect, *rigorous* measures to secure same.

"In its finality, based on the preponderance of evidence, I voted with the majority here to levy only economic and diplomatic sanctions on Iran – trade and visa restrictions, isolation of its government officials. In effect, we denied President Vander Kamp's authority under the War Powers Act to engage in yet another open-ended conflict."

Trembling fingers sent a sheet of Rosenbaum's remarks errantly to the floor. Instantly a young page scrambled to retrieve it.

"While we looked on with disdain at Iran for laboring to construct its first 'conventional' nuclear warhead, our attention all the while fixated on those underground plutonium-generating facilities, someone built two backyard nukes and set them off. But we couldn't prove who.

"To a nation such as ours, bound by a marvelous constitution, rules of evidence and the principles of fairness, the interruption of Israel's heartbeat on our watch was a *fait accompli*: no solid evidentiary trail, universal denials, and America's unwillingness to reengage that area of the world so soon.

"As we stood befuddled then, now here we are again at the precipice, beset by a momentous decision: whether and how to use America's might and righteousness to pummel Iran, presumably. This time we ponder whether that nation is responsible for dismembering our longtime ally of convenience, Arabia – which today seeks a new prefatory surname.

"Once more we have, for the moment, meager evidence: a few slain attackers dressed as harmless nomads, some assault weapons and vehicles purportedly of Chinese design, and the shards of three destroyed gunboats in Persian Gulf waters. Our adversaries sell those wares to Iran but to others as well.

"And once more voices are heard in the Senate cloakroom and in our offices: 'We will survive this.' 'Tighten the sanctions.' 'China is flying sorties near Hawaiian airspace.' 'The North Koreans are acting up.' 'Russia is calling for multinational talks.'

"As President Seymour expressed during his campaign, we certainly have the firepower to bring the ayatollahs to their knees. There has never been any question of that.

"The people of Iran have known a very long and proud history. Some of the greatest artists, mathematicians and, yes, warriors have hailed from that land. Always the warriors, on the high seas and across the desert, looking for an advantage. Iran, a principal adversary of Israel in the '67 War, has never ceased plotting its next conquest, it seems, looking across decades and centuries to come. The ayatollahs are not even feigning ignorance this time by trotting out their nominal head of state.

"The rest of the world cannot abide any nation dismantling an entire region, one piece at a time. Fool me once, as the saying goes. This time we must act without delay on only circumstantial evidence, for we all know in our hearts and minds this was Iran's doing – with a little help from their friends.

"I came here over two generations ago to help win the peace. With a broken heart, grieving for relatives I never knew who lost their lives in Israel to Iran's last great adventure, and recognizing all the innocents in Iran now who do not yet know their fate, I will vote for coordinated Israeli-American incursions as necessary to crush the Iranian threat for the conceivable future. Jehovah's justice, God's will be done."

At 9:35 PM, after every senator who wished to had spoken his or her piece, by an electronic vote of 96-0 with two abstentions, the Senate adopted Joint Resolution 265, authorizing President Seymour "to take all necessary and prudent military actions in his discretion" to throttle Iran.

Three hours later, amid custodians on overtime emptying wastebaskets and dusting desks, the U.S. House of Representatives passed the same measure on a voice vote, with no request for a roll call.

Grandstanding aside, representatives of both houses and both parties were of a single mind: Get the bastards.

The situation room surroundings were all too familiar of late to most of the dozen faces around the conference table. The 7 AM discussion was just underway but already spirited. Roles were long since cast, personal agendas known.

"Sir, recognizing the swift authorization from congress for offensive actions, I hope everyone here maintains perspective on what has happened," National Security Advisor Davis Conklin offered. "Iran isn't swallowing the planet, after all; it's not a Fourth Reich. I believe they do wish to dominate the region, restore some long-lost Persian glory."

"What a curiously secular analysis as always," came the quick rejoinder from Admiral Jonathon Cleveland, CIA Director, "considering they look at the world in terms of a jihad."

Conklin ignored the swipe. "As I attempted to emphasize in this room several months ago, Arabia has been tapping its last major reservoir of oil for a while now. Iran still has huge reserves because it was slow to develop them, to acquire hardware to extract and process them. Had its council of ayatollahs shown a little more patience, the House of Sa'ud was going to run out of product in a handful of years. Nonetheless, Russia now provides all the drilling equipment and facilities Iran needs. With these strikes on the Arabian pipelines and elimination of its civilian leadership, Iran has positioned itself to step into the breach."

"I agree, but that's not the entire story, Mr. President." Cleveland took the reins. "We're piecing together some chatter about a secret gathering back on Halloween day. A lot of important Shi'ite belligerents from the region didn't show up for work that day, as it were. Sir, this is Shi'a on Sunni more so than about Iran cornering oil markets."

Secretary of State Rutherford B. Hayes VI spoke up. "Whatever the impetus, Mr. President, we're here to determine an immediate response. A total blockade, incoming and outgoing, would piss off Moscow mightily, but it can work in the short run and that must be our focus now. Despite what went on in Ukraine, we have a strong and growing relationship with the Russians in manufacturing and general commerce. They won't break those deals over this."

Rudy Hayes was the great great great great grandson of the 19th American president known mostly for being less tolerant of corruption than his predecessor, Ulysses S. Grant. Hayes was the one true blue blood in this assemblage.

"Furthermore, they benefit immensely from the Saudi developments. Hardware for Iran's oil fields aside, Russia itself has moved up the short list of leading natural gas and oil suppliers to both Europe and Asia."

"Fine. What about China?" Seymour's eyes shifted to his Defense Secretary Williams.

"Following that line of thought, sir, on the commercial spectrum of suppliers and consumers, as mentioned previously China has been sucking up almost half of Iran's oil exports in return for missiles made to order, fighter jets, assault vehicles, small arms – the *comprehensive* plan." Williams was his usual droll self.

The President glowered at the ceiling. "I could just wring Ho Deng Hua's neck."

"Sir?"

"Never mind. Anyway, if we put a blockade on Iran, what's Beijing gonna do, close our McDonald's franchises?"

Treasury Secretary Veronica Huff saw an opening to justify her invitation to this war party. "You're getting into my field, Mr. President. Yes, the Chinese might well throw Ronald McDonald out on his ear, but far more importantly they've been our Mastercard for quite a while. We all recall too well that we conducted the Iraq and Afghanistan wars and occupations almost entirely on credit. Our bonds on the open markets to cover the annual deficits were devoured mostly by China and Saudi Arabia, as were the deficits we were running in the first years of a long recession a decade ago. Recalling if you will, sir, from awhile back, the Chinese economy is almost as big as ours now and still growing at a faster rate. Beijing can threaten to sell off well over two trillion dollars whenever they decide the timing to wreck our currency."

"That would be a bluff," voiced Areum Park – or Park Areum in her grandparents' native South Korea. The President's Advisor on Asian affairs was a slight, middle-aged woman. Her dancing eyes belied an icy resolve. "China is in a continuing struggle to simply feed its people. It *relies* on the U.S. for wheat, corn, rice, soybeans and oilseeds. Food is the *first* commodity in China. If they were to balk at an Iranian blockade, we remind them that our grain ships can be called back to port. That would be felt severely in a matter of weeks."

Hayes poked an index finger onto the table's surface, having found his ally at the table. He looked at her as he said, "We make some noise about going after the oil, shutting the faucet off ..."

Park nodded. "And Beijing will understand that our hole card is the bulk grains and oils."

Seymour broke in. "Bottom line, this isn't Moscow's or Beijing's call, and they've sure as hell done enough to put us in this bind. I like the blockade idea. Rudy, I'd like you to work the Chinese ambassador. Tell him we'll help them arrange other sources of oil for the time being.

"Okay, we can keep China sitting on its hands, and Russia should be kissing our ass. So we isolate Iran, then what? I'm trying to find an alternative to nuking the sons o' bitches. If we go with a total shutdown in and out of their ports, how fast can we put it together and how quickly would it break them? General Yarbrough?"

Mason Yarbrough, chairman of the Joint Chiefs, leaned forward, cleared his baritone and spoke with characteristic gravity. "A carrier group is already in the Gulf of Oman. Inside 24 hours we can smother Iran's coastline. As to how quickly the Council of Ayatollahs would yield, well, Iran fought Iraq to a standstill for nine years. I think the ayatollahs would put their citizenry through hell before giving in."

"We'll see," the President replied. "All right, unless I hear a better option...." He looked around the group but found no takers. "Then set the blockade in motion.

"But," he pounded heavily on the table, "they have to pay a fine immediately. Mason, send our burliest missiles – but no nukes – raining down on that Natanz place. Their finished warheads are elsewhere, right, Jonathan?"

"That's correct, Mr. President." Cleveland tapped a folder

before him. "We plot them every ninety minutes from circumpolar orbit."

"All right, people, this'll be the shock-and-awe moment we're famous for." Having reached that decision, only now did Seymour ask about the physical consequences. "We'll be blowing up lots of centrifuges, Stan Van. Can we expect much fallout from partially processed plutonium?"

Science advisor Stanford Van Fossen pulled nervously at his bow tie. "On a given day very little of the material should be fully enriched. The remainder is radioactively modest. Expect the equivalent of a medium-sized power plant erupting – a Chernobyl. Natanz is located quite a distance from any population center; most of it should climb into the stratosphere fairly rapidly.

"Lots of nations will surely complain and vigorously so, Mr. President. I wouldn't count on the environmental vote next time around."

"That's okay, I'm willing to trade in some tree huggers. Besides, they don't even hunt.

"Thank you, Stan Van. Folks, I'm thinking a little theatrics along the way might help." Seymour drifted into a wry smile. "Make 'em wonder if I'm a little bit of a loose cannon, unpredictable. I just thought of something, a little reprise from the Nixon years. Hell, yeah.

"Y'know, a couple of those Saudi royals were acquaintances of mine. We had dinner here, met the wives, showed 'em around the gardens out back. Nice folks, sincere, reasonable. And now they're gone, along with their whole extended family, butchered. Lots of 'em were stabbed in the belly, I'm told, just to inflict the pain before their throats were slashed. These are animals we're dealing with."

Seymour stood. "Thank you, that's all." With that he stalked out of the room.

*   *   *

Kenna Nowitzky's schedule of meetings was a shambles before she set her bag on the desk. She struggled to prioritize all the Persian Gulf-related secure transmittals she'd been cc'd on, let alone more routine messages detailing other hotspots around the globe.

Politicians of every stripe and nation were raising fists, supporting or decrying the charge that Iran had provoked a regional, if not wider, war. Overnight China's foreign ministry had warned the U.S. State Department not to overreact, employing diplomatic speak to suggest a potentially harsh response. And a squadron of North Korean Migs had briefly shadow boxed with its counterpart from an American air base outside Seoul. Meanwhile, heretofore inactive insurgencies in a score of countries were on the move, taking advantage of the distraction in the Middle East.

At precisely 9 AM, Kenna's programmed TV, perched high in a corner of her office, switched on for the President's emergency address to the nation.

The oval office camera came to life in confusing fashion. The high-backed leather chair embossed with the presidential seal was empty. A step behind it, Seymour was seen in mid shove, and his press secretary, Chip Cullen, stumbled out of view. The President then seated himself. He was solemn now, elbows on the desk, a single sheet of handwritten notes before him.

"My neighbors and fellow patriots, as you all know by now, I'm a plain-spoken Missourian. To some in the media and in the other party, that means inept. Well, I'll be speaking plainly to you this morning; you decide. Those of you with younger children in the room, please remove them now. I'll wait a moment."

He reached for a glass of water. Withdrawing a tissue from a pants pocket, he dabbed at a light coating of what appeared to be perspiration reflected on either side of his widow's peak.

"A friend and ally of the United States has been viciously attacked. By now you've no doubt heard about the cowardly acts of a few radical Muslims against the monarchy of Saudi Arabia. There was absolutely no provocation."

Seymour took another sip of water and swallowed hard. "The royal house of Sa'ud is no longer a reality. Overnight, aggressors mutilated the bodies of even grandchildren and distant cousins of the ruling family, over four hundred men, women and youngsters in all. The horror that these provocateurs inflicted on their victims is unspeakable and unforgivable."

He took a deep breath and continued. "Before I sat in the chair, the previous holder of this office spoke to you after America's great friend, Israel, was likewise victimized by unprovoked attacks. Today, we continue to host over two million Israeli refugees on our shores, and we're proud to do so. One day they'll all return to their homeland, with their industries, their confidence and resolve fully restored.

"The last administration dawdled when retribution was in order, assembling a commission to determine what happened. It leaned on the Israeli military to keep its guns holstered, promising justice ultimately. By the time the facts were settled, all but proving the rogue state of Iran was behind it, the United States capitulated. After plenty of talk, America never took concrete steps on Israel's behalf to punish those responsible. Justice was simply not served. We might not be where we are today if adequate measures had been taken then."

Seymour's hands seemed to tremble slightly with barely contained rage. "At this hour, various investigations are underway to positively determine the source or sources of these latest, craven acts. But that is a formality, really, for we all know who performed them or was behind them.

"Iran began installing centrifuges to capture plutonium years ago, then added more and more, all ostensibly to fire nuclear power plants but really intended for weapons. America said it wouldn't allow a nuclear armed Iran, yet it happened.

"Feeling all muscled up as a 'nuclear power,' I guess, in their bid to become the dominant player in the Persian Gulf the religious cult that rules Iran decided to strike at a second peace-loving nation, Saudi Arabia. They figured they can just step in and take over the Arabian oil markets.

"These ayatollahs in Tehran think of themselves as the righteous inheritors of the earth, but you and I know they're not. They and the militias they control in Lebanon, Syria and Iraq preach hate and intolerance. They are plainly zealots, and now they must be stopped.

"Ambassadors of goodwill from various Middle East countries, plus a series of United Nations special envoys, have tried repeatedly to impress upon the puppet Iranian government that, frankly, America and the rest of the world are not going to sit back like pitiful helpless giants forever. There comes a time when righteous indignation must rule the day. And today is that day.

"Accordingly, and with the advice and consent of Congress last night, early this morning I commissioned air strikes on the underground nuclear enrichment facilities at Natanz, in the Iranian desert. I'll pause here for a few moments while you watch those precision strikes carried out in near-real time."

As Seymour turned his head to the side to watch a monitor, a portable green screen behind him switched from a lazily flying, electronic American flag to a direct feed from inside the cockpit of the American strike force leader. Three Boeing-built, B-6 Motherload fighter-bombers in formation, protected by two squadrons of F-24 Python interceptors, were in range of the Natanz complex. From the air it was a distant shallow mound of earth hazily visible in the desert's fading light.

Momentarily a muffled voice was heard: In rapid succession, the first B-6 released its four super-bunker-busting, laser-guided missiles.

At five-second intervals came missiles-away affirmations from the other B-6s. Twelve armaments, each packing the equivalent of over thirty tons of TNT, hit their tightly-arranged underground targets. While the attack proceeded, several of the F-24s broke away to chase down Iranian fighters scrambled to offer token resistance.

An extraordinarily deep, wide crater, along with a massive cloud of debris flying high into the early evening Iranian sky, as if in slow motion, constituted the final scene. The green screen returned to the waving flag.

"Good!" Seymour resumed, satisfied, turning back to the camera. "*That* should've been done a long time ago. Rest assured, the radioactive fallout from that site will be nominal and won't threaten any population center beyond Iran's borders. The three completed nuclear warheads in Iran's so-called arsenal are not at Natanz. Those are scattered and sitting atop short-range missiles Iran purchased from China. We know where they are and we can blow them up on the ground in a variety of ways or out of the sky from our U.S. Navy anti-ballistic missile batteries in the Persian Gulf and the Gulf of Oman. And that's a fact.

"If Iran's Grand Ayatollah Shirazi and President Fadavi have any thoughts of retaliation for today's necessary action, they should be mindful that we do control lots of nuclear-tipped short-range missiles across their border in Arabia and in Israel – close enough to reach them."

Seymour took another sip of water and set the glass aside. "My fellow patriots, Iran's leaders must decide whether they want their nation to survive or not. They've been villains in our world, and it's time for the last twenty minutes of the movie to play out. Now, I'm not talking about the great majority of Iranians – fine people who only want to live out their lives and practice their faith. But Ayatollah Shirazi and President Fadavi have put them at grave risk.

"Neighbors, as of today Shirazi, Fadavi and their henchmen will realize they're playing in the majors now. Their curveballs have been wicked, for certain, but not so sharp that we can't hit them and hit them hard. They're bush league. Until today they were all puffed up about themselves. Welcome to the big leagues, Iran.

"From this moment forward, that country will no longer be allowed to pose a military threat to anyone – *any peace loving people*. And if its leaders have aspirations of continuing to exist as a nation in *any meaningful* way, Shirazi, Fadavi and their cronies must come forward right now.

"They have to do three things: First, admit their treachery; second, offer up every bit of their nuclear hardware for destruction under international supervision; and third, prepare to empty their treasury as reparations to Arabia, Israel and the other nations harmed. *America* will decide when those conditions are met.

"In support of this situation, I've also called upon the Fifth Fleet of the U.S. Naval Forces Central Command to intensely patrol the region until further notice, and I am ordering a blockade of Iranian commerce from sea and air. As of this date, other than food and medicine by ships we first inspect, we won't allow one pound of commodities to enter Iran's ports or one ounce of its oil to leave.

"Furthermore, today your government is initiating charges before the International Court of Justice against the entire Iranian leadership, including Grand Ayatollah Shirazi, his council of ayatollahs and President Fadavi, for crimes against humanity.

"Also, at America's request the United Nations Security Council has scheduled an extraordinary session for next week, December 23rd, to review Iran's membership privileges in that international body of peace-loving countries.

"Our ambassador to Arabia, Dorsey Peterson, and a full diplomatic corps are already on the scene there, working with their parliament. And our Secretary of the Navy is meeting with their military commanders, just as we undertook before with the remaining Israeli leadership.

"As good neighbors do, the United States will be offering a full complement of emergency and ongoing assistance to the stricken Arabian people. Neighbors, this wasn't just about oil; many people beyond the Saudi royal family were killed in the clashes or wounded financially as well as emotionally. We'll help in every way possible to put that nation back on its feet, just as we're now doing for our great friends in Israel.

"Moreover, I know the International Red Cross and many other fine charitable organizations worldwide are already pitching in.

"Meanwhile, the United States of America calls upon friendly nations across the Middle East, especially our close allies Egypt and Jordan, to be vigilant but cautious militarily about Iran. We want to avoid any mistakes or overreaction that might lead to another senseless tragedy."

The frank-talking Missouri Valley farm boy had just thrown a change-of-pace on the inside corner to Shirazi, a called strike by Egypt and/or Jordan on the Persians whenever the President chose.

Seymour looked deeply into the camera before him. "Rest assured, fellow patriots, these disruptions in America's oil supply won't come close to crippling us. Our strategic petroleum reserve will be tapped as necessary to carry us through this winter. I'm authorizing an initial disbursement today, and I'll be speaking to you soon on further steps your government sets in motion.

"God bless you all, and God bless America."

Weak on foreign policy? J.T. Seymour had shown his countrymen a thing or two about handling world affairs, he assured himself as the camera went dark.

Kenna switched off the set and shook her head slowly over long seconds. Iran was following some spurious call to centuries-old glory, to rule the Persian Gulf again, to control the region's primary resource, namely its diminishing oil supply. Arabia, until yesterday America's foremost supplier, was castrated: Its pipeline arteries were severed at many points, fires out of control. Its key decision-makers, royal family members all, lay dead.

Maybe that was a key, she thought further. *Of course!* Shirazi and his council of ayatollahs were primarily interested in destroying the Saudi leadership structure; the pipelines were secondary, a diversion. Better said, their purpose was to emasculate Arabia, home to the world's Sunnis. And judging by Seymour's final statement, Jordan's monarchy, Egypt's fledgling democracy and their respective Sunni cultures might have been next in Shirazi's sights.

This wasn't primarily about Middle East dominance or the world's petroleum supply, she concluded. This was centuries-old vengeance, a Shi'ite stick thrust into the eye of perceived Sunni infidels. She cringed at the potential reverberations.

The president, she knew, still confused Sunni and Shi'a-dominant countries. He'd never bothered to learn even fundamentals about either sect, why they regarded each other as unworthy. They were all, frankly, "rag heads" to J.T. Seymour's simplistic thinking, all adherents to a false faith, end of discussion.

Seymour's ploy in Iran was exceedingly dangerous, Kenna reasoned. He saw himself as an Old West sheriff of sorts, staring down the bad guys, wrenching justice from a street fight, restoring order from chaos. But a few of the players in this drama didn't necessarily acknowledge his starring role – namely Iran, North Korea, Russia and no doubt China. The hours or days ahead would determine whether his script played out as written.

Chapter Sixteen

Johnson Selby padded barefoot into the theater of his suburban Albuquerque estate, a steaming mug of black coffee in one hand, the L.A. Times in the other. As usual he flipped on the BBC for its less Ameri-centric world view.

Grim faces were engaged in the studio's round table discussion, reviewing President Seymour's bold action and threat of more. No one disagreed that the tumult in the Middle East would spawn, if not a new world war, at the very least a wider outbreak.

Asian and European financial markets, meanwhile, were plummeting – except for certain commodities, predictably. Precious metals and light sweet crude were hitting all-time highs.

Dating back to the seventies, first waterbeds and futons then foam and air mattresses had made inroads into the bedding industry. But a majority of consumers still preferred an inner-coil mattress. With daily use, those needed to be replaced within ten years, and Selby, Inc. still sold the most. Consequently its stock had always remained stable in the face of market downturns. Johnson's family had chosen well, an industry which, like bread or coffins, never knew a severe slump.

The day after witnessing that globe of light at the Sisters the previous July and sensing a great upset soon to come, Johnson had converted most of his portfolio – other than Selby shares – into secure bonds and Treasury bills. At Monday's opening bell, his overall holdings were valued at just over $152 million. He was not among the super-rich; he was merely rich.

Following the round table, amid the BBC's commentaries and features came word that Sheikh Nawaf Khalid al-Dakhil, Arabia's preeminent Sunni mullah, was rumored to be proceeding to an undisclosed location in Turkey for a meeting with Grand Ayatollah Alireza Vahid Shirazi, Iran's foremost Shi'a cleric and overseer of its governing council. If true, the correspondent added, this would mark the first such one-on-one between Sunni and Shi'a heavyweights in over sixty years.

Johnson flipped open his cell phone.

"Estefan, my main man, how are you?"

"Well, actually, I'm dicing onions at the moment and a little teary eyed. With Christmas coming, foot traffic increases here. Fences be damned, people who want to be with relatives find a way across, the dedicated ones. We feed them as they pass through."

"That's … You're where it's really at, Padre. But, hey, I expect your thoughts have been on the solstice as well."

"Yes, it's troubling me. Thank you very much, by the way, for the camera phone. That was very generous of you."

"Feliz Navidad, my friend. One more step for you into the 21st century. By the way, be sure to stuff it in your overnight bag." Johnson proceeded to relate the BBC account.

"Izmir?" the cleric suggested.

"Smyrna by any other name, eh? This certainly sounds like another—"

"Sign, yes," the priest completed his friend's thought.

"Listen, I'll send my Beechcraft twin down to pick you up in Deming. The airfield there doesn't accept jets. How about if I meet up with you at my hangar here?"

"You have *two* planes?"

"And a small Bell helicopter, actually," Johnson confessed. "Told ya' I'm a hedonist. Can you leave soon?"

"It's not that simple. I need to phone the bishop and ask for emergency leave, locate a volunteer to take over meals here, plus arrange transportation to Deming for Sunday Mass for my parishioners."

"And find Miguel," Johnson added.

"This is finals week at the high school. I'll have to talk to his parents and the principal."

"So, one o'clock at the Deming airport, then?"

"Rosalinda, Renaldo, good morning. I hope I haven't come at a bad time."

"Not at all, Father, come in out of the wind. Have you eaten? We're having a late breakfast. Little ones, go play in the other room. Please sit down, Father. Coffee?"

Renaldo broke into his wife's chatter and extended a hand. "Hello again, Father. And thank you again for visiting us when I first returned."

Estefan nodded. "Have you found work for the off-season?"

"Part time, at the farmer's market in Deming, like last year."

"Good, good." The priest's expression now grew serious. "I'm afraid I can only stay a moment. Something more has happened, much like what Miguel and I shared at the South Sister."

"Santa Maria!" Rosalinda blurted as she reached for the

rosary in her apron pocket.

"Perhaps," was the priest's honest if veiled answer. "I can tell you that there is a matter of some urgency I must attend to. With your permission I'd like to take Miguel along. There may be a role for him."

Renaldo's brow knitted, the creases deepened from all the years of squinting under the sun. "Will it be dangerous?"

"I wish I could tell you no with certainty. I don't want to deceive either of you. If you're reluctant, that's fine, he'll remain here."

"We know you will watch over him," Miguel's mother reasoned. She raised her rosary in the sign of the cross. "Where must you take him?"

"To a city in Turkey."

"Oh, Mother of mercy," she hushed.

"Rosa, Turkey is not the same as Iraq or Lebanon," Renaldo comforted. "I keep up with the news, Father. Things are very bad again in that part of the world, we know. Now there's all the murders and the pipelines that were cut. Very bad."

Estefan tried a bit of reassurance. "I agree, of course. But as you say, Turkey has been stable. The city we'll be visiting is called Izmir, on the Aegean Sea. It's a tourist destination, really. My friend Johnson Selby from Albuquerque will be flying us there. And if I know Johnson, our accommodations will be more than comfortable."

Rosalinda brightened a bit. "When must you leave?" As always, she was willing to put her trust in Father and the Lord.

"Right now, as soon as possible. Again, I'm sorry this is so sudden; it couldn't be avoided."

"Miguel is taking his last exam this morning." Rosalinda looked back at their wall clock. "In fact, he should be done by now. It is their final school day before Christmas, you know, so not much class work the rest of the day. I will write a note to the principal to let him out early."

While she reached for a pad and pen, Miguel's father engaged his pastor. "This is my only son, Father. His mother and I, we want him, and our girls, too, to have a more prosperous life to justify our labors."

Estefan in turn had great admiration for the legal émigré and grizzled laborer before him. This man was forging a simple but solid life for his family on the strength of his back and the quickness of his hands.

"Miguel can be anything he chooses to be, Renaldo. His curiosity, his determination – and hopefully his legs – will carry him far. You should know there were college recruiters at the state meet. Miguel was certainly noticed."

Renaldo beamed and nodded. "A ticket out."

Rosalinda finished her note and looked up into her spouse's eyes with the admiration of a newlywed. "He still refuses to buy anything for himself when he's on the road, Father." Holding his gaze, "My husband, this must be God's work. Our Savior and Father Estefan will keep Miguel safe."

The cleric was gratified. "Thank you both for your trust. We hope to be back in just a couple of days. I'll call you when we're settled over there."

"Oh!" Rosalinda fairly shouted. "We almost forgot, Father!" She dashed to a back bedroom. In just over half a minute she emerged again with Miguel's duffle. It was stuffed with changes of under and outer clothing and his running shoes.

"We are all very proud of you here in Columbus, Father," this mother of five said. "You are Puerto Rican, a Spaniard, not of Indian blood. You are highly educated. Yet you came to this place and gave your heart to us and to all who pass by here. I want you to know we all appreciate you. We love you, Father."

Tears welled in six eyes as Renaldo spread an arm across her shoulders.

"She says it better than I can, Father." Holding her look, Renaldo grinned. "Now, Rosa, let our pastor leave!"

Chip Cullen strode into the White House press room for the noon briefing. Considering the gravity of the world's affairs just now, he was a little surprised that this would be the very first question, posed by an AP reporter. The president was counting on him to snap off a theatrical sharp curveball of his own.

"I ... uh, stumbled. It was just a momentary miscommunication. President Seymour has been dealing with very stressful circumstances these past three days. He hasn't slept much, understandably. It was my fault entirely. I, uh, miscalculated the time left before we went live." Then two lines to seal the feint: "The President is calmly engaging world leaders at this hour, listening to all viewpoints before deciding America's further course of action. He is himself, I assure you."

Cullen proceeded to inform the assembled press that China was closing its D.C. diplomatic offices and had expelled all American diplomats from Beijing. He deferred to the later Pentagon briefing all questions regarding a possible U.S. response to China's continuing brushes with American air space over Hawaii and North Korea's violation of the 38th Parallel. In wrapping up this brief session, he emphasized that Britain,

France and Germany had all expressed unqualified support for Seymour's forceful actions regarding Iran.

Sidebar stories on the evening news and in the morning papers would produce the intended effect. In the wake of "The Shove," was President Seymour losing his grip, crumbling under the pressure of the crisis, about to "jump the tracks," as a London Times correspondent put it? Was this "mad as hell" American executive taking the West into all-out war with Iran and to the brink with China and/or Russia?

Chapter Seventeen

The Citation's twin Rolls Royce jet engines propelled the aircraft at a cruising speed of over 600 mph, easily the fastest business jet on earth. In fact, since the retirement of the Concorde, it was also swifter than any commercial plane. The Citation climbed easily to over fifty thousand feet where thinner air improved its fuel efficiency. Its sleek contours, with royal and Kelly trim over white, captured the spirit of Johnson's moniker. "Sky Candy" was splashed across the tail section.

The shortest route from Albuquerque to Izmir would take its passengers first to Atlanta's Hartsfield International, America's busiest airport, for refueling.

Miguel had quickly mastered the controls built into his right armrest. The 18-inch pop-up monitor before him now displayed a Formula 1 racing game he had pulled up from Johnson's software storehouse onboard. He was in the cockpit of the number 14 car, that of the famed Mexican driver Hector Valenzuela. The men traded a smile as Miguel's face repeatedly contorted, the console's shifter in his right hand, a small steering wheel in his left. He was negotiating the tight turns at Monaco.

When ordering the Citation from Cessna's Kansas City plant, Johnson had requested just a few custom features to complement its already well-appointed cabin. The most conspicuous concerned the seating.

Years before, an older Selby family acquaintance, a man who could afford far more, had instead built a one-bedroom, 900-square-foot retirement home. With numerous siblings, nephews, nieces and cousins, most of whom he preferred not to entertain overnight, the man had expressed to Johnson, "If you don't build it, they won't come."

The photographer and world traveler had that thought in mind when choosing Sky Candy's interior layout. The 24-foot cabin was designed to accommodate eight to twelve passengers. Johnson instead had four seats spread about plus one at the rear for the flight attendant.

He enjoyed the company of a lovely travel companion or perhaps a two-couple arrangement, nothing more. He had observed more than enough socializing, glad handing and gamesmanship as a youth in the company of his late grandfather, John Franklin Selby, founder and board chairman of Selby Mattress, Inc. Now Johnson preferred more intimate settings.

Beyond their gadgetry, these custom seats incorporated Selby spring coil technology, adjustable lumbar and neck supports and kid leather. Each was fully berthable for long hauls such as this.

While Miguel continued his race, Estefan reviewed nuances in Arabic syntax from an old text he'd brought along.

Suki rose and turned to the galley and its array of cabinets in natural cherry. Into the convection oven she slid refrigerated plates from Mr. Seth's, a downtown Albuquerque landmark: giant scallops over wild rice, with sides of spicy-cheese broccoli and lemony greens. Fine dining was minutes away.

Miguel's car finished fourth. Out of the medals again, he mused. He looked over at his priest seated a few strides away. "Father, can I ask you something?"

"Sure, what?" setting his tutorial aside.

"Well, y'know how you explained before about Christmas

and everything being maybe not really when Christ was born and all that. So, it's just a date on the calendar we celebrate, like Memorial Day maybe."

"Good comparison."

"Thanks. So, I get that, but I still don't understand this winter solstice deal, y'know? I mean, I was there at the South Sister; I heard her say you have to do something before the solstice. And that's in three more days. It sounds like otherwise something really bad is gonna happen."

"We don't know that, Miguel," Estefan replied. He was now convinced that the adolescent hadn't seen the awful images of destruction and despair projected into his own mind out there. "But, yes, there's some logic to concluding that some change might be coming, and our world is certainly crazy right now."

Johnson turned away from a ceiling screen showing repetitive coverage of the American air strikes at Natanz. "Excuse me, Estefan, the Iranian president hasn't made an appearance yet and it's been several hours. I'm thinking he's waiting on instructions from Shirazi and those apparently aren't forthcoming yet. It's late evening in Izmir now, so a meeting with al-Dakhil might happen tomorrow or maybe a day or so down the road."

Estefan looked back at his young charge. "As I mentioned when I picked you up at school, I've been asked to deliver a message, and thanks to this very generous man," sending a smile to Johnson, "I will try to do that. The rest really is in God's hands, Miguel. Now, as to how the winter solstice in particular might—"

"Can I have a part of that one?" Johnson broke in. "I've been to a couple of the places in question." He lowered his leg rest and sat forward. "Ever hear of Stonehenge, Miguel?"

"It's a monument or something, I think, in England maybe."

"Good job, yeah, in the southwest part of England, near the River Avon. But did you know Stonehenge was erected with the winter and summer solstices in mind?" He glanced at Estefan and winked. "This takes a bit of telling."

The adolescent touched a button and a motorized mechanism slid his monitor over and down, where the support snapped it into place below his seat cushion. He liked Johnson and wanted to hear more.

"As 3,000 BC approached, well before the Egyptians began building pyramids, way north of there, tribes in Western Europe and offshore – in what we now call England, Wales, Scotland and Ireland – had pretty much settled down from their roaming ways. No doubt they still had hunting excursions, of course, but they also farmed. They domesticated oxen and wild plants like wheat and potatoes and onions. Sounds like a meal already," he grinned.

"Life was hard, for sure. Yet, first around 3,100 BC, something – *something* – possessed those hunter-farmers on the Salisbury Plain in southwest England to take the considerable time and effort necessary to build a series of big circular ditches across a very wide area, miles apart – what we now call henges. These ditches were good size, some maybe fifty or a hundred feet across. The dirt they dug up formed a continuous mound around the henge. For what purpose, who knows? Maybe something religious for their time.

"A few centuries later, those early Celts on that English plain started spacing tall posts carved from nearby trees to form circles inside their henges. Carbon dating shows that sometime between 2,400 and 2,200 BC, those folks decided on something more permanent and turned from wood to hard rock at the

Stonehenge site. They built another, less elaborate henge with stones at a relatively nearby place called Avebury.

"Now, here's one curious part. The inner circle of stones within what we now call Stonehenge could come from only one place, the Preseli Mountains in Wales – a *long* distance away. These slabs were found along a mountainous cliff there that sheds them from time to time.

"They're called 'bluestones' because when wet they take on a deep bluish-gray hue. My young friend, these were mighty rocks, up to six feet long and four *tons*. That's twice the weight of a 4x4 pickup – and without those convenient wheels.

"This region of Wales, so you know, is dotted with primitive, ancient stone circles – but not on the scale of Stonehenge.

"The shortest route from that Preseli Mountain cliff to the Salisbury Plain is around 250 miles and that'd include what is today a wide channel."

Johnson smiled at Miguel. He had the youth's total interest. "So, here's your challenge: You're the team leader of, oh, a dozen guys on an expedition to retrieve one three-ton bluestone from the Preseli Mountains. How do you get it from Point A to B?"

Miguel thought for a moment. Even if they could make ropes from some vegetation, dragging seemed out of the question. Then it hit him.

"Were there lots of trees around?" he asked Johnson.

"Ah-hah! I think you're onto something, my man. Yes, there would've been plenty of trees along the way."

"Then they'd need maybe stone axes to cut some smaller trees down and cut off the limbs and make them into rollers. I mean, it'd still be slow going, but they could do it, right?"

"Yes, they could. Except for that big body of water – unless it wasn't there four thousand years ago. But if it was there back then, how would you get across it?"

Miguel responded without hesitation: "You'd need to build a really big raft, using trees and tying them together somehow, maybe with strips of bark the way the Indians used to strap things together."

Johnson looked over at Estefan. "Do we have a budding engineer in our midst or what?" Back to Miguel, seriously now, "However they did it, felling lots of trees to use as rollers, probably, maybe also fashioning ropes from hemp or whatever for the men or oxen to pull, plus huge rafts to cross the water, that herculean effort got those bluestones all the way back to that barren plain near the Avon. This was around 2300 BC.

"They set them upright, evenly spaced, to form two concentric circles inside the henge.

"Later they added two more rings – one between the rings of bluestones and another outside all three of those. Now, these were slabs of hardened sandstone, *outrageously* gigantic, from a quarry twenty-some miles away. The heaviest of those were *twenty to forty tons* or more. Just enormous weights to haul, even with today's heavy machinery."

"The trees for rollers would need to be bigger," Miguel considered aloud.

"You got that right! Then they topped off all these spectacular sandstone uprights with still more that they shaped to fit laterally across their tops to form arches."

"Sweet," Miguel smiled. He was clearly impressed and intrigued.

"Yeah, sweet. Now, about those lintels, the horizontal

stones taller than a man's reach. Elevating them into place was a gargantuan feat by itself because, as far as we know, pulleys hadn't been invented yet. It must've been done with brute strength somehow."

"Or maybe a ramp," Miguel offered. "They did that with the pyramid stones."

"So they did," Johnson smiled again. "However they 'pulled' that one off, altogether the slabs then formed four concentric circles of bluestone pillars and sandstone arches – some eighty slabs in all. But for what purpose or purposes, today no one is quite sure."

Miguel subconsciously leaned forward, rather spellbound.

Johnson went on. "A couple hundred scattered graves have recently been discovered nearby, but that's not nearly enough to account for all the tribal people who lived in that general vicinity over the many centuries to follow. Maybe burials there were reserved for tribal elders, chieftains, medicine men, that sort of thing, or possibly a particular family line, royalty of sorts. We just don't know.

"Then more recently and a few miles away, archaeologists came upon what they think was a summer encampment for hundreds of people. No permanent moorings, but there were charcoal remains and other trappings of a temporary settlement. It looks like families from a wide area came there year after year during the warmer months to drag those stones and finally erect this monument.

"Now I'm finally getting around to partially answering your question. See, there must've been some powerful belief about the sun behind all that phenomenal physical effort over centuries, because those rings of great stones are positioned precisely. As the sun sets on December 21, the winter solstice, and at sunrise on June 21, the summer solstice, the sun's rays would've streamed in between all those circles of stones to the very center. On no other days of the year would that occur."

"Wow. ... But why is that important?" Miguel was willing to be wowed, yet he also wanted to genuinely understand.

"Well, there would've been one practical reason, at least: for their farming. By counting the days *after* the winter solstice, the shortest day of the year, and no doubt with some trial and error, they would've learned when to plant their crops in the spring. Too early invited a killer frost, after all; too late and the young plants would wither in the summer heat. Plus, they likely learned, relative to the *summer* solstice, when to expect cycles of rain and dry spells.

"I think you could say that calculating the shortest and longest days comprised the first calendar, the first farmer's almanac." Johnson paused to allow it all to sink in.

Estefan picked up the discussion with Miguel. "It was natural for them to have a certain reverence for the sun. Try to suspend for a moment what you've learned in school. We know it's one of 250 billion or so stars in the Milky Way alone, which in turn is one of a hundred billion galaxies. The early Britons didn't have that sophistication. To them the sun was plainly the giver of life: It warmed them, grew their crops; by their reckoning it had to have magical powers.

"And so the solstices – plotted at each village according to where the sun rose and set relative to, say, a particular tree or a hill on the horizon – must have had great significance for them. We know the Egyptians came to call the sun Ra, their highest god." With that, the priest passed the baton back to Johnson.

"Stonehenge wasn't the first of its kind, only the most durable. Avebury, some dozen miles away, also had huge slabs, several hundred in ten concentric rings. An enormous henge surrounded them all.

"Yet another henge not too far away is called Durrington Walls. Instead of stupendous rocks, those builders constructed rings of timbers, so it's likely older. Probably finished it in a season or two. Only the post holes remain today, of course. But the spaces through the entrance to the center captured the winter solstice sunset."

Estefan took another turn. "Archaeologists around the world have uncovered evidence from thousands of years earlier still of ritual burials – laying the remains of elders to rest with their tools or jewelry. It's only a small jump to say that, well before Stonehenge was erected, there was some manner of belief in an afterlife. These were spiritual places."

Miguel sat perfectly still, attentive. For his meager years of life, he was wise enough to know he had much to learn.

"But there's a related line of reasoning, too, about Stonehenge," Johnson continued. "They've studied the skeletons in those scattered graves nearby, and a high proportion showed signs of injury or disease. They discovered small chips of bluestone at lots of the gravesites. Well, guess what? The bluestones forming those rings have plenty of man-made chip marks. The stone chips may well have been treasured artifacts that they carried in an amulet – that's a pouch worn around the neck. So, Stonehenge in particular may well have been regarded as a place of healing."

"As with Lourdes," Estefan added. "Which is again to say, Stonehenge was probably considered sacred by those who went there." He saw the boy's wonderment and a warmth filled him.

Johnson jumped back in. "Britain, by the way, isn't the only place where the solstices came to be revered. The Mayans flourished along Mexico's Yucatan Peninsula from about 200 BC until their society finally collapsed around 900 AD. They built ceremonial temples and plazas with the sun in mind. At Palenque, the Temple of Inscriptions is aligned to the winter solstice. As the sun crosses the sky that day, its rays hit the back wall and descend a stairway into the tomb of their greatest leader."

Miguel's inquisitive mind stirred again. "Okay, I get that the ancient people thought of the sun as God or something, that's sweet. But we know that the solstices come around just because the earth's axis is tilted. I mean, I learned that way back in fourth grade."

The photographer looked over at Estefan and nodded. He liked this kid, too. There was an innocence about him, refreshing in a hard-bitten world of cynical teens.

Miguel took a long pull on his cola then looked up again. "So, Father, how does any of that make the solstice a special day?"

Estefan clasped his hands on his lap. "There's a reason why the early Christian church marked the 25th of December as the day Jesus was born. It was intended to overshadow and displace the winter solstice as a meaningful day, to dismiss it and all the rituals and celebrations that accompanied it across many societies."

Johnson added, "Even if the winter solstice wasn't really spiritual to them, they knew that the days to follow would have more and more light, more warmth. For sure that'd be a reason to party."

"So, Father, the lady out there," the youth suddenly referred back to the South Sister, "or I don't know 'cause she wasn't really real, but she was dressed like the Virgin Mary and everything, y'know? Except she didn't act like it."

"I know. That bothers me, too. The voice from the light said the figure would be familiar to me. And, obviously, it was. But, Miguel, it wasn't the Virgin Mary as we think of her."

"A fake like Our Lady of Guadalupe in Mexico City, then?"

"From different motivations, but yes."

"So, at the South Sister, was that, uh, maybe a Mother Earth or something?"

"Or something," Estefan evaded.

Johnson broke the pregnant pause that followed. "Miguel, you originally asked whether the solstice could hold something bad in store. Here's a bit of information that might help.

"The Mayans carved elaborate stone calendars dating back many centuries and into the future as well. The calendars were highly accurate, especially considering this was before the first telescope. They plotted and recorded the movements of not only the sun but the moon and Venus, the next brightest light in the night sky which they thought of as their primary god. They were even able to predict solar eclipses. Impressed?"

"Yeah," Miguel said with a broad expression. He had no idea some of his Indian ancestors had put together so much with so little.

The youth's enthusiasm prompted Johnson further. "Y'know that smear of faint light you see across the sky on a really clear night? That's actually looking through billions of stars toward the center of the Milky Way. Well, for centuries and from year to year, the Maya plotted imperceptible movements of that elongated mass across the sky. They used real principles of astronomy and geometry to calculate the year when Earth was last in the exact center of it – and when we would be again. They called this period an Age, and it was about 25,700 years. They recorded all this on what they called the 'Long Count' stone calendar.

"The current Age, they measured and carved, would end in 2012. They chose the winter solstice as a representative day and made it the last day of that calendar. Their medicine men wove stories of human strife expected to surround that day."

Estefan added, "Try to always keep in mind, Miguel, that just a little bit of knowledge is dangerous. Back in the 1990s, word traveled around on the Internet that the end of the Mayan calendar meant the end of times."

He passed a wry smile to Johnson who dribbled it. "Yeah, December 21, 2012. Kids everywhere were probably making presents for their parents out of construction paper and crayons, and their moms made a fine meal that evening. ... Anything missing? Oh, that's right, a catastrophe!

"The winter solstice of 2012 obviously came and went without a ripple. And y'know what? Considering their lack of resources, those Mayan priests over a thousand years ago were amazingly accurate in plotting the end of that Age. They were off by only fifteen years. The actual year when Earth crossed what we call the midpoint of the galactic equator – the middle of that smear in the night sky – was 1997. Nothing happened then, either."

"Another grand alignment," Estefan posited.

"Correct, my friend. In May 2000, a fluke occurred, Miguel, where Mercury, Venus, Earth and our moon, Mars, Jupiter and Saturn all fell into a nearly straight line in their respective orbits. It's happened many times in history and will again. But astrologers and spiritualists of all sorts got carried away speculating about it. There were claims that the cumulative gravitational pull in that line would cause *untold* carnage on our planet. Others suggested that the combined holistic energies could transform humans to a greater purpose, tra la la. Again, we know now, nothing unusual took place.

"And that's all to suggest that our planet endures. So, my advice to you, my young friend, is don't believe everything you see or hear."

"Father already told me that last summer."

Johnson turned to Estefan with mock disgust. "Whattya, stealin' my lines now?"

"I don't think you can claim ownership of that one," Estefan replied with a broad smile.

"Miguel," Johnson concluded, "what your pastor and I have been getting at is that the winter solstice has only a technical meaning today. But to our forebears, it had a very powerful meaning."

"So, then, why did the lady – er, the figure – make a big deal of it?"

The two men traded glances. "I don't know, son," the priest answered quietly.

The petite Suki brought a huge cheeseburger deluxe and fries for the youth and seafood for Johnson and Estefan. Miguel noticed her eyes shine as she set Johnson's plate on his fold-out tray. Call me, they seemed to convey.

Chapter Eighteen

The Air Force Office of Special Investigations (OSI) was headquartered at Andrews Air Force Base – more prominently known for housing the traveling White House, Air Force One. Over six decades, OSI's central charge had been to investigate, and neutralize as necessary, all criminal, terrorist and espionage threats to USAF and other military personnel and resources.

Including reservists, OSI employed over 2,000 trained investigators scattered across three continents – co-located with but independent of their base and command-center hosts.

Over seventy years, OSI had distinguished itself in a myriad of testy circumstances as an unbiased and productive body. But it *was*, after all, part of the military high command. Accordingly, the one stain on its record had been the occasional, if intentional, non-conclusion whenever it was pulled into the UFO quagmire.

A Navistar GPS satellite had lain strewn in the southwestern New Mexico desert. Retrieved by USAF security personnel, standard procedure in space-junk recovery operations called for OSI processing of all collateral contacts, including personal interviews where warranted.

To that end, the young first lieutenant on hand from an Air Force Reserve unit had drawn the short straw on this occasion. He pulled into the gravel driveway at the Flores home in Columbus, New Mexico, having concluded the long trip down from Boulder – slowed by snow squalls in the early going. It was now approaching 9 PM.

"Senora Flores?" the reservist half shouted through the

glass storm door. He summoned a cheerful spirit. "My name is Lieutenant Morris, LaShawn Morris. I'm with the Air Force Office of Special Investigations."

Rosalinda instinctively put a hand to her mouth. "Please, please come in," as she pushed the door open against a gust of wind. "Has something happened to Miguel?"

"No, ma'am. There's nothing to be alarmed about." The tall muscular officer stepped in and removed his cap. "Actually, it's your son Miguel I'm here to see. The other day, ma'm, some hardware came to rest in the desert near here, and a security officer at the site took down Miguel's name. I guess he approached the officer on foot out there."

"Sure, sure, by the Sisters. He is a runner, you know. He runs out there and back sometimes. I tell him he pushes himself too hard with this running all the time." She turned to address her daughters. "Girls, please take your game to the kitchen table. Ten more minutes and then to bed." Dutifully, the oldest picked up the Shoots and Ladders board from the floor and removed it to the other room.

"So, I take it he's not home now? When do you expect him back, ma'am?"

"Not for a couple of days, I think. He left with Father Tolavares, our parish priest."

"I see, to a church retreat or something?"

"No, no, nothing like that. It is about what happened there at the South Sister last summer when Miguel and then Father, too, saw the Virgin Mary. And then Father saw her again a few days ago in a vision, and he came to us and told us he needed to take Miguel with him and another man, uh, Mr. Selby, Johnson Selby, yes, that is his name."

She bit her lip, fretting at the quizzical look on the kindly dark brown face of the visitor. "We are Catholic," she offered by way of summary explanation. "And you?"

"Baptist, ma'am, but would you mind if we go back to the beginning? I confess to being a little confused."

"I wish Renaldo were here. He is working in Deming tonight, unloading and setting up poinsettias at the farmers' market – for Christmas."

Rosalinda briefly recounted Miguel's encounter with the Marian figure that morning in July, his return to the South Sister the following day in the company of their priest, then Estefan's sudden arrival this very morning, seeking their permission to take Miguel overseas.

Lieutenant Morris continued to stare into the naive eyes of this Latino mother. On its surface, her story had the earmarks of an abduction: spiriting a youth, even if willingly, to a faraway country for suspect purposes. Notions of past scandals within the Catholic Church, possibly an international sex slave trade, came to mind. Still, the woman's knowledge of supposedly miraculous events five months before at the very place where the satellite had crashed last week was confounding to him.

"Just where will they be staying in this city in – you said Turkey?"

"Izmir, yes, that is what Father Estefan said. I don't know where. He said they would phone when they arrive."

"*Uh-huh*," Morris gruffed. "Well, thank you very much, senora." He managed another smile as he reached into a breast pocket for a calling card. "Do me a favor, if you would, and call me collect at this number when you hear from either your son or Father Tolavares. And please get a number where they can be reached."

Morris drove around the corner and stopped, shaking his head at the woman's ignorance. If not related to the sex market, the priest and this Selby fellow flying to Turkey might well involve the boy as a mule. Both the heroin and hashish trades had picked up lately.

Whatever the scenario, he had come away with a whole different impression than expected. This might have nothing to do with crime, terrorism or espionage involving the Air Force directly, but it did smell to high heaven. Maybe Interpol needed to be alerted. Three days into his annual two-week stint of active duty, the young Air Force Reserve officer was convinced he had stumbled onto ... something.

While winds near gale force buffeted his dark blue sedan, Morris placed a call to his superior in Boulder.

As the Citation slipped eastward through failing light, a furious battle continued to rage in the Persian Gulf and the Gulf of Oman. With night-goggled pilots at the wheel, ubiquitous Iranian gunboats, powered by 600-horsepower turbocharged engines of Russian design, darted across the long expanse in bursts eclipsing 100 knots.

Ignoring frantic hails from their targets, oil laden supertankers all, fat cannons bolted to the gunboat decks aimed just below the waterline. From 500 meters, they lobbed "goo balls," as U.S. Navy personnel would soon tag them. The petro-chemical mass, heated to super-sticky as it left the barrel, slammed into and adhered to the ship's hull with a thud. Half a second later twenty kilograms of high-energy plastic explosives buried within the waxy orb opened a gaping maw in the outer shell. Repeated rounds aimed at the same location carved crevices into the inner hull as fire broke out and tons of crude spilled forth.

Between volleys, the gunboats raged back and forth through the waters, constantly zigzagging to avoid surface-to-surface missile lock-on by the Navy's protective cruisers and destroyers, their artillery slow to react. Underpowered PT boats, meanwhile, were left in the attackers' fading wakes. Small-barrel guns fired from their decks had only intermittent success.

Two hours into the engagement, four supertankers bound for the U.S., including the Exxon Cartwright and the Chevron Victoria, the pride of their respective fleets, were dead in the water and sinking. Nine others bound for Europe, Japan and Australia were listing, trying to limp to safety at ports in Qatar and Dubai. Three of those would not survive the night. Dozens of lives were lost among the various merchant fleets in the explosions and fires that ensued.

Notable in the rampage, the Iranian Quds Force ignored two tankers bound for China and one for North Korea. The predators were skilled in identifying their prey.

Then, as suddenly as they had appeared, the gunboats were gone, racing back to separate ports along the Iranian coast.

Several oil slicks soon spread to alarming proportions. Iran's own extended shoreline would not be spared. An ecological disaster loomed.

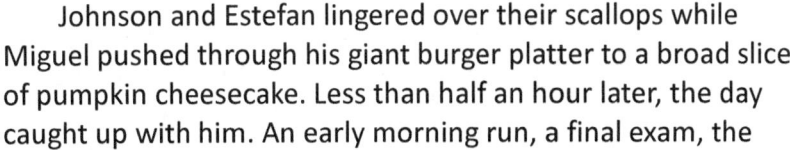

Johnson and Estefan lingered over their scallops while Miguel pushed through his giant burger platter to a broad slice of pumpkin cheesecake. Less than half an hour later, the day caught up with him. An early morning run, a final exam, the exhilaration of a sudden trip and now this massive diversion of blood from brain to digestive tract conspired to engage his auto-pilot. The adolescent's head slumped in the seat.

Johnson wanted to probe Estefan's mind again. "Any advanced thoughts, bud, on what might lie ahead?" The whisper of jet pods outside disguised his hushed voice.

"You're the one flying me across continents. What's your thinking?"

"Oh, put it back on me, right." He considered for a brief moment. "Pardner, I stared down a cougar in the Canadian Rockies once – with nobody around, frankly. In the Outback I stumbled onto a pack of wallabies protecting a female in labor. I wouldn't wanna do that a second time, either. And the reindeer in Norway, when you see them thundering by, a herd of a hundred or more, it's a rush. It can also be damn dangerous without a tree nearby to climb. But this, this has me a little spooked.

"By the way, I was surfing the networks and the Web while you were practicing the linguistic arts. Hey, guy, the world could be at Beelzebub's door. There's a naval battle going on right now in the two connected gulfs, Oman's and the Persian. Iran, they think, is sinking oil tankers headed for the West. It doesn't look good."

Suki glided silently by with dinner trays for the pilot and co-pilot. Raven hair extending beyond her waist caught the fading, deep yellow sunlight streaming through the portals as she went.

"Keep the pilots well nourished, that's my policy," Johnson joked while unabashedly swiveling his head to take in her receding form. Turning back, "She's Hawaiian; we met on the Big Island. Suki is her given name; she goes by Susan in most settings. Lovely girl."

"If I may be so bold, my bachelor friend, you've had lots of lovely girls. You might want to consider a woman."

The priest's telling remark shoved Johnson back into his seat. "Ooh, good one. And I do admit to a degree of commitment phobia. Hey, all I'm looking for – when I'm looking – is that girl next door, a great snuggler who prefers movies with happy endings but also has a wanderlust for exotic places. Oh, and a great body would be persuasive, too."

The freelancer grimaced as he stroked a still-tender quad, a leftover from his October trip to Glacier National Park for the color change. He was hopeful of publishing the spread under the title, "Glacier Post-Glacier," in recognition of the receding ice.

"But what about you, my honorable traveling companion? It's been most of a year now since the Vatican released the priesthood from that damn vow of chastity. You're free to marry – so long as she's a Catholic, eh? So, any prospects? Wait, I take that back. Luna County is indeed an appropriate name for your base of operations; it really is like the moon's surface. You gotta get out more, guy."

"A vow is a vow," Estefan replied softly. "I didn't take it with the prospect of a change in the rules. This is permanent."

"Now, why am I not surprised you'd say that? Anyway, I was just curious, 'cause I've never had the sense that you're gay."

"Good, because I'm not. I admire Suki's tush as much as you. But as you'll recall from the old Baltimore Catechism, I try not to dwell on it."

Johnson broke into a grin. "You're a throwback, you know that?"

"I'm a priest," Estefan responded evenly, his words barely heard.

Suki closed the cockpit door and moved back down the aisle, collecting dishes. Her winning smile revealed orthodontically perfect white teeth. "After-dinner wine?"

"Not for me," Estefan replied.

Johnson insisted. "Two pinot noirs, thanks. And could you find a couple ibuprofen back there?

"So, all right," returning his attention to Estefan, "if I have a cogent thought in all this, here it is:

"As to the true nature of the figure you saw, I agree it was probably a holographic projection – invisible to me and to the cameras somehow. I think it's noteworthy that the figure only directed statements to you and didn't react to your firing the stone. She or it was programmed. Advanced technology, then, to be sure, but not supernatural.

"Still, hey, I wouldn't discount entirely that it was metaphysical in the truest Church sense, a direct call placed from heaven to you, my friend – however well or poorly legends have defined such events up to now. As you well know, the crowds at Lourdes and Fatima didn't see a figure, either. But they sure as hell saw that globe of light you witnessed and I did, too. And so did the cameras, and that means something in our physical world, compadre. You and Miguel and I, we didn't all hallucinate at the same time. It's real in some sense.

"You mentioned the absence of love and compassion that Bernadette and Lucy were so impressed by back when, and I see that as a yellow flag regardless of whatever else is going on here. Yet, if we've both pretty much concluded this projection of Miriam wasn't the real article, then why the ruse – and on whose part? Didn't it know you'd see right through that? I mean, the light only gave the excuse of offering a 'familiar' image after you'd already called it out. Frankly, that whole sequence has had me shaking my head."

Estefan leaned forward. "I've had those thoughts, too." Gesturing, "Please go on."

"All right, well, I could make the case for an ET hypothesis, for sure, as Paul Palmatier did about Fatima: an intelligence superior to humans in mechanization, and no doubt raw intelligence, which hijacked the Church's reverence for Mary and maybe employed it occasionally to cover its real purposes. Whatever those are.

"For that matter, it could be some sort of inter-dimensional traveler. Y'know, physics is on the brink of proving parallel universes in that mysterious eleventh dimension. But of course you've read that, too."

"Yes," the cleric responded honestly. "But what about a potentially demonic presence?"

Johnson caught the expression and stifled a laugh. "Well, ya' got me there, fella. I thought hell left the building last year at Vatican III along with the ban on priests marrying."

The two held a long and mutually trusting gaze.

Johnson went on. "Whatever the true source of the Marian medium through the centuries, the message has always been about maintaining a steady state in the world, warning of impending instability or chaos. In that sense your own experience here was really typical.

"No one can win, it said. Now, you can interpret that two ways. It might mean neither antagonist is capable of winning – a stalemate. Or it could mean neither side should be *allowed* to win.

"However a standoff is achieved, both sides will ultimately back away when they realize it's pointless. And that's not usually a bad thing. Anyway, the last I knew, promoting stability wasn't exactly a satanic trait. So, that's gotta be a factor in its favor when you're evaluating the motives of this light or its underlying intelligence."

"Yes, my friend. Good observations." Estefan was pondering why he happened to know this adventurer, this old roommate, who served not only as his transportation but also a foil on this journey. Could it have been preordained? "You agreed to this," the voice from the light had said, implying something was planned long ago, possibly even before this lifetime.

Johnson looked across with compassion. "All that said, I doubt that it matters. Even if you've been communicating with a *mere* representative of a more advanced life form than us, I really think you need to go with it. It's not just that you're a Jesuit, my man." His voice took on a whispered intensity. "You're a *seeker*.

"Estefan, nothing you've told me suggests any evil intent, okay? This sorry ass world of ours has shown over the last five thousand years that we just can't get our act together. Here and there a Rodney King gets our attention, asking can't we all just get along, y'know? But there's as much cruelty and discrimination in the world today as there ever was, by my accounting. Maybe more.

"So, if an advanced intelligence – or a higher power, whatever – has decided to intervene when we're on the brink of calamity, I for one am not prepared to object.

"Now, regardless of why the Marian theme, it seems to me this intelligence expects you to fulfill your Jesuit duty, to obey regardless, to do whatever you're led to do without complete and convincing evidence that it's for the best. ... I guess they call that faith."

"Well put," Estefan smiled.

The photographer leaned forward, elbows on knees, forming a tent with his spread fingertips. "Okay, here's something else that's bugged me about all this. The light told you in the desert that you'd become aware of a message to deliver – to someone, sometime, no specifics expressed.

"So on the 8th of this month you're told to look for signs. I'm good with that; I think we've interpreted them correctly. But lots of things had to come together to put us here on this aircraft right now."

Estefan tried on an explanation. "Maybe the intelligence knew the sequence that would follow. The voice did recite lots of moments from my past, after all." He looked away, reviewing in his mind odd yet significant events from so many years before that the presence was aware of.

"Ah, but that's different. Those were subconscious memories stored in your brain, man, ready to be picked off."

"That'd be one method of retrieval, yes, I agree." The priest sighed, knowing he couldn't know how any nonhuman would think or reason.

"Hmmm, okay, I'm there. So, you're saying this amber light – or some underlying intelligence if the light was merely a taxi – maybe didn't tap your memories, it just *knew* everything about your past. Cool, that'd be close to god-like, I guess. But that still doesn't account for something that hasn't happened yet."

"I'm not so sure it doesn't," the priest replied, folding his arms. "The light said, 'You will become aware of a message to deliver. Now you must forget. When you remember, it will be your time; then you will act.' Plus the mention that a 'tall woman' would assist me to remember. I can certainly interpret all that as predicting events yet to unfold, that Ricki would help bring my bedroom encounter out in the open. Knowing the past, the future, isn't it all just about time?"

"Whoa, stop the boat, I think I just fell overboard." Johnson's brow creased as he struggled to get mental arms around the concept.

The two men sat in silence for a long moment before Estefan spoke. "If we have the opportunity – and that's a big if – it would be easier if I could just tell Sheikh al-Dakhil and Ayatollah Shirazi that one of them has it basically right and the other has a pants full." Johnson snorted at the imagery. "But that wasn't the message. 'No one can win' is all I've got to go on."

"Awhile back," Johnson responded, "I was in Sarajevo doing a shoot. That city was beautiful before their civil war. They hosted the '84 Winter Olympics, remember? It was still kind of torn up when I was there, only partway back. The countryside, though, which I came for, was stunning. Anyway, I was in a downtown tavern one night, and over a couple pints I had an insightful talk with a middle manager in the city's water and sewer department. He was a Christian, Russian Orthodox.

"We talked about the old days, under the Soviet regime. Pieter summed up the way it was then: 'They pretended to pay us, and we pretended to work.'"

Estefan laughed at the stranger's poignant word play.

"He said, after the civil war, the city had a humongous task just restoring services from all that shelling. They didn't have enough serviceable equipment to dig up all the streets and retrofit all the buildings; it took many years. The people got impatient and took it out on the Serbian-controlled government, he said.

"At another point Pieter remarked, and this is a close

paraphrasing, 'Look what we have done to the old Yugoslavia? It was a political creation from the beginning, but now Croatia, Bosnia, Herzo-Govina, they all broke away from Serbia. The world is fracturing into smaller pieces. Politicians try to keep them together, but ultimately the people decide. Cultures, religions – people want to be with and want to be governed by their own kind, their own tribe."

Estefan looked out a portal at distant puffy clouds set against the darkness below as the Citation continued east across the Atlantic. "What about the European Union? Disparate cultures came together for a common purpose."

"Ah, no, I don't think that fits. The E.U. is essentially a commercial venture. More and more, civil disturbances across every one of those countries involves immigrants – victims, aggressors, it varies. And I don't think the U.S. is a shining example of tolerance, either, for that matter. Muslim-Americans haven't exactly been the toast of the town since 9/11."

"Christian with Christian, Shi'ite with Shi'ite, Sunni with Sunni, then," Estefan now extended the earlier analogy. "And on and on it goes." He let out a deep breath. "The human condition still centers around fear and suspicion."

Johnson lifted his wine glass. "Well, good luck with that, bud. But this is what I keep coming back to. If I could pick anyone in the world to handle what we might get into – a selfless person with the compassion, brains and innate savvy to do some good – it'd be you.... But I'm thinking the pants-full remark would be over the top."

Suki collected the stemware for insertion into the steam dishwasher with the other dishes and flatware. A light hiss from the machine ensued.

Johnson moved the discussion this time. "Okay, first of all, I made the assumption that the topdog Shi'ite, Shirazi, and the Sunni, al-Dakhil, wouldn't choose Istanbul as the place to meet – too obvious and hard to keep the secrecy lid on. An out-of-the-way city like your Smyrna – Izmir – makes sense.

"I also figured they're probably meeting in a mosque. It could be a hotel or someplace else, but my guess is a mosque."

"They'd logically meet at a house of worship," the cleric agreed.

He accepted Suki's offer of a pillow and a finely woven Scottish wool blanket in navy and forest green plaid. She handed a second set to Johnson and draped another over the slumbering Miguel.

Johnson continued. "The Hisar mosque, next to the Kemeralti market square downtown, was built in 1597, so I guess it meets the historical-places test. It has a large central dome for prayer that's surrounded by seven smaller domes, open courtyards between and lawns beyond. It'll be easy to locate. And it's reasonably close to where we're staying. I figure we'll know if that's the right place, 'cause if it is, there's liable to be guards posted. This is a secret meeting and all, but I doubt they'd abandon security entirely.

"Just so you know, two other locations are possible as well. Isa Bey Mosque is in the Seljuk district of the city; that's a cab ride away. It's one of the last structural remains of the Ottoman Empire, built in 1375 – near St. Jean basilica, actually."

Estefan cast a glance at Miguel's peaceful face. "A city divided by faith but living together peacefully, after all. That has to be encouraging."

"Christian and Sunni, sure. But add some Shi'ites to the mix and the pot can boil over, my friend. Anyway, a third possibility is called Birge, outside town. It's also of Ottoman architecture. On the grounds are the tomb of an ancient imam named Birgivi, plus not one but two small mosques and a madrasa, a Muslim elementary school.

"By the way, you might not know that outside Izmir, on Nightingale Mountain, are the ruins of a house where the Maron Christians believe Mary fled to after the crucifixion to avoid the Romans – as well as idolatry by some of her son's followers. Legend has it that Jesus entrusted his mother to a male friend named Jean, who transported her from Jerusalem all the way to Ephesus, near Smyrna. He built her a small house there, and they say she lived out the rest of her life in it and reached 100. Back in 1967, Pope Paul declared it a holy site."

Estefan smiled then yawned. "Excuse me," clapping his mouth shut. "I did know that, but thank you for reminding me. I'd love a chance to see it."

"Ah, you're no fun, you know everything. But could that be another one of these signs? I mean, otherwise, it's a strange coincidence, eh?"

"Hard to say, maybe. Where do you keep your manual on signs?" The two stifled laughter so as not to rouse Miguel.

"Hey, you're yawning and we should wrap this up soon, anyway. It's only 8 PM Mountain but already 6 AM in Turkey. We still have some hours left before wheels down. We'll need the rest."

"Good point. And thanks for not asking, incidentally."

"About what, a plan?" Johnson's face broadened, knowing that was what Estefan meant. "I figured if there was a plan, I'd know about it by now. So, we're pretty much winging it, eh, Padre?"

"I do apologize if this only wastes your money and time."

The priest removed the white collar tab from his black shirt and pulled at the button behind. "As you say, I guess I'm taking it on faith. If it's meant to be – if, in Rosalinda's words, this is God's work – then circumstances will favor us."

"Well, I'm not Indiana Johnson, and you're not Zorro, friend. This could be the stuff of comedy routines, y'know."

Estefan paused a few seconds, a serious smile lining his lean face. "It was terrific of you to introduce me to some towering intellects these past months. I want you to know how much I appreciate that; their perspectives were beyond valuable.

"This figure, Johnson, it's not truly Mary, I recognize. But we agree the light is, or represents, an intelligent life form – perhaps a vastly superior intelligence – which came in a form that's familiar to me, to get my attention. As for the absence of a rosary and roses, well, maybe that was intentional."

"So, by that reasoning, showing you the rosary in your room wasn't a belated addition but instead, what, a confirmation? That you recognized this as a power that could create just about anything? That you passed the test?"

The priest nodded.

"Well, I gotta say, in my book you sure as hell passed one when you threw that rock and the light didn't throttle you on the spot. Estefan, you're a quiet man and a deep thinker, but you do have a way of rising to the occasion."

The priest touched his left armrest controls, spreading his seat completely horizontal, and reached for his pillow. He looked at the ceiling and offered a final thought. "I suspect the intelligence is without emotions as we know them. Yet it shows a desire to prevent a great catastrophe on Earth. I can't ignore that."

"Angel, then? I hear they come in lots of flavors." From a year at the seminary Johnson was drawing on his own considerable knowledge of Church lore, of mystical interventionists under the broad category of angels, ranging from amorphous presences to fierce warriors.

Estefan lifted his head and fixed his eyes on Johnson a final time before dropping his eyelids. "I've considered that as well."

Suki darkened the cabin lights.

Chapter Nineteen

Something had occurred at Latitude 16 N, Longitude 9 E on the sun's Earth-facing side. The high-arcing flare spawned a solar storm to rival classic recorded events in the planet's instrumented history.

Solar flares were normally associated with clusters of sunspots, the relatively cooler, quixotic points in the sun's corona. This rogue flare had spiked the solar wind from a pedestrian 800,000 mph to over 2 million and would last several hours.

Earth's magnetosphere would bend the stream of super-hot ionized gases to the north and south poles. There, a portion would rush down into the ionosphere, impaling any unprotected satellites, disrupting radio signals at all bands, savaging electrical substations on the ground, and coincidentally creating a widespread colorful aurora – the Northern Lights.

The Space Weather Prediction Center was a little known but vital arm of the U.S. government. Located in Boulder, the center employed solar astronomers and physicists and hosted USAF techs from Space Command. SWPC reported jointly to the Air Force and to the expansive National Oceanic and Atmospheric Administration (NOAA). Their diligence generated timely alerts in order to reposition, shield or shut down space hardware in the event of a heightened solar storm.

Major Julie Mendenhall looked at the digits on her chronograph: 0328 Wed 12-19. Before sending out the dispatch in her hand, she reviewed it with her sergeant and the SWPC's overnight civilian director.

"This is a head-on in two days and change, gentlemen, and there's lots of machinery to attend to. We can expect widespread power outages along the grids. Somebody else will decide whether those are voluntary or otherwise.

"Okay, we're solid that this doesn't follow any repeating pattern? And there were no sunspots near this flare?"

The men nodded in sober agreement. Flares were nearly always associated with nearby sunspots and occurred at regular intervals, from a month to a century or more apart.

"I'm thinking 1859," she offered.

In that year, before the electrification of America, a flare's vicious solar storm created an aurora that even Mexicans observed. That would have decimated modern power grids. This imminent and powerful storm would rush past our planet, on to Mars and beyond at roughly 2.4 million mph.

"This is damn peculiar. Okay, let's push it out the door." Mendenhall turned to her sergeant. "Update Space Command first. Wait for a reply before general distribution."

She pulled at the small hole in her thermos cup of tea and stared at the blackness beyond her fourth-floor windows. She worked at one of the world's most spectacular locations, in a handsome brick building cut into the Rockies outside Boulder, Colorado. The snowy ribbons on towering slate-gray ridges outside, though, were invisible to her; she worked the graveyard shift.

Half an hour later, the Center's provocative message went out via secure network, an official alert outside its normal schedule:

```
Joint USAF/NOAA Special Report of Solar and
Geophysical Activity
```

WINTER SOLSTICE

SDF Number 353, 19 Dec, 0344 MT

1A. Analysis of Solar Active Regions and
Activity: An unexpected, highly significant
flare erupted at Lat. 16:21 N, Long. 9:14 E
at 1003 GMT. No other activity of concern in
the remaining observed regions.

1B. Solar Activity Forecast: Activity in
stated heliosector is expected to return to
quiet over the next six hours.

2A. Geophysical Activity Summary: Earth's
geomagnetic field is quiet to moderately
unstable at this hour.

2B. Geophysical Activity Forecast: Solar
stream winds associated with the flare will
increase progressively. The ionosphere is
expected to be unsettled on the first day
(20 Dec) as the stream advances from 300
km/sec to 380 km/sec; highly unstable on the
second day (21 Dec) as the stream surges to
1070 km/sec; and unstable to quiet on the
third day (22 Dec) after the stream surge
has passed.

The SWPC report's attachment contained projected sets of
numbers showing the chance of significant ionospheric
disturbance at 30 to 60 degrees North latitudes. For late
afternoon and evening on December 21, the Center's readings
projected a 99-percent chance of "active" storm-related
conditions at the 30th parallel – northern Florida - and "severe"
conditions for all points above a line extending roughly from
Norfolk through Nashville, Oklahoma City and Fresno.

Too soon after dropping off to sleep, Ray Washburn suddenly awoke. Instinctively he looked over at the adjacent pillow where Peggy's head had rested for 38 years. In that first second rousing from slumber, ovarian cancer had taken her only last week. But it was eight years ago now.

The i-pod was incessantly vibrating on his nightstand, an SWPC alert. He coughed her night-gowned image out of his thoughts and read the message from Major Mendenhall on the incoming solar storm. His still sleepy eyes strained to focus on the major's feminine hand in the margin: "Centuries event. No sunspot near flare."

Washburn scanned the numbers on the attachment and agreed with the officer's cryptic assessment. He punched in a five-word reply: "Got it. Hold general distribution."

Something was goddamn wrong about this, he knew, another incongruity. He was a patriot, first and always, and he was worried. He touched the keypad again to reach Space Command and set in motion the repositioning and masking of satellites in the way.

This violent escalation of the solar stream would begin two and a half days hence, just short of 4 PM Eastern on the 21st, and continue well into the night. By laser-guiding as many satellites as possible out of harm's way and activating the Cocoon shielding on those in geosynchronous orbit, physical damage from the incoming torrent could be minimized.

For six hours, perhaps more, GPS, internet, TV and nearly all radio communications would be lost across a wide expanse of the U.S. and Canada. AA and AAA batteries would sell out as tens of millions dusted off battery-operated radios to find those stations at the ends of the AM dial, the Emergency Alert System (once the Emergency Broadcast System), their sole source of news.

Air traffic would be another complication, given the interruption in GPS and air traffic control communications. Setting a time to order all planes out of the sky needed to be handled pronto as well.

Following programmed systems checks on all satellites, the only question would be when to come about. Two o'clock Eastern on the 21st would be a minimally safe choice, he believed. The networks especially would raise holy hell for every hour lost. But he was more interested in saving expensive machinery.

Washburn forwarded the SWPC dispatch to Kenna Nowitzky's email box. With no text, he titled his email "Duck."

December 19, 6:50 AM EST. Kenna held her standard-issue i-pod at arm's length for a second and sighed. Annoyed once again, she knew at least that a permanent record of this private-line call would exist – relative to a potential badgering charge. She had come to liken Ray Washburn to an earlier male friend who just didn't get it. While deciding how to respond to his latest tempest, she opened a folder and hit the print key for all its files. Then she phoned the general.

"The president has a lot on his plate right now, Ray, and I've got a second helping for him on my desk. Tom and I are due at the White House very shortly." She refused to let this intrusion define her day.

"Seymour wouldn't recognize a Navistar if it flew down and bit him on the ass. It's all *that stuff* to him. The man is flat-out incompetent."

Kenna exhaled audibly. "Do you want me to tell him that, too?"

"Very funny, little lady," Washburn admonished.

"I try, fat old man," she countered his chauvinistic quip. "Listen, the president may be a little challenged technologically, but he's still our commander in chief. And right now I think he's trying to get through today and still have a world left to greet tomorrow's sunrise. In that context, I'll express your concern if and when there's an opportunity. Best I can do."

"My 'concern' *is* the context, Kenna. Last night was not a mainframe problem; it wasn't a software problem. That kind of event doesn't just happen because somebody substituted a one for a zero. The whole GPS array doesn't just *hiccup* all at once! This was a 10-second freeze in every Navistar satellite the world over."

"I realize that." If only she could nail him on a point of logic.

"But that was just a teaser. Two hours ago there was a solar flare, an especially *big* one. We've got a several-hour burst in the solar wind racing to Earth at almost two and a half million miles an hour – maybe not the fastest ever but certainly the fastest this place has ever recorded. It's carrying quadrillions of charged particles to run roughshod over every satellite in the way and the power grids below.

"We've got two days to swivel and shield some our machines in the sky and move the rest away from the worst of the onslaught. That or we're gonna have one helluva junkyard up there. As for the power stations below, well, in the northern tier states, if they don't shut down, they'll be cooked. Not that anyone should *pay attention*."

"Will you be able to get everything moved or protected in time?" She did want him to know she was taking this threat from the sun seriously.

"Maybe, I don't know; it'll be close. But these are just two more bizarre 'coincidences,' given what we've talked about before and all the rest, don't you think?"

Kenna didn't respond, partly because her one-time weekend paramour, she suspected, wasn't finished, but also in recognition of a watershed moment descending on her. He was right fundamentally, she knew. Coincidences were piling up.

"So that you know," the general broke their silence, "these past couple days it's taken a world crisis to keep UFOs out of the headlines. They've been seen over metro areas, some daylight sightings as well. Thousands of witnesses. Cell footage is going up on YouTube."

Kenna's instinct was to counter his claims with a "ufonut" label, as she had before, but it wouldn't advance the discussion of why the entire GPS system had blinked inexplicably. That incident followed so soon by this sudden threat posed by a solar storm — a threat to those very machines and others — was straining her usual cynicism toward conspiracy theories.

"Now we can add Tulsa's brownout just last evening," Washburn continued. "That happened to coincide with a saucer hovering over the city's main electrical station, according to guards and a security camera there. At the same hour a Milwaukee FM radio outlet pulled in the audio of a televised jai alai match in Buenos Aires. A few hours later, the Chattanooga NBC affiliate flipped from its eleven o'clock news to the Cartoon Network.

"The FCC is getting all kinds of crazy ass reports — satellite-related but nothing to do with the storm approaching. It's all tied into that hiccup; there's some level of outside manipulation going on, Kenna, maybe a distance-early warning. But not of our doing, not of any human's doing."

"Can you prove that?"

"Hah! With what? We've seen how the debunking officialdom tears down every form of evidence imaginable: UFOs couldn't possibly be real, therefore they're not.

"Anyway, no, on a moment's notice I can't document any of it. What are you looking for, bells and whistles?"

Washburn looked out his office window at the faint, predawn Rocky Mountain light. He was certain of only one reality in all this, the itch he was trying to scratch. Some kind of intelligence was here, monitoring – and now disrupting. He should've retired five years ago, he knew, and saved himself the hassle.

"Ray, I'm open to some insight."

He caught the conciliatory tone. "I call it science and technology beyond our imaginations – maybe beyond what we *can* imagine. But if by chance you're adopting an open mind, all I can tell you is that we can't mix and match modes of communication like we've just seen. And now with what looks like an unprecedented solar storm ..." Washburn's voice trailed off. "These were warnings, Kenna, I'm sure of it. There's something bigger going on here."

"I'll keep that in mind." This time she meant it.

Minutes later Nowitzky jammed a dozen flashpoint folders into her briefcase, grabbed her laptop and moved into the hallway. "Hold that elevator!" she cried out at hearing the chime eighty feet away. She barged through her building's exit door and slipped into the waiting DHS limo on the heels of HSA Director Hagelthorne. A light cold rain was falling.

The West Wing's situation room was smaller than Kenna remembered from a single previous occasion, a courtesy visit during a quiet hour when she was first hired. The mahogany conference table dominated, seating twelve. Another fourteen chairs tightly lined two walls. The ceiling was uncomfortably low.

Though compact and space-efficient, the surroundings were lush for their purpose, thanks to some recent retrofitting. The back wall opposite the President consisted of eighteen monitors: real-time satellite feeds; maps of U.S. and foreign ballistic missile sites, movements of ground troops and PAVs (potentially aggressive vehicles); plus more screens for the wealth of other data available for call-up.

Side walls manifested the international markets, worldwide weather, major television networks across six continents, smart boards and a projection screen for non-electronic media. Overlooking the president's chair was a splash of quotes on the front wall from earlier commanders in chief in times of war and near-war, meticulously painted in beautiful script and intended to bolster the courage and patriotism of everyone present. J.T. Seymour had requested that enhancement himself.

Ten minutes into the discussion, called upon to discuss border security, Hagelthorne spoke from Kenna's synopses of possible terrorist threats and vulnerabilities along the Canadian and Mexican borders and America's coasts. He then turned to Kenna on his left. She nodded, her face a little tight.

"Sir, this is Dr. Kenna Nowitzky, my eyes and ears, as it were. She sniffs out fires before they become infernos. You may have seen her previously, seated along a wall at several cabinet meetings."

Throughout every department and agency of federal government, an informal but ironclad rule had always applied to room seating: Decision makers sat at the table and spoke. Support staff sat along the walls, reports and notes at the ready in case called upon. For the first time, Kenna had a seat at the table.

"I trust her judgment implicitly, Mr. President. And though I'm unclear on the exact tenor of her input, it will assuredly be insightful."

"Pleased to make your acquaintance, I'm sure, Dr. Nowitzky," the portly executive offered, gesturing cordially while sending a hard glance at the DHS director for the gap in his preparedness. "What do you have to add? Please be succinct." Seymour looked at his watch.

Suddenly Kenna was a bit overwhelmed. The rigid squares of service ribbons adorning the generals' and admirals' breasts, the flashing screens along the walls together with a palpable tension in the room had dried her throat. She coughed and bore down mentally.

"Mr. President, I shall indeed be brief. On the morning of July 21, NORAD picked up an unknown intruder from deep space. It wasn't a foreign missile, a comet, meteor or any form of debris. It changed course, narrowly missing one of our thirty-six Navistar GPS satellites then plummeted to the surface at an improbable angle, taking it to west Texas. It was detected by satellites and ground radars en route, but no vapor trail, disintegration or impact was reported.

"Shortly thereafter two F-22s scrambled from Holliman Air Force Base spotted a glowing ball of light rising up from the desert floor in southwest New Mexico. It ascended at great speed and out of sight before they could engage their weapons."

She mentally shuddered at what she had just said to the president.

Seymour looked to his right. "Mason, you know anything about this?"

General Mason Yarbrough, chairman of the joint chiefs, demurred. "Not a thing, Mr. President."

Seymour looked at his Air Force secretary. "Sandy, how 'bout you?"

General Sanderson Townsend expressed ignorance as well. "If there was an incident, sir, it was handled, as are those infrequent occasions when a satellite gets tangled up with debris in space. And frankly, sir, that speaks to part of our budget request for next year.

"But Mr. President, if Ms. Nowitzky is suggesting something supposedly from beyond our solar system, well, we haven't investigated anything like that in half a century. We shut down Project Bluebook in 1969. Official findings were published after twenty years of chasing down claims of flying disks and whatnot. Optical illusions, mostly, normal things seen in the sky but maybe from a bad angle, that sort of thing. Whatever else was claimed, no threat was posed to national security and the so-called UFOs didn't seem to have a technology beyond our own.

"Those were the Air Force's conclusions then and we stick by them today. In short, Mr. President, there's nothing to that whole business."

Seymour looked back at Kenna. "Nothing to it, he's telling me, Dr. Nowitzky."

"Yes, well, sir, Bluebook did leave 900 cases unidentified. Those were mostly encounters by military and commercial pilots as well as ground-level close encounters by base security and credible civilians such as policemen, town mayors, college professors – a collective of people who put their careers on the line to come forward.

"Further, Bluebook was often bypassed when direct threats occurred: base intrusions, including ballistic missile sites and nuclear weapons depots."

God help me, what am I doing? Kenna looked around the room and knew she should not have gone there. She just had to pick up that book Ray had sent through inter-departmental mail last month. Now she found herself practically reciting from it.

She took a deep breath before continuing. *This one's for you, bud*, as she saw Ray's face drift over a jigger of Dewar's on ice at the Marriott three years before. She fully realized both his career and her own were on the line with what she would say next. *In for a penny ...*

"Mr. President, a week and a half ago, that same GPS satellite, the one that was buzzed by a bogey in July, abruptly dropped out of orbit and crashed in southwest New Mexico – within a few hundred yards of where our pilots had spotted that globe of light in July."

"Sandy?" The President again looked to his Air Force Secretary.

"So what, Mr. President? The *strong* chance of coincidence aside, we recovered the remains of that machine, as she describes. It was past its projected life. Lab analysis will determine whatever structural or internal damage prior to impact might have contributed to its demise."

"Well, I imagine *impact* was quite enough for its demise, wouldn't you say?" Seymour was curious now. "So, we know a meteor didn't knock it down. Are you saying it just ran out of juice, then?"

Kenna jumped in. "It was operating flawlessly, Mr. President – sufficient fuel and no sign of decaying orbit."

She forced the issue because Townsend was trying to cover his ass. This for her now was about winning a good scrap. Exchanges with sharp-edged callers from her radio appearances back in Illinois had honed her debating skills and her resolve.

She raised her right hand over the table, stabbing a finger at Townsend while answering for him to the president. "It shouldn't have de-orbited, sir, and certainly not at that declination. First, it had a flawless record, no sign of impending trouble, no degradation of its orbit. And those life spans are calculated conservatively; it had fuel to last several more months." She glared at the general "Second, it came down at an angle that defied its expected trajectory, even in a situation of catastrophic shutdown."

"How could you know all that?" the general demanded.

"I got it from the horse's mouth, Ray Washburn at Space Command." Turning back to the President, "Sir, General Washburn has been trying for years to get someone to listen that there's something out there, something more powerful than the Iranians or the North Koreans or the Chinese or Russians, something that's technologically superior to us all."

Seymour waved off Townsend's facial protest then folded his arms to listen as Kenna continued.

"When the Navistar GPS satellite abruptly left orbit, one of four backups from the array was maneuvered into place to integrate with the other thirty-one positioned around the world. The system was soon operating optimally again.

"Then, last night, for precisely ten seconds every one of those satellites and all GPS worldwide went off-line. There's no explanation for it; they were all functioning perfectly. Besides, the individual machines are quasi-independent of one another."

Kenna looked from one set of eyes to another around the room, receiving a bland composite "no thanks" in return. Her boss, Tom Hagelthorne, looked away. She grasped the futility of her argument; they were not buying it. But now there was a damn *point* to be made.

"When they snapped back on in unison, their internal clocks were all exactly ten seconds slow. These are cesium clocks, not electric; they operate no matter what. Which is to say, from the satellites' perspective, Mr. President, it was as if time itself had paused for those ten seconds."

"Your point?" Seymour, unaccustomed to satellite-related jargon, was growing restive at the noticeable absence, as the military brass was fond of saying, of actionable assertions in Nowitzky's storyline.

"Sir, just this morning, NOAA's Space Weather Prediction Center found something disturbing. The near face of the sun issued a solar flare, an especially menacing one consisting of many trillions of charged particles – radiation, essentially. The force of the flare nearly tripled the speed of the solar wind headed toward Earth.

"There will be some mayhem in two days, Mr. President. As we speak, all of our satellites in the way are being programmed to move or pivot to show their backs to the solar wind, but at least a good portion of our communications on the ground will be lost – the northern half of the country. It'll be very widespread and extend to Europe and beyond as well. I'm sure you'll be hearing more soon."

"Sandy?" Seymour looked quizzically.

The Air Force Secretary was bewildered. "I'll need to get in touch with my staff."

Nowitzky plunged ahead. "That said, sir, the ten-second GPS snafu last night was not the result of this solar storm to come; it was too early for that. Mr. President, I prefer deductive reasoning to speculating, but all of this strains coincidence.

"General Washburn sees a relationship: the intrusion over southwest New Mexico last July, that same satellite crashing last week at that very site, now the coordinated GPS blip and the solar storm. He called them warnings."

"And what about you, Dr. Nowitzky? What do *you* call them?"

"I ... I believe they defy explanation." Then she crossed a fatal line. "Mr. President, I grew up in a rational household. My parents were scholars in their own right, and they taught me, among many other things, that talk of UFOs was nonsense. Until now I accepted that premise.

"General Washburn also mentioned other violations of U.S. airspace in recent days – intrusions by unconventional aerial vehicles seen by the public."

"Unconven–... It sounds to me like you're in league with this Washburn." Seymour straightened in his chair, looking hard at her. "Well, I have to say, it's a novel approach, Dr. Nowitzky, blaming a few systems failures on space aliens."

Kenna's face reddened noticeably at the rebuke.

"Sandy, he's your man. What's the story on this guy?"

Townsend stayed with his CYA posture. "Washburn is a 40-year man, came up through the Academy and into NORAD. He knows radar, sir. But, ah, the scuttlebutt has always been that he interprets the occasional odd return as, well, an extraterrestrial presence. Not officially, of course."

Kenna's shoulders slumped. Townsend was all too willing to

take her down along with Washburn, and there was nothing she could say in retort. Ray did support the ET hypothesis; her own disparaging words to him washed over her now.

Seymour smirked. "Well, it might be time for a performance review for the general, eh, Sandy? All right, I trust you'll all be on top of this solar storm thing. Find Chip Cullen before you leave. We need to coordinate on getting the word out."

Returning his attention to Kenna, the president narrowed his gaze and said, "Thank you for your input, Dr. Nowitzky, it was, um, entertaining. Enjoy your day."

As if she had already left, Seymour looked around the table. "Now, if we're finished with the 'woo woo' take on matters, I'd like to hear how we intend to counter these damn 'goo balls'."

Kenna slipped out the door and into a tear-blurred elevator. *You stupid fool!* she screamed silently at herself while trying to maintain a semblance of outward composure. Head downcast, eyes glistening, she sped past uniformed guards into the persistent cold rain and a vacant taxi.

Tom sat there the whole time looking at his hands, embarrassed. Well, there ya' go, Ray. Told ya' the subject is poison.

Despite her protests and warnings each time Washburn had phoned, in the end it was she who swallowed the kool-aid. *Fool*, she repeated. Civilization might survive the days to follow; her latent career as a civil servant would not. She gave the driver directions to her condo; tomorrow was soon enough to clean out her office.

Chapter Twenty

The Citation touched down at Adnan Menderes Airport on Izmir Bay at 9:43 AM IRST. As they taxied toward the private aircraft hangar, the cockpit door opened and the co-pilot poked his head into the cavity. "We have a greeting party, Mr. Selby. I don't think it's very welcoming."

Moments later the three tourists were seated in the office of Banu Pamuk, the Izmir airport manager. Johnson looked to Estefan, who took the lead in responding to the opening question posed by the Turkish Army colonel.

"We are here in the liberal traditions of Roman Catholic faith, to visit the home where Turkish legend suggests the mother of Jesus spent the later years of her life." The priest was fully aware that an entire "sura," or chapter, of the Qur'an was devoted to Mary's miraculous birth to an important prophet, Jesus, and to his teachings. He was also aware that he was shading the truth at best.

Fortunately the colonel knew of Nightingale Mountain and the Christians' devotion to Mary. The ruins drew a few thousand visitors a year, from Europe mostly.

"Plus we wish to visit your city's beautiful mosques and synagogues, of course," Johnson hastened to add. He held a practiced neutral face, the one he utilized on occasion in Selby, Inc., board meetings.

"Mm-hmm," Pamuk responded, likewise without expression. "What about the boy?"

"Oh, Miguel," Johnson grinned innocently. "You wouldn't know this, but Miguel is a fine distance runner – and a devout

Catholic, a member of Father Estefan's parish. We wish to show him your stadium where the World University Games were held in 2005. We're hoping it serves as an inspiration to him." He looked at the colonel's suspicious face and plunged ahead.

"It's Christmas this coming week – for more than a few Turkish citizens as well. Sir, I'm a wealthy man. I've been fortunate to see many of our world's wonders and beautiful cities. Izmir is a place I have long wanted to visit. This holiday season I decided to share my good fortune with an old friend, Father Tolavares, whose wisdom I admire."

Noting the still protruding dark eyebrows before him, Johnson tried, "This for us is mostly a spiritual journey."

The colonel looked over at Estefan, who gazed back dispassionately while fingering his rosary. Standing next to the cleric, Miguel tried to look friendly.

"Attempts are made to traffic contraband through these facilities," the colonel said, glancing at the boy. "And other cargo." Looking down at his clipboard again, "Mr. Selby, I see you acquired passports for Reverend Tolavares and Miguel Flores, plus visas for all three of you, within the past 24 hours. Was this a last-minute decision to visit our country?"

"Oh, no, indeed not," Johnson earnestly lied. "I had planned this for several weeks – as a surprise Christmas gift. But I *forgot* about the travel documents until yesterday. Completely my oversight."

Banu Pamuk stared bullets at Johnson.

"I have a friend in the U.S. government who can dispatch those quickly, that's all. I assure you they are legitimate." Johnson's ears were brightening within his tangled web.

"And so, since you have nothing to conceal, you will not

mind that my staff searches your plane's interior and cargo hold."

"Of course, not." Johnson looked at Estefan and Miguel and smiled weakly.

The colonel pondered the Arabic script on his clipboard for a long moment before raising his head. "Provided nothing illegal is found on your plane, you and your companions may enter this country. Be aware that you will be watched."

"I hope you like it. The Ontur only has six floors and eighty rooms, but it's probably nice enough."

Johnson was offering faint praise to the Ontur Izmir Boutique Hotel, a five-star establishment in the center of the city on Lamet Kaplan Mah Gazi Boulevard, next to the famed international fairgrounds. A mile away rested the city's historic district and centuries-old Hisar Mosque.

Their cab driver, Ahmed, had torn through the city's streets with a relish, weaving across lanes to gain whatever minor advantages along the route from the airport. The aging but sturdy Toyota minivan now moved into the hotel's semi-circular drive, where two bellmen were at its doors before the cab reached a complete halt.

Johnson pulled out a money clip thick with euros overnighted to him and peeled off 300. "Stay with us all day?"

"At your service, Yankee gentleman," the driver said appreciatively, folding over a week's salary into his pocket. He pulled his cab to a spot out of the way. Johnson knew Ahmed was good for it; were he to drive off, he'd never work this hotel again.

The Ontur's bright lobby featured a luscious marble floor, very high ceiling, extraordinary crystal chandeliers yet contemporary furnishings. Instantly a host rushed to greet them.

"Mr. Selby, I presume, hello, welcome to the Ontur Boutique. I trust you had a safe journey." He waved at one of the bellmen. "Suites 610 to 612."

Johnson passed his American Express card to the host, who grinned and continued. "I am Safak. Please mention my name if you have any question or concern whatsoever."

The photo-journalist now flashed ten 100 euro notes at Safak. "We'd prefer our presence to remain discreet. Will there be a higher bidder?"

"No, indeed, sir. You are a guest at Izmir's finest hotel. Your anonymity is assured," he replied with a curt bow. For a tip such as this, Safak would maintain a servile posture. Money trumped both civil authorities and ethnicities.

Miguel had recently stayed in a cheap room for the state cross-country meet, his only other time at any motel or hotel. He gawked at the king-size bed in his suite, the 72-inch LCD screen on one wall, framed prints of local archaeological finds on another. Estefan and Johnson, trailing behind, chuckled as the youth tossed his duffel onto a chair and looked out at the cityscape below, beyond which the bay spread out magnificently.

"It's almost 10:30," Johnson offered, "I think we can still catch some of that breakfast buffet. Then we'll see what the day holds."

The young athlete turned to his pastor with a suddenly anxious face and repeated a line from the summer before: "Father, is it time to be scared yet?"

"Are you nervous?"

"Maybe a little."

"Well, I've found that, when you're nervous, you should just concentrate on what you're good at. And what would that be in your case?"

"Running," Miguel said without hesitation.

"And what make you a good runner are your stride, keeping your oxygen debt in check, the confidence you have to remain strong to the finish. Keep a solid thought on those strengths you have. But you're also very intelligent, Miguel; you can think on your feet. Don't sell yourself short on that.

"We're keeping a low profile here, okay? Just act normally but be observant."

"Okay. Uh, Father?"

"Yes?"

The adolescent stood straight and faced his pastor. "Why are we really here?" As before, the youth sought bottom-line answers.

"To deliver a message to two important people – if we can find them and somehow are allowed to," the cleric replied matter-of-factly. "And maybe to stop a conflict. But do understand, Miguel, this may amount to nothing, just a bit of foolishness. I hope that's enough of an explanation."

Miguel looked back at his priest admiringly, still puzzled but proud to be included in whatever lay ahead.

With no fanfare the holy men, Sunni and Shi'ite, entered the Hisar mosque's smallish domed meeting room from separate interior doors.

The stout, aging Saudi Sheikh Nawaf Khalid al-Dakhil was dressed in a fine white linen robe and white corded shora. He trailed half a dozen advisors and two body guards who positioned themselves evenly along one side.

The younger, wiry Ayatollah Alireza Vahid Shirazi, chosen Iran's supreme leader five years before by the Assembly of Experts, was by now the unchallenged head of all Shi'ite faithful. As leader of his nation's judiciary, he was an ardent champion of its morality police. Dressed in a black wool robe and black turban, Shirazi was accompanied by an equal number of supporters – all members of the Islamic Revolutionary Guard Corps. In the hastily planned protocols, the Arabian contingent had failed to anticipate this Iranian show of force.

The two imams grunted into place, cross-legged and opposite one another on a tapestry rug, no table to separate them.

As the one who called this extraordinary meeting of Muslim minds, Sheikh al-Dakhil spoke first – in classical Arabic. Raising hands to chest in the Sunni prayerful pose, Dakhil spat a perfunctory greeting: "May the blessings of Allah and the wisdom of the Prophet descend over this gathering."

Though Farsi was the Persian Shirazi's native tongue, the tri-lingual (including Urdu) scholar needed no translation to detect the bitterness in his adversary's voice and body language. "I concur in their sacred names and truths," he replied, arms held to his sides in traditional Shi'a prayer posture.

The necessary if minimal pleasantries were out of the way.

"Why have you fractured the Sa'ud nation, the home to Islam?" Dakhil demanded, glaring across at the Shi'ite with coals of fire. The images of slain Saudi family members and oil pipelines in ruins seared into his mind, fanning the anger in his voice.

Shirazi's three-point reply came with cool dispatch:

"Be mindful that Mecca was left untouched.

"The House of Sa'ud has been concerned far more with wealth and power for the few than with serving Allah. The clan dealt openly with the Great Satan for *many years*," Shirazi hissed. "Their hands were imprinted with green ink. Their investments accounted for ten percent of the Great Satan's total worth. They donned Satan's principles. Their god was not Allah but gold."

In driving home the point, Shirazi wagged an index finger and invoked the sacred book. "The Sa'uds tied a knot with the West, alliances in which you are complicit. 'Put not with Allah other gods, or thou wilt sit despised and forsaken,' Muhammad warned us.

"Your so-called royalty was despotic. The Sa'ud clan scorned the Prophet's instruction to aid those in distress. Amnesty International condemned the kingdom as a major violator of human rights. All Arabians can now rejoice at the riddance of blasphemers."

Shirazi held Dakhil's gaze. He had made his case as a plain man with a plain message: The Sa'uds were corrupt; they deserved to die – all of them.

Dakhil consulted briefly at a whisper with one of his subordinates while digging into bowls of dried apricots and figs by his knee. Swallowing the greater part of his temper for the moment, the Sunni offered his own take on the slaughter.

"I believe your actions were borne of vengeance. It did not go unnoticed that the only official outside the royal family to be murdered was Pachachi," a reference to the Saudi oil minister, Abu Bakr Pachachi. The minister had been found slain in his bedroom, his hands shackled to a ceiling fixture, a gaping knife wound from sternum to pelvis.

"He made sport of you at an Arab League meeting, yes? And thus have you delivered retribution in your typically barbarous fashion. One must wonder whether Shehab and Cairo are next on your 'to-do' list."

Ammon Farouq Shehab, the Egyptian foreign minister, had also been caught unaware on an Al Jazeera camera and live microphone that night as he and Pachachi ridiculed the grand ayatollah.

Returning to the matter at hand, Dakhil offered a scriptural observation of his own. "The Prophet made clear on many occasions that violence against a Muslim neighbor is justifiable only with cause. The House of Sa'ud gave Iran no such reason to react outside the bounds of international diplomacy."

"When the brave students of Tehran rose up and seized the American embassy in 1979, what camp did the Sa'ud family retreat to?" Shirazi scowled.

Dakhil raised a cup of mint tea then stabbed the Shi'ite a second time with Muhammad's counsel on respecting neighbors and their business: "The Prophet has declared, 'Make not thy hand fettered to thy neck, nor yet spread it out quite open, lest thou shouldst have to sit down blamed and straightened in means.'"

Shirazi smiled tightly in return. "The Prophet has also said, 'Verily, thy Lord spreads out provision to whomsoever He will or however He doles it out. Verily, He is ever well aware of and sees His servants.' Allah has overseen these necessary actions and approves."

Dakhil gathered himself up and strode silently around the room, his considerable bulk brushing against his handlers. He reached the other side and approached the Shi'ite, leaving Shirazi to wonder whether this moment was one borne of weakness or strength. Finally, the Sunni sheikh leaned down, his full face not two feet from the lean contours of the ayatollah. An Iranian guardsman flinched, anticipating the possibility of close-quarters combat.

Shirazi straightened, tilting his head upward to meet the Sunni's eyes.

Dakhil, arms extended, quoted from the Qur'an once more, savaging the Shi'a faith as a cult: "'Kill the idolaters wherever ye may find them; and take them, and besiege them, and lie in wait for them in every place of observation; but if they repent, and are steadfast in prayer, and give alms, then let them go their way; verily, Allah is forgiving and merciful.'

"You have made a grave miscalculation," the Sunni seethed. "Persia will not reclaim its glory by these roads. And Shi'a will never displace Sunni as the one true way."

Dakhil straightened but continued. "You must pay for the damage you have done, as the Prophet prescribes. If you do not, you force the Sunni hand to arrange once more with the West. Be aware, you will thereby be annihilated. But at the risk of boring you by repetition, why did you attack the sovereign state of Arabia, home to Islam?"

Shirazi sprang up, thrusting a finger into the Sunni's girth. "'But if they break faith with you after their treaty, and taunt your religion, then fight the leaders of misbelief; verily, they have no faith, happily they may desist.'

"You have abused the followers of Shi'a for many centuries. Now other forces in this world and beyond decree it is our turn. The pendulum has swung."

"All very persuasive in your mind, no doubt," Dakhil countered. "But beyond that simplistic answer, you did after all attack the birthplace of Islam. So you have eliminated the House of Sa'ud; another house will take its place in time. The pipelines will be rebuilt. The ministries will form a new government – one not at all to your liking. Which leaves the only tenable reason: Was this not to avenge your personal embarrassment from Pachachi's words and those of Shehab? To this you owe an honest answer."

Each glared coldly at the other but the Shi'ite said nothing.

The scriptural stalemate, even this tacit admission of personal guilt by the Shi'ite, left the sheikh dissatisfied. Shirazi's continued cold silence sent a chill across the Sunni's neck at what might transpire next. He motioned for an early recess. He, his aides and bodyguards filed out with barely a rustle.

When they were gone, Shirazi strutted about the room with contrived buoyancy, assuring his guards that the events of this day were going well.

Johnson instructed Ahmed to pull over at a taxi stand on a street bordering the Kemeralti open-air market. Beyond the bazaar rested the Hisar mosque. He looked across the roof of the car at Estefan. "This is only one of three, remember," reminding the cleric that two other places of note were potential sites for a meeting between the mullahs.

"This will be the one, I'm quite sure," the cleric said quietly with a look curiously removed from the moment. Johnson bent one eyebrow at Miguel for a second, wondering where that response came from.

The three walked across the expanse of shops, tents and umbrella-shaded carts offering everything from pirated PhotoShop software to Syrian dates and vine-ripened tomatoes from Algeria. Minutes later the large, glittering golden dome and some of its seven surrounding domes came into view.

"Okay, Padre, it's your show. Lead on."

They walked as inconspicuously as possible along sidewalks bordering one side and the rear of the mosque's property. Johnson unfolded a tourist map along the way, an impulse buy in the market. He made a minor production of unfolding it, poking at the print and pointing silently in one direction and another. Then he pulled his Nikon PalmCorder from a cargo pants pocket and panned their surroundings. This tourist ruse, he knew, was probably superfluous and lame, evoking scenes from black-and-white movies on Classic Flix. He chuckled to himself at the absurdity. Then again, the colonel at the airport did say they'd be watched.

The tall, heavy wooden doors at the main entrance were closed and unattended, as were those of first one then a second, third and fourth satellite dome.

Miguel turned to his pastor as they continued ambling around the perimeter. "I don't see any soldiers or anything, Father."

"Yeah," Johnson agreed, "y'know, it might've been a stretch on my part to presume there'd be an armed presence outside. You may wanna consider just strolling into the sanctuary. It's between prayer calls now, there won't be many inside."

Estefan shook his head curtly, adjusted the white tab at his throat, and spoke softly. "I ... there's a feeling – familiar.... Just before the light appeared over the Sisters, it's like that. Remember, Miguel?" He was looking above tall palm trees and the tops of buildings in the distance.

Miguel looked at Johnson and shook his head; he didn't know what Father was talking about. But he wondered to himself whether this was about that sixth sense his pastor had brought up to him before – just knowing.

The photographer in turn was recalling Estefan's oblique reference earlier on the flight over and concluded this was a feature only the cleric had experienced.

As the fifth satellite dome came into view along the far side of the sprawling mosque property, Estefan caught a slight movement in the shadows some 200 feet away. He halted abruptly and turned away to face his friend. Johnson instantly grasped the situation. The two men feigned conversation while Johnson stared past the priest's ear at the smallish dome.

There were six uniformed men in total at the dome's entrance: Two Turkish Army guards, in jet-black dress uniforms with white belt, sash and helmet, stood at parade rest on either side of the double doors. Their right hands were comfortably outstretched, holding the muzzles of Kalekalip Avunya sniper rifles that rested on the stone slabs. In camo fatigues, two elite members of the 150,000-strong Iranian Revolutionary Guard Corps crouched with Khaybar assault rifles strapped to their backs. Several feet away and standing together, a pair from the Saudi Royal Guard Regiment wore their traditional flowing white *thaub*, *kaffiyah* and *qutrah* (robe, skullcap and scarf). They loosely held lightweight Slovenian tactical assault rifles, grenade launchers attached.

Boxes of ammunition were visible behind the six, stacked against the stone wall.

As he surveyed the situation, Johnson's mind turned whimsically to a series of films from generations before. "Well, as Oliver Hardy used to say to Stan Laurel, this is another fine mess you've gotten us into," he grinned. "Friend, it seems we're outnumbered six to three. In terms of firepower, well, they have lots of it, we don't. I think that about sums it up."

"That's all right," Estefan replied soberly, "something will happen." He continued to look blankly past his friend's shoulder at the sky, as if he were both here and in some faraway place.

Half a minute passed. Johnson noticed first one then a few of the guards turn heads their way and take notice. He lifted his map again, but they needed to move.

Estefan turned around and looked higher in sky. A smile crossed his lips. The amber light appeared several hundred feet over the mosque for half a second then vanished. Simultaneously all three American visitors felt a strong indefinable presence.

"I believe we can proceed now," the priest announced distantly. His thoughts had turned to the New Testament's Book of Acts, when the apostle Peter was delivered from prison by an angel. The guards had not taken notice of their passage.

They moved onto a sidewalk leading to the dome and the guards there. "It'll be okay," Estefan assured his companions as they proceeded tenuously forward.

Something extraordinary was transpiring, Johnson knew now. The armed men continued to stare at the spot on the adjacent sidewalk where the three had stood a moment before. *It can't be this easy*, the adventurer thought.

They approached the inlaid-stone landing. All six guards were in some trance-like state, apparently, dead in their tracks, their breathing shallow. An old line Johnson had scribbled on a notepad back at the seminary during an especially boring lecture came to mind: "What is the taste of music, the sound of a sunset, the touch of blue, the scent of love, the sight of magic?"

The aging Sunni mullah, Sheikh al-Dakhil, had taken his

place again at one end of the beautiful carpet, waving off an outstretched bowl of figs. His heart was heavy with the consequences of what he must do. He snorted lightly through his thick white facial hair as his counterpart lowered a lithe frame onto an ornately woven pillow placed for him during the break. Dakhil spoke first, his Arabic intonations dipped in bitterness.

"When you destroyed the Jewish entity, Allah and the Prophet smiled, for the Zionists put their faith in false prophets. Yet yours was a reckless action. You relied on confusion to shield you in the first days. When the trail of evidence inexorably led to your door, you guessed – *guessed* – that the Americans would forestall the Israeli military from raining bullets and missiles on Tehran.

"If you failed to notice, Arab nations engaged in only talk," the Sunni intoned, "raising no arms against you, resisting participation in the embargoes and boycotts that followed. For your deed against the Zionists was not without benefit to all Muslim peoples.

"Instead, it was the parliaments and tribunals from other continents that condemned you, imprisoned your officials within your borders, sanctioned your commerce. This is not what the people of Iran desire. In ever greater numbers they seek to be part of a wider world, yet you render them outcasts.

"Now you attack your Muslim brothers, just as you did in Iraq, just as you have at every opportunity since your Persian clans first took up the sword and sail."

The Shi'ite Shirazi retorted, "Yours is a dying culture," a smear on all things Arabic, "and a dying, false religion."

Dakhil sighed and closed his eyes for a second. When he spoke again, it was with a resigned spirit and hushed voice. "The

Prophet tells us at many points in the Qur'an that those who admit to trespassing then perform works of amends may be forgiven by Allah. You, however, are unrepentant, it is clear."

The time for fulminations and admonishments had passed. Now Dakhil summoned the courage to wage war. "I have prepared a fatwah calling upon all nations of the Arab League to rise as one – jihad against the Persian Shi'ite infidels. The fatwa will be delivered in three days at the League's emergency meeting in Cairo."

"You hang by mere strings orchestrated by the Great Satan, your puppeteer," Shirazi spat.

Dakhil ignored the epithet. "I will inform American and Israeli officials of this exchange and request their military intervention. I tell you this directly so there is no misunderstanding."

"That will not happen," Shirazi shot back. "The Great Satan is weak willed. Its youth shy from serving their nation. It is fat from greed and reeling in debt. Its time has passed, and its mouth holds an acrid taste for this region.

"The Israelis remain without leadership, disorganized. Their forces would confront a stronger Iran this time, with weapons from allies and pledges of more.

"Be mindful also that Iran is now a nuclear nation. What Arabic capital will answer your call to arms, knowing it will be slaughtered in return?

"It is you who cast your fate to the winds of the past. Now you pay the price."

Suddenly came the sound of heavy locks spontaneously snapping open. The entrance doors behind Shirazi swung out and in strode Estefan Tolavares, Johnson Selby and Miguel

Flores.

Estefan found a vacant space near the edge of the woven carpet and paused. A pale shimmering aura of yellow-white encased his entire torso.

"Guards!" Shirazi screamed.

There was no response whatsoever. Lesser Sunni clerics and trained Iranian killers alike around the room, just as the guards outside, were in a mental stupor, frozen in place, staring blankly ahead. Not a single weapon was raised. Only Dakhil and Shirazi remained alert, and both were aghast at this powerful development.

"My identity is unimportant," Estefan began in Arabic, looking into Shirazi's eyes then Dakhil's.

The two glanced at each other with identical looks, beyond astonished.

"I am a messenger. The message is this: 'You have lost your way. Your hateful paths lead to Allah's wrath upon all Muslims.'"

Dakhil looked about at his stricken contingent. He eyed the priest's well-worn black shoes, pants and shirt, the Roman collar. *This has to be a papist trick!*

Estefan himself was amazed to realize he had picked up the Sunni's emphatic thought. Cloaking his surprise in bland facial features, he spread his open palms and looked directly at him.

"No, this is not a papist trick." The mullah's fleshy jaw fell slack, his dark eyes widening. "You are confronting a power beyond your imagination," Estefan added.

He turned to ensnare Shirazi's frightened but suspicious look. "You must cease your conflict – Shi'a and Sunni, Persian and Arab – or you will all perish in mere days."

Shirazi looked across at Dakhil and spat, "This is Satan's messenger!"

The old Sunni looked back quizzically, not at all sure what to believe. "He read my mind," his voice barely managed.

Weakling, the Shiite mentally sneered before turning his attention again to the intruder.

"Sheikh al-Dakhil is no weakling," Estefan implored.

It was now Shirazi's mouth that dropped. But his misgivings were not yet allayed. This was neither saint nor angel.

"Be gone, Christian devil!" the Shi'ite barked, his eyes bulging. *Prophet, protect your loyal servant from this infidel.*

"'Prophet, protect your loyal servant from this infidel.' That was your wording, yes?" Estefan held a stone face as Shirazi's bravado dissolved into bewilderment and stark fear. Like his Sunni adversary a moment before, he was now convinced that this interloper could truly read their minds.

The priest continued. "You are warned. End this conflict now and render justice or all Muslims will perish." *Not to mention all of humanity*, he reminded himself.

"The remainder of the message I am here to deliver is thus: 'Allah controls the sun, all the stars and all life. Look to the northern sky in the mid of solstice night for proof that His wrath is near.'"

Johnson, his left hand still at his side, quietly closed the PalmCorder and slipped it into a pants pocket. With a trained eye for angles, he had captured the mullahs' reactions and slowly panned half the room as well. The entire scene and verbal exchange was now a permanent record.

Miguel was still processing what he had just seen and

heard: the glow surrounding his priest, all the men motionless around the room – including one caught scratching his scalp – plus Father's stern warning. He thought again of those first days at the South Sister. *I just knew this was about you, Father.*

Estefan turned and headed for the double doors, Johnson and Miguel on his heels. As they moved over the threshold, the aura surrounding the Jesuit disappeared. But the guards outside remained motionless as before, staring at the same spot on the far walkway where they first spotted the three visitors minutes earlier.

"Friend, why don't we cut across the lawn instead of using the sidewalk? We don't know how long these guys will be out of it."

"Agreed," Estefan replied.

They jumped a hedge and trotted past a flower garden, reaching an adjoining sidewalk street-side, across from the Kemeralti plaza. Just then an Izmir city police cruiser pulled up nearby and the officer jumped out.

"You there, halt!"

The young runner seized the moment. He reached into the priest's back pocket and lifted his wallet. "Forgive me, Father," he hurriedly said, "tell him I'm a thief." With a wrestler's move he'd seen at a high school match a month before, he lifted and thrust a foot behind Estefan's right knee, buckling him instantly. The priest toppled backward and landed on the plush grass, buttocks first.

Miguel darted across traffic and fled down the opposite sidewalk.

"He stole my wallet!" Estefan bellowed at the officer in Arabic.

In his confusion, the cop instinctively ran across the street in pursuit of the boy, lifting a cell phone from his belt as he went.

"We gotta go, guy," Johnson said to Estefan as Miguel raced around a corner. He glanced down at his watch while they ran in the opposite direction – 11:25 local. They weaved between passing cars and into the labyrinth of carts and shops at Kemeralti.

Take the boy. He will clear a final hurdle. The words came back to the priest repeatedly as they ran.

Once within the shopping maze they slowed to a brisk walk to avoid any more undue attention. The market was modestly busy this late morning. In moments they reached the far side and the taxi stand there. Ahmed stood leaning on the front fender of his cab, a not-for-hire placard attached to the windshield's down-turned visor. A few cigarette butts lay at his feet.

"Take us back to the hotel," Johnson directed.

"What about Miguel?" Estefan asked with alarm.

"If he's as smart as you say, he'll know to double back and find us there."

The cleric didn't press the point. But a 14-year-old he had promised to watch over was out there on unfamiliar streets, trying to evade the police and in possession of a wallet that was obviously not his own. This could end badly.

En route to the Ontur, Johnson was on the phone instructing his pilot and co-pilot in turn to meet them at the Citation's hangar ASAP. They pulled into the hotel's horseshoe drive minutes later. The men looked anxiously around the grounds – no Miguel.

"Mr. Selby, Father Tolavares, welcome home to the Ontur

Boutique," Safak greeted the men out of rote, without his customary broad smile.

Estefan inquired, "Have you seen the boy Miguel who was with us earlier – Hispanic, thin?"

"No, I have not, I apologize. Mr. Selby, may I have a word with you?"

"With both of us, sure. What's up?"

"Two men came here not long ago. They are from an agency of my government – the Milli Istihbarat Teskilati."

"The National Intelligence Organization," Estefan interpreted.

Johnson's brow furrowed. "Have they left?"

"They demanded pass keys to your rooms. They are up there now. I am sorry, if it were anyone else, I would of course deny that you are staying here."

Damn! "Safak, you are a good man. I personally assure you we have done nothing wrong." He retrieved the clip and peeled off five more 100 euro notes. "I would ask only that, if they inquire further, you will not recall seeing us since we left the hotel earlier."

"Absolutely, Mr. Selby. Discretion is paramount at the Ontur Boutique. Have a safe journey."

The men strode back outside, hoping to find Miguel lurking around a corner or perhaps beyond a parked car. But he was nowhere in sight.

Ahmed's old Toyota raced again through Izmir's streets, headed out of downtown toward the airport.

"Johnson, we can't just leave Miguel here. He's not street

savvy like I had to be at fourteen. There are risks worse than the police for him."

"I know, Estefan, but I think we need to be with the plane for now. We did agree we're winging it, right? Just call upon some of that faith, my friend."

The priest nodded and looked away, his eyes filling up.

The photo-journalist heaved a heavy sigh. "Okay, here's the deal. We're not headed back to the states, at least not yet. If we get to the hangar and they've seized the plane or any authorities at all are present, we say uncle, sure. If not, my guys can take us to, say, Tierra del Fuego out in the Atlantic on the excuse of refueling. Or there's lots of tourist cities north of here. We can grab visas and Euro passes and come back by rail. We *will* surely find him."

"And where should we begin, at the police lock-up? Plus, what about Suki?"

"Aaaaah!" Johnson's face contorted. In the rush of events, he'd forgotten about their flight attendant, who, like the pilots, had checked into an airport hotel, on call.

Estefan had a stranglehold on his rosary, the pewter crucifix burning into his hand. "Johnson, I know you mean well, but we're looking and sounding like fugitives. We should end this now."

"All right, all right. Sorry, yes, you're right. You did what you were called here to do. Now it's Pilate's turn, if that's what has to be."

Ahmed cruised up to the smallish hangar reserved for private aircraft. There didn't seem to be anything afoot, no activity other than a few mechanics doing routine maintenance on small prop-driven planes. The scene was not unlike the service area at any auto dealership.

Johnson handed the driver a thousand euros. "Lose this day on your log, yes?"

"You got it!" Ahmed beamed through brown-stained teeth and sped off.

As the men moved under the open bay door and toward the Citation, an office door opened to their left and two figures walked through – Johnson's pilots. Apparently the airport manager, Pamuk, was yet unaware.

Now another figure emerged at the far end of the hangar, from behind a stack of barrels.

"Miguel!" Estefan cried out. "Oh, thank you, Teacher!"

The young distance runner came forth in limp damp shirt and cutoffs. His black hair was matted and sweat glistened from his face and neck. He was spent but buoyant at seeing his pastor again. They stood on the concrete floor next to the Cessna and all three embraced for a brief eternity.

"Padre," Johnson broke in, "are we back in fugitive mode or not?"

"I don't care to meet up with that colonel again, either, not to mention Turkish intelligence agents."

"Then let's go now. I'll get Suki on a train to Istanbul and a flight out from there."

They proceeded up the staircase and into the cabin as first one then the other jet pod sprang to life. While they strapped themselves in, the sleek white "Sky Candy" moved out of the hangar toward the dual runways.

Seconds later the co-pilot, J.D. Stovall, reopened the cockpit door. "Mr. Selby, we're being hailed."

"By whom?"

"The airport manager, Banu Pamuk."

"Look at your radar. Is there any traffic incoming?"

Stovall looked at his screens then back. "No, sir, it's a slow day here."

"Then let's boogie. I know it's not kosher. I'll make this up to you."

"Yes, Mr. Selby," he said soberly. Then, with a smile creasing his lips, "It'll be a brief walk down memory lane." For Stovall, air chauffeuring had been an uneventful gig these past several years. Midway through a stellar career as a Navy pilot, he'd achieved Top Gun status.

The door closed and at 12:07 PM IRST the Citation blasted down the westward runway. The pilot raised its nose into a steep ascent, the twin Rolls Royce engines responding beautifully.

Just seconds aloft, the cockpit door opened again and Stovall poked his head out. "Mr. Selby, we're tracking two aircraft in pursuit, probably Turkish Air Force."

"What are they flying these days?"

"F-16s, mostly."

"And how far back are they at this point?"

"They're still about 40 miles inland but closing fast."

"Well, they can out-climb us, but Turkey only claims six nautical miles of territorial airspace. Level out and bust a gut. We don't need to beat them across the ocean, only to international waters."

Stovall spoke to the pilot then turned back into the doorway again. "We'll be there momentarily, Mr. Selby, but they're no doubt armed. We're already in range of an air-to-air missile."

"That's not gonna happen. Hang in there, pardner, we've done something righteous. I'll surely make this worth your while."

Johnson trusted in the notion that Turkey's military wouldn't shoot his plane out of the sky, creating an international incident with an important ally in the process, over what would ultimately amount to a misunderstanding. At best, from the Turks' perspective, this was a potential heroin interdiction or the like, he reasoned. They'd alert American authorities instead.

By whatever means, Johnson was determined to remove his friend and quiet hero from harm's way.

The three passengers sat in tense silence, listening to the pronounced roar from the straining engines outside. Seconds stretched to a minute as Johnson reminded himself of a newswire feature: Turkish jets had recently flown over several Greek islands in an ongoing dispute over territorial boundaries, regulations be damned.

He groaned silently and tried to dismiss the thought. *They won't do this*, he repeated in his mind but without his normally strong resolve. He was risking four other lives and he knew it.

Finally Stovall's voice came softly over the cabin speakers, "We're clear, Mr. Selby, they've broken off. Course laid in to Atlanta."

Johnson unbuckled and walked back to the galley's cabinetry for something stronger than red wine. He pulled out a 35-year-old, single-malted scotch and two jiggers then reached for ice and a cola from the refrigerator for Miguel. He passed the drinks around, hoisted his own aloft and proclaimed, "Job well done, gentlemen, I'm so damn' proud of you both."

"You may be a little premature," Estefan said with a still worried look.

"We're small potatoes, compadre. It was a calculated risk. But still it was a risk and I apologize to you both.... And I do expect a reception committee in Georgia."

"Johnson, it was a situation that I put you in. Miguel is the one deserving an apology." Estefan looked at the youth with a serious smile. "I'm sorry that I endangered you."

"Are you kidding, Father? It was a rip!"

Johnson spoke. "Unfortunately, young man, it's a story you're not gonna be free to tell your friends."

At Estefan's eager questioning, Miguel proceeded to explain how he had managed to elude the police and make his way to the airport.

"At first I just needed to get away, and the policeman, he wasn't so fast. I turned left and right and left and lost him, y'know? Then I ducked into an alley and hid behind a trash container. He ran by and then back again a minute later with a second cop. After they were gone I started out, using the sun as a guide to the airport. I remembered the way once I got out on the main streets.

"A bus stopped ahead of me and the rear door opened, so I sneaked on. That saved a lot of time. I ran the rest of the way and got to the hangar just before you did. I figured it was best to just hide there and wait.

"Oh, here's your wallet, Father," as he reached into a rear pocket. "Sorry about knocking you down."

"That's quite all right, young man!" Estefan grinned broadly. This lad would've survived south Chicago just fine, he figured.

"You didn't think to go back to our hotel?" Johnson asked.

"Are you kidding? That's the *first* place they'd look! Don't you ever watch old movies?"

Johnson and Estefan shrieked in duet.

Chapter Twenty One

December 19, 6:30 PM IRST (10:30 AM EST). Two hours short of Atlanta, Johnson broke into their continuing banter, releasing the mute button on a remote. A monitor embedded in the rear wall of the cabin immediately riveted their attention.

"In breaking news, the National Oceanic and Atmospheric Administration has issued a bulletin concerning a severe electrical threat from space. We take you to Boulder, Colorado, where Heidi Hutchinson from our affiliate KBLD is on the scene."

Bundled in a heavy hooded parka against a whistling wind and swirling snow, the young reporter stood before a low brick office building set against a Rocky Mountains backdrop. Her mittened hands held a slightly trembling mic. The wind chill index was minus 7. White streams of her breath flew to one side with each exhale.

"Brad, NOAA's Space Weather Prediction Center behind me is responsible for tracking activity on the sun and its effects on our planet. Just an hour ago the Center confirmed a total of four unexpected eruptions in the sun's corona in rapid succession. They occurred around the 3AM hour Mountain time in a heliosector identified as Latitude 16 North, Longitude 9 East on the sun's Earth-facing side.

"The resulting flare – an arcing plume from the sun's surface that everyone is familiar with from science programs – has greatly increased the solar wind headed toward Earth.

"The solar stream's normal speed is a *mere* half million to a million miles per hour, and it's mostly deflected by Earth's blanket of protection, the magnetosphere.

"Two days from now, shortly before 4 PM Eastern, a supercharged solar storm will strike a blow to our planet at 2.4 million miles per hour. It'll continue at that rate for several hours, raining down countless trillions of charged particles into Earth's atmosphere.

"Minutes ago, I spoke with the Center's spokesperson, Air Force Major Julie Mendenhall. She confirmed that the oncoming burst of energy will inevitably pose havoc to U.S. commercial and military satellites in orbit as well as to major portions of North America's electrical grids. Power outages for many millions are expected. Local and regional utility companies across the northern tier of states are being alerted to the risk of equipment failure if they do not shut down voluntarily before the solar storm hits."

"Sounds like one heckuva way to celebrate the winter solstice, eh, Heidi?" the news reader quipped.

Off camera, Hutchinson accepted congratulations from her cameraman for a smooth piece. She was glad she'd only nodded curtly at the final flip comment by the network's anchor. This was serious business.

The three passengers on the Citation, meanwhile, looked at one another after Johnson muted the broadcast. Miguel was the first to break the silence. He recalled his pastor's warning in that mosque hours before: "Look to the northern sky in the mid of solstice night for proof that His wrath is near." He directed his question to Johnson.

"Mr. Selby, do you really think the aliens knew that? Did they predict somehow that it would happen? Did they, y'know, figure out ahead of time, from the physics of the sun, that it was gonna happen? Or did they make it happen?"

Johnson glanced over at the cleric and winked. "Estefan, we gotta make sure this kid gets into a great college." Looking back at the youth, with a wry expression he spoke for his friend.

"3 AM Mountain Time, my youthful friend, that's when the flare burst. And that was 1 PM in Izmir – *after* we left the mosque and well after your pastor's message was delivered. Cool. And the public is just now hearing about it.

"So, Miguel, did they know ahead of time that it would happen, or did they *make* it happen? Great question. And who could know? But I think back to a conference on UFOs I attended. Some guy I met there said over late night drinks, 'Hey, they can get here and we can't get there. That said, all other bets are off the table.'

"Young man, we just don't grasp the outer limits of their intelligence. But what we *do* know is that, for whatever reason, they appear to care about what happens to us. They don't want us to annihilate each other to the point where we vanish from this planet. Why? Well, maybe we're somehow their genetic cousins, millions of years less evolved than they are, and they step in from time to time to shepherd us along. Maybe they're what we've always called angels, here to deliver some tough love. We just don't know, and in all probability we *can't* know."

The priest nodded, recognizing the significance, but his thoughts were already elsewhere.

Johnson tried to reel him back to buoyancy. "You rock, my friend. I mean, you nailed it! 'Look to the northern sky in the mid of the solstice night.' Our experts say it'll strike on the 21st around 4 PM on the east coast – midnight in the Middle East. I'll just bet that blast of solar wind is gonna give a fine Northern Lights show. How very cool is that?"

Estefan shook his head at his traveling companion and

confidant, contemplating further moves on the chess board. "It may not matter. I gathered that Ayatollah Shirazi is a stubborn man."

"But what if he is?" Johnson pressed, his face darkening. "Ya' think if the worst comes to pass, your childhood walk-up in Chicago would really be blown away?"

The priest's brow pinched tight. "The light said the scenario I was shown doesn't have to be. Maybe that suggested alternate futures."

"Whoa, you're rockin' my boat again." Never a student of the sciences, he needed a better explanation.

This wasn't a notion easily absorbed, Estefan knew. "It's been postulated in chaos theory that the future can go in different directions. Isn't it free will that affects our future? That was part of the Teacher's message. We do have free will; we're not chained to playing out a given script."

"Then, normal diplomatic contacts and the rest could've settled things out as well? Without your meeting with Shirazi and Dakhil?"

"In one iteration, yes."

"And in another?

"In another, we're flying back home in your beautiful jet to witness the final days."

Four Atlanta Hartsfield security officers stood at the bottom of the Citation's lowered staircase. The crewmen and passengers were marched to a pair of waiting dark sedans that sped them off to the main terminal.

Rafael Dominguez, the airport's chief inspector, was in practiced form as he entered the interrogation room. "Johnson Selby, Reverend Estefan Tolavares and Miguel Flores, correct?"

The three nodded.

"Miguel, this woman is going to take you down the hall to another room and she'll talk to you there, okay?

"Gentlemen, be seated. Mr. Selby, your plane is receiving a thorough inspection as we speak. If contraband is discovered, you are both in a world of hurt, as are your pilots."

"Yeah, right, your inspectors are more thorough than the ones in Turkey," Johnson retorted coldly. "So, go for it." This interview was off to a poor start.

"At the airport in Izmir, your aircraft ignored a hail and directive to return to the terminal. Were you aware of that?"

"Yes, I was. I directed my crew to take off. This isn't their fault."

Dominguez adjusted the knot in his tie. "A noble gesture, but it's not quite that simple. Departing from an FAA-recognized airport without permission is a Class-A felony under Turkish law or anywhere else. A certain military officer there, Colonel Pamuk, whom I'm told you both are familiar with, was *very* displeased by your actions. If they seek extradition, well, have you ever spent time in a Turkish prison?"

Ah, the scary part, Johnson mentally smirked. "No, I haven't. I've never been arrested."

"We're checking on that, too," Dominquez smiled malevolently. "Father Tolavares, I verified that you are indeed a Jesuit priest, and I spoke with your bishop. He had *no idea* where you were. What do you say to that?"

"Bishop Stevens gave me permission to leave," Estefan responded minimally. He well understood this could still end badly.

"Mm-hmm, well, please allay my confusion, if you would. Bishop Stevens told me you were on some 'mission of discovery.' And Colonel Pamuk said you told him you were on a Christmas *excursion*. Yet, after checking into your hotel, you failed to attend the one site you mentioned to him in particular, the ruins of the Virgin Mary's home. And yes, Turkish authorities stationed men there to monitor your visit."

"I told him that, actually. I said it was my Christmas gift to Estefan and Miguel and that we intended to visit the ruins – it was me," Johnson offered for clarity.

"Does it *matter*?" Dominguez said dismissively. "You were both in Izmir. Whatever your actual purpose, it seems you weren't in the city long, around two hours. Further, you were seen running from a mosque. Then, without so much as returning to your hotel to gather your belongings, you left the airport without filing a flight plan or waiting for take-off instructions."

The inspector pulled a menthol cigarette from a breast pocket and lit it. He let out a long exhale and struck a bit softer tone. "Father Tolavares, I am a Catholic, too. But certainly you can understand my doubts." He leaned back against a heavy metal desk, folded his arms and turned his attention back to Johnson. "Were you attempting to sell the boy by some arrangement?"

Estefan gasped lightly, his face paling. "No, no! Nothing like that!"

Johnson kept his demeanor in check. "Mr. Dominguez, I am very well off financially, all right? I have no interest in selling a child for a few thousand dollars or whatever the going rate is. That question offends my intelligence."

Their eyes met icily before Dominguez turned back to the cleric.

"The boy is being examined as we speak. If anything – *anything* – suspicious arises from that examination, well, Father, you can surely envision the scandal. For the present, both of you wait here."

Dominguez stalked out of the room and the men sat without speaking.

Forty-five minutes later the door opened. Miguel walked in with a long face.

"Miguel, how are you?" Estefan rose to greet his charge.

"I'm fine. Father, they thought you or Johnson did something bad to me, like sexually."

"I apologize for all this, Miguel."

"Don't be sorry, Father, it's not your fault."

Johnson wondered aloud, "Did the woman question you about why we were there?"

"No, she didn't – I think because I'm a kid and everything. She was more concerned with doing a physical. I told her nobody's touched me but me."

"Were you okay with it, I mean, being examined by a woman?"

"Yeah, it was all right, y'know, not too embarrassing or anything. If it was, y'know, our nurse at school, that'd be different. She's kinda hot."

Johnson smiled ruefully at the characteristic remark of a

healthy adolescent. "Well, just keep in mind, we haven't done anything wrong. And we're not under arrest." He looked up again at the half-globe of smoked glass centered in the ceiling, identical to the "eyes in the sky" in Vegas casinos. He wondered where the microphones were hidden, there or elsewhere. "Let's just continue to wait quietly."

Fully an hour passed before Dominquez reentered the room, followed by two U.S. Air Force officers.

"Your plane is free of contraband, Mr. Selby," he began.

"Imagine that!" came Johnson's rejoinder. "And here I was, with *nine figures* in the bank, trying to become a drug mule for a few thousand bucks." Estefan gained his attention with his hand in a subtle tamping-down motion.

"And our nurse determined that Miguel has not been violated."

Johnson ignored the priest's caution. "You had a *female* nurse examine a 14-year-old boy?"

"There are psychological factors which I will not go into. Regulations give us some latitude in these cases."

"*These* cases, I see." Johnson was getting testy once more. Estefan caught his eye and shook his head slightly. He'd always known that, when pushed, his roomie from the seminary was capable of a sarcastic temper.

The inspector continued. "As for the Turkish authorities, no extradition has been sought as yet. You and your pilots may well have to answer in an American court, nonetheless. You will be notified.

"That is all I have. But we've been joined by Air Force General Raymond Washburn, director of Space Command, and Air Force Reserve Lieutenant LaShawn Morris from the Office of

Special Investigations. They would like to have a word with you in private."

"In private?" Johnson repeated, looking up at the ceiling camera.

"That'll be turned off. If they are satisfied with the information you provide relative to national security concerns, you will be free to depart." Dominguez proceeded out of the room.

With a sweep of his head, Washburn peered at the three travelers in turn. "Gentlemen, I am authorized to tell you that what you witnessed near the Mexican border last July was a sentient drone, the product of a Department of Defense black budget program intended for use in drug surveillance and interdiction. The Air Force fighters you saw were engaged in a reconnaissance exercise with that drone."

Johnson swayed back in his straight-back chair and let out a whoop. "And I was born yesterday! Oh, General, you came all this way just to get laughed at?"

Washburn didn't accept such a sharp retort lightly. He wasn't about to let a civilian's dismissive put-down go unrecognized.

"Lieutenant Morris spoke with someone on your board of directors, Mr. Selby. Apparently you have something of a reputation as aloof, a playboy of sorts, cocky. So it's understandable that you'd dismiss something you know absolutely nothing about. But I know something about what you three have been up to recently. Tell me the rest – *now*."

Johnson, Estefan and Miguel traded glances. Johnson took the lead, cautiously.

"We flew to Izmir, Turkey, to, ah, meet with some people, to deliver a message. General, we didn't do anything illegal."

Idiot. "I *know* where you went. Who did you meet with?"

Estefan looked warmly at his longtime friend. He blinked, nodded, turned back to the general and spoke. "We met with Sheikh Nawaf Khalid al-Dakhil and Ayatollah Alireza Vahid Shirazi."

Washburn was taken aback, unconsciously shifted his feet but maintained his characteristic gruffness. "Just like that, you met with the supreme leaders of the Sunni and Shi'ite religions?" Throwing his arms out, he mocked, "And *I* was born yesterday, too! Try again."

Johnson spoke now, deciding to lay the truth bare. "General, I could regale you with some harrowing adventure, but really it was pretty easy. They were meeting in the Hisar mosque in Izmir, no doubt to try to settle their differences. A light appeared overhead in the sky and we just walked right in, past some guards who were sorta stunned and out of it. Then Father Estefan spoke to them. He told them to back off their sectarian war. He warned them of God's wrath and annihilation of all Muslims if they didn't. Then we left. And that's what *really* happened."

Washburn sniffed loudly. "Uh-huh. Sounds a lot like a Harry Potter tale so far." The general decided to play along for the moment. "And how did you happen to know where to look there for these holy men? *ESP*?"

Johnson reached into his left pants pocket, pulled out his PalmCorder, thumbed a short sequence and offered the device to Washburn.

"Hit the Play button. The date-time stamp is Mountain Standard."

Lt. Morris looked on as Washburn's skepticism soon turned to amazement. The three-minute scene clearly showed Dakhil and Shirazi and panned slowly back and forth across a domed room. All others in the viewfinder stood transfixed along the walls, motionless. The voice doing most of the talking, though in Arabic, was quite obviously the priest's. The remaining utterances by appearance matched the lip movements of Shirazi and Dakhil. If this was a fake, it was a damn good one, Washburn knew.

Washburn handed the device to Morris, who popped out the mini-disk before handing the device back to Johnson. "I'll have our lab in Boulder process this right away, sir."

"Ah, folks, that's my property," Johnson barked. "But I'd accept at least a copy, eh?"

"You'll get a copy," Washburn sneered. He turned his attention to the Jesuit, who maintained a passive expression. "What did you say at the end, again?"

"The words were, 'Look to the northern sky in the mid of solstice night for proof that His wrath is near.' I took that to mean around midnight on the 21st."

"That'd be about 4 PM Eastern. Well, isn't that convenient," Washburn replied with now-forced cynicism. "We just happen to be expecting a major solar storm to hit at that hour. The aurora borealis this time, they say, will be practically unprecedented. In fact, they'll even see it in the Middle East. Yes, how convenient for you."

The date-time stamp on the video, he noted, was an hour before the sun's first disturbance in the heliosector and almost two hours before the Space Weather Prediction Center issued its first alert. He had paid attention to the time-stamp numbers throughout, realizing the odds against either a prank or random prediction of this coming celestial event.

He looked for a crack in either man's armor but found none. "Reverend, the stamp on Mr. Selby's camera suggests you made your little speech before anyone, even our solar astronomers, knew about the impending storm. Did you?"

"No."

"Well, what if I said this is sounding more and more like a cock-and-bull story?"

"You'd be wrong. General, I didn't know what was meant by proof in the sky until we saw the news bulletin on our return flight."

"So, humor an old man. Just who told you about some 'proof in the sky'?"

"That's a personal religious matter."

Washburn was befuddled. But for now there was a related matter to address, and he aimed to get a more reasonable answer. Softening his tone a bit for effect he continued.

"Father Estefan, the OSI and Lieutenant Morris recently followed up on the reentry of a satellite that came to rest not far from your home. The boy," glancing at Miguel, "was apprehended near that scene. His mother told the lieutenant that you and he had, let's say, an experience there last summer. Is that correct?"

"Yes, that's right, in late July."

"Am I getting into something here that you'd say is Roman Catholic Church business?"

"No, only reconciliations – confessions – are privileged."

"Good. Now, back on July 21, two Air Force pilots out of

Holloman airbase encountered what they described as a glowing light in that same vicinity, a light that rose into the sky at great speed." He scowled at Johnson then returned his attention to Estefan. "I presume you're not buying the drone explanation, either."

"I have reason to believe otherwise," the priest said cautiously.

"The pilots that day also said that, on their flybys, they observed two people and a Jeep there. Was that you and the boy?" glancing at the youth.

"Father hasn't done anything wrong!" Miguel suddenly blurted, unable to sit in silence any longer. "He was just told to deliver a message, that's all!"

"By a *light*?" Washburn asked, now genuinely intrigued.

Miguel drew a breath. "There was the ball of light; it was a perfect sphere except it glowed. And then the Virgin Mary came out of it – or what looked like the Virgin Mary except it wasn't. It was just a projection that vanished. And then we knew it was the ball of light that was the, uh, ..."

"Intelligence," Estefan finished Miguel's thought. "I was instructed by whatever source that underlay the light to deliver a message of peace – just before the solstice. A few nights ago I received further instruction at my home on where to go – to Izmir. My friend Johnson generously arranged to take me there."

The general slowly shook his head and sighed, not knowing quite what to believe. "Are you aware that the United States is at the brink of war?"

"Yes, General," the priest replied, "I think that's why I was dispatched when I was.

"There was more to the encounter last summer. I was

shown a future scene in my mind of total annihilation, what I interpreted as the aftermath of an East-West nuclear exchange. I saw my own childhood street in Chicago destroyed, death and destruction everywhere. My olfactory system was made to smell putrid odors accompanying the scenes. This intelligence can assault at least two human senses, General, and perhaps all five. It conveys information telepathically. It also knew my thoughts and my entire life history."

Washburn scratched the prickling goose bumps at the back of his neck. He tossed his hat onto the desk and sat down heavily in a swivel chair behind it. Memories came flooding back: the military base intrusions in '67 and '75 and '80, all the unidentifiable radar returns, the thousands of calls to NORAD from worried civilians nationwide. He ran a hand across a grey-white temple.

Miguel took the opportunity to speak up again in his pastor's defense. "When we were inside there, in that mosque, there was a glow all around Father, like an aura, maybe, just like there was around the young woman, y'know, the projection at the mountain, the South Sister."

"An aura, you say, around your priest. And a young woman. So, am I to believe not only this fantastic story but now that Reverend Tolavares is a holy man?"

"Nah, he's just Father Estefan. He's cool and everything, but I think the light we saw drop over the mosque before we went inside, that's what made Father glow."

Washburn stared at the teen for a long moment without detecting a hint of deceit.

"Reverend, what exactly was the nature of this message you were so hellfire worked up over delivering?"

"Exactly as you'll hear on the disk when your people

interpret it, General. I spoke the words to the mullahs precisely as I received them in my room, only in Arabic. To paraphrase, Sunnis and Shi'ites must end their conflict and make amends or all Muslims will be destroyed by God after this week."

Estefan knew, though, that he had manipulated the message, misstating the scenes of total extermination as affecting Muslims alone.

He continued for the general's benefit. "What I saw in my mind in the desert and the words I telepathically heard imply that all of humankind will be destroyed. But I didn't tell them that."

"Oh? Why not?"

"I thought it best that they focus on each other and the task at hand."

Washburn stroked his chin. "Uh-*huh*. You're Secretary of State Tolavares, then. So, did they heed your warning?"

"We don't know, we left."

"I see." The general leaned in toward the priest, his sarcasm gone, his voice lowered. "Reverend Tolavares, what are the *capacities* of this light source?"

"I wouldn't know the full extent. It didn't fire a laser beam at anything, if that's what you mean. But it did issue a holographic projection, a realistic appearing figure of the Virgin Mary."

"Father threw a rock right through her!" Miguel interjected. "That's how we knew she wasn't real."

"At short range," Estefan went on, "the projected figure cast some kind of depressive force, something like greatly elevated atmospheric pressure or gravity that also affected my awareness; it slowed my thought stream.

"The light source read my long-term memories as well as my extant thoughts. And it seemed to know our future. General, I don't think there's any weapon today or tomorrow that could counter those powers."

Johnson piped up. "I have another disk and eight rolls of film showing the ball of light and its departure. But neither the camcorder nor the SLR picked up this image of the woman he's talking about. And I didn't see it, either."

"You were there?"

"A few miles away – with telephoto equipment."

Washburn crossed his legs and internally smiled. If he had a mind to, he could save the wench Nowitzky's job. If he had a mind to.

"We'll need to borrow those as well, Mr. Selby."

"Well, I've heard that in years gone by people gave up their photos and home movies of UFOs to the Air Force and either didn't get them back at all or got a substitute that was blurry, washed out, less compelling."

"A copy – a good copy – of everything will be returned to you. But if you're thinking of selling them to the highest bidder in the media, think again. This is a national security matter, mister, and all of you are subjects of interest. Do you take my meaning? You will not, *any* of you, speak of this to any reporter or publish any of the material before you hear from me personally. As they say, we know where you live."

Washburn abruptly rose to his feet. "Mr. Selby, if you were under my command, I'd take you down a couple pegs."

"And you wouldn't cut it as a mattress salesman in one of

my stores, General. Gotta work on those customer relations, eh?"

Washburn glared at Johnson's insolence before extending a bit of cordiality to the cleric. "I hope you did some good over there, Father Estefan. I know a few folks at State. If this disk pans out, I'll arrange to have any charges against you three and your pilots dropped. For now you may go home."

Washburn clomped out of the room, and minutes later the captives and their crew were on their way. The Citation rose splendidly to fifty thousand feet, pointed west to Albuquerque.

Chapter Twenty Two

President Seymour had found success in at least one respect. Detroit was well on its way to making his natural-gas forecast a reality, retooling plants to build millions of methane-burning cars and light trucks. The Motor City had a head start on Toyota and Honda; hope was in the air again in the long-suffering city.

That good news aside, Seymour's itinerary for December 20 was dominated by a stream of advisors from inside and outside government regarding the second crisis competing with the Middle East for news cycle airtime. Widespread blackouts stemming from the solar storm would disrupt commerce, catapult crime and stress hospital emergency rooms. Moreover, despite an onslaught of hastily prepared PSAs to find a local warming center, hundreds or more likely thousands would freeze to death in the Midwest, Northeast and across Canada; this was late December.

More so than even automotive fuel, America was dependent on electricity. The wind-generating super farms and electrical superhighways were at early to middle stages of construction. A coordinated startup of both was still two years out.

MagneRail technology and the hundred thousand miles of roadbed to pave its way, meanwhile, were roasted on the coals of unsurpassed national debt, its annual interest payment, and congressional inaction on both.

None of that, though, would have prevented what was in store. The very last thing North America needed right now was a power disruption affecting upwards of 150 million of its citizens.

As to the first crisis, the mouths of the Persian Gulf and the adjoining Gulf of Oman were deemed disaster areas by UN inspectors aloft. Lakes and snaking rivers of crude oil spread by a westerly wind would soon reach Iran's own broad shores. Qatar, and the United Arab Emirates remained in ecological peril as well in the aftermath of the supertanker attacks. Curiously, all the havoc had been well removed from the shores of Oman and Bahrain, both Shi'a-majority countries.

The 21st of December was heavy with intrigue and speculation in Washington and throughout the nation's media. At 2:30 PM in Tehran (6:30 AM Eastern), Iranian President Nazila Fadavi made a very brief, awkward, if compelling statement to his nation's press. He expressed "compassion for the lives lost in Arabia" and announced, ambiguously, a "statement tomorrow." His remarks were released just in time for America's morning TV, grist for those knights of the roundtables.

The west wing of the White House was restless all day as analysts huddled to decipher the meaning of the Iranian Fadavi's words. Was this truly a concession? He appeared to be stalling for time – which only played into America's hand, after all. Evidence was mounting to condemn Iran for the wanton attack on the Sa'ud family and its waning oil empire. But conventional wisdom argued that Fadavi was only a tool of the ayatollahs, in particular Grand Ayatollah Shirazi who, the day before, had met secretly in (now confirmed) Izmir, Turkey. Would that "statement" come from Fadavi or the ayatollah directly?

As a result of backchannel communications with Iran, the Chinese and North Koreans had simultaneously chosen to suspend their harassing flights over American spheres of influence.

Late in the day, the Russian ambassador to the U.S., Antonin Fyodorov, met with the president's national security advisor and secretaries of state and defense to press for a pause in the buildup to a war no one wanted.

"Let this moment of decision not pass hastily," Fyodorov said in conversation. "The Persians are a breed apart. Allow Grand Ayatollah Shirazi, his council and President Fadavi to collect their thoughts. Otherwise, my government must act to protect our vested interests. We do not wish to ponder where adventurism would lead."

Iran, by all appearances, had disrupted the oil flow from Arabia, slain its entire hierarchy then asked for a timeout. Seymour listened to all views. Though rankled ("pissed off" in his own words privately), he decided that a day or two wouldn't alter his nation's resolve to smite the bastards. He'd wait a bit longer.

Financial markets worldwide had already nosedived on speculation of further interruptions in world shipping and general worry over the prospect of war, a conflict employing the most wanton of weapons, a war never experienced in full scale. On the further news that Iran's brinkmanship might be faltering, the Dow and NASDAQ now held steady, still down ten percent each for the week. The dollar, from all-time lows, had rallied slightly.

A state dinner that evening with the Norwegian ambassador and his wife was postponed. The president went ahead with greetings of an eighth grader – the National Geography Bee champion – plus the Western Michigan Broncos football team, winners of the NCAA playoffs for mid-level programs. The balance of his day and evening would again witness a parade of cabinet secretaries, generals and admirals, with his national security staff perpetually on the scene.

WINTER SOLSTICE

December 21, 23:30 IRST (Tehran), 11:00 PM Asia/Riyadh, 3:30 PM EST. Sheikh Nawaf Khalid al-Dakhil stepped from the elevator and strode purposefully, arms swaying angularly outward from his girth. The north-facing atrium windows near the peak of Kingdom Tower were a breathtaking 300 meters above the streets of Riyadh. Arabia's tallest skyscraper was also host to the world's highest mosque just a few floors below, where the sheikh had moments before prayed to Allah once more for guidance. A wing-back leather chair was placed behind him; lights were darkened. Dakhil stared out across the vast desert night.

By prearrangement, at virtually the same moment and with the pilot's assistance, Grand Ayatollah Alireza Vahid Shirazi snapped his double harness into place. The Elburz Mountains blocked horizons north and east of Tehran. That plus equal measures of wonder, fear and skepticism had propelled Shirazi's Citroen to Mehrabad International and the waiting military chopper. He would go aloft personally to witness whatever, if anything, might transpire.

From separate inquiries, science advisors to both holy men had relayed newswire stories predicting a strong display of the age-old aurora borealis this night, including disruptions of electricity in Europe and North America. The aurora was primarily a September-October and March-April phenomenon, they explained, but winter Northern Lights were not uncommon; our sun was unpredictable.

Even if such a demonstration were cast across the entire Caspian Sea to Tehran, it would be perhaps strange to behold but explainable, counselors to the ayatollah insisted. Still, it could serve as amusement. No such exhibition had been viewed from the Iranian Plateau for generations.

Riyadh, removed another ten degrees in latitude, might well

host a barren night sky despite astronomers' predictions, the sheikh's counselors reasoned. This was to suggest, they cautioned, the disturbance by that priest at the Hisar Mosque two days before had been nothing more than a bold ruse by a clever charlatan employing parlor tricks.

Dakhil and Shirazi, though, knew the hour at which the Hispanic priest without a name, the priest who spoke in American-accented Arabic, had broadly implied an appearance by the aurora. He had told them this even before the sun's eruption and well before the first announcement anywhere. How could he possibly have known, that priest set aglow?

In the nearly 60 hours since, the imams had been forced to confront their uncomfortable shared experience. The stranger had somehow unlocked bolted doors and bedazzled their entourage inside and out. More disturbingly, he had read their minds, their very phrasings, they could not deny. Whatever the veracity of the priest's remarks, those factors were seemingly beyond any stage magic either one could conjure.

This self-proclaimed "messenger" had invoked Allah's name in threatening their entire followings, then invoked some celestial event in the northern sky this night as his proof. Had the intruder's prediction come only hours later, any spectacle tonight could be dismissed, but the timing was disturbing. In response, their respective advisors could only suggest a coincidence, chance, a lucky guess.

Now Shirazi sat alone in the unadorned cabin of the Shabaviz chopper as the Mehrebad tarmac fell away. Eight minutes later and five thousand feet above the airport, the aircraft came to a hover. Most of the Elburz peaks loomed below him in the distance.

From their disparate locations, the two sects' supreme

representatives proceeded to stare for long silent minutes at the same region of black sky.

Shirazi noticed it first – a dim yellowish flicker beyond some distant unnamed peak, then another. In minutes a psychedelic river of yellow, green and off-white hues flowed across the top of the Elburz range.

The sight resolved into a shimmering, undulating curtain rising slowly, inexorably skyward. Within half an hour it had graduated to spectacular proportions, setting ablaze the lower third of the northern sky – impressive even by Alaskan-Canadian standards. But this was Tehran, the latitudinal equivalent of Raleigh, North Carolina.

From Dakhil's more southerly locale (sharing a latitude with Tampa, Florida), the drapery of light, while still impressive, was somewhat less intense in its colorful striations. It stretched roughly twenty degrees above the desert floor at its apex.

They had agreed to remain at their respective locations for one full hour, more if called for. In reality, like all first-time observers, they were mesmerized by the eery beauty of it. Though addressed in science's words outside the Qur'an, this was in truth a demonstration of Allah's mighty hand in all things. Neither spoke; the visual experience captivated.

When the hour had expired, with no further advance in the splendor, having been told the exhibit might last until dawn, Shirazi and Dakhil were giving thought to ending the vigil. The Iranian Revolutionary Guard pilot and Sheikh al-Dakhil's handlers in the Riyadh hotel awaited a signal.

Just then another effect took form before the eyes of the ayatollah and the sheikh. As if drawn by the finger of Allah, the curtain's central portion suddenly coalesced into a single white spear-like band, sharply defined. It thrust upward into the sky in seconds until nearly overhead. As quickly, the shaft retreated down into the wall of light and disappeared.

While the two stricken adversaries looked on in renewed awe, the menace re-formed and shot forward toward the zenith of the firmament again. Shirazi and Dakhil craned their necks upward at their respective windows.

The spear of light retracted once more. Now forming a brilliant red tip, the white shaft streaked overhead a third time. As it did, both holy men witnessed a further anomaly: From its point cascaded thousands of individual blood-red anomalies – points of light directed downward. The small red teardrops cascaded over their cities, vanishing just above rooftops all around them. The two imams were aghast anew.

The rogue auroral sword now slipped back into the overall display a final time.

The symbolism of this final demonstration had a palpable and chilling effect, the warlike imagery not lost on either. It was no magician's trick; only Allah was capable of such a miracle. That priest's words of warning flooded back to them now.

Dakhil stood and looked at the others standing beside him. They uniformly smiled, but none of them otherwise reacted – impossible given the absurd spectacle he had just witnessed. "The white sword, the red anomalies!" he proclaimed aloud. Puzzled looks were all around.

Shirazi in turn lifted his handset and spoke with the helicopter pilots, who conveyed nothing unusual beyond from the ongoing curtain of light. The bloody sword and rain of blood were the province of the imams alone.

Chapter Twenty Three

"Hey, fella, how's my favorite man of the cloth? Did you catch the Northern Lights last night? They didn't start to die down here 'til nine o'clock. Wow, talk about a show! I was up on my roof. Used up thirty rolls of ultraviolet and 1600 ISO; I guess I'll be in the darkroom awhile."

Estefan laughed anew at his friend's enthusiasm. "I joined the Flores family to watch. It really was beautiful. But millions of people have been suffering in the cold, my friend. Churches all across the Midwest and Northeast were set up as warming centers, but I'm afraid that wasn't enough."

"Yeah, lots of areas along the electrical grid failed, plus all the utilities that were shut down intentionally beforehand. They're saying 80 million across the country are still without power. Portable generators sold out everywhere in a matter of hours, I heard. Europe's been hit big-time, too.

"But the reason I called is that there seems to be something afoot, guy. The BBC just announced it's carrying a live feed from Al Jazeera within the hour. Would you believe our two boys will be making some sort of joint statement?"

"Sheikh al-Dakhil and Ayatollah Shirazi?"

"You got it."

"Hmmm." Estefan's heart wanted to rejoice but his head paused. The auroral exhibition was an inspiring and colorful sight, for sure, but the Northern Lights were a known commodity, and the curtain of wavy bands everyone witnessed was really a typical sight farther north. Could his "prediction" alone have made a difference? "Johnson, what are you thinking?"

"I don't know what to think, man, except that you know and I know, whatever the odds of the aurora – out of season – stretching that far south, well, you called it, roomie, right in front of them before anyone else knew about it. And if they've pulled their noses out of the Qur'an for a minute since then, they know that, too. They've got solar scientists of their own, y'know."

"But I didn't know that's what it involved when I recited the words. And I still don't know that what I said was enough."

"Maybe not. But you gave it your best shot, Estefan. You do rise to the occasion, man. Anyway, I guess we'll know shortly if it worked.

"But whatever develops, you're never gonna get a lick of credit, you know that – not that you'd ever ask for any."

"Or blame? I drove to Las Cruces to see Bishop Stevens yesterday and reconciled everything."

In his own conscience, Estefan had lied. While he had carried forward the message verbatim, in so doing he led the imams to believe that God the Father would punish Islam. He knew that went beyond shading the truth; the destruction he'd been shown was seemingly worldwide. He had succumbed to his ego – and to his trust in an intelligence he knew virtually nothing of.

"Okay. Yeah, I hear ya'. You're one stickler for the truth, my man. So, uh, not to intrude on a 'confession,' but how'd Stevens react?"

Estefan flashed a quick smile. "Well, he sat kind of wide-eyed for quite a while. I can tell you he didn't discount what I said. He left it to me to decide. No rosaries as penance or anything."

"And?"

"Johnson, if what I did causes any harm, any complication, I really have to notify the authorities. I've been giving plenty of thought and prayer to all this. My actions were rash and brash. I'm truly sorry I had to involve you."

"Now, don't be saying sorry to me, I won't hear of it. I did this willingly. Besides, we did nothing wrong – except maybe trespass, elude the cops and secret police, and outrun a couple F-16s to open water." He laughed out loud.

The adventurer's wry tone was infectious. Estefan smiled again for a second.

"And I'm thinking, between Colonel Pamuk, Inspector Dominguez and General Washburn, we have *done* the authorities route. Like Washburn said, they know where we live. But hey, let your conscience be your guide, man; I'll be there with you."

"And I'm so very grateful. But it's not just that. Johnson, I trusted in a *nonhuman* intelligence."

"One you originally threw a rock at, so there you go. To remind you of your own words, Estefan, this intelligence may or may not be of *God* as you define it, but it didn't appear malevolent, either. My great friend, you reacted to what your gut – your id, your soul, maybe – told you was right. And you did so with the most honorable intentions." Johnson broke into a wide grin. "Then again, I'm speaking as the captain of your cheerleading team."

"Thank you, dear friend," came the cleric's hushed response. He grew misty at his good fortune to have such a confidant and foil.

"Hey, I think what we both understand is that this ... species, or intelligence, whatever, is interested in maintaining some semblance of order amid all the chaos on Earth. I look at it as a kind of sentry, a fail-safe arrangement. We can't wipe ourselves out, fella; it won't let that happen – whatever it is. And I for one find that rather comforting in an odd way. Estefan, I've got a good feeling about this."

"Keep that positive thought. Goodbye, friend." The priest clicked off and returned to chopping vegetables for the mid-day meal at St. Javier's.

At the stroke of 20:00 IRST in Tehran (7:30 PM Asia/Riyadh; noon EST), December 22, an Al Jazeera feed to CNN, MSNBC and Fox began with split-screen images of the two imams, Shirazi and Dakhil, principals in an impending major escalation of their many-centuries-old sectarian feud.

Across six continents, the assembled commentariat had filled the airwaves and Web for hours, notions of hope mixing with cries of doom on the planet's doorstep.

From his administrative offices in downtown Tehran, the wiry Grand Ayatollah Shirazi would speak first, in his native Farsi. An assembly of studio linguists at keyboards would inform the rest of the world in five languages with near-instant captions.

Dressed in the same simple black cloak and piled turban, Shirazi was seated behind a modest wooden desk. A large framed painting behind him of a dour Ayatollah Ruhollah Khomeini looked over the proceeding. Journalists and bloggers would debate for weeks whether the visual presence of that theocratic ruler and spiritual leader of the Iranian revolution constituted a *faux pas*.

Through semi-gritted teeth, Shirazi read a prepared text.

"Adherents of Islam and citizens of the world, I extend the mercies of Allah to you. His wishes be ever our devotion."

Talking heads would likewise debate whether Shirazi's seemingly fearful eyes offered a clue. His features were otherwise muted.

"Recent events on the Arabian Peninsula have transpired outside the bounds of the Prophet's words expressed in the Qur'an. For incidents in which the Iranian Guardian Council may bear some responsibility, atonement is the reasonable explication under Muhammad's guidance.

"Arabia is a sovereign land, recognized in our sacred writings. At this hour its people call out for the vast mercy of Allah, as prescribed in the Prophet's teachings. The people of Iran and Shi'a believers everywhere offer great sympathy and alms to the Arabian people.

"Accordingly, the nation of Iran will henceforth share its natural resources generously with the Arabian people until further notice. Compensation will also be made to other interests for their losses.

"To allay misgivings concerning Iran's peaceful intentions and that of all Shi'a faithful, President Fadavi will decommission elements of the Iranian Revolutionary Guard and order the dismantling of certain advanced weapons on our soil.

"The Guardian Council recognizes the authority of international bodies in secular affairs. Yet the Council must answer only to Allah. May His blessings shower us all."

These final lines were apparently Shirazi's attempt to shield himself and his council of ayatollahs from the World Court and UN. Fadavi was left to take the fall in the tribunals certain to follow. Nonetheless, Shirazi's sudden turnabout was stunning.

Al Jazeera's cameras shifted to Mecca and Sheikh al-Dakhil. He stood at the pulpit of an empty Masjid al-Haram, the Grand Mosque, Islam's largest. Resplendent in fine white linen, he had waited passively during Shirazi's brief address. Now the tenor of his reply – from a fatwa potentially to an olive branch – would determine whether the world was dragged into irretrievable war.

His initial words left no doubt.

"Allah and the Prophet Muhammad have heard the supplications of Grand Ayatollah Shirazi and are satisfied, I am confident. Let arrangements be made to render the Arabian Peninsula and its people whole.

"To preserve continuity, the bin-Laden family, one of Arabia's oldest and most distinguished, has claimed temporary leadership responsibilities, with other families' support, to administer internal and external affairs. Let those with eyes to see and ears to hear accept this arrangement."

Dakhil's expression changed, akin to the vague look of fear seen in Shirazi's eyes a moment before. "This is not a time for vengeance against Iran or Shi'ite Muslims. I call upon all Sunni faithful and all peace-loving nations to leave your scimitars banded at the waist. Praise and all glory to Allah."

The screen returned to the Al Jazeera logo.

J.T. Seymour flipped the TV remote onto his desk, swung open the Oval Office door and, with a beaming expression, accepted congratulations from his ecstatic staff. Shouts rang forth of "You did it, Mr. President!" and "Shirazi got your musical 'bomb bomb Iran' message loud and clear, sir!" Vigorous applause and laughter fairly shook the old walls.

Above the tumult Seymour exclaimed, "Well, I guess that rascal Shirazi figured out which side of his bread was buttered, anyway." The president accepted an offer of a cold Michelob and hoisted it to more loud cheers. "Hey, somebody said Tehran saw the Northern Lights for the first time in God knows how long. Maybe that spooked him," he said to more uproarious laughter and cheers.

When the shouts and applause finally died down, Seymour became serious. "For dang sure, we're going forward with those criminal sanctions, that's a fact. Shirazi will find out he's answerable to a few folks besides Allah – not that we can really haul his ass to prison, which would be too good for the son of a bitch.

"Hey, somebody tell Tom Hagelthorne he can take us off red status and back to orange." The President turned to his appointments secretary. "I'll need all the usual suspects over here, let's say three o'clock, to run through the particulars of standing down."

"You'll go up twenty points in the daily tracking polls," someone yelled.

Seymour glanced over that way with another grin then winked. "Well, that's not all that important. I want to thank each of you for your hard work to make this happen. The good Lord was looking over us and allowed us to prevail."

To a cascade of final applause, he swung the door closed behind him, mentally clicking his heels as he waddled back to his desk, quite pleased with himself. It was still a dangerous world out there, he knew, but his gambit with Iran had paid handsome dividends.

Within the hour, however, word arrived of something awry; two hours later the confirmations were complete. From U.S.

Navy ships in the two gulfs and across Arabia's and Israel's expanses, the computerized targeting mechanism of every missile, nuclear-tipped or not, was corrupted. No explanation was available other than that it happened to all such weapons simultaneously. Word of the phenomenon would not reach the public.

Morning editions of the Tehran and Riyadh newspapers carried accounts of the aurora, despite its rare appearance, as page-two stories behind the immediate news of potential war thwarted. No reporter or street interviewee in either city mentioned a spear of light or a myriad of red lights falling to earth.

A pajama-clad Estefan dropped onto the kneeler before his bedroom crucifix. *Teacher, this has been sobering. In our Creator's vast universe, undoubtedly there are forces of darkness. I chose to believe – I guessed – that this intelligence wished to protect humanity.*

In my ignorance I guessed, yet I told the holy men it was our Father who would strike them down if they didn't make peace. I falsely invoked His name. Please forgive me, Jesus. Please forgive me, Father.

He turned back the covers, extinguished his bedside lamp and drifted off to the sounds of a blustery wind outside.

Was it only a moment? Estefan suddenly came to full consciousness – and to the feeling he alone had experienced in the desert back in July, then again outside the mosque – an expectancy. He looked at his clock's LED: 3:20A 12 23.

He sat up in bed and rubbed the sleep away, listening

intently. The wind had died down, but still he heard nothing. His eyes adjusted to the darkness and the scant moonlight seeping through his window. A minute passed then five. *Allow me to remain lucid*, he repeated in his mind.

It came through the wall to his left, passing directly through the crucifix. This was not a jerry-built projection of Miriam, it was the luminous ball of amber light – now less than a foot in diameter. As he had noted about the niche at the South Sister, none of its brilliance now reflected off the surrounding walls of his room – impossible according to known optical physics.

You performed well, priest, Estefan heard telepathically. *Your species is safe from extinction for a brief period.*

The cleric gathered a bit of courage. "Who are you?"

This concerns you more than the restoration of order. Examine why.

"I, uh ...," Estefan wasn't expecting the directive. "I need to know you are in league with the Teacher."

You fathom civilizations without number in your universe. Yet you do not fathom universes.

Estefan contemplated the enormity of the rejoinder. He thrust back the Indian quilt and stood up. "That aside, a straight answer: Assure me that you represent good. Surely the concept is not foreign to you."

In your limited grasp, this unit represents the purpose: furtherance of life.

Estefan let out a pent-up breath. "Then are you of God?"

We are all what you identify as God, priest. All life is God. You knew this.

"So, I should believe you because ..."

CHAPTER TWENTY THREE

You wish to believe.

In seven of your years, you will be called again.

The amber light abruptly receded through the bedroom wall and was gone.

Author's Note

In an interview printed in the Vatican's newspaper, *L'Osservatore Romano*, in May 2008, the Argentine Jesuit Jose Funes, director of the Vatican Observatory, declared:

> *"Just as there is a multiplicity of creatures over the earth, so there could be other beings, even intelligent, created by God. This is not in contradiction with our faith, because we cannot establish limits to God's creative freedom."* Asked in the article whether a nonhuman life form could be more evolved than humans, this science advisor to Pope Benedict XVI added, *"Certainly, in a universe this big you can't exclude this hypothesis."*

Source: www.catholicnewsagency.com